Praise for Alexander McCall Smith

'The suspense lasts till the end; and McCall Smith has the gift of evoking an entire social atmosphere in very few and simple words' *Sunday Telegraph*

'McCall Smith's greatest gift as a writer – and God knows this is just one of many – is that he can write likeable characters' *New Statesman*

'One of the most entrancing literary treats of many a year . . . a tapestry of extraordinary nuance and richness' *The Wall Street Journal*

'Has the power to amuse or shock or touch the heart, sometimes all at once' *Los Angeles Times*

'Alexander McCall Smith's subtle, gentle stories are works of art' *Daily Telegraph*

' . . . with a mastery of comic understatement and a powerfully evident sympathy for his subjects and their milieu, Alexander McCall Smith sets out a world where the old rituals of politeness and respect hold sway. His unassuming, carefully voiced tour of the small things that make life worth loving is a quiet delight' *The Times*

'Infinitely touching, beautiful novels, each of which is a miracle of gentle wit and perception' James Naughtie

'The writing is unfussy, the voices clear and unique, filled with a sort of grave, humorous directness which is refreshing and charming' *Scotland on Sunday*

'Highly amusing, intelligent and heart-warming' *The Scotsman*

Alexander McCall Smith is the author of over sixty books on a wide array of subjects. For many years he was Professor of Medical Law at the University of Edinburgh and served on national and international bioethics bodies. Then in 1999 he achieved global recognition for his award-winning series *The No. 1 Ladies' Detective Agency*, and thereafter devoted his time to the writing of fiction, including the *44 Scotland Street*, and the *Portuguese Irregular Verbs* series. His books have been translated into forty-five languages. He lives in Edinburgh with his wife, Elizabeth, a doctor.

ALEXANDER McCALL SMITH

44
SCOTLAND
STREET

Illustrations by
IAIN McINTOSH

This is for Lucinda Mackay

ABACUS

First published in Great Britain in 2005 by Polygon
This paperback edition published in August 2005 by Abacus
Reprinted 2005 (nine times), 2006 (three times), 2007, 2008 (twice), 2009 (twice)

From the daily novel published in

THE SCOTSMAN

Grateful acknowledgement is made to Macmillan Ltd for permission to quote
from 'The Onion Memory' by Craig Raine.

Every effort has been made to trace the copyright holders of work quoted in this
book. Please contact the publishers if there are any errors or omissions and these
will be put right in future editions.

A CIP catalogue record for this book
is available from the British Library.

ISBN 978-0-349-11897-0

Typeset in Janson by Palimpsest Book Production Limited, Polmont, Stirlingshire
Printed and bound in Great Britain by Clays Ltd, St Ives plc

Papers used by Abacus are natural, renewable and recyclable
products sourced from well-managed forests and certified
in accordance with the rules of the Forest Stewardship Council.

Mixed Sources
Product group from well-managed
forests and other controlled sources
www.fsc.org Cert no. SGS-COC-004081
© 1996 Forest Stewardship Council
FSC

Abacus
An imprint of
Little, Brown Book Group
100 Victoria Embankment
London EC4Y 0DY

An Hachette UK Company
www.hachette.co.uk

www.littlebrown.co.uk

Preface

Most books start with an idea in the author's head. This book started with a conversation that I had in California, at a party held by the novelist Amy Tan, whose generosity to me has been remarkable. At this party I found myself talking to Armistead Maupin, the author of *Tales of the City*. Maupin had revived the idea of the serialised novel with his extremely popular serial in *The San Francisco Chronicle*. When I returned to Scotland, I was asked by *The Herald* to write an article about my Californian trip. In this article I mentioned my conversation with Maupin, and remarked what a pity it was that newspapers no longer ran serialised novels. This tradition, of course, had been very important in the nineteenth century, with the works of Dickens being perhaps the best known examples of serialised fiction. But there were others, of course, including Flaubert's *Madame Bovary*, which nearly landed its author in prison.

My article was read by editorial staff on *The Scotsman*, who decided to accept the challenge which I had unwittingly put down. I was invited for lunch by Iain Martin, who was then editor of the paper. With him at the table were David Robinson, the books editor of the paper, Charlotte Ross, who edited features, and Jan Rutherford, my press agent. Iain looked at me and said: "You're on." At that stage I had not really thought out the implications of writing a novel in daily instalments; this was a considerable departure from the weekly or monthly approach which had been adopted by previous serial novelists. However, such was the air of optimism at the lunch that I agreed.

The experience proved to be both hugely enjoyable and very instructive. The structure of a daily serial has to be different from that of a normal novel. One has to have at least one development in each instalment and end with a sense that something more may happen. One also has to understand that the readership is a newspaper readership which has its own very special characteristics.

The real challenge in writing a novel that is to be serialised in this particular way – that is, in relatively small segments – is to keep the momentum of the narrative going without becoming too staccato in tone. The author must engage a reader whose senses are being assailed from all directions – from other things on the same and neighbouring pages, from things that are happening about him or her while the paper is being read. Above all, a serial novel must be entertaining. This does not mean that one cannot deal with serious topics, or make appeal to the finer emotions of the reader, but one has to keep a light touch.

When the serial started to run, I had a number of sections already completed. As the months went by, however, I had fewer and fewer pages in hand, and towards the end I was only three episodes ahead of publication. This was very different, then, from merely taking an existing manuscript and chopping it up into sections. The book was written while it was being published. An obvious consequence of this was that I could not go back and make changes – it was too late to do that.

What I have tried to do in *44 Scotland Street* is to say something about life in Edinburgh which will strike readers as being recognisably about this extraordinary city and yet at the same time be a bit of light-hearted fiction. I think that one can write about amusing subjects and still remain within the realm of serious fiction. It is in observing the minor ways of people that one can still see very clearly the moral dilemmas of our time. One task of fiction is to remind us of the virtues – of love and forgiveness, for example – and these can be portrayed just as well in an ongoing story of everyday life as they can on a more ambitious and more leisurely canvas.

I enjoyed creating these characters, all of whom reflect human types I have encountered and known while living in Edinburgh. It is only one slice of life in this town – but it is a slice which can be entertaining. Some of the people in this book are real, and appear under their own names. My fellow writer Ian Rankin, for example, appears as himself. He said to me, though, that I had painted him as being far too well-behaved and that he would never have acted so well in real life. I replied to him that his self-effacing comment only proved my original proposition. Then there are some who appear as themselves, but have no speaking part. That great and good man, Tam Dalyell, does that. We see him, but we do not hear what he says. We also see mention of another two admirable and much-liked public figures, Malcolm Rifkind and Lord James Douglas Hamilton, who flit across the page but who, like Mr Dalyell, remain silent. Perhaps all three of them could be given a speaking part in a future volume – if they agree, of course.

I enjoyed writing this so much that I could not bear to say goodbye to the characters. So that most generous paper, *The Scotsman*, agreed to a second volume, which is still going strong, day after day, even as I write this introduction to volume one. In the somewhat demanding task of writing both of these volumes, I have been sustained by the readers of the paper, who urged me on and provided me with a wealth of suggestions and comments. I feel immensely privileged to have been able to sustain a long fictional conversation with these readers. One reader in particular, Florence Christie, wrote to me regularly, sometimes every few days, with remarks on what was happening in *44 Scotland Street*. That correspondence was a delight to me and helped me along greatly in the lonely task of writing. I also had most helpful conversations with Dilly Emslie, James Holloway and Mary McIsaac. Many others – alas, too numerous to mention – have written to me or spoken to me about the development of characters and plot. To all of these I am most indebted. And, of course, throughout the whole exercise I had the unstinting daily support of Iain Martin and David

Robinson of *The Scotsman*. I was also much encouraged by Alistair Clark and William Lyons of the same newspaper.

But the most important collaboration of all has been with the illustrator of this book, Iain McIntosh. Iain and I have worked together for many years. Each year for the last twenty years or so I have written a story at the end of the year which has been printed for private circulation by Charlie Maclean and illustrated by Iain. Iain then illustrated my three novels in the *Portuguese Irregular Verbs* series. His humour and his kindness shine out of his illustrations. He is the modern John Kay, and Edinburgh is fortunate to have him to record its face and its foibles.

Alexander McCall Smith, January 2005

1. Stuff Happens

Pat stood before the door at the bottom of the stair, reading the names underneath the buttons. *Syme*, *Macdonald*, *Pollock*, and then the name she was looking for: *Anderson*. That would be Bruce Anderson, the surveyor, the person to whom she had spoken on the telephone. He was the one who collected the rent, he said, and paid the bills. He was the one who had said that she could come and take a look at the place and see whether she wanted to live there.

"And we'll take a look at you," he had added. "If you don't mind."

So now, she thought, she would be under inspection, assessed for suitability for a shared flat, weighed up to see whether she was likely to play music too loudly or have friends who would damage the furniture. Or, she supposed, whether she would jar on anybody's nerves.

She pressed the bell and waited. After a few moments something buzzed and she pushed open the large black door with its numerals, 44, its lion's head knocker, and its tarnished brass plate above the handle. The door was somewhat shabby, needing a coat of paint to cover the places where the paintwork had been scratched or chipped away. Well, this was Scotland Street, not Moray Place or Doune Terrace; not even Drummond Place, the handsome square from which Scotland Street descended in a steep slope. This street was on the edge of the Bohemian part of the Edinburgh New

Town, the part where lawyers and accountants were outnumbered – just – by others.

She climbed up four flights of stairs to reach the top landing. Two flats led off this, one with a dark green door and no nameplate in sight, and another, painted blue, with a piece of paper on which three names had been written in large lettering. As she stepped onto the landing, the blue door was opened and she found herself face-to-face with a tall young man, probably three or four years older than herself and wearing a rugby jersey, his dark hair *en brosse*. *Triple Crown*, she read. *Next year*. And after that, in parenthesis, the word: *Maybe*.

"I'm Bruce," he said. "And I take it you're Pat."

He smiled at her, and gestured for her to come into the flat.

"I like the street," she said. "I like this part of town."

He nodded. "So do I. I lived up in Marchmont until a year ago and now I'm over here. It's central. It's quiet. Marchmont got a bit too studenty."

She followed him into a living room, a large room with a black marble fireplace on one side and a rickety bookcase against the facing wall.

"This is the sitting room," he said. "It's nothing great, but it gets the sun."

She glanced at the sofa, which was covered with a faded chintzy material stained in one or two places with spills of tea or coffee. It was typical of the sofas which one found in shared flats as a student; sofas that had been battered and humiliated, slept on by drunken and sober friends alike, and which would, on cleaning, disgorge copious sums in change, and ballpoint pens, and other bits and pieces dropped from generations of pockets.

She looked at Bruce. He was good-looking in a way which one might describe as . . . well, how might one describe it? Fresh-faced? Open? Of course, the rugby shirt gave it away: he was the sort that one saw by the hundred, by the thousand, streaming out of Murrayfield after a rugby international. Wholesome was the word which her mother would have used, and which Pat would have derided. But it was a useful word when it came to describe Bruce. Wholesome.

Bruce was returning her gaze. Twenty, he thought. Quite expensively dressed. Tanned in a way which suggested outside pursuits. Average height. Attractive enough, in a rather willowy way. Not my type (this last conclusion, with a slight tinge of regret).

"What do you do?" he asked. Occasions like this, he thought, were times for bluntness. One might as well find out as much as one could before deciding to take her, and it was he who would have to make the decision because Ian and Sarah were off travelling for a few months and they were relying on him to find someone.

Pat looked up at the cornice. "I'm on a gap year," she said, and added, because truth required it after all: "It's my *second* gap year, actually."

Bruce stared at her, and then burst out laughing. "Your *second* gap year?"

Pat nodded. She felt miserable. Everybody said that. Everybody said that because they had no idea of what had happened.

"My first one was a disaster," she said. "So I started again."

Bruce picked up a matchbox and rattled it absent-mindedly.

"What went wrong?" he asked.

"Do you mind if I don't tell you? Or just not yet."

He shrugged. "Stuff happens," he said. "It really does."

After her meeting with Bruce, Pat returned to her parents' house on the south side of Edinburgh. She found her father in his study, a disorganised room stacked with back copies of the *Journal of the Royal College of Psychiatrists*. She told him of the meeting with Bruce.

"It didn't last long," she said. "I had expected a whole lot of them. But there was only him. The others were away somewhere or other."

Her father raised an eyebrow. In his day, young people had shared flats with others of the same sex. There were some mixed flats, of course, but these were regarded as being a bit – how should one put it? – *adventurous*. He had shared a flat in Argyle Place, in the shadow of the Sick Kids' Hospital, with three other male medical students. They had lived there for years, right up to the time of graduation, and even after that one of them had kept it on while he was doing his houseman's year. Girlfriends had come for weekends now and then, but that had been the exception. Now, men and women lived together in total innocence (sometimes) as if in Eden.

"It's not just him?" he asked. "There are others?"

"Yes," she said. "Or at least I think so. There were four rooms. Don't worry."

"I'm not worrying."

"You are."

He pursed his lips. "You could always stay at home, you know. We wouldn't interfere."

She looked at him, and he shook his head. "No," he went on. "I understand. You have to lead your own life. We know that. That's what gap years are for."

"Exactly," said Pat. "A gap year is . . ."

She faltered. She was not at all sure what a gap year was really for, and this was her second. Was it a time in which to grow up? Was it an expensive indulgence, a *rite de passage* for the offspring of wealthy parents? In many cases, she thought, it was an expensive holiday: a spell in South America imposing yourself on a puzzled community somewhere, teaching them English and painting the local school. There were all sorts of organisations that arranged these things. There might even be one called *Paint Aid*, for all she knew – an organisation which went out and *painted* places that looked in need of a coat of paint. She herself had painted half a school in Ecuador before somebody stole the remaining supplies of paint and they had been obliged to stop.

Her father waited for her to finish the sentence, but she did not. So he changed the subject and asked her when she was going to move in. He would transport everything, as he always did; the bundles of clothing, the bedside lamp, the suitcases, the kettle. And he would not complain.

"And work?" he asked. "When do you start at the gallery?"

"Tuesday," said Pat. "They're closed on Mondays. Tuesday's my first day."

"You must be pleased about that," said her father. "Working in a gallery. Isn't that what most of you people want to do?"

"Not in particular," said Pat, somewhat irritated. Her father used the expression *you people* indiscriminately to encompass Pat, her age group, and her circle of friends. Some people wanted to work in a gallery, and perhaps there were a lot of those, but it was hardly a universal desire. There were presumably some people who wanted to work in bars, *to work with beer*, so to speak; and there were people, plenty of people, who would find themselves quite uncomfortable in a gallery. Bruce, for instance, with his rugby shirt and his *en brosse* haircut. He was not gallery material.

That had been another interview altogether. She had seen the discreet, hand-written notice in the window of the gallery a few streets away. *A bit of help wanted. Reception. Answering the phone – that sort of thing.* The wording had been diffident, as if it was almost indecent to suggest that anybody who read it might actually be looking for something to do. But when she had gone in and found the tall, slightly lost-looking young man sitting at his desk – the wording had seemed perfect.

"It's not much of a job," he had said. "You won't have to sell any paintings, I expect. You'll just be providing cover for me. And you'll have to do the occasional other thing. This and that. You know."

She did not know, but did not ask. It looked as if he might have found it tedious to give the details of the job. And he certainly asked her nothing about herself, not even her name, before he sat back in his chair, folded his arms, and said: "The job's yours if you want it. Want it?"

2. A Room With a Smell

Bruce had shown Pat the vacant room in the flat and this had brought home to him what a complete slut Anna had been. He had asked her to clean the room before she left – he had asked her at least twice – and she had assured him, twice, that it would be done. But he should have known that she did not mean it, and now, looking at the room with a visitor's eyes, he saw what she had done. The middle of the carpet had been vacuumed, and looked clean enough, but everywhere else looked dirty and neglected. The bed, pulled halfway away from the wall, had large balls of dust under it, as well as a collapsed stack of magazines. A glass of water, with lipstick stains on the rim, had been left on the bedside table. She had moved out a week ago and he should have checked, but he had always hated going into the room while she was there and her presence somehow lingered. So he had left the door closed and tried to forget that she had ever lived there.

Pat stood still for a moment. There was a musty odour to the room; a smell of unwashed sheets and clothes.

"It's got a great view," said Bruce, striding across to draw the curtains, which had been left half-closed. "Look," he said. "That's the back of that street over there and that's the green. Look at the pigeons."

"It's big enough," said Pat, uncertainly.

"It's not just big, it's huge," said Bruce. "Huge."

Pat moved over towards the wardrobe, a rickety old oak wardrobe with half-hearted art nouveau designs carved up each side. She reached out to open it. Bruce drew his breath. That slut Anna, that *slut*, had probably left the cupboard full of her dirty washing. That was just the sort of thing she would do; like a child, really, leaving clothes on the floor for the adults to pick up.

"That's a wardrobe," he said, hoping that she would not try to open it. "I'll clean it out for you. It might have some of her stuff still in it."

Pat hesitated. Was the smell any stronger near the wardrobe? She was unsure.

6

"She didn't keep the place very clean, did she?" she said.

Bruce laughed. "You're right. She was a real slut, that girl. We were all pleased when she decided to go over to Glasgow. I encouraged her. I said that the job she had been offered sounded just fine. A real opportunity."

"And was it?"

Bruce shrugged. "She fancied herself getting into television journalism. She had been offered a job making tea for some producer over there. Great job. Great tea possibilities."

Pat moved towards the desk. One of the drawers was half-open and she could see papers inside.

"It almost looks as if she's planning to come back," she said. "Maybe she hasn't moved out altogether."

Bruce glanced at the drawer. He would throw all this out as soon as Pat went. And he would stop forwarding her mail too.

"If there's any danger of her coming back," he said, smiling, "we'll change the locks."

Later, when Pat had left, he went back to the room and opened the window. Then he crossed the room to the wardrobe and looked inside. The right-hand side was empty, but on the left, in the hanging section, there was a large plastic bag, stuffed full of clothes. This was the source of the musty odour, and, handling it gingerly, he took it out. Underneath the bag was a pair of abandoned shoes, the soles curling off. He picked these up, looked at them with disgust, and dropped them into the open mouth of the plastic bag.

He moved over to the desk. The top drawer looked as if it had been cleared out, apart from a few paper clips and a chipped plastic ruler. The drawer beneath that, half-open, had papers in it. He picked up the paper on the top and looked at it. It was a letter from a political party asking for a donation to a fighting fund. A smiling politician beamed out from a photograph. *I know you care*, said the politician, in bold type, *I know you care enough to help me care for our common future.* Bruce grimaced, crumpled up the letter, and tossed it into the black plastic bag. He picked up the next piece of paper and began to read it. It was handwritten, the second or subsequent page of a letter as it began halfway through a sentence: *which was not very clever of me! Still, I wasn't going to see them again and so I suppose it made no difference. And what about you? I don't know how you put up with those people you live with. Come through to Glasgow. I know somebody who's got a spare room in her flat and who's looking for somebody. That guy Bruce sounds a creep. I couldn't believe it when you said that you thought he read your letters. You reading this one, Bruce?*

It was settled. Pat had agreed to move in, and would pay rent from the following Monday. The room was not cheap, in spite of the musty smell (which Bruce pointed out was temporary) and the general dinginess of the décor (which Bruce had ignored). After all, as he pointed out to Pat, she was staying in the New Town, and the New Town was expensive whether you lived in a basement in East Claremont Street (barely New Town, Bruce said) or in a drawing-room flat in Heriot Row. And he should know, he said. He was a surveyor.

"You have found a job, haven't you?" he asked tentatively. "The rent . . ."

She assured him that she would pay in advance, and he relaxed. Anna had left rent unpaid and he and the rest of them had been obliged to make up the shortfall. But it was worth it to get rid of her, he thought.

He showed Pat to the door and gave her a key. "For you. Now you can bring your things over any time." He paused. "I think you're going to like this place."

Pat smiled, and she continued to smile as she made her way down the stair. After the disaster of last year, staying put was exactly what she wanted. And Bruce seemed fine. In fact, he reminded her of a cousin who had also been keen on rugby and who used to take her to pubs on international nights with all his friends, who sang raucously and kissed her beerily on the cheek. Men like that were very unthreatening; they tended not to be moody, or brood, or make emotional demands – they just *were*. Not that she ever envisaged herself becoming emotionally involved with one of them. Her man – when she found him – would be . . .

"Very distressing! Very, very distressing!"

Pat looked up. She had reached the bottom of the stair and had opened the front door to find a middle-aged woman standing before her, rummaging through a voluminous handbag.

"It's very distressing," continued the woman, looking at Pat over half-moon spectacles. "This is the second time this month that I have come out without my outside key. There are two keys, you see. One to the flat and one to the outside door. And if I come out without my outside key, then I have to disturb one of the other residents to let me in, and I don't like doing that. That's why I'm so pleased to see you."

"Well-timed," said Pat, moving to let the woman in.

"Oh yes. But Bruce will usually let me in, or one of his friends . . ." She paused. "Are you one of Bruce's friends?"

"I've just met him."

The woman nodded. "One never knows. He has so many girl-friends that I lose track of them. Just when I've got used to one, a quite different girl turns up. Some men are like that, you know."

Pat said nothing. Perhaps wholesome, the word which she had previously alighted upon to describe Bruce, was not the right choice.

The woman adjusted her spectacles and stared directly at Pat. "Some men, you see, have inordinate appetites," she remarked. "They seem to be genetically programmed to have a rather large number of partners. And if they're genetically predisposed to do that sort of thing, then I wonder whether we can actually blame them for it. What do you think?"

Pat hesitated. "They could try a bit harder not to cheat."

The woman shook her head. "Not easy," she said. "I believe that we have much less free will than we think. Quite frankly, we delude ourselves if we think that we are completely free. We aren't. And that means if dear Bruce must have rather a lot of girlfriends, then there's not very much he can do about it."

Pat said nothing. Bruce had said nothing about the neighbours, and perhaps this was the reason.

"But this is very rude of me," the woman said. "I've been talking away without introducing myself. And you'll be wondering: *Who is this deterministic person?* Well, I'm Domenica Macdonald, and I live in the flat opposite Bruce and his friends. That's who I am."

Pat gave the woman her name and they shook hands. Her explanation that she had just agreed to take the spare room in Bruce's flat brought a broad smile to Domenica's face.

"I'm very pleased to hear that," she said. "That last girl – the girl whose room you'll be taking . . ." She shook her head. "Genetically programmed to have lots of boyfriends, I think."

"A slut? That's what Bruce called her to me."

This surprised the woman. "Male double standards," said Domenica sharply, adding: "Of course, Edinburgh's full of double standards, isn't it? Hypocrisy is built into the stonework here."

"I'm not sure," ventured Pat. Edinburgh seemed much like anywhere else to her. Why should there be more hypocrisy in Edinburgh than anywhere else?

"Oh, you'll find out," said Domenica. "You'll find out."

3. We See a Bit More of Bruce

"Terrific!" said Bruce, unbuttoning his Triple Crown rugby shirt. "That looks just terrific!"

He was standing in front of the mirror in the bathroom, waiting for the bath to fill. It was a favourite mirror of his, full-length – unlike most bathroom mirrors – which made it possible to inspect at close quarters the benefits of his thrice-weekly sessions in the gym. And the benefits were very evident, in whatever light they were viewed.

He pulled the shirt up over his head and flung it down on the top of the wicker laundry basket. Flexing his biceps, he stared back at the mirror and liked what he saw. Next, by crouching slightly, as if poised to leap forward, the muscles that ran down the side of his trunk – he had no idea what they were called, but could look them up in the chart his personal trainer had given him – these muscles tensed like a series of small skiing moguls. Moguls, in fact, might be a good word for them, he thought. Biceps, pecs, *moguls*.

He removed the rest of his clothes and looked again in the mirror. Very satisfactory, he thought – *very* satisfactory. Reaching up, he ran his fingers lightly across the top of his *en brosse* haircut. Perhaps a little off round the sides next week, or, again, perhaps not. He might ask his new flatmate what she thought. Would I look better with longer hair? What do you think, Pat?

He was not sure about this new girl. She was not going to be any trouble – she could pay the rent and he knew that she would keep the place clean. He had seen her look of concern over the state of the room, and that had been a good sign. But she was a bit young, and that might be problematic. The four years that separated them were crucial ones, in Bruce's mind. It was not that he had no time for twenty-year-olds, it was just that they talked about different things and listened to different music. He had often had to hammer on Anna's door late at night when he was being kept awake by the constant *thump thump* of her music. She played the same music all the time, day-in day-out, and when he had suggested that she might get something different, she had looked at him with what was meant to be a patient expression, as one might look at somebody who simply did not understand.

And of course Bruce could never think of anything to say to her. He would have loved to have been able to come up with a suitable put-down, but it never seemed to be there at the right time, or at any other time, when he came to think of it.

He tested the temperature of the bath and then lowered himself into the water. The cleaning of Anna's room had made him feel dirty, but a good soak in the bath would deal with that. It was a wonderful bath in which to soak; one of the best features of the flat. It must have been there for fifty years, or even more; a great, generous tub, standing on four claw-feet, and filled from large-mouthed silver taps. He very rarely saw a bath like that when he did a valuation, but when he did, he always drew it to the attention of the client. *Fine bathroom fittings*, he would write, knowing that he could be writing the epitaph of the bath, which would be removed and replaced by something half its weight and durability.

He lay back in the water and thought of Pat. He had decided that she was not his type, and in general he preferred to keep relationships with flatmates on a platonic basis, but one should not make absolute rules on these matters, he thought. She was attractive enough, he reflected, although she would not necessarily turn his head in the street. Comfortable, perhaps, was the word. Undisturbing. Average.

Perhaps she would be worth a little attention. He was, after all, between girlfriends, now that Laura had gone down to London. They had agreed that she would come up to Edinburgh once a month and he would go down to London with the same frequency, but it had not worked out. She had made the journey three months in a row, but he had been unable to find the time to do the same. And she had been most unreasonable about it, he thought.

"If you cared anything about me, you would have made the effort," she had said to him. "But you don't and you didn't."

He had been appalled by this attack. There had been very good reasons why he could not go to London, apart from the expense, of course. And he had had every justification for cancelling that weekend: he had entered the wrong date for the Irish international at Murrayfield in his diary and had only discovered his error four days before the event. If she thought that he was going to miss that just to go down for a weekend which could be rearranged for any time, then she was going to have to think again, which she did.

He stood up and stepped out of the bath. As he did so, he caught a glimpse of himself in the mirror, and smiled.

4. Fathers and Sons

Somebody had pushed a bundle of advertisements into the mail box of the Something Special Gallery, which irritated Matthew Duncan. It was Tuesday morning, and the beginning of another working week for Matthew, who took Sundays and Mondays off. He was early that morning – normally he opened at ten o'clock, as it was unheard of to sell a painting before ten, or even eleven. He believed that the best time to make a sale was just before lunch, on a Saturday, to a client who had accepted a glass of sherry. Of course, private views were even better than that, because crowd behaviour then entered into the equation and red spots could proliferate like measles. That, at least, was what he had been told when he had taken over the gallery a few weeks previously. But he could not be sure, as he had so far sold nothing. Not one painting; not one print; nothing at all had been bought by any of the people who had drifted in, looked about them, and then, almost regretfully in some cases, almost apologetically in others, had walked back out of the front door.

Matthew flung the advertisements into the wastepaper bin and walked into the back of the gallery to deal with the alarm, which had picked up his presence and was giving its first warning pips. The code keyed in, he flicked the light switches, bringing to life the spotlights that were trained on the larger paintings on the walls. He enjoyed doing this because it seemed to transform the room so entirely, from a cold, rather gloomy place, inadequately lit by natural light from the front window, into a place of warmth and colour.

It was not a large gallery. The main room, or *space* as Matthew had learned to call it, stretched back about thirty feet from the two wide display windows that looked out onto the street. Halfway down one side of this room there was a desk, which faced outwards, with a telephone and a discreet computer terminal. Beside the desk there was a revolving bookcase in which twenty or thirty books were stacked; a *Dictionary of Scottish Artists*, bound catalogues of retrospectives, a guide to prices at auction. These were the working tools of the dealer and, like everything else, had been left there by the former owner.

Matthew had acquired the gallery on impulse, not an impulse of his, but that of his father, who owned the building and who had repossessed it from the tenant. Matthew's father, who was normally unbending in his business deals, had been an uncharacteristically tolerant landlord to the gallery. He had allowed unpaid rent to mount up to the point where the tenant had been quite incapable of paying. Even then, rather than claim what had been owing for more than two years, he had accepted gallery stock in settlement of the debt and had paid rather generously for the rest.

Matthew's father despaired of his son ever amounting to much in the world of business. He had started Matthew off in a variety of enterprises, all of which had failed. Finally, after two near-bankrupt stores, there had been a travel agency, a business with a promising turnover, but which under Matthew's management had rapidly lost customers. His father had been puzzled by this, and had eventually realised that the problem was not laziness on his son's part, but a complete inability to organise and motivate staff. He simply could not give directions. He was a completely incompetent manager. This was a bitter conclusion for a father who had dreamed of a son who would turn a small Scottish business empire, the result of decades of hard work, into something even bigger. So he had decided that he might as well accept his son's limitations and set him up in a business where he would have virtually no staff to deal with and where there was very little business to be done anyway –

a sinecure, in other words. A gallery was perfect. Matthew could sit there all day and would therefore technically be working – something which he believed to be very important. He would make no money, but then money appeared not to interest him. It was all very perplexing.

But he's my son, thought Matthew's father. He may not be good for very much, but he's honest, he treats his parents with consideration, and he's my own flesh and blood. And it could be much worse: there were sons who caused their fathers much greater pain than that. He's a failure, he thought; but he's a good failure and he's *my* failure.

And for Matthew's part, he knew that he was no businessman. He would have liked to have succeeded in the ventures that his father had planned for him, because he liked his father. My father may have the soul of a Rotarian, thought Matthew, but he's *my* Rotarian, and that's what counts.

5. *Attributions and Provenances*

It was not Pat's first job, of course. There had been that disastrous first gap year, with all the varying jobs that *that* had entailed. She had worked for the person she could now only think of as *that man* for at least four months, and had it not been for the fire – which was in no sense her fault – then she might have spent even longer in that airless, windowless room. And one or two of the other jobs had hardly been much better, although she had never encountered employers quite as bad as he had been.

This was clearly going to be very different. To start with, there was nothing objectionable about Matthew. He had been offhand at the interview, quite casual, in fact, but he had not been rude to her. Now, as she reported for work on that first Tuesday, she noticed that when she came into the room Matthew stood up to greet her, holding out his hand in a welcoming way. The standing up was something that her mother would have noticed and approved of; if a man stands up, she had said, you know that he's going to respect you. Watch your father – when anybody comes into the room he stands up, no matter who they are. That's because he's a . . . She had hesitated, looking at her daughter. No, she could not bring herself to say it.

"Because he's a what?" Pat had challenged. It was always gratifying to expose parents as hopelessly old-fashioned. She was going to say *gentleman*, wasn't she? Hah!

"Because he's a psychiatrist," her mother had said quickly. There! She would find out soon enough, the difference between the types of men, if she did not already know it. And I will not be patronised by her, just because she's twenty and I've reached the age of . . . My God! Have I?

Matthew, sitting down again, unaware of the memory he had triggered, indicated the chair in front of his desk.

"We should talk about the job," he said. "There are a few things to sort out."

Pat nodded, and sat down. Then she looked at Matthew, who looked back at her.

"Now then," Matthew said. "The job. This is a gallery, see, and our business is to sell paintings. That's it. That's the bottom line."

Pat smiled. "Yes." This was surprising. But why was the sale of paintings the bottom line? She was not at all sure what bottom lines were, although everybody talked about them, but perhaps he would explain.

Matthew sat back in his chair, propping his feet on an upturned wastepaper basket at the side of the desk.

"I freely admit that I haven't been in this business for very long," he said. "I've just started, in fact. So we'll have to learn together as we go along. Is that all right with you?"

Pat smiled encouragingly. "I like paintings," she said. "I did a Higher Art at school, at Edinburgh Academy."

"The Academy?" said Matthew.

"Yes."

He looked thoughtful for a moment. Then he said: "I used to go there. You didn't hear anything about me there, did you?"

Pat was puzzled. "No," she said hesitantly. "Not that I remember."

"Good," said Matthew, with the air of one changing the subject. "Now, the job. You need to sit here when I go out. If somebody comes in and wants to buy a painting, the prices are all listed on this piece of paper over here. Don't let a painting out of the gallery until they've paid and the cheque has cleared, so tell them that they can collect the painting in four or five days, or we'll deliver it. If we know them, we can take their cheques."

Pat listened. Matthew was making it clear enough, but surely there must be something else to the job. He could hardly be expected to pay her just to watch the shop for him when he went out.

"Anything else?" she asked.

Matthew shrugged. "Some bits and pieces."

"Such as?"

He looked about him, as if searching for ideas. He looked at the paintings and then turned his gaze back on Pat. "You could do a proper catalogue of stock," he said, and then, warming to the idea, explained: "I had something like that, but I'm afraid that it got lost somewhere. You could go through everything and find out what we have. Then make a proper catalogue with the correct . . . correct . . ." What was the word they used? "Attributions. Yes, attribute the paintings. Find out who they're by."

Pat glanced at the wall behind her. There was a painting of an island, in bright colours, with strong brush strokes. She could just hear the voice of her art teacher at school, intoning, reverentially: "That, boys and girls, is a Peploe."

But it couldn't be a Peploe. Impossible.

6. Bruce Takes a Look at a Place

Bruce worked in a firm of surveyors called Macaulay Holmes Richardson Black. In spite of the name, which implied at least four partners and a global reach, it was not a large firm. There were in fact only two partners, Gordon Todd and his brother, Raeburn, known to the staff as Gordon and Todd. They were good employers, and both of them were prominent in the affairs of their professional association, the Royal Institution of Chartered Surveyors. Gordon always wore a tie with the Institution crest on it, and Todd had a gold signet ring on which the same crest had been engraved. Both were strong golfers. Gordon had become a member of Muirfield (after a rather long wait), and Todd was hoping that the same honour would one day befall him.

"I can't understand why I have to wait longer than he did," Todd said to his wife, Sasha.

"Does it matter?" she asked. "What's so special about that place? Surely one golf course is much the same as another. Fairways, greens, holes. What's so special about Muirfield?"

Todd had looked at her with pity. "Women don't understand," he said. "They just don't."

"Oh yes we do," she said. "We understand very well."

"Then explain it!" Todd had crowed.

"But that's what I just asked you to do," she said. "I asked you what the difference was, and you don't answer that question by batting it back to me. What's the difference? You tell me."

Todd had said nothing. He was confident that Muirfield was special, but he was not sure that he could explain it. Ultimately, it had something to do with the people who played there; special people. But that was not something one could put into words – without a measure of embarrassment – and it was certainly not something that his wife would understand. She would not think of these people as special; that was her mistake.

The firm preferred, if at all possible, to employ sporting assistants. Both brothers found that they could relate easily to sporty types, and such people were also rather good at generating business. Business was done on golf courses (or some of them), and it helped to have sociable employees who would meet clients at parties and in pubs. It was a sociable profession.

Bruce was popular in the firm. Both brothers liked him, to an extent, and Todd had given him a spare seat at Murrayfield on several occasions. Todd had a daughter, Lizzie, who might be suitable for Bruce, so Todd thought, if only she would get over her unreasonable prejudice about him. She seemed to have taken against him on first meeting, and it was quite unfair, although there was perhaps something about this young man which was not quite right – something to do with the way he preened himself? Todd had seen him preening once, looking at himself in the rearview mirror of the firm's Land Rover, and he had been slightly surprised by it.

"Satisfied?" he had said to him, in a joking tone, and Bruce had leapt up, surprised, and muttered something about needing a haircut. But there had been something else going on, and Todd had remembered it.

Now, as he arrived in the office that morning, the morning on which Pat began at the gallery, Bruce saw that Todd had put a file on his desk, to await him. He was to do a survey by eleven o'clock that morning, to report back to the client by eleven-thirty. The property in question, a large top-floor flat overlooking the Dean Valley, had offers closing at noon and the client wanted to bid. This was tight, as he would need to pick up the keys, inspect the property, and dictate a short written report within half an hour of returning to the office.

Bruce took a taxi to the firm of solicitors in York Place. It did not take long to sign for the keys, go back to fetch the company car, and then make his way over the Dean Bridge to the quiet terrace where the flat was located. Once inside, he moved from room to room, noting the condition of the floors and the many other things which it had become second nature to observe. Power points. Fireplaces. The state of the cornices (if any).

He walked through to the kitchen, which was the last room he inspected. There was nothing exceptional about it. The cupboards were in bad taste, of course, because they had stinted on the joinery, but the floor (a sealed cork) was new, and that would not need replacing for some years. So you could live with this kitchen.

He walked past a large microwave oven, which had been placed at eye-level. Its wide, opaque door of smoked glass made him stop. There was something inside it. No. Just me.

He stood still for a moment, and then smiled.

Nice micro-onde, he wrote in his notebook. Bruce liked to give French names to certain things, if he knew the words. Of course he would use English terms in his official report. Imagine Todd wrestling with words like *micro-onde*!

Now for *le toit*, Bruce said to himself.

7. *A Full Survey*

The flat which Bruce was surveying was on the top floor of a four-storey, late-Georgian tenement. The way into the roof space was through a trapdoor in the ceiling immediately above the top landing of the common stair. A stepladder was needed to reach this trapdoor, but there was one conveniently to hand in the hall cupboard of the flat. Bruce set this up below the trapdoor and climbed up to open it.

He pushed against the trapdoor, but it would not budge. He tried again, and this time it opened, reluctantly, but only halfway. Something – a heavy object of some sort – was preventing the trapdoor from opening inwards into the roof space. Bruce lowered it, and then tried again. Still it would not open sufficiently for him to crawl through.

Bruce swore softly under his breath. Looking at his watch, he realised that he now had only fifteen minutes or so to finish the survey if he was going to have sufficient time to write it up by the deadline. Looking up, he peered through the half-open trapdoor into the darkened roof space. He sniffed: if there was rot he might be able to smell it. He knew surveyors who could diagnose the various forms of rot merely by smelling. He could not yet trust himself to rely on that, but he was still able to recognise at least some of the musty smells that could mean that something was wrong. He sniffed again. The air was quite fresh. There was no rot up there.

Closing the trapdoor, Bruce climbed down the ladder. He would have a look from outside, he decided. He had a pair of binoculars in the car and he could use those. He would be able to see if there was anything that needed to be done, which he was sure that there wasn't.

He replaced the ladder, locked the flat, and then made his way downstairs. On the other side of the street there was a set of gardens which sloped steeply down the hill to the Water of Leith below. Bruce crossed over and stood on the pavement, his binoculars trained on the roof of the building. It was by no means ideal, he thought; the angle from which he had to observe the roof made it impossible for him to see more than the first third of it, but that seemed perfectly all right. He ran the binoculars over the stonework along the front of the roof. That seemed fine as well. *Roof inspected and found to be in good condition*, he dictated to himself. He looked at his watch. He had ten minutes to get back to the office, twenty minutes to dictate the report, and that would mean that the client would get it just in time. There was the valuation to think about, of course, but that was not going to be a particular problem. The location was good: the flat was a ten-minute walk from Charlotte

Square; the street was quiet, and there was nothing to suggest that the neighbours were difficult. A flat three doors down had gone recently for three hundred and eighty thousand pounds (Todd had told him about that transaction) but that was on the first floor, which added to the price, and so: *Three hundred and twenty thousand pounds*, thought Bruce, and then, feeling benevolent to the purchasers and their mortgage needs, he added a further eight thousand pounds for good measure. *A fine, late-Georgian flat with many original features. Superb cornice in the south-facing drawing room; wainscoting in all public rooms; a fine bath which a purchaser might wish to preserve, and a decorated fireplace in the rear bedroom depicting the Ettrick Shepherd, Walter Scott and Robert Burns in conversation with one another in a country inn.* These reports wrote themselves, thought Bruce, if one was prepared to loosen up one's prose a bit.

He drove back to Queen Street, parked the car in the mews garage (for which the firm had paid the equivalent price of a small flat in Dundee) and made his way into the office. There the report was dictated, presented to the secretary, and delivered to Todd in a crisp blue folder.

Todd gestured for Bruce to sit down while he read the survey. Then, looking up at his employee, he asked him quietly: "You inspected the roof, did you?"

"Yes," said Bruce. "Nothing wrong there."

"Are you sure?" asked Todd, fingering the edge of the folder. "Did you get up into the roof space?"

Bruce hesitated, but only for a moment. There was nothing wrong with that roof and it would have made no difference had he been able to squeeze through the partly-blocked trapdoor. "I went up," he said. "Everything was fine."

Todd raised an eyebrow. "Well," he said. "It wasn't when I went up last week. I looked at it for another client, you see. He lost interest in offering before I wrote a report, and so I thought a fresh survey appropriate. Had you really gone up, you might have seen the fulminating rot and also noticed the very dicey state of one of the chimney stacks. But . . ."

Bruce said nothing. He was looking at his shoes.

8. Hypocrisy, Lies, Golf Clubs

The silence lasted for several minutes. Todd stared at Bruce across his desk. I trained this young man, he thought; I am partly responsible for this. I had my reservations, of course, but they were about other things, about more general failings, and all the time I was missing the obvious: he's untruthful.

Bruce found it difficult to meet his employer's gaze. I tell far fewer lies than most people, he thought. I really do. Everybody – *everybody* – has cut the occasional corner. It's not as if I had made a report in bad faith. That roof looked fine to me, and I *did* open that trapdoor and look inside. Fulminating rot? Surely I would have smelled it.

Todd drew in his breath. He was still staring at Bruce accusingly, a gaze which was unreturned.

"If surveyors lie," said Todd, "then whom can we believe?"

Bruce said nothing, but shook his head slightly. Self-reproach?

"You see," said Todd, "when a client approaches a professional person, he puts his trust in him or her. He doesn't expect to be misled. Hmm?"

Bruce looked up briefly. "No," he said. "You're right, Todd."

"We rely on our reputation," went on Todd. "If we lose that – and you can lose that very quickly, let me tell you – then we have nothing. Years and years of hard work by my brother and, if I may say so, by me, go out of the window just because somebody is found to be misleading a client. I've seen it happen.

"And there are much broader considerations," he went on. "All of our life is based on acts of trust. We trust other people to do what they say they're going to do. When we get on an aeroplane we trust the airline to have maintained its aircraft. We trust the pilot, who has our lives in his hands. We trust other people, you see, Bruce. We trust them. And that's why what you've done is so dreadful. It really is. It's unforgivable. Yes, sorry, but that's the word. Unforgivable."

It was at this point that Bruce realised that he was about to lose his job. Up to now, it had been one of the little lectures that Todd occasionally gave his staff; now it was something different. He looked at his employer, meeting his gaze, hoping to read his intentions.

Todd's face registered not anger, but disappointment. This confirmed Bruce's fears. I'm unemployed, he said to himself. As of five minutes from now, I'm an unemployed (and unemployable, he suddenly realised) surveyor.

"So when you went into that building at No. 87 Eton Terrace, you were doing so on trust. You were . . ."

Bruce sat up straight. "Number 78."

Todd paused. "Number . . ." He looked at the file in front of him. "Number . . ."

Bruce closed his eyes with relief. Yes, there had been a flat for sale at No. 87. He remembered somebody saying something about it over coffee. Todd had confused the two.

Todd had now extracted a diary from a drawer and was checking a note. He closed the book, almost reluctantly, and looked up at Bruce.

"I'm sorry," he said quietly. "This is my mistake. I'm very sorry. I was mixing up two properties. You see . . ."

Bruce shook his head. "You don't need to apologise, Todd," he said. "We all make mistakes. All of us. You really don't need to apologise to me." He paused, before continuing. "The important thing is to remember that, and to own up to one's mistakes when one makes them. That's the really important thing. To tell the truth. To tell the truth about one's mistakes."

Todd rose to his feet. "Well," he said. "We can put that behind us. There's work to be done."

"Of course," said Bruce. "But I was wondering whether I could possibly have the afternoon off. I'm pretty much up to date and . . ."

"Of course," said Todd. "Of course."

Bruce smiled at his employer and rose to leave.

"A moment," said Todd, reaching for the file. "Was there an old or a new tank in the roof space? Some of those places still have the lead tanks."

Bruce again hesitated, but only for an instant. "It was fine," he said. "New tank."

Todd nodded. "Good," he said.

Bruce left the room. He was trying to trap me, he thought. One would have imagined that he had learned his lesson, but he was still trying to trap me. As if I would lie, *as if*. He felt angry with Todd now. What a hypocrite! Sitting there lecturing me about lies when he comes from a whole world of lies and hypocrisy. What hypocrites! Masonic lodges! Golf clubs! – even though he's not a member of the golf club he really wants to be a member of, thought Bruce, with a certain degree of satisfaction.

9. SP

Pat was hardly surprised when Matthew announced that he was going to take a coffee break. She had been sitting in her cramped office at the back of the gallery, retyping the now somewhat grubby list of paintings which Matthew had handed her. Matthew had been reading the newspaper at his desk in the front, glancing at his watch from time and time and sighing. It was obvious to Pat that he was bored. There was nothing for him to do in the gallery and his mind was not on the newspaper.

Shortly before half-past ten, Matthew folded up his newspaper, rose to his feet and announced to Pat that he was going out.

"I go to that place on the other side of the road," he said. "The Morning After, it's called. Not a very good name, if you ask me, but that's what it's called. Everyone calls it Big Lou's. If you need me, you can give me a call."

"When will you be back?" asked Pat.

Matthew shrugged. "Depends," he said. "An hour or so. Maybe more. It all depends."

"I'll be fine," said Pat. "Take your time."

Matthew gave her a sideways glance. "It is my time," he muttered. "It goes with being your own boss."

Pat smiled. "Sorry, I didn't mean to be rude. I just wanted you to know that I think I'll be all right."

"Of course, you will," said Matthew. "I can tell you're going to be a great success. I can tell these things." He touched her lightly on the shoulder. "Smart girl."

Pat said nothing. She was used to condescension from a certain sort of man, and although she did not like it, it was better than what she had experienced on her gap year – her first gap year.

Alone in the gallery, Pat seated herself at Matthew's desk and looked out onto the street. She watched Matthew cross the road and disappear into The Morning After. She would make herself a cup of coffee in a few minutes, she thought. She rationed herself to three cups a day, and eagerly looked forward to the first cup of the morning.

Matthew had left his newspaper on the desk, and she picked it up. The front page was filled with political news, which she skipped over, in favour of an article on an inside page about a new film which everybody was talking about but which nobody, apparently, had seen. The violence in this film, it was said, was particularly graphic. There were severed heads, and limbs, and the breaking of bones. This, the writer said, was all very exciting. But why was it exciting, to see others harmed in this way? Were we addicted to fear, or dread? Pat was reflecting on this when she heard the muted note of the bell which announced that somebody had entered the gallery. She looked up and saw a man of about forty, wearing corduroy trousers and a green sweater. He was not dressed for the office, and had the air of a person with no pressing engagements.

"May I?" he said, gesturing at the paintings.

"Of course," said Pat. "If there's anything you want to know . . ." She left the sentence unfinished. If there was something he wanted to know it was unlikely that she would be able to give him any information. She could call Matthew, of course, but then he appeared to know nothing as well.

The man smiled, looking about him as if deciding where to start. After a few moments he went up to a small still-life, a Glasgow jug into which a bunch of flowers had been stuffed at a drunken angle.

"Not the way to arrange flowers," he said, and then added: "Nor to paint them . . ."

Pat said nothing. It was an unpleasant, amateurish painting; he was quite right. But she said nothing; she felt vaguely protective of Matthew's paintings, and it was not for customers to come in and criticise them, even if the criticism was deserved.

The man moved over to the painting which looked like a Peploe; school of Peploe perhaps. He stood in front of it for a few moments and then turned to address Pat.

"Very nice," he said. "In a derivative sort of way. Peaceful. Shore of Mull from Iona, or shore of Iona from Mull?"

Pat picked up the list from her desk and walked over to join him. "According to this, it's Mull," she said. "Mull, near Tobermory, by, and then there's a question mark."

"It's not a Peploe," the man said. "That's pretty obvious. But it has its points. Look over there, that nice shading. Confident brush strokes."

Pat looked. How can he be so sure it's not a Peploe, she wondered. Particularly since there were the initials SP painted in the bottom right-hand corner. Then it occurred to her: SP – School of Peploe.

10. The Road from Arbroath

Matthew felt that he was the discoverer of Big Lou's coffee bar, although, like everything that is discovered (America or Lake Victoria being examples), it had always been there; or at least it had been there for the last three years or so. Before that it had been a second-hand bookshop, noted for its jumbled stock, that observed no known principle in the shelving of its collection. Topography rubbed shoulders with poetry; books on fishing and country pursuits stood side-by-side with Hegel and Habermas; and nothing was too recondite to find a place, even if no purchaser. Nobody wanted, it seemed, a guide to the walking paths of Calabria, to be found, quite fortuitously, next to an India-paper edition of *South Wind* by Norman Douglas, signed by the author, and forgotten.

Only the proprietor loved these books, so fiercely and possessively, perhaps, that he discouraged purchasers. At length, as if crushed by the sheer weight of his duty and slow-moving stock, he died, and the shop was sold by his executors to Big Lou, together with its books. And then, in a gesture which was to change her life, she took all the books home to her flat in Canonmills and began to read them, one by one. She read the Norman Douglas, she read the guide to Calabrian walking paths, and she read the Hegel and the Habermas. And curiously enough, she remembered the contents of all these books.

Big Lou came from Arbroath, and that was all that anybody knew about her. Questions about what she had done before she arrived in Edinburgh were ignored, as if they had not been asked, and as a result there was some speculation. She had been married to a sailor; no, she was a sailor herself, having gone to sea dressed as a man and never been unmasked; no, she had been a man, who had gone to Tangier for an operation and returned as a woman. None of this was correct. In fact, Big Lou had done very little with her life. In Arbroath she had looked after an aged uncle until she reached the age of thirty. Then she had left, but the leaving had been ill-starred. Having decided to go to Edinburgh on the death of the demanding uncle, she had shut up the house, handed the keys to a relative, and walked to the station with her suitcase. Arbroath Station is not complicated, but Big Lou had nonetheless mistaken the north-bound platform for the south-bound one, and had boarded a train to Aberdeen. She had been tired; the carriage was warm, and she almost immediately went to sleep, to wake up shortly before the train reached Stonehaven. She alighted at Aberdeen Station and felt too discouraged to return immediately. Somehow, Aberdeen was less threatening than she suspected Edinburgh might be. Directly outside the station there was a small café, and in the window of this she saw a notice advertising a vacancy for care assistants at a nursing home. That, she thought, is what I am. I am a carer. I care for others, which is exactly what she did for the next eight years in the Granite Nursing Home.

Although it was in some respects discouraging, this job ultimately proved to be extremely lucrative. One of the residents, a retired farmer from Buchan, had named her as the principal beneficiary in his will, and she had come into a substantial sum of money. This was the signal to stop caring for people in Aberdeen – in every sense – and to take the train that she had missed those eight years before. She was now in a position to buy the coffee bar and the flat in Canonmills, and to start a new life.

The coffee bar had been designed for her by a man she had met in a launderette. Like most of the things that had happened in Big Lou's life, she was not properly consulted. Things happened to her; she did not initiate anything. And so she was never asked whether she wanted the booths that this man designed and constructed for her; nor whether she approved of the large and expensive mahogany newspaper rack which he installed near the front door. This was all done without anything having been agreed, and she appeared to accept this, just as she had accepted that she should devote the early years of her adult life to looking after her uncle, while her friends from school had gone off to Glasgow or to London and had all led lives of their own making.

There had been men, of course, but they had treated her badly. One had been a married man who had harboured no intention of leaving his wife for Big Lou; another had been a chef on an oil rig, who had left her to take up a job in Galveston, cooking for Texan oilmen. He had written to tell her about his life in Texas and also to tell her not to come out to join him. Galveston was no place for a woman, he had said.

Big Lou kept this letter, as it was one of the few personal letters she had ever received. She wanted to keep it, too, because she loved this man, this oily cook, and she hoped that one day he might return, although she knew this would never happen.

11. The Origins of Love and Hate

Matthew negotiated his way down the stairs that led to Big Lou's coffee bar. They were hazardous stairs, down which Hugh MacDiarmid had fallen on at least two occasions in the days when the bookshop had been there. Then, it had been the unevenness of the tread; now, to this peril was added the hazard of a collapsed railing. Big Lou had intended to fix it, but this had never been done.

The coffee bar had been divided into booths – low divisions that enabled the tops of heads to be seen above the wooden partitions. The booths were comfortable, though, and Big Lou never encouraged her customers to hurry. So one might sit there all day, if one wished, and not feel any of the unease that one might feel elsewhere.

Matthew usually stayed for an hour or so, although if the conversation was good he might sit there for two hours, or even more. He was joined each morning by Ronnie and his friend Pete, furniture restorers who occupied a workshop in a lane off an elegant New Town crescent. Ronnie specialised in cabinet work, while Pete was a French polisher and upholsterer. They had worked together for two years, having met in a pub after what had been a traumatic afternoon for their football team. Matthew knew nothing about football, which interested him not at all, and by unspoken agreement they kept off the topic. But Matthew sensed that there were unresolved football issues somewhere beneath the surface, as there so often are with upholsterers.

Ronnie was married; Pete was not. Matthew had only known Ronnie since he had taken over the gallery, and during this time he had not had the opportunity to meet Ronnie's wife, Mags. But he had heard a great deal about her, some of it from Pete, and some from Ronnie himself.

When Ronnie was not there, Pete was voluble on the subject of Mags.

"I wouldn't bother to meet her," he said. "She'll hate you."

Matthew raised an eyebrow. "I don't see why she should hate me. Why?"

"Oh, it's not you," said Pete. "It's nothing personal. Mags could even like you until she found out."

Matthew was puzzled. "Until she found out what?"

"That you're a friend of Ronnie's," explained Pete. "You see, Mags hates Ronnie's friends. She's jealous of them, I suppose, and she can't help herself. She looks at them like this. See? And they don't like it."

Matthew winced. "What about you? Does she hate you?"

"Oh yes," said Pete. "Although she tries to hide it. But I can tell that she hates me."

"What's the point?"

Pete shrugged. "None that I can see. But she does it nonetheless."

Big Lou had been listening to this conversation from behind her counter. Now she chipped in.

"She hates you because you threaten her," she said. "Only insecure people hate others. I've read about it. There's a book called *The Origins of Love and Hate*. I've read it, and it tells you how insecurity leads to hatred."

The two men turned and looked at Big Lou.

"Are you sure?" asked Pete after a while. "Is that it?"

"Yes," said Big Lou. "Mags hates Ronnie's friends because she's afraid of losing him and because they take him away from her. How much time does Ronnie spend talking with Mags? Have you ever seen him talk to her?"

"Never," mused Pete. "Never."

"Well, there you are," said Big Lou. "Mags feels neglected."

Pete was about to say something in response to this when he suddenly stiffened and tapped Matthew on the forearm.

"They're here," he whispered. "Ronnie, with Mags in tow."

Matthew turned round to look. Ronnie was making his way down the steps, followed by a woman in a flowing Paisley dress and light brown suede boots. The woman was carrying a bulging shopping bag and a folded copy of a magazine. As they entered the coffee bar, Ronnie exchanged a glance with Pete and then turned to Mags to point to the booth where his two friends were sitting. She followed his glance and then, Matthew noticed, she frowned.

Ronnie approached the booth.

"This is Mags," he said, almost apologetically. "Mags, this is Matthew. You haven't met him before. Matthew's a friend of mine."

Matthew stood up and extended a hand to Mags.

"Why do you stand up?" she said sharply. "Do you stand up for everybody, or is it just because I'm a woman?"

Matthew looked at the floor. "I stand up because I intend to leave," he said evenly. "Not wishing to be condescended to, or whatever, I intend to leave. You may have my seat if you wish."

He walked out, and started up the perilous steps. He was shaking, like a boy who had done something forbidden.

12. Chanterelles Trouvées

Bruce had offered to cook dinner for Pat that evening. The offer had been made before he left the flat in the morning as he popped his head, uninvited, round her half-open door.

"I'm cooking anyway," he said. "It's as easy to cook for two as it is for one."

"I'd love that," said Pat. She noticed his glance move around her room as they spoke, resting for a moment on her unmade bed before moving to the suitcase which she had not yet fully unpacked.

Bruce nodded. "You will," he said. "I'm not a bad cook, if you don't mind my saying so. I could teach Delia a thing or two."

Pat laughed, which seemed to please Bruce.

"Only about surveying," he went on. "Not about cooking." He finished, and waited for Pat to laugh again, but she did not.

"I'm sure it'll be very good," she said solemnly. "What will we have?"

"I only cook pasta," said Bruce. "Pasta with mushrooms probably. Chanterelles. You like mushrooms, don't you?"

"Love them," said Pat.

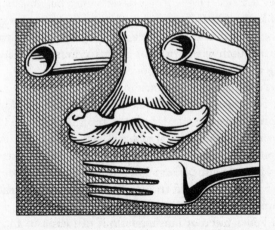

"Good. Chanterelles in a butter sauce, then, with cream. Garlic. Black pepper and a salad dressed with olive oil and a dash of balsamic

33

vinegar. Balsamic vinegar comes from Modena, you know. Has to. How about that?"

"Perfect," said Pat. "Perfect."

When she returned to Scotland Street that evening, late – because Matthew had asked her to show a painting to a client who could only come in after six – Bruce had laid out the ingredients of his pasta dish on the kitchen table. She sat there as he cooked, explaining as he did so some troubling incident at work that day, a row over defective central heating and a leaky cupola.

"I told them they'd have trouble with these people," he said. "And I was right. It always happens. You get people moving up in the world and they start putting on airs. They probably had to look up the word 'cupola' in the dictionary before they complained about it. Cup-er-lah. That's what they call it. *I've got a leaky cup-er-lah.*"

"It can't be any fun having a leaky cupola," Pat pointed out, mildly. "You can't blame them."

"All cup-er-lahs leak," said Bruce. "People who have cup-er-lahs are used to that. It's just when you get promoted to having a cup-er-lah that you get all uptight about it. *Nouvelle cup-er-lah.* That's what they are."

The pasta cooked, he had tipped helpings onto two plates, had added the yellow sauce, and sat down at the table opposite her. The sauce, although too rich for her taste, was well-made, and she complimented him.

"Where did you get the mushrooms?" Pat asked.

"From my boss," said Bruce. "Mr Todd. He found them and gave them to me."

Pat paused, looking down at her plate.

"He picked them?"

"Yes. He picked them on a golf course up in Perthshire. He hit a ball off the fairway and it landed in the middle of these mushrooms, under a tree."

Pat fished a piece of mushroom out of the pasta and looked at it. "Does he know what he's doing?"

Bruce smiled. "No. He's pretty ignorant. Useless, in fact."

"Then how does he know that these are chanterelles? How does he know these aren't . . . aren't poisonous?"

"He doesn't," said Bruce. "But I do. I can tell chanterelles. I know they're all right. I've only been wrong about mushrooms once – a long time ago."

"And you were ill?"

"Very," said Bruce. "I nearly died. But I'm right about these. I promise you. You'll be fine."

They continued with the meal in silence.

"You don't have to eat this if you don't want to," Bruce said sulkily.

Pat thought for a moment, but shook her head and finished her helping, rather quickly, thought Bruce. Then, over coffee, which Bruce brought to the table, they talked about Matthew and the gallery.

"I've met him," said Bruce. "His old man's a big Watsonian. Rugby. The works. Lots of tin. But the son's useless, I think."

"You seem to find a lot of people useless," remarked Pat. She did not want to sound aggressive, but the remark came out as a challenge.

Bruce took her observation in his stride. "Well, they are. There are lots of useless people in this city. It's the truth, and if it's the truth then why bother to conceal it? I spell things out, that's all."

They finished their coffee and then Bruce explained that he was going to meet friends in the Cumberland Bar. Pat was welcome to come if she wished. They were interesting people he said: surveyors and people from the rugby club. She should come along. But she did not.

13. You Must Remember This / A Kiss Is Just a Kiss

After Bruce had left the flat for the Cumberland Bar, Pat went back into her room and lay down on her bed. It was proving to be a rather dispiriting evening. It was not easy listening to her flatmate and his opinionated views, and she wondered if she was beginning to feel queasy. Those mushrooms had tasted all right, but then that was often the case with poisonous fungi, was it not?

She lay on her bed and placed a hand on her stomach. What would the first symptoms be? Nausea? Vomiting? Or would one simply become drowsy and fade away, as Socrates had done when given hemlock? She should have refused to eat them, of course; once Bruce had announced their origins she should have had the courage of her convictions. She would have to change. She would have to stand up to him.

She picked up her mobile phone and opened the lid. She had told herself that she would not phone home at the first sign of feeling miserable, because she had to learn to stand on her own two feet. But phoning home was always so reassuring, particularly if she spoke to her father, who was so calm about everything and had an outlook of cheerful optimism – a vindication of the proposition that the one requirement for a successful career in psychiatry is a sense of humour.

Pat started to key in the number but stopped. Somebody was playing a musical instrument, a clarinet, or was it a saxophone? Yes, it was a saxophone; and it seemed that it was being played directly outside her door. She listened for a moment, and then realised that the sound was coming up through the wall beside her bed. It was not bad; there was the occasional stumble, but it was no rank amateur playing.

She continued dialling and heard her father answer at the other end. He asked where she was.

"I'm in my room. I'm lying on my bed listening to somebody downstairs play the sax. Listen." She put the mobile up against the wall for a few moments.

"'As Time Goes By'," said her father. "From *Casablanca*. And it sounds as if it's being played on a tenor sax. Not badly either."

"It's very loud," said Pat. "It comes right up into my room."

"I suppose you must expect *some* saxophone music if you live in a flat," he said. "Still, you could ask them to keep it down, couldn't you? Didn't Tommy Smith learn to play the sax with socks stuffed down it because of the neighbours? I think he did."

"I don't really mind," said Pat. "It's better than listening to Bruce."

"Your flatmate?"

"Yes," said Pat. "But I suppose he's not too bad."

There was a short silence at the other end of the line. "You don't want to come home, do you?"

"No. I don't."

14. The Smell of Cloves

Pat switched off the mobile. The saxophone player had stopped, and only silence came through the walls.

She began to think of Bruce, and how she should deal with him. It was not that he had been rude or stand-offish; it was more a question of his having *patronised* her. That might have been something to do with the fact that he was a crucial few years older than she was, but somehow it seemed to be more than that. It would be better, she thought, when the other two flatmates, Ian and Sheila, arrived, as Bruce would perhaps be a little bit less overbearing. But where were these other two? Bruce had said that they were away travelling, but had not been specific. He thought that they were in Greece, but he was not sure. And he had not said what they were doing there.

Pat got up from her bed and closed the curtains. Her room still had a musty smell to it, and she had left the window slightly open to freshen the air. She had also bought a supply of joss sticks, and she lit one of these now, savouring the sharp sandalwood smell of the curling wisp of smoke.

Picking up her towel from where she had draped it over the back of her chair, she made her way through to the bathroom. It was a good opportunity to use it; Bruce tended to monopolise it when he was in, and the previous evening, when she had been trying to luxuriate in the bath, he had knocked on the door and asked her when she would be coming out. This was a small thing, perhaps, but it was irritating.

Pat closed the bathroom door behind her and began to run a bath. Putting her towel down on the bentwood bathroom chair, she slipped out of her shoes and was about to get undressed when her eye was caught by the mirrored cupboard above the hand-basin. This was a large cupboard, and she noticed that there were greasy fingerprints on the mirror near the handle where somebody, presumably Bruce, had touched the mirror as he opened the cupboard door.

A shared bathroom is not a place of secrets, and Pat felt quite entitled to open the cupboard. After all, she might store her things there too; Bruce did not have an exclusive claim to storage space, even if he was the senior resident.

There were three shelves in the cupboard, and all of them were virtually full of jars and tubes. Pat peered at the labels on the jars nearest the front: *après rasage pour hommes actifs*; *restoring cream for the masculine face*; *gel pour l'homme sportif*. Pat leaned forward and made a closer inspection. She knew that men used cosmetics, but this, surely, was an over-abundance. And did men actually use body butter? Bruce apparently did.

Pat reached forward and took out the jar of *gel pour l'homme sportif*. Opening it, she stuck a finger into the oleaginous substance and sniffed at it. It was not unpleasant; redolent of cloves perhaps. She took a further sniff at the gel, and then the jar slipped out of her hands and fell to the floor. It bounced once and shattered, leaving a circle of green gel on the floor, like a small inverted jelly, covered with fragments of glass.

She stared at the broken glass and the now useless gel. A spicy smell hung in the air. So might Zanzibar smell, on a hot night, or an Indonesian bar with its cloud of clove tobacco smoke in the air; or the bathroom of a flat in Scotland Street. She left the mess where it was, intending to clear it up after her bath. And she thought of her father, and a remark he had made about accidents and how they reveal our repressed wishes. *We destroy that which we love*, he had said. Had she intended to destroy Bruce's hair gel, because she was falling in love with him? Impossible. She could not fall in love with Bruce. She simply could not.

15. 560 SEC

Pat left the flat the next morning at precisely the time that Domenica Macdonald opened her door onto their mutual landing. Domenica, wearing a green overcoat and carrying a scuffed leather bag, greeted her warmly and enquired about her settling in.

"I'm very happy," said Pat, but thought immediately of the fact that she had not told Bruce about the dropping of the gel. "It's all going well, or . . ." *Quite well* was what she meant to say.

"I know," said Domenica, lowering her voice. "Bruce might be a little bit, how should we put it? Difficult? Is that the right word, difficult?"

"Different," suggested Pat.

Domenica smiled, and took Pat's arm as they went downstairs. "Men *are* different, aren't they? I remember when I first lived with a man – my husband, in fact, things being somewhat more *respectable* in those days, I found it very strange indeed. Men are so . . . so . . . well, I must say I don't quite know the word for men, do you?"

"Masculine?" suggested Pat.

Domenica laughed. "Exactly. That says everything, doesn't it? Bruce is masculine. In a way." She looked at Pat in a shared moment of feminine understanding. "They're little boys, aren't they? That's what I think they are."

They were now on the landing of the floor below, and Domenica gestured at the door of the flat on the right. "Speaking of little boys, that's where young Bertie lives. You will have heard him playing the saxophone last night, I assume."

Pat glanced at the door, which was painted light blue and bore

39

a sticker indicating that no nuclear power was produced, nor used, within.

"Yes," she said. "I heard him."

Domenica sighed. "I don't object to the noise. He plays remarkably well, actually. What I object to is his age."

Pat was uncertain what this meant, and looked at Domenica quizzically. It was difficult to imagine how one might object to the age of another person: age was something beyond one's control, surely.

Domenica sensed her confusion. "Bertie, you see, is very young. He's about five, I believe. And that's too young to play the saxophone."

"Five!"

"Yes," said Domenica, looking disapprovingly at the landing behind them and at the light blue door. "Very pushy parents! Very pushy, particularly her. They're trying to raise him as some sort of infant prodigy. He's being taught music and Italian by his mother. Heaven knows why they decided on the saxophone, but there we are. Poor child!"

Pat found it difficult to imagine a five-year-old boy playing "As Time Goes By" on the saxophone. If it was a tenor instrument, then it would be difficult to see how his fingers would span the keys. And a saxophone would be almost as tall as the boy himself. Did he stand, then, on a chair to play it?

"The whole point about childhood," Domenica went on, "is that it affords us a brief moment of innocence and protection from the pressures of the world. Parents who push their children too hard intrude on that little bit of space. And of course they make their children massively anxious. You weren't pushed by your parents, were you?"

Pat shook her head. "Not at all. I was encouraged, but not pushed."

"There's a big difference," said Domenica. "And I could tell that you weren't pushed. You're too calm and sensible. You seem to be a very balanced person to me. Not that I know you terribly well. In fact, I don't know you at all. But one gets that *feeling* about you."

Pat felt vaguely embarrassed by this conversation, and was about to change the subject, but they had by now reached the front door and Domenica had disengaged her arm.

"You're on your way to work?"

"Yes," said Pat.

"I could give you a lift," Domenica offered. "My car is right there in the street. It would be no trouble."

"Work is just round the corner," said Pat. "It's kind of you, though."

Domenica paid no attention to this refusal. "That's it over there," she said. "That custard-coloured Mercedes-Benz 560 SEC. That's my car."

Pat stared at the car which was being pointed out by Domenica. It was a sleek-looking coupé with gleaming silver hub caps and a proud Mercedes circle worked into the grille. "It's a very beautiful car," she said. "A lovely car."

"It's a dream to drive," said Domenica. "It has a double kickdown feature. You press your foot right down and it shifts the automatic gear-box down, twice, if you need it. And the power! The engine capacity is five point six litres, which gives it the power of five Minis!"

"Five Minis!" exclaimed Pat.

"Yes!" said Domenica. "Five Minis! Now come, my dear, let's get in it!"

16. *Irrational Beliefs and the Mind of the Child*

Bertie and his mother came out of the front door of 44 Scotland Street just after Domenica and Pat had strapped themselves into the front seats of the custard-coloured Mercedes-Benz. Neither couple noticed one another: Domenica was busy with the starting of the engine, while Pat was looking with admiration at the plush off-custard leather upholstery and the polished walnut dashboard. For their part, the two members of the Pollock family, young Bertie, aged five, and his mother, Irene, aged thirty-four, were concerned about getting to the East New Town Nursery in good time. For Bertie, an early arrival was important if he was to secure the train set before other boys, with lesser moral entitlements, claimed it; for Irene, an early arrival meant that she could speak to the supervisor, Miss Christabel Macfadzean, before she became too distracted by children and parents to give her any attention. There were several matters which she wished to raise with her, and it was no good writing to her as she never gave anything more than a brief acknowledgment of the note.

Irene did not like Christabel Macfadzean, even if she had to admit grudgingly that the teacher had a few good points – she was conscientious enough, and the children seemed quite attached to her. The trouble was, though, that she did not appear to realise just how gifted Bertie was and how much extra stimulation and attention he needed. This was not to say that other children did not have their needs – of course they did – it's just that Bertie's needs were special. The other children could not read, for instance, while Bertie read English well and was making good progress with Italian. He had a well-used Italian children's book, *Le Avventure del Piccolo Roberto* which he could now read in its entirety, and he had moved on to an Italian translation of *Max und Moritz* (not something with which Irene saw eye to eye ideologically, but it was better, she decided, than the *Struwwelpeter* with its awful cruelties).

As they walked through Drummond Place, Bertie held onto his mother's hand and desperately tried to avoid stepping on any of the cracks in the pavement.

"Do come along, Bertie," said Irene. "Mummy has not got all day. And why are you walking in that silly way?"

"Cracks," said Bertie. "If I step on the cracks, then they'll get me. *È vero.*"

"What nonsense!" she said. "*Non è vero!* And who are *they* anyway? The CIA?"

"Bears . . ." Bertie began, and then stopped. "The CIA? Do they get you too?"

"Of course they don't," said Irene. "Nobody gets you."

They walked on in silence. Then Bertie said: "Who are the CIA? Where do they live?"

"The CIA are American spies," said Irene. "They watch people, I suppose."

"Are they watching us?"

"Of course not. And they don't mind if you step on the cracks. Plenty of people step on the cracks and get away with it."

Bertie thought for a moment. "Some people get away with it? And other people? What happens to them?"

"Nothing," said Irene. "Nothing happens to anybody if they step on the cracks. Look, I'm stepping on the cracks, and nothing is happening to me. Look. Another crack, right in the middle, and nothing . . ."

She did not complete her sentence. Her heel, caught in a rather larger than usual crack, became stuck and she fell forwards, landing heavily on the pavement. Her foot, wrenched out of its shoe, twisted sharply and she felt a sudden pain in her ankle.

Bertie stood quite still. Then he looked up at the sky and waited for a moment. If there was to be further retribution, perhaps it would be from that quarter. But nothing came, and he felt safe enough to bend down and take his mother's hand.

"I've twisted my ankle," said Irene, miserably. "It's very sore."

"Poor Irene," said Bertie softly. "I told you, didn't I?"

Irene rose to her feet tentatively. The twisted ankle was painful, but not too painful to walk upon, and they could continue their journey, although more slowly than before.

"It's very important that you don't think that was anything but

43

an accident," she said firmly, a few minutes later. "That's all it was. I don't want you developing magical ideas. Belief in fairies and all the rest."

"Fairies?" asked Bertie. "Are there any fairies?"

They were now at the end of London Street. The nursery was not far away.

"There are no fairies," said Irene.

Bertie looked doubtful. "I'm not so sure," he said.

17. *An Educational Exchange*

Miss Christabel Macfadzean, proprietrix of the East New Town Nursery, looked concerned when she saw Irene limp through the front door. "You've hurt your ankle?" she asked solicitously. "An accident?"

"Not an accident," muttered Bertie, only to be silenced by Irene.

"Yes, an accident," she said. "But a very minor one. I tripped on the pavement in Drummond Place."

"So easily done," sympathised Christabel. "You take your life in your hands walking anywhere these days. If one doesn't fall into a hole, then one might get stuck to the pavement because of all the discarded chewing-gum. One might just stand there, stuck and unable to move."

Irene smiled tolerantly. Although Christabel was surely no more than forty-five, she was very old-fashioned, she thought, with remarks like that about chewing-gum – *anti-youth* remarks, really. In normal circumstances she might have been inclined to challenge her on that and say, *Is that remark really about chewing-gum, or is it directed against teenagers in general?* but the conversation had to be brought round to Bertie.

"I wanted to discuss Bertie for a moment," she said. "I know you're busy, but . . ."

Christabel glanced at her watch. "A few minutes. I really must . . ."

Irene seized her chance. "You'll have noticed how bright he is," she said.

Christabel looked away for a moment. Of course Bertie was bright – frighteningly so – but she was not going to encourage this pushy woman. There was nothing worse in her view, nothing, than a pushy parent.

"He's not slow," she said, carefully.

Irene's eyes widened in surprise. "Not slow? Of course he's not slow. He's gifted."

"In what respect?" asked Christabel evenly. "Most children have gifts of one sort or another. That little boy over there – that tall one – he's very good with a ball. Gifted, in fact."

Irene's lips pursed. "That's different, quite different. Gifted is a term of art in developmental psychology. It should only be used for children who have exceptional intelligence."

"I don't know," said Christabel casually. "I haven't had all that much experience of young children, I suppose – no more than twenty-two years – but I do think that most children have their little gifts. Certainly Bertie is quite good at assembling the train set. And he's not bad when we have our little sing-songs."

Irene struggled to contain herself. "And his Italian?" she blurted out. "His Italian? Have you noticed that he speaks Italian?"

Miss Macfadzean had, but too much was at stake now to tell the truth.

"Italian?" she said. "How interesting. Are you Italian? Or your husband? We often get bilingual children in – when one of the parents speaks another language. Children pick it up so readily in the home. They're remarkable linguists. All of them – not just Bertie."

"I am not Italian," said Irene. "Nor is my husband, for that matter. Bertie has *learned* Italian. It is an accomplishment he has – one of a number of accomplishments."

"How useful," said Miss Macfadzean coolly. "He will be well placed should he go on holiday to Italy."

"That's not the point," said Irene. "He has learned Italian to read it and appreciate the culture."

"How nice," said Miss Macfadzean, glancing at her watch. "Such noble people the Italians, sometimes."

"Yes," said Irene. "And he's recently passed Grade six saxophone. Grade six."

"What an active little boy!" said Miss Macfadzean. "I'm surprised that he finds time to come to playgroup! We're obviously very lucky to have him."

"He needs more stimulation," Irene pressed on. "If you could find the time to work with his reading . . ."

"Out of the question," said Miss Macfadzean. "There are all the other children to think about. I'm sorry." She paused for a moment. "Anyway, I did want to have a word with you about Bertie's behaviour. He needs to work a bit more on his co-operation with other children. He's not exactly gifted in that respect. Sometimes there are *incidents*."

"Incidents?"

"Yes," went on Miss Macfadzean. "He likes the train set. But he must learn to share it a bit more. He destroyed a rather nice little station set-up that one of the other children had made. He said that he had blown it up. He said it was something to do with politics."

Irene smiled. "Dear Bertie! That's the trouble, you see. He's so much more advanced than the other children. They won't know anything about politics. They won't even know the word."

"No, they won't," agreed Miss Macfadzean. "But he shouldn't really spoil their games. We have to teach them how to live and let live. We have to encourage socialisation."

"Bertie knows all about socialisation," said Irene quickly. "The problem is that all the other children are . . . well, sorry to have to say this, but they're just not up to him. They won't understand him. And that means he gets frustrated. You have to see it from his point of view."

Miss Macfadzean glanced at her watch again. "Perhaps he needs to be left alone a bit more. Perhaps he needs a little more space to be a five-year-old boy. Do you think . . . ?" She tailed off weakly, disconcerted by Irene's stare.

"Bertie is a very special child," Irene said quietly. "But not everyone seems to understand that." She glanced at Miss Macfadzean, who looked away again. It was hopeless, Irene thought; hopeless.

18. The Works of Melanie Klein

The unsatisfactory interview over, Irene walked back to Scotland Street, giving a wide berth to the section of pavement which had been the cause of her downfall. She knew very well what Miss Macfadzean had thought of her; it had been apparent in her every look and in her every insulting remark. She thought that here was another pushy mother – one of those women who thinks that their child is special and is not getting enough attention. That's what she thought about her, and it was all so wrong, such an unfair judgment. They had never pushed Bertie – not for one moment. Everything that they had done with him had been done because he wanted it. He had asked for a saxophone. He had asked to learn Italian after they had gone to buy sun-dried tomatoes at Valvona and Crolla. They had never pushed him to do any of this.

And what did that woman mean when she talked about the space to be a five-year-old boy? What exactly did that mean? If it meant that they had to deny Bertie's natural curiosity about the world, then that was outrageous. If a child asked about something, you could hardly deny his request for information.

There are certain difficulties with Christabel Macfadzean, thought Irene. Firstly, she's a cow. Now, that was putting it simply. But even as she thought this – and it gave her some satisfaction to think in these terms – Irene realised that such thoughts were unworthy of her. That's how ordinary people thought. She knew that the real difficulty lay in the fact that this woman purported to run an advanced playgroup (the brochure claimed that they adhered to the latest educational principles, whatever those were). In spite

47

of these claims, this woman knew nothing about how children behaved. She had made some sarcastic reference to her *mere* twenty-two years' experience, but no amount of experience, not even fifty years, could make up for her complete ignorance of Melanie Klein. That was the astonishing thing, in Irene's view: to claim to be able to look after children and not to have read a page, not one single page, of Melanie Klein. It quite took one's breath away.

Had Christabel Macfadzean been familiar with the merest snippets of Kleinian theory, she would immediately have understood that when Bertie blew up that other child's train station, this was purely because he was expressing, in a person-object sense, his fundamental anxieties over the fact that society would never allow him to marry his mother. This was obvious.

It was remarkable, when one came to think of it, that Bertie should behave so like Richard, the boy whom Melanie Klein analysed during the war. Richard had drawn pictures of German aeroplanes swooping in for attack, thus expressing the anxieties he felt about the Second World War, and about his mother. In destroying the train station, Bertie had merely acted out what Richard must have felt. Irene stopped. A remarkable thought had occurred to her. Had Bertie read Klein? He was an avid reader, but probably not, unless, of course, he had been dipping into the books on her shelves . . . If he had been reading Klein, then he might unconsciously have mirrored Richard's behaviour *because he realised that his anxieties so closely matched Richard's*. This, then, was his way of communicating, and it had gone completely unnoticed by the very adult who was meant to be guiding him through these first, delicate steps towards socialisation.

It angered Irene just to think about it, and for a few moments she paused, standing quite still in the middle of the pavement, her eyes closed, battling with her anger. She had been going to the Floatarium recently and she imagined herself back in the tank, lying there in perfect silence. This sort of envisioning always helped.

She would take Bertie to the Floatarium next time and put him in the tank. He would like that, because he had an interest in meditation. And he might go to yoga classes too, she thought. He had asked her about yoga recently and she had made enquiries. There was a yoga class for children in Stockbridge on a Monday evening, Bendy Fun for Tots, it was called, and Bertie was always free on a Monday evening. Any other evening would have been difficult, but Monday was fine. She would pencil it in.

19. A Modest Gift

The custard-coloured Mercedes-Benz drew up outside the gallery and Pat stepped out. She waved her thanks to Domenica Macdonald, who waved back, and then drove off down the hill.

Matthew had not yet arrived, but Pat had a key and had been instructed in the operation of the alarm. Scooping up the morning's mail from the floor, she placed it on the front desk before she went through to the back of the gallery to make herself a cup of coffee.

Matthew had told her to open the mail, which she now did. There was a bill from the electrician for a new light switch which he had installed and an enquiry from a prospective customer who was interested in purchasing a Hornel. *Had they anything in stock*, he asked, and Pat reflected that an honest answer would be: *We have no idea*, as they did not know what they had. There could be a Hornel, for all she or Matthew knew, although it was unlikely. She suspected that there was nothing of any great value in the gallery, although even as she thought that she looked at the painting of Mull/Iona and wondered. How much was a Peploe worth these days? The day before she had paged through a magazine which she had found in the back of the gallery and which had featured the previous year's auction prices for Scottish art. A large Peploe had gone for ninety thousand pounds, and so if the painting at which she was now staring was indeed a Peploe then it would be worth, what, forty thousand pounds?

The door chime sounded and Pat looked up. It was the man who had called in yesterday – the man in the casual sweater who had examined the painting and pronounced on it with such authority.

He walked over towards the desk.

"I was just passing by and I thought I might take a quick look at one or two other things. I have a birthday present to buy, and that's terribly difficult, you know. A little painting perhaps – nothing too pricy, but something that will hang on any wall without *shouting*. You know what I mean."

"Please look around," said Pat, gesturing at the display on the walls. "You might find something."

The man smiled and sauntered over to the wall to Pat's right.

"D.Y. Cameron prints," he muttered, just loudly enough for her to hear. "Not bad for one's aunt, but not really suitable for one's lover. Know what I mean?"

Pat was not sure how to respond; she had an aunt, but no lover, and so she laughed. This made the man turn round and look at her with a raised eyebrow.

"You think otherwise?" he asked.

"No," said Pat. "I'm sure you're right."

He resumed his browsing, now moving over to the wall on which the Peploe imitation hung. He stopped and peered down at it more closely.

"How much are you asking for this . . . this Saturday afternoon work?"

"Saturday afternoon?"

"It's when amateurs get their paints out," he explained. "This person, for example, was probably a retired bank manager from Dumfries or somewhere like that. Painted a bit. Like our friend Mr Vettriano."

Pat caught her breath. She had seen the comments about Mr Vettriano and she knew that some people had a low opinion of his work, but she did not share these views. She rather liked pictures of people dancing on beaches in formal clothes, with their *butlers*; she had never seen this happen, of course, but it was always possible. Just.

She reached for the list which Matthew kept in the top drawer.

Running her eye down the figures, she came to the appropriate entry. *Scottish school – Unknown: initials SP – Some Person? One hundred and fifty pounds.*

"One hundred and fifty pounds," said Pat.

The man stood back and stroked his chin. "One hundred and fifty? A bit steep, isn't it? But . . . but, maybe. It would be a nice little gift for my friend." Then, turning to Pat, he said decisively: "I'll take it. Wrap it up please. I'll pay in cash."

Pat hesitated. "On the other hand," she said, "if it's a Peploe, then one hundred and fifty might be a little bit low. Perhaps forty thousand would be more appropriate."

The man, who had been crossing the floor towards the desk, stopped.

"Peploe? Don't be ridiculous! Would that it were! But it isn't. Out of the question."

Pat watched him as he spoke. She saw the slight flush of colour to his brow and the movement of his eyes, which darted sideways, and then returned to stare at her. She was convinced now that she had taken the right decision. The painting was no longer for sale.

20. The Boys Discuss Art

Matthew arrived in the gallery just before it was time for him to cross the road for morning coffee at Big Lou's. Pat started to tell him of the two visits of the would-be purchaser of the Mull/Iona painting, but he stopped her.

"This is big," he said. "Come and tell me about it over coffee. The boys will want to hear about this. We'll close the shop for an hour. This is really, really big."

They made their way over the road to Big Lou's, crossing the cobbled street down which the tall buses lumbered. At the bottom of the street, beyond the rooftops of Canonmills, lay Fife, like a

Gillies watercolour of sky and hills. Matthew saw Pat pause and look down the road, and he smiled at her.

"Yes," he said. "It's beautiful, isn't it?"

She nodded. She had not thought that he would notice something like that, but then she knew very little about him. Matthew was not like Bruce, who would never notice a view. There was something more to Matthew, a gentle quality that made her feel almost protective towards him.

They turned away from Fife and made their way down Big Lou's dangerous stairs. Ronnie and Pete were already in the coffee bar, sitting in their accustomed booth. Matthew introduced Pat to his friends.

"This young lady has just made a major discovery," he said. "There's a very important painting in the gallery. I missed it. I would have sold it for one hundred and fifty and it's worth . . . ?" He turned to Pat. "Ten thousand?"

"Forty, maybe."

Ronnie whistled. "Forty grand!"

Big Lou came over with coffee and set mugs in front of them.

"I'm reading Calvocoressi's book about Cowie at the moment," she said. "Very interesting."

"Yes," said Pete. "You bet. But this painting, how do you know that it's whatever you think it is? How can you tell?"

Pat shrugged. "I can't tell," she said. "I don't know very much about all this. I did Higher Art, I suppose, and we learned a little bit about Scottish painters. We learned about Peploe, and I think this looks like a Peploe."

Ronnie said: "Lots of things look like something else. Lou looks like the Mona Lisa, don't you, Lou? But you aren't. You have to know about these things." He turned to Matthew. "Sorry, pal, but you may be jumping the gun a bit."

This remark seemed to worry Matthew, and he turned to Pat anxiously. "Well, Pat, how can you be sure?"

"I can't," said Pat. "I've just said that. But I'm pretty sure that this man who came in had recognised it as being something valuable. He was pretending – I could tell. He was pretending not to be too interested in it, and when I said that it might be a Peploe he almost jumped. I could tell that he was . . . well, he was annoyed. He thought he had a bargain."

"Sounds good," said Pete. "Remember when we bought that table, Ronnie, and that dealer pretended not to be interested in it? We saw him looking underneath it before he came to us and offered us twice what we'd paid. We could tell."

"Yes," said Ronnie. "You can tell." He paused. "But how are you going to be sure? You can't put it in the window as a Peploe or whatever unless you know what you're talking about."

"I'll get an opinion," said Matthew. "I'll take it to somebody who knows what they're talking about."

"Unlike you?" said Pete.

"I've never said that I know anything about art," said Matthew. "I've never made any claims."

Ronnie looked down at his coffee. "So who do we ask? Lou?"

"I know more than you do," said Lou from behind the counter. "You know nothing. Both of you. You and your friend, Pete, you know nothing. You're just *afa feels*. "

"Let's not fight over this," said Matthew quietly. "Even in the Doric. I think that what we need to do is to take this to somebody else on the street here – another dealer. And we'll ask what they think."

"Good idea," said Ronnie. "Just take it down to that what's his name – that one on the corner there. Ask him."

"I can't do that," said Matthew. "He'd laugh at me. And he'd tell everybody else that I don't know what I have. No, we need to get somebody else to do it." He looked at Pat. "Pat? What about you? You take the painting down to him and say that it's yours. Ask him for an opinion. Is that all right with you? Do it tomorrow?"

"I suppose so," said Pat. This involved her telling a lie, even if it was a small one. But she was truthful by inclination, and the thought of telling any untruth made her feel uncomfortable. And she did not feel easy in the company of Ronnie and Pete. There was something unsettling about them, something of the late afternoon perhaps, even if not quite something of the night.

21. A Daughter's Dance Card

It was not a particularly busy day at the offices of Macaulay Holmes Richardson Black, Chartered Surveyors and Factors. The senior partner, Gordon, had gone to London to look at a commercial property in Fulham which a client of the firm had just inherited from a relative. The client wanted to sell the building, but distrusted London agents, a view with which Todd had readily agreed.

In Gordon's absence on this inspection trip, the firm was run by his younger brother, Raeburn Todd, who was spending the day going through the files in his brother's filing cabinet. Bruce pretended not to notice. It was information which he could perhaps use one day, if it were necessary. One never knew when one might be in a tight corner, and it was useful to have some *cover*.

Bruce had very little to do that day and he was bored. After twenty minutes of the newspaper, he rose to his feet and went to look out of the window. It had turned into a wet day outside, although the showers were light and sporadic. From their offices, on the fourth floor of a building in Queen Street, they could look out over the roofs of Heriot Row and Great King Street, down to the distant greens of Trinity, and beyond. Although he was a relatively junior member of staff, Bruce had a room with this view, and he was staring at it absently when the telephone rang and he was summoned to Todd's room. He's finished snooping, thought Bruce. Now he wants to interfere with my work.

He picked up a file on a Lanarkshire fencing project and walked through.

"How is Gordon getting on in London, Todd?" asked Bruce.

"Fine, as far as I know," said Todd. "He'll probably phone me at lunchtime. He'll have taken a look at that Fulham place by then. Three thousand square feet in a good part of London, just off a main shopping street. Do you know what that's worth?"

Bruce shrugged. "I haven't looked at the recent tables," he said.

54

"I don't deal with anything in London. I can tell you what that would be in Edinburgh or Glasgow. But not London. Lots of boodle, though. Lots."

Todd frowned. "You should keep an eye on things, Bruce. You should read the trade press. You should keep an eye on London."

Bruce thought: he's brought me here for a lecture, and his eyes glazed over.

"Yes," said Todd. "It's important to keep abreast of changing values in London, because that affects us. Business relocation is all about comparing prices. You know that, don't you?"

"Yes," said Bruce, patiently, and then: "Have you been busy yourself, Todd? Catching up on paperwork?"

Todd looked at him warily. "A bit of reading," he said. "Keeping current, you know."

Bruce smiled. "Good policy," he said.

Todd stared at him for a moment, and then continued: "But I didn't ask you in here to discuss work," he said. "This is a personal matter. I hope you won't mind if I raise it."

Bruce was intrigued. "I don't mind at all. Fire away."

"You know that Mrs Todd and I enjoy quite a full social life." There was a note of pride in Todd's voice.

"Yes. I saw your picture in *Scottish Field*. A party somewhere."

"Indeed," said Todd. "A party. Max Maitland-Weir's fiftieth. But that wasn't the only one we've been to. We go out a great deal."

Bruce nodded politely. He was not sure where this conversation was going, but it seemed to him that a proposition was about to be made.

"We've got tickets to a ball," said Todd. "I'm not so wild about it, but my wife is dead set on getting a party together. My elder daughter's keen, too, but the problem is, well, we don't exactly have anybody to partner her. And so I wondered whether you would be good enough to join us and perhaps have the odd dance with my daughter." He paused, and for a moment Bruce felt a surge of sympathy for him. Poor man! That awful wife of his and that dreadful daughter of his. They were very heavy going – Bruce was well aware of that – but it seemed as if he would have to accept the invitation. It would not be easy to say no.

"I'd be honoured," said Bruce. "What ball is it?"

"The South Edinburgh Conservative Association," said Todd. "I'm convener of the ball committee, and we're having a bit of a battle getting enough people to come to it. We've hired the hotel, so it's going to have to go ahead, but we're a bit thin on the ground. In fact, it's only going to be the four of us so far."

Bruce stared at him mutely. Was this a social problem, he wondered, or was it a political one?

22. Bruce Comes Under Consideration

After Bruce had left his office, Todd sat back in his seat and stared at the ceiling. For a few minutes he did nothing, but then he reached for the telephone, pushed a memory button labelled *domestic bliss* and called his wife.

Todd had married Sasha when they were both in their mid-twenties. She had just completed her training as a physiotherapist and had been one of the most popular and sociable students at Queen Margaret College. At their first meeting, Todd had decided that this was the woman whom he wished to marry, and, as he said to his brother, he had never regretted the decision for one moment.

"Really?" Gordon had said. "Are you sure?"

The question had not been intended as a slight, even if it had sounded like it. It had made Todd think, though. Was his wife as attractive and compelling a personality to others as she was to him? People had different tastes, and it might be that there were those who found her too . . . well, what could they possibly object to in her? Sasha had opinions, of course, but that was far better than being a passive, reflective sort.

Of course there was jealousy to be taken into account. Sasha was undoubtedly attractive, with her blonde hair in bouffant style and her trouser suits. She never looked anything but well turned-out, and this could attract envy. That is the problem with this country, thought Todd. We sneer at people who do well, and who want to make something of their lives. Look at the remarks which a certain sort of person makes about Bearsden. What is wrong with living in Bearsden, or, indeed, with having the sort of attitudes that go with living in Bearsden? Nothing.

The people who ridicule people like us, thought Todd, are making up for their own failure. And there are plenty of people – Labour politicians, for example – who *want* people to remain thirled to poverty, who do not want them to have any spirit or independence. These are the sort of people who think that there's something good about having a limited life.

As he pondered these matters of political philosophy, Sasha picked up the telephone at the other end.

"Honey bunch?" she asked.

"Sugar," replied Todd.

"Is everything all right?"

"Yes. I'm sitting here in my office thinking. Things are a bit quiet. Gordon is in London looking at a building down there, and nothing much is happening in the office."

"Come home, then."

"I can't. I can't leave the office in the hands of the staff. On which subject, that young man, Bruce Anderson. You've met him."

"The one in your office?" said Sasha. "The good-looking one?"

Todd paused, tripped up by the taboo that prevents one man from commenting, except adversely, on the looks of another. You couldn't say it – you just couldn't.

"Hah!" he said. "I suppose the girls might say that. I don't know about these things."

"He is rather dishy," said Sasha. "Dark hair. Lovely shoulders. Well-shaped . . ."

Todd felt slightly irritated. "Well-shaped what?" he asked. "He's got a well-shaped what?"

"Nothing. I just said well-shaped. *He's* well-shaped. That's what I meant to say."

Todd moved the conversation on. "Anyway, that's the one. I've asked him about the ball. He says that he can come. He'll be happy to dance with Lizzie."

"That's wonderful! Lizzie met him once at that Christmas do and I think he made a bit of an impression on her. Good."

Todd sighed. "But there's still this wretched problem with the tickets. Has anybody else said that they can come?"

"No," said Sasha. "I phoned around again this morning. A lot of people are tied up in one way or another that weekend. Archie and Molly said that they might think about it, but I hear he's just been carted off to hospital again and so that's them out. Perhaps we should call it off."

"No we won't," said Todd firmly. "That's the last thing – the last thing – we'll do. It would be a total admission of failure. We have the prizes for the tombola and the band booked. Deposits paid. We're going ahead, even if it's only us. That's it."

"All right. And we'll enjoy ourselves even if it's a small party."

"That's the spirit," said Todd, now mollified.

They rang off and he returned to staring at the ceiling. He was pleased that Sasha had approved of his decision to invite Bruce – which he had not previously consulted her about. Lizzie would like it, he was sure, and although there was something odd about that young man – the mirrors and that substance on his hair – he was probably perfectly all right under the surface. Todd was concerned about Lizzie: she wanted a boyfriend, he knew, but did not seem to have had much success in finding one. Most young men went out with one another these days, he had observed, which meant that there were rather few young men left over for the girls. Terrible pity.

Perhaps something would come of this. And what would be wrong with that? If Bruce and Lizzie made a go of it, then they could take him into the partnership and the succession would be assured. And the responsibilities of marriage would soon sort Bruce out. Yes. Not a bad idea at all.

23. Goings-on in London

Gordon Todd stood by a window on the first floor of the building he had been inspecting in London. The position of the property impressed him – tucked away in a mews avenue off the Fulham Road, but close enough to really fashionable parts of Chelsea and South Kensington to attract tenants with the means to pay a substantial rent. It would be a good office, he thought, for a design studio or an advertising agency.

His client, who had inherited the property, was wondering about selling it. That would not be difficult, Gordon thought, because the place was in good condition and he could not imagine any obvious planning drawbacks. But it might be better to hold on to it for a couple of years and see whether its value went up appreciably. He could do the arithmetic after he had spoken to his London contacts and worked out just what might be paid for a place like this.

Gordon looked out of the window. The street was quiet – a good sign, he thought, as it suggested that the mews houses on the other side of the road were still being used as houses rather than as offices. And they were attractive, he thought, with their white-painted fronts and their panelled doors. London was full of pleasant corners, he reflected, even if there were trackless wastes further out. One might even live in London, at a pinch, provided that one were not too tall and in danger of bumping one's head at every turn on their ridiculously low ceilings, and provided one were not too readily shocked by what one saw in the street.

As he thought about this, he noticed that a light had gone on in a room in the opposite house. It was a living room, not very large, he thought, although it was comfortably furnished with a few easy chairs and a sofa . . . Gordon stopped. There were two people on the sofa, a man and a woman, and . . .

Well really! You would think that people would close the curtains if they proposed to engage in that sort of thing. Of course they must have thought that the building opposite was empty – that was reasonable enough – but how would they know that there might not be a surveyor in it, or a possible purchaser? And there they were, obviously on very close terms, completely unaware of the fact that anybody might be able to see them.

He was about to turn away when he saw a small and expensive sports car draw up in front of the house in question and a man step out. The man reached into his pocket, took out a key, and opened the front door. Gordon caught his breath. The window at which he was standing afforded a good view not only of the living room, but of the hall outside it. Now, as he watched, he saw the man's head appearing above the level of the stairs and then, a few moments later, he was standing in front of the door to the living room, his hand upon the doorknob.

The man paused. Then, leaning forward slightly, he appeared to put his ear to the door. Gordon stood quite still. This was the husband, obviously, and he had arrived home unexpectedly, to find his wife *in flagrante* with a lover. It was a very trite scene, but seeing it enacted in front of him seemed quite extraordinary. Would he knock on the door, or would he creep away, shocked and disappointed?

The man did neither. Slowly he tried the handle of the door, twisted it, and found it locked. He stood back, appeared to think for a few moments, and then moved towards the hall window – the window through which the unobserved observer was now watching him.

Gordon looked on in amazement as the man opened the window – which was a large one – and began to climb out onto the small ironwork window box. Then, very slowly, the man inched himself towards the neighbouring window – the window of the room in which the woman and the man were still unaware of the danger of discovery.

Gordon thought: so this is the sort of thing one sees in London! It's obviously a hotbed of adultery and goings-on. And then the man on the ironwork window box slipped. Gordon saw him grab at the brickwork and, quite slowly at first, topple backwards. Gordon gave a cry, involuntarily, and closed his eyes. Then he leaned forward and saw the man lying on the top of the canvas roof of the small sports car, which had been parked directly beneath him. He was staring up at the sky, and for a moment their eyes met. Then, without moving the rest of his body, the man raised a hand and waved to Gordon, a wave that one might give to a friend one has just noticed in a café, or on the other side of the street.

24. Unwelcome Thoughts

That morning, when Pat had been given the unnecessary ride in the custard-coloured Mercedes-Benz belonging to Domenica Macdonald, an invitation to dinner had been extended, and accepted.

"I'll knock together a few bits and pieces," said Domenica airily. "I'm not a very good cook, I'm afraid. But we can talk. *Sans* Bruce."

They had exchanged a look.

"He's all right," said Pat. "But it would be nice to talk."

"I can tell you all about everyone on the stair," promised Domenica. "Not that there's much to relate, but there is a bit. You may as well know about your neighbours before you meet them."

Pat had been told to ring Domenica's doorbell at six-thirty, which gave her time to get back from the gallery and have a bath before she crossed the landing. Bruce had already arrived at the flat when she came home and he was sitting in the kitchen reading a catalogue.

"Sold any paintings today?"

"No." She paused. "Well almost, but not quite."

Bruce laughed. "I don't think that gallery is going to do spectacularly well. I was hearing about him, you know, your boss, Matthew. Walking cash-flow problem. It's only the fact that his old man pays the bills that keeps him going."

"We'll see," said Pat.

"Yes," said Bruce. "We'll see. And if you need a new job, I can get you one. A friend of mine needs somebody to do some market research. He said . . ."

"I'm fine," said Pat.

"Well, just let me know," said Bruce, returning to his catalogue. "And by the way, have you seen my hair gel?"

For a few moments Pat said nothing. She opened her mouth, but then closed it again.

"Well?" asked Bruce. "Have you seen it?"

Pat swallowed, and then replied. "I broke it," she said. "I'm very sorry. I'm going to buy you some more. I'll get the same stuff if you tell me where to get it."

Bruce lowered his catalogue. "Broke it? How did you do that?"

Pat looked up at the ceiling. She was aware that Bruce was staring at her, but she did not wish to meet his gaze.

"I was looking at it," she said. "It fell out of my hands and it broke. I was going to tell you."

Bruce sighed. "Pat," he said. "You know that it's very important to tell the truth when you're living with people. You've got to tell the truth. You know that. Now, what really happened? Were you using it?"

The accusation made her feel indignant. Why should he imagine that she would use his hair gel? And why would he imagine that she would lie about it? "No," she said. "I did not use it. I was looking at it."

"Is hair gel that interesting?"

"Not yours," she snapped.

Bruce looked at her and wagged a finger. "Temper!" he said. "Temper!"

Pat looked at him scornfully, and then turned and made her way back into her room slamming the door behind her. He was impossible; he was self-satisfied; he was smug. She could not live with him. She would have to move.

But if she moved, then it would be his victory. She could just imagine what he would say when he showed the next person her room. *There was a girl here, but she didn't stay long. Very immature type. Second gap year, you know.*

She sat down on her bed and stared down at the bedside rug. There is no real reason to feel unhappy, she thought, but she did. She had a job, she had the place at St Andrews for next October, she had her supportive parents: she had everything to look forward to. But somehow her life seemed to be slow and pointless: it seemed to her that there was a gap in it, and she knew exactly what that gap was. She wanted a boyfriend. She wanted somebody to phone up, right then, and tell about what Bruce had said. And he would sympathise with her and ask her to meet him for dinner, and they would laugh about Bruce over dinner, and she would know that this other person – this boy – regarded her as special to him. But she had none of that. She just had this room, and this emptiness, and that sarcastic, self-absorbed young man out there, with that look of his, and his eyes, and his *en brosse* hair, and . . .

She stopped herself thinking about that. Her father had once spoken to her about unwelcome thoughts; thoughts that came into one's mind unbidden. They were often rather disturbing thoughts – thoughts about doing something outrageous or shocking – but this was not something to be too concerned about. The whole point about these thoughts was that they were never translated into action because they did not represent what one really wanted to do. So one never discarded one's clothes and ran down the street, nor jumped over the waterfall, nor over the cliff for that matter, even if one thought how easy it would be to throw oneself over the edge, and to fall and fall down to the very bottom. So easy.

25. Dinner with Domenica

"Now," said Domenica with a gesture that embraced the room. "This is where I work. I sit at that desk over there and look out over Scotland Street. And if I run out of ideas, I go and sit in that chair and wait."

"Until an idea comes along?"

"In theory. But I might just fall asleep or become restless. You know how it is."

Yes, Pat did. She felt restless. The encounter with Bruce had unsettled her and her spirits had been low when she had knocked at Domenica's door on the other side of the landing. Domenica, looking at her guest over her half-moon spectacles, could tell that something was wrong. So she asked Pat what it was, and Pat told her the story of the hair gel.

Domenica smiled. "Hair gel! All over the floor? The best place for it, in my opinion!" But she saw that Pat was worried, and her tone became concerned. "That young man, you know, is a narcissist. It's perfectly obvious. Clear as day. And the point about narcissists is that they just can't see anything wrong with themselves. They're perfect, you see. And they are also quite incapable of laughing at themselves. So he would never think it remotely funny that his hair gel had come to an unfortunate end."

"He didn't make it easy for me," said Pat.

"Of course he wouldn't. He expects you to admire him, and he's annoyed that you don't appear to be falling at his feet. So he's a bit uncertain how to deal with you."

This discussion with an ally made Pat feel more cheerful and she put Bruce out of her mind. Domenica was far more interesting, she thought, with her sharp comments and her book-lined study. She wanted to find out more about her neighbour, and what she did. Did Domenica have a job? She kept odd hours, she had noticed, and when she had driven her off in the custard-coloured Mercedes-Benz that morning she had not appeared to be going to work. And if she sat at her desk waiting for ideas, what were these ideas about?

"You're wondering what I do," said Domenica abruptly. "How rude of me. I know that you work in a gallery, so I have the advantage of you. And I have kept you guessing about me."

"Well," admitted Pat, "I suppose I was wondering."

"I'm not gainfully employed," said Domenica. "I'm a bit of a dilettante. I do this and that. Which doesn't tell you very much. I produce the occasional article for obscure journals and I act as secretary for a society. And I write a great number of letters to people. And that, I suppose, is it."

"Your articles?" asked Pat.

"Anthropological. I trained as an anthropologist, and I've dabbled in it on and off for years. But I'm not very professional about it and I imagine that the real anthropologists – the ones in institutes and universities – rather turn their noses up at me. Not that that ever bothered me in the slightest."

Domenica gestured to a chair and invited Pat to sit down. Fetching an empty glass, she poured a generous helping of sherry into it and offered it to her guest.

"I take it that you drink," she said. "This is a very dull sherry but it will have to do. It's the sort of sherry that ministers serve in the manse. But let's persist with it nonetheless, in the sure and certain knowledge that things will improve at dinner. I have a very nice bottle of something much less dull which we can drink at the table."

Pat raised her glass and they toasted one another. So Domenica was an anthropologist. She had expected her to be something exotic, and an anthropologist seemed about right. "I've never met an anthropologist," she said hesitantly. "It sounds so . . ."

Domenica interrupted her. "Sounds so, but isn't. Anthropologists are really rather mundane people, for the most part. They used to be interesting in the days of Pitt-Rivers and Margaret Mead and all the others. But now it's all very dry and technical. And of course they've run out of people to study. Everybody is more or less the same these days. I expect that if one went to New Guinea, for example, one would find that all those people who used to have a resident anthropologist attached to them are watching American television through their satellite dishes. No time for inter-group warfare or initiation rites when you have all that popular culture to absorb. So the anthropologists have a rather thin time of it."

"That's rather sad," remarked Pat. "Who wants everywhere to be the same?"

Domenica shrugged. "The European Commission, I suppose. But back to anthropology. It used to be such fun when you chose your field work, back in the heyday of the subject. Everybody wanted to go to New Guinea, of course, and many did. But there were other places. Hill tribes in India were a good choice. Or the Bushmen of southern Africa. Everybody knew about them after Laurens van der Post wrote all his nonsense."

"Where did you go?" asked Pat.

Domenica looked into her glass of sherry. "I went here and there," she said. "Mostly in India, though. You see, I worked on feral children and I went to visit a number of communities where there were claims of feral children being found."

Pat was unsure of what she meant. "Feral children?"

"You've heard of Romulus and Remus?" asked Domenica. "They were brought up by wolves. Well, they were feral. And there were many others. Wolves, monkeys, even gazelles. Animals can make very good parents, you know. And they tend not to be too pushy – unlike those people downstairs."

26. A Room, a Photograph, Love and Memory

Pat looked around Domenica's room. Two of the walls were covered with bookshelves, towering up to the ceiling, and the others were liberally hung with framed photographs and paintings.

"Yes," remarked Domenica, noticing Pat's interest. "It is a bit of a mess this room. That wall over there, with its photographs, is a bit like one of those Italian restaurants where they have pictures of the well-known people who have eaten there. Usually these days it's Sean Connery, but I really can't imagine that he's spent all hours in those Italian restaurants. Where would he find the time to get on with being famous, poor man? And if you go to Italy, all the restaurants have photographs of Luciano Pavarotti, who also couldn't possibly have been to all the places which claim him. It's rather like the cult of saints and their bones. There are so many bits of the more popular saints that one could assemble several hundred skeletons of each of them. St Catherine of Siena for example – she of the miraculous water barrel – must have had *numerous* fingers. I've seen at least twenty in various churches in Tuscany. Quite miraculous!"

Pat laughed. "I find those old bones a bit creepy," she said. "But I suppose that some people like them."

"Yes, I understand that Neapolitans and the like find great consolation in such things," Domenica said. "But you are a most tolerant girl. Yours is a tolerant generation. The religious enthusiasms of others can be a bit trying, but they are important, don't you think? They allow people to express their sense of the spiritual."

Domenica took a sip of her sherry. "I don't mind a good-going religious ritual of the sort you see in India," she continued. "You know, something with coloured smoke and elephants – though the Scottish Episcopal Church doesn't go in for elephants very much, alas. I can see a bishop on an elephant, can't you?"

Pat had noticed the prints on the wall, and the metal candlestick on the table, in the shape of a three-headed cobra. And on Domenica's desk, in a small porcelain pot, a bundle of joss sticks.

"Yes," said Domenica, who seemed to have an uncanny facility for guessing exactly what it was that Pat was going to ask. "Some mementoes from India. But actually I was born right here in Scotland Street."

"Right here? In this building?"

Domenica nodded. "In those days people were born in places where people lived. Astonishing, but true. I came into this world, would you believe it, in this very room. It was my parents' bedroom and their bed was over there, against that wall. I was born in that bed. Precisely sixty-one years ago next Friday afternoon. There was a war on, as you may recall, and I had been conceived when my father came back on home leave from convoy duty. He did not survive the North Atlantic, I'm afraid, and so I never knew him." She pointed to a photograph above a small, corner fireplace. "That's my father there."

Pat got up and crossed the room to stand before the photograph. A tall man was standing on what seemed to be a dune, the grass about his feet bending in the breeze. The face was an intelligent one, the mouth relaxed into a smile. His hair was ruffled, blown by the wind.

"I loved him very much," said Domenica. "Although I never knew him, I loved him very much. Does that sound odd to you? To love somebody you never knew?"

Pat thought for a moment. "No, I don't think so. People fall in love with all sorts of people. People write letters to one another and fall in love even if they never meet. That happens."

Domenica nodded. "It's a special sort of love that one has for such a person. It's an idealised love, I suppose. You're in love with a memory, with an idea of somebody. And I suppose that for some people that's all they have."

For a short while there was silence. Pat looked again at the picture of Domenica's father and then returned to her seat. She had always imagined that the saddest fate for a child would be to have no parents. But perhaps it was sadder still to have parents who did not love you. At least, if you had no parents you could think that they would have loved you, if they had been there. But if you knew your parents did not love you, then you would be denied even that scrap of comfort.

She looked at Domenica. "I'm sure he would have loved you," she said. "I'm sure that he would have loved you a great deal."

"Yes. I think he would."

They said nothing for a moment. Then Domenica looked at her watch. "We must go through to the kitchen," she said. "And then while I'm getting dinner ready, we can talk a little more. I don't want to bore you, though. Sixty-one can be very boring for twenty whatever it is you are."

"Twenty. Just twenty."

"A good age to be," said Domenica. "As is every age, I imagine, except for the years between fourteen and seventeen and a half. An awful time for everybody. Were you a dreadful teenager? I was, I think. In fact, I was exactly the sort of person I would not have liked to be. Does that make sense? Let's think about it."

27. *The Electricity Factory*

Domenica chopped the onions with a large-bladed knife, while her guest sat at the scrubbed-pine table and watched her.

"When did you live in India?" Pat asked.

Domenica tipped the onions into a saucepan. "I shall explain," she said. "It will be simpler if you get the whole story. Reduced, of course, to five minutes. Time marched on, and it continued to do so until I was eighteen, when my mother suddenly decided that she wanted to go off to India. She had been offered the job of principal at a school for girls in south India. It was run by a Scottish charity, some people in Glasgow. I stayed behind – I was about to go to university – and she went off. When I had finished my degree, I went out to see her. You travelled by ship in those days – a tremendous thrill for me.

"Her school was in the hills above Cochin, in Kerala. It's a lovely state, Kerala – all that greenery and those waterways and those cool towns up in the Western Ghats. I fell in love with the place immediately, and begged her to let me stay with her, which I did. I had no idea what I was going to do at home, and Scotland was pretty dull, remember, in the early Sixties. I suppose we were still in the Fifties while everybody else had moved on.

"So I stayed with my mother in the principal's lodge at the school. It seemed very grand to be living in a lodge, but it was quite a modest house, really. There was a verandah which ran round two sides of the house and a garden with fire coral trees. There were pepper vines growing up these trees and we used to harvest our own pepper and let it dry on banana leaves on the ground.

"I loved living there, as you can imagine, although I didn't have all that much to do. I was taken on as a teacher, but I was not paid for this, and the duties were pretty light. But it was easy work, because the girls at the school were all very well-behaved and wouldn't dream of being rude to the staff. Nobody was rude then. Rudeness was invented much later.

"And that's where I stayed for three years. Then, at a lunch party held by the manager of a tea company, I met the man who became my husband. He came from Cochin, where his father had owned a business – more of that in a moment. He was called Thomas, as many people are in that part of the world because, as you know, it's a largely Christian state – Thomist Christians. Very ancient communities. In fact, you get all sorts of churches, including the Syrian Orthodox Church, which goes in for fireworks in a big way on important saints' days. Quite wonderful.

"Thomas asked me to marry him, and I said that I would. I had fallen for India, you see, and the idea of marrying into the country was a very exciting one. And Thomas was a good man – very quiet and thoughtful, and very kind. Of course, I hadn't realised that I would have to put up with his mother too, who would live with us in our house in Cochin. But that's what happens when you marry into an Indian family. You get the whole lot.

"Thomas told me that he had a job in the business that his father had set up, but he didn't explain what the business was. He would show me the factory, he said, and I would see. But before that, when I met his mother for the first time and I was drinking tea under her enquiring eye, I asked what the family factory made.

"She looked at me in surprise, and then said: 'Why, we make electricity. It's an electricity factory. We make very fine electricity. Everybody knows that.'

"I was surprised. I thought that power stations would belong to the government, or to very large companies, but, no, it seemed that there was a role for a few private generating companies, and we were one of them. Varghese Electricity was the name of the company and the factory, as they called it, was a large building to the east of Cochin. It had a railway line running into it, and the trains brought loads of coal into our private siding.

"Thomas went to the factory every morning, but did not stay long, as there was nothing for him to do. He had an office there, but there never seemed to be any papers on the table and the whole place was run by very efficient managers. So he used to go off to his club and read the newspapers until it was time to come back for lunch. Then he would supervise the gardener in an orchid-house which we had at the back of the property, and after that he would go and sleep for an hour or so until the worst of the after-noon heat was over.

"That was our life, and I suddenly realised that this was what I was going to be doing for the rest of my days. Suddenly, India did not seem quite as beguiling and I began to wonder whether I had made the most awful mistake."

Domenica looked at Pat. "What would you have done in my circumstances? Married to a nice man who owned an electricity factory, but with a great emptiness of years stretching out ahead of you? What would you have done?"

28. Thomas is Electrocuted

"No, that's unfair," said Domenica Macdonald, withdrawing her own question. "Nobody *really* knows how they would react to hypothetical situations."

"I don't know," said Pat. "We can imagine what we would do. I think that if I found myself in your position, I would possibly have . . ."

Domenica raised a hand. "You don't know, though. You don't really know what you would do. But I can tell you what I did. I left Thomas. I remained with him for five years, and then, shortly after my thirtieth birthday, I asked him what he would feel if I left him.

"Of course he said that he would be very upset. My light would go out, is what I think he said. The whole family talked like that. They used the metaphors of electricity. I am a bit below my normal wattage. I feel like shorting out. That sort of thing.

"That made me hesitate, but I persisted. I explained to him that I was not cut out for the sort of life that we were leading. I wanted to travel. I wanted to get to know people. I couldn't face the prospect of sitting there on the verandah for the next goodness knows how many years, drinking afternoon tea with his mother while she went on and on about some complicated injustice that had been done to her family twenty years before. I just couldn't face it.

"He tried to persuade me to stay. He offered to build a new house next to the existing one, which I could then live in and not have to share with his mother. He said that he would pay for people – educated people, he said – to come and talk to me during the day. He made all sorts of offers.

"I became more and more depressed at the thought of what I was doing. Thomas was such a good man, and I was behaving as if I was some petulant Madame Bovary. But I couldn't stop how I felt. I couldn't work up any enthusiasm for a life which I found so completely unfulfilling and so I eventually gave him a date on which I proposed to leave.

"Two days before I was due to go – I had already packed every-thing and had the flight from Bombay all organised – two days before, there was the most awful kerfuffle. One of the managers from the factory arrived and he was sobbing and waving his arms about. It took some time before I managed to work out what it was all about. There had been an accident at the factory. Thomas had taken it upon himself to inspect a piece of equipment and had inad-vertently touched a live wire. They had tried to revive him, the manager said between his sobs, but it had been to no avail. 'You are widow now,' he said. 'I am very sorry, but now you are widow. Your husband has died of electricity.'

"You can imagine how guilty I felt. And I still do, to an extent. That man had offered me nothing but affection and support, and I had repaid him with what I suppose he must have viewed as contempt. That is not what I felt, of course, but that is what he must have seen it as.

"His mother now became mute. She looked at me, but then looked away, as if it was painful even to see me. I did my best to speak to her, but she simply didn't seem to hear me. And in the meantime, I had to deal with the lawyers, who informed me that I now effectively controlled the electricity factory, as Thomas had left his entire shareholding to me. This was worth quite a bit of money. The family was well-off anyway, but the factory, it turned out, had some very valuable land attached to it. I could easily live very well on the income which the shares produced, even if we sold none of the extra land. And I could live on that not only in India, where things are cheap, but back in Scotland.

73

"To begin with, of course, the thought of controlling the factory appalled me, as it tied me down even more. But I did make an effort, and I stayed for a further few years, getting the hang of how the business worked. Eventually, I decided that I had done enough and that I could leave without feeling too guilty. The old woman – Thomas's mother – had become demented by now, and spent her time wandering around the garden with a long-suffering attendant, chopping the heads off flowers. I returned to Scotland for a while, and then went off on further adventures for quite some time, which I regret that I can't tell you about just now because this risotto I'm making is requiring my complete attention and I cannot talk about anthropology and make a proper risotto all at the same time. So the rest of my life will have to wait for some other occasion."

29. Friendship

Pat left Domenica shortly after ten, crossed the landing to her flat, and went straight to her room. Bruce's door was shut, but the narrow band of light from beneath it told her that he was in. And there was music too; in the hall she could just make out the faint sound of the Cuban bands that he liked to play. He was considerate in that respect, at least, as he was always careful to keep the volume low.

She closed her door behind her and prepared for bed. The evening had started badly with that exchange over the hair gel – she would replace that tomorrow, she had decided – but Domenica's company had soon made her forget her irritation. Domenica and Bruce were polar opposites: she represented wit, and subtlety; Bruce represented . . . well, what did he represent? She closed her eyes and thought of Bruce, to see what free association might bring, but she opened them again sharply. A jar of hair gel.

She had been unsure what to expect of Domenica. On the face of it, dinner with a sixty-one-year-old neighbour might have been a dull prospect, but it had turned out to be anything but that. There were, presumably, dull sixty-one-year-olds, but there were also plenty of dull twenty-year-olds. It might even be, thought Pat, that there were more of the latter than the former. Or did it not matter what age one was? If one was dull at twenty, then one would still be dull at sixty-one.

Age was not of great importance to Pat. The secret, she thought – and she had read about this somewhere – was to talk to people as if they were contemporaries, and that was something that Domenica obviously understood. Her older neighbour had not talked down to her, which she might easily have done. She had treated her as somebody with whom she could easily share references and common experiences. And that had made it all seem so easy.

She had found out a certain amount about Domenica – about India and anthropology and, tantalisingly, a few snippets about feral children – but she was sure that there was much more to come. During dinner, their conversation had not let up, but Domenica had said little more about herself. Rather, she had told Pat something of the neighbours: of Tim and Jamie, who lived in the flat below, of Bertie's parents, Irene and Stuart, and of the man in the ground-floor flat, the man whom nobody saw, but who was there nonetheless.

"There may be a perfectly simple explanation," said Domenica. "Agoraphobia. If he suffers from that, poor man, he won't want to go out at all."

Pat noticed that Domenica spoke charitably, but when it came to Irene and Stuart, her tone changed.

"That poor little boy is nothing but an experiment to them," she said. "How much music and mathematics and so on can be poured into him before the age of seven? Will he compose his first symphony before he starts at primary school? And so on. Poor little boy! Have you seen him?"

"I've heard him," said Pat.

And Tim and Jamie downstairs? "There are many different

recipes for unhappiness in this life," said Domenica, "and poor Tim is following a very common one. To love that which one cannot attain. It's terribly sad, really. But people persist in doing it."

Pat said nothing. She had seen a young man walking up the stairs in front of her, but by the time she reached the landing he had disappeared. That, she assumed, was Tim or Jamie.

"Tim is very attached to Jamie," Domenica went on. "And Jamie is very keen on a girl who's gone to Canada for a year. So that's that, really."

"It can't be easy," said Pat.

Domenica shrugged. "No, it can't. But sometimes people decide to be happy with what they've got. I've known so many cases like that. People hold a candle for somebody who's never going to be for them what they want them to be. It's hopeless. But they carry on and on and make do with the scraps of time and attention that come their way."

"Sad."

"Very," Domenica replied, and then thought for a moment. "When I had him up here one evening for sherry, all he wanted to talk about was Jamie, and what Jamie was doing. Jamie was going to Montreal to see this girlfriend of his. And all that Tim was thinking of was this. His sadness was written large for me to see. He was losing his friend.

"And what made it worse for him was that there were so few people he could talk to about this, because he feared their lack of understanding, or their scorn. People are cruel, aren't they?"

After that they had sat in silence for a while and Pat had thought, and thought again, now that she was back in her room: we love the unattainable. Yes, we do. Foolishly. Hopelessly. All the time.

30. Things Happen at the Gallery

Pat arrived at the gallery slightly early the next morning, to find that the postman, a cheerful man with a weather-beaten face, had already been and there was a letter on the floor. She opened it and saw that it was an invitation to an opening to be held in a gallery further down the road. They were always getting this sort of thing, and it struck her that there was a lot of this in the art world: dealer sells to dealer, round and round in a circle. Eventually a genuine customer would have to buy a picture, but where were they? So far they had sold nothing, and the only person who had shown the slightest interest in buying something had turned out to be intent on obtaining a bargain. Perhaps things would change. Perhaps somebody would come and buy one of the D.Y. Cameron prints; somebody who would not make a dismissive remark about Mr Vettriano; somebody who liked pictures of hills and glens.

She put the gallery invitation on Matthew's desk and was about to go through to the back, when she stopped. Usually, when she came in in the morning, she would hear the alarm signal and have to key in the security number to stop it. This had not happened this morning, or had it? It was perfectly possible to go through the motions of a familiar action and not remember that one had done it. But Pat was sure that she had not attended to the alarm this morning. She had come in, opened the letter, and then walked over to Matthew's desk, where she now stood. The control box was on the other side of the gallery, near the light switch, and she had definitely not been over there.

Had the alarm been set? Pat tried to remember who had been last to leave the gallery last night. It was not Matthew. He had gone off to meet his father shortly after four and she had stayed at work until five. She remembered leaving the gallery and when she had done so, because she had been concerned about being in time for Domenica's invitation.

She glanced towards the control box, across the semi-darkened gallery. Two small red lights blinked regular pulses back at her. That was different. Normally, when she came in a single red light flashed until the code was keyed in. Now there were two.

Pat looked about her. The gallery had a large expanse of glass at the front, and this gave out onto the street. There were people on the pavement, traffic on the road. The door was only a few feet away. But even so, she felt suddenly uneasy, and now she saw that the door that led to the room at the back was ajar. She closed that door – always – before she left. She would not have left it open like that, as the alarm system depended on its being closed.

Now she felt frightened, and she ran across the room to switch on the lights. Then, with the gallery bathed in light, each of the larger pictures illuminated by their spotlights, she found the courage to walk over to the inner office door and tentatively push it open.

The intruder had managed to raise the lower panel of the back window about eighteen inches. The glass was not broken, but the catch had been forced and there were splinters of wood on the floor – she saw those immediately.

She stood in the doorway, quite still, her feelings confused. There was a feeling of intrusion, almost of violation. They had been burgled at home once, and she remembered how *dirtied* she had felt at the thought that somebody had come into their house and just *been* there, just been physically present and uninvited. She had spoken to her father about it, and he had simply nodded and said: *Yes, that's how it feels.*

She stepped back from the doorway and walked calmly to Matthew's desk, where she picked up the telephone and dialled the emergency code. A comforting voice told her that the police would arrive within minutes and that she should not touch anything until that happened. So she stood there, her heart pounding within her, wondering what had happened. Why had the alarm not gone off? Why was the office door ajar? It suggested that the intruder had managed to get in through that small opening and had then been disturbed, perhaps by the sounding of the signal on the control box. That would have made a perfectly audible sound, even if the main part of the alarm, the siren, had failed to go off.

Or perhaps Matthew had come in last night for some reason, set the alarm improperly, and then left the door ajar; he was the only other person with a key, as far as Pat knew. But then if he had done this, why would he have forced the window?

It suddenly occurred to Pat that a break-in could be quite convenient for Matthew. He was having difficulty in selling any of his paintings; perhaps it would be easier to arrange an insurance claim.

31. The Lothian and Borders Police Art Squad

A few minutes later, as promised by the calm voice on the telephone, a police car drew up outside the gallery and two uniformed officers, generously equipped with radios, handcuffs, and

79

commodious pockets, emerged. Pat went to the front door and opened it to them.

"An art gallery?" asked one of the policemen, the younger one, as they came in.

"Well it's not a supermarket," said the older one. "Pretty obvious."

Pat saw the younger policeman look down at the floor. He had been embarrassed by the put-down, but said nothing.

She showed the two men the alarm control unit, which was still flashing mutely.

"Can't have worked properly," said the younger policeman.

"Pretty obvious," said the older one.

Pat said nothing. Perhaps it was the end of a long shift for them and they needed their sleep. But even if that were the case, she did not think that the young man deserved this humiliation.

She led them through to the back room and pointed at the fragments of wood on the floor. The younger policeman bent down and picked up one of the splinters.

"From the window," he said.

The older policeman looked at Pat, who met his gaze briefly, and then he turned away. He peered at the window glass and shook his head.

"No prints there," he said. "Nothing. I should think that whoever it was who wanted in was disturbed by something. It happens all the time. These people start an entry and then something gets the wind up them and they're offsky."

"Offsky?" Pat asked.

"Yes," said the policeman. "Offsky. And there's not much we can do, although I can probably tell you who did this. All we can suggest is that you get your alarm seen to. And get a new catch – a more secure one – and put it on this window at the back. That's about it."

Pat listened in astonishment. "But how do you know who did it?" she asked.

The older policeman looked at her patiently. Then he raised his wrist and tapped his watch. "I retire in six hours' time," he said. "Thirty-six years of service. In that time, I've seen everything –

everything. Horrible things. Sad things. And in my time in the Art Squad, aesthetically disturbing things. And after all that time I've reached one conclusion. The same people do the same things all the time. That's how people behave. House-breakers break into houses. Others break into shops. It's no mystery. I can take you right now to the houses of the house-breakers in this city. I can take you to their actual doors and we can knock on them and see if they're at home. We know exactly who they are – exactly. And we know where they live. We know all that. And so if you think I'm picking on anybody, then let me tell you this. This was probably done by a man called Jimmy Clarke – James Wallace Clarke, to be precise. He's the person who steals paintings in this city. That's what he does. But of course we can't prove it."

Pat looked at the younger policeman, who returned her glance impassively.

"It must be frustrating for you," she said.

The older policeman smiled. "Not really," he said. "You get used to it. But my colleague here has it all in front of him. I'm offsky this afternoon. My wife and I have bought a bed-and-breakfast in Prestonpans. That's us fixed up."

The younger policeman raised an eyebrow. "Will anybody want to stay in Prestonpans?"

"It gets visitors," said the older policeman curtly.

"Why?"

The question was not answered, and they moved back into the main gallery. The older policeman walked about, looking at the paintings, leaving the younger man by Pat's side.

"My name's Chris," said the policeman, his voice lowered.

Pat nodded. "Mine's Pat."

"He's very cynical," said the policeman. "You know what I mean?"

"Yes," whispered Pat. "I do."

"Not everyone I meet in this job knows what cynical means," said Chris. "It's nice to come across somebody who does." He paused. "Would you like to go for a drink tonight? That is, if you're not doing anything."

Pat was taken by surprise and it was a few moments before she answered. She was free that evening, and there was no reason why she should not meet Chris for a drink. She had only just met him, of course, but if one couldn't trust a policeman, then whom could one trust?

"I wouldn't mind," she said.

He was visibly pleased with her response and he gave her the name of a wine bar off George Street. He would be there at seven o'clock, he said, adding: "Not in uniform, of course. Hah, hah!"

Pat winced. She suddenly realised that she had made a terrible mistake. She could not go out with a man who said *hah*, *hah* like that. She just could not. *Offsky*, she thought.

32. *Akrasia: the Essential Problem*

Before Matthew came into Big Lou's coffee bar that morning, full of the news of the attempted break-in at the gallery, Big Lou had been engaged in conversation with Ronnie and Pete about the possibility of weakness of the will.

"Ak-how much?" asked Ronnie.

"Akrasia," said Big Lou, from her accustomed position behind the counter. "It's a Greek word. You wouldn't know about it, of course."

"Used in Arbroath?" asked Ronnie coolly.

Big Lou ignored this. "I'm reading about it at the moment. A book on weakness of the will by a man called Willie Charlton, a philosopher. You won't have heard of him."

"From Arbroath?" asked Ronnie.

Big Lou appeared not to hear his remark. "Akrasia is weakness of the will. It means that you know what is good for you, but you can't do it. You're too weak."

"Sounds familiar," said Pete, stirring sugar into his coffee.

"Aye," said Big Lou. "You'd know. You're a gey fine case of weakness of the will. You know that sugar's bad for you, but you still take it. That's weakness of the will. That's what philosophers call incontinence of the will."

Pete glanced at Ronnie. "That's something else. That's diarrhoea of the will."

Big Lou sighed. "Diarrhoea and akrasia are different. But it's useless trying to explain things to you."

"Sorry," said Ronnie solemnly. "You tell us about akrasia, Lou."

Big Lou picked up a cloth and began to wipe the counter. "The question is this. Does weakness of the will make sense? Surely if we do something, then that means that we want to do it. And if we want to do it, then that means that must be because we think that it's in our best interests to do it."

Ronnie thought for a moment. "So?"

Big Lou intensified her rubbing of the counter. "So there's no such thing as a weakness of will because we always do what we want. All the time. You see?"

"No," said Pete.

Big Lou looked at Ronnie. "And you? Do *you* see?"

"No."

Big Lou sighed. It was difficult dealing with people who read nothing. But she chose to persist. "Take chocolate," she began.

"Chocolate?" said Ronnie.

"Yes. Now imagine that you really want to eat chocolate but you know that you shouldn't. Maybe you have a weight problem. You see a bar of chocolate and you think: that's a great wee bar of chocolate! But then something inside you says: it's not good for you to eat chocolate. You think for a while and then you eat it."

"You eat the chocolate?"

"Yes. Because you know that eating the chocolate will make you happier. It will satisfy your desire to eat chocolate."

"So?"

"Well, you can't be weak because you have done what you really wanted to do. Your will was to eat the chocolate. Your will has won. Therefore your will has been shown not to be weak."

Ronnie took a sip from his sugared coffee. "Where do you get all this stuff from, Lou?"

"I read," she said. "I happen to own some books. I read them. Nothing odd in that."

"Lou's great that way," said Ronnie. "No, don't laugh, Pete. You and me are ignorant. Put us in a pub quiz and we'd be laughed off the stage. Put Lou on and she'd win. I respect her for that. No, I really do."

"Thank you," said Lou. "Akrasia is an interesting thing. I'd never really thought about it before, but now . . ."

She was interrupted by the arrival of Matthew, who slammed the door behind him as he came in and turned to face his friends, flushed with excitement.

"A break-in," he said. "Wood all over the place. The cops have been."

They looked at him in silence.

"The gallery?" asked Pete.

Matthew moved over towards the counter. "Yes, the gallery. They were disturbed, thank God, and nothing was taken. I could have lost everything."

"Bad luck," said Ronnie. "That might have helped."

There was a silence. Big Lou glared at Ronnie, who lowered his gaze. "Sorry," he said. "I didn't mean that. I meant to say that it was bad luck that they tried to break in. That's what I meant." He paused. "What else could I have meant? Why the sensitivity?"

Matthew said nothing. "They could have taken the Peploe. In fact, I reckon that's what they were after."

Pete looked up. "The one worth forty grand?"

"Yes," said Matthew. "They must have been after that. All the rest is rubbish."

Ronnie looked thoughtful. "That character wanting to buy the painting the other day – he must be the one. Who else knows about it?"

Matthew frowned. "Nobody, as far as I know. Just us."

"Then, it's him," said Ronnie.

"Or one of us," said Big Lou, looking at Pete.

Nobody spoke. Big Lou turned to make Matthew his coffee. "Not a serious remark," she said. "It just slipped out."

"Weakness of the will?" said Ronnie.

33. Peploe?

"This is no time for levity," said Matthew. "The fact is, somebody is after my Peploe."

"*If* it's a Peploe," interrupted Ronnie. "You don't know, do you? So far, the only person who's said it's a Peploe is that girl, Pat. And what does she know about it? And you know nothing, as we all know."

"All right," said Matthew. "We'll call it my *Peploe?* That is, Peploe with a question mark after it. Satisfied? Right then, what do we do?"

"Remove it from the gallery," suggested Pete. "Take it home. Put it in a cupboard. Nobody's going to think there's a Peploe? in your cupboard."

Big Lou had been following the conversation closely and had stopped wiping the counter. "That's where you're wrong," she said. "If this person – the one who was interested in it – is really after it, then he'll have found out who Matthew is. Are you in the phone book, Matthew?"

Matthew nodded.

"Well, there you are," said Lou. "He'll know where you live. And if he was prepared to break into your gallery, then he'll be prepared to break into your flat. Take the Peploe? somewhere else."

"The bank," said Pete. "I knew this guy who kept a Charles Rennie Mackintosh bureau in the Bank of Scotland. It was so valuable that he couldn't afford the insurance. It was cheaper to keep it in the bank."

85

"What's the point of that?" asked Lou, frowning. "What's the point of having a bureau if you can't use it?"

"They'd keep kippers in it up in Arbroath," said Ronnie. "Smokies even."

"What do you know about Arbroath?" asked Lou. "You tell me. What do you know about Arbroath?"

Pete answered for him. "Nothing. He's never been there."

Matthew was becoming impatient. "I don't think that we should be talking about Arbroath," he said, irritably. "You two should stop needling Lou. The real question is: what do I do with my Peploe??"

They sat in silence, the three of them at the table, and Lou standing at her counter. Ronnie glanced at Matthew; he might have arranged the break-in to claim insurance. But if he had done that, then why had none of the paintings disappeared? There were several possible answers to that, one of which was that this was just the cover – the real stealing of the painting would come later. But if the Peploe? were to prove to be a Peploe, then why would he need to have it stolen in the first place? He would get his forty thousand or whatever it was by taking the picture to an auction. Why go to all the trouble of claiming the insurance, particularly when he would have no evidence of value to back up his claim?

Lou, too, was thinking about the situation. Pete had been right to suggest that the painting should be removed from the gallery. But they would have to ensure that it was kept somewhere else. Should she offer to look after it for him? It would be safe in her flat, tucked away behind a pile of books, but did she want to have something so valuable – and so portable – sitting there? Forty thousand pounds could buy a perfectly reasonable place to live in Arbroath. No, it would be better for the Peploe? to go elsewhere.

"Pat!" she said abruptly. "Get that girl to take the painting back to her place. She's the one who identified it. Let her look after it."

"John won't know who she is," said Pete. "She won't have told him . . ."

Matthew turned to Pete. "Who's John?" he asked.

Pete looked down at his coffee. "John? I didn't say John."

"You did," said Matthew. "You said something about John not knowing who Pat was. But why did you call him John? Do you know him?"

Pete shook his head. "You misheard me. I didn't say anything about a John. I don't know any Johns."

"Rubbish," said Lou. "Don't know any Johns? Rubbish."

"What I said was that *he* – this man who wants the Peploe? – whoever he is, and how would I know he's called John? – *he'll* not know who Pat is and won't know where she lives. Which is, where?"

"No idea," said Matthew.

Pete shrugged. "All right. Tell her to take it back to her place and keep it in a cupboard until you've decided what to do with it. It'll be safe there."

"Good idea," said Matthew. "I'll speak to her about it. I'll ask her to take it home this evening."

They finished their coffee in silence. Matthew was the first to go, leaving the other two men at their table.

"I suppose we have to get back," said Ronnie after a while. He looked at Lou. "Perhaps I should have been a philosopher instead, Lou. Easier job, I think."

Lou smiled. "I wouldn't know. But I suspect that it's not as easy as you think. They worry a lot. Life's not simple for them."

"Nor for us," said Pete, rising to his feet.

"Maybe," said Big Lou. "But then, ignorance can be comfortable, can't it?"

34. On the Way to the Floatarium

Irene had an appointment at the Floatarium, but with a good half-hour in hand before she was due to submit to the tank's womb-like embrace, she had time to enjoy the bright, late spring day. Strolling along Cumberland Street that morning, she noted the changes brought by relentless gentrification. A few years back there had been at least some lace curtains; now the windows with their newly-restored astragals were reassuringly bare, the better to allow, at ground level at least, expensive minimalist or neo-post-Georgian furniture to be admired. Irene paused before the windows of one flat and pondered the colour scheme. No, she would not have chosen that red, which was almost cloying in its richness. Their own flat was painted white throughout, apart from Bertie's room, which they had chosen to paint pink, to break the sexist mould. Or, rather, she had chosen to paint the walls pink. Stuart, her husband, had been less certain about this and had argued for white, but had been overruled. Irene was not sure about Stuart's commitment to the project of Bertie's education, and she had even wondered on occasions whether he fully understood what she was trying to do. The discussion over colour schemes had been a case in point.

"Boys don't like pink," he had observed. "I didn't, when I was a boy."

Irene had been patient. "That, of course, was some time ago, and your upbringing, as we both know, was not exactly enlightened, was it? Attitudes are different now."

"Attitudes may be different," said Stuart, "but are boys? Boys are much the same as they always were, I would have thought."

Irene was not prepared to let such a patently false argument go unrefuted. "Boys are not the same!" she said. "No! Definitely not! Boys are constructed socially. We make them what they are. A patriarchal society produces patriarchal boys. A civilised society produces civilised boys."

Stuart looked doubtful. "But boys still want to do boyish things. If you put them in a room with dolls and toy cars, won't they choose the cars? Isn't that what they do?"

Irene sighed. "Only boys who have had no other options will go for cars. Some boys will go for other things."

"Dolls?"

"Yes, dolls. If you give them the chance. Boys love playing with dolls."

"Do they?"

"Yes. As I said, if you make the environment right."

Stuart thought for a moment. "Well, look at Bertie. He loves trains, doesn't he? He's always going on about the train set at the nursery school. He loves it."

"Bertie loves trains because of their social possibilities," said Irene quickly. "The train set enables him to act out social dramas. Bertie likes trains for what they represent."

Matters had been left at that, but doubts about Stuart's commitment had lingered in Irene's mind, and she often reflected, as she was doing now on her stroll down Cumberland Street, that raising a gifted child was not easy if one did not have the complete support of the other parent. And this difficulty was compounded, surely, by the absence of support from that nursery school woman, Christabel Macfadzean, *that cow*, thought Irene, who clearly resented Bertie's talents and seemed determined to prevent him from developing them – all in a spirit of misplaced egalitarianism. Irene, of course, was deeply committed to egalitarianism in all its forms, but this did not prevent the paying of adequate attention to gifted children. Society needed special people if egalitarian goals were to be met. Unexceptional people – ordinary people, as Irene called them – were often distressingly non-egalitarian in their views.

She reached the end of Cumberland Street and decided not to take the more direct route along Circus Lane, but to make her way along Circus Place, where she might just treat herself to a latte before the Floatarium. There was a café there she liked, where she could read the papers in comfort and occasionally make a start on one of the more challenging crosswords. Irene had thought of teaching Bertie how to do crosswords, but had decided that his programme was probably a bit too full at the moment. What with his Grade seven music theory examination coming up – Bertie was the youngest Scottish entrant for that examination that the Royal College of Music had ever registered – and with his new course of mathematics tutorials, there would be little time to take him through the conventions of crosswords. Perhaps he should learn bridge first, although it might be difficult to find partners for a bridge four. Stuart was not keen, and when Irene had raised the possibility of playing the occasional hand with that woman upstairs, that Macdonald woman, she had actually laughed at the thought that Bertie might play.

There was something odd about that woman, thought Irene. She was a type which one often encountered in Edinburgh. A woman with intellectual pretensions and a haughty manner. There were so many of them, she reflected; so many.

35. Latte Interrupta

It was while she was sitting in the small café in Royal Circus with her generous cup of latte, skimming through the morning newspaper, that Irene's mobile phone (with its characteristic Stockhausen ring) notified her of the incoming call from the East New Town Nursery. Christabel Macfadzean came right to the point. Would Irene mind coming round to the nursery immediately? Yes, Bertie was perfectly all right, but an incident had nonetheless occurred and it would be necessary to discuss it with her.

Irene thought that she might finish her latte. It was an imposition to be summoned back to the nursery, and she would have to cancel her appointment at the Floatarium. But Christabel Macfadzean would not think of that, of course; in her view, parents had nothing better to do than drop everything and listen to her complaints. Obviously there had been some little spat between Bertie and one of the other children, presumably over that wretched train set. That was no reason to drag her into it. If Christabel Macfadzean had bothered to acquaint herself with the works of Melanie Klein, then she would have been in a position to understand these so-called "incidents" and she would not over-react – as Irene was fairly certain she was doing right now.

Irene's growing irritation prevented her from enjoying the rest of her coffee. She folded the newspaper and tossed it onto a side table. Then, having exchanged a few brief words with the young woman behind the counter, she began to make her way to the nursery. As she walked, she rehearsed what she would say to Christabel Macfadzean. She was adamant that she would not allow Bertie to be victimised. An incident, as Christabel Macfadzean called them, required two participants, and there was no reason to imagine that Bertie had started it.

By the time she arrived at the nursery, Irene was ready for whatever conflict lay ahead. So when Christabel Macfadzean's assistant opened the door and ushered her in, Irene was ready to go on the offensive.

"I'm surprised that you deemed it necessary to call me," she said to Christabel when she appeared from behind the water-play table. "I was actually rather busy. This is not really convenient."

Christabel Macfadzean dried her hands carefully on a small red towel.

"There has been an incident," she said calmly. "It is always my policy to involve the parents when an incident is sufficiently serious. I would be failing in my duty if I did not do so."

She looked up and fixed Irene with a firm stare. She knew that this woman would be difficult, but she was looking forward to the encounter with all the pleasure of one who knew that her position was quite unassailable.

"Incident?" said Irene sharply. "Surely the life of a nursery school is filled with incident. Children are always acting out little dramas, aren't they, as Melanie Klein pointed out. You're familiar with the works of Melanie Klein, I take it?"

Christabel Macfadzean closed her eyes for a few moments. Ignoring the question, she said: "There are little dramas and big dramas. Then there are incidents. This is an incident which requires parental involvement. We can't cope here with serious bad behaviour all by ourselves. We have to invoke parental assistance."

Irene drew in her breath. "Serious bad behaviour? A little spat over the train set? Do you call that serious bad behaviour? Well, really . . ."

Christabel Macfadzean interrupted her. "It has nothing to do with the train set – nothing at all."

Irene glared at her. "Well, something equally trivial, no doubt."

"No," said Christabel Macfadzean. "It's by no means trivial." This is most enjoyable, she thought. This particular galleon is having the wind taken right out of her sails, and it is a most agreeable experience, for me at least.

"Well," said Irene. "Perhaps you would be good enough to let me know what it is. Has Bertie been involved in a fight? Fighting is to be expected of little boys, you know, particularly if they are not adequately supervised . . ."

This last remark drew an angry snort from Christabel Macfadzean. "I shall pass over that comment," she said. "I shall assume that I misheard you. No, there has been no fighting. What there has been is vandalism."

Irene laughed. "Vandalism! Children break things all the time! There's no call for a fuss!"

"No," said Christabel Macfadzean. "This incident did not involve the breaking of anything. It involved the writing of graffiti. In the toilet – all over one wall – in large letters."

"And what makes you assume that it was Bertie?" Irene asked belligerently. "Are you not rather jumping to conclusions?"

Christabel Macfadzean put down the towel and looked at Irene in triumph. This was a sweet moment for her, and she prolonged it for a few seconds before she answered.

"Two things compel that conclusion," she said solemnly. "Firstly, he's the only one who can write." She paused, allowing just the right interval to heighten the dramatic effect of her revelation. "And then it happens to be in Italian."

36. Bertie in Disgrace

Irene, somewhat deflated, followed Christabel Macfadzean down the corridor, with its colourful examples of juvenile art pinned on the walls. An open doorway led to a room with a row of tiny washbasins and small stalls, and there, across the facing wall, was the graffiti, in foot-high letters.

Irene gasped as she saw what Bertie had written. LA MACFADZEAN È UNA VACCA!

"You see!" said Christabel Macfadzean. "That is what your son has done."

Irene nodded. "A very silly thing to do," she said quickly. "But I'm sure that it will wash off easily enough. It's probably washable marker pen."

Christabel Macfadzean bristled. "That's not the point," she said. "The real offence lies in the fact that he has written it at all. And, may I ask – since presumably you know Italian – may I ask what it means?"

Irene blinked. It was going to be extremely difficult to explain. The word *vacca* had two meanings, of course: cow (the common meaning) and woman of ill repute (the rude meaning). She assumed that Bertie had intended the more innocuous of these, but even that one could hardly be admitted. Then an idea came to her, and at a stroke she was rescued.

"It means *La Macfadzean* – that's you, of course – is a . . . *vacuum cleaner*. What a silly, childish thing for him to write, but not insulting, of course."

Christabel Macfadzean looked puzzled. "A vacuum cleaner?"

"Yes," said Irene. "Isn't that ridiculous? It's just a piece of childish nonsense. A vacuum cleaner, indeed! Innocent nonsense. Almost a term of endearment. In fact, in Italy it probably is. I shall look it up in the *Grande Sansoni*."

"But why would he call me a vacuum cleaner?"

Irene frowned. "Do you use a vacuum cleaner here? Have the children seen you vacuuming? Could that be it?"

"No," said Christabel Macfadzean. "I never vacuum."

"Perhaps you should. Perhaps the children should see you doing these ordinary tasks, dignifying them . . ."

"Well, may I suggest that we return to the subject of this . . . this incident. We cannot tolerate this sort of thing, even if the insult is a piece of childish nonsense. What will the other children think?"

Irene sighed. "I'm sorry that you're taking this so seriously," she said. "I thought that all that would be required would be for Bertie to be told not to do this sort of thing. There's no need to over-react."

Christabel Macfadzean turned to Irene. "Over-reaction, did you say? Is it over-reaction to nip juvenile vandalism in the bud? Is it over-reaction to object to being called a vacuum cleaner? Is that an over-reaction?"

"But nobody will have understood it," said Irene. "If the other children can't read – nobody yet having taught them – then they won't have understood. None of the children will know the first thing about it. They'll assume that the writing is just another notice. No real harm's been done."

Christabel Macfadzean led the way back to the small office that she had at the front of the building. Gesturing for Irene to take the uncomfortable straight-backed chair before her desk, she herself sat down and rested her folded arms on a large white blotter.

"I very much regret this," she said evenly, "but I'm going to have to suspend Bertie for a few days. It seems to me that the only way in which we can bring home to him the seriousness of what he has done is to suspend him. It's the only way."

Irene's eyes opened wide. "Suspension? Bertie? Suspend Bertie?"

"Yes," said Christabel Macfadzean. "If he's as advanced as you claim he is, then he will need to be punished in an advanced way. It's for his own good."

Irene swayed slightly. The idea that Bertie – who was effectively doing the nursery a favour by attending it – the idea that he should be suspended was quite inconceivable. And that this pedestrian woman, with her clearly limited understanding of developmental psychology, should be sitting in judgment on Bertie – why, that was quite intolerable. It would be better to withdraw Bertie, thought Irene, than to leave him here. On the other hand, this nursery was convenient . . .

Irene closed her eyes and mentally counted from one to ten. Then she opened her eyes again and stared at Christabel Macfadzean. "I was proposing to take him out of nursery for a few days anyway," she said. "He needs a bit of stimulation, you know, and I thought that I might take him to the museum and the zoo. He doesn't appear to get much stimulation here, and that, incidentally, may be why he called you a vacuum cleaner. It's his way of signalling his boredom and frustration."

"You can call it taking him out of school," said Christabel Macfadzean. "I'll call it a suspension."

Irene did not wish to continue with the exchange. Fetching Bertie from the corner where he was playing with the train set, she retrieved his jacket and half-marched him out of the room.

"Bertie," she said, as they walked back along London Street, "Mummy is very, very cross with you for writing that Miss Macfadzean is a cow. You should not have said it. It's not nice to call somebody a *vacca*."

"You do," said Bertie.

37. *At the Floatarium*

The curious thought occurred to Irene, as she lay in her supporting Epsom salts solution, that they were both suspended. Bertie was suspended from nursery over that ridiculous graffiti incident, and she was suspended, almost weightless, in her flotation chamber. Her suspension was for no more than an hour, though, whereas Bertie was to be suspended for three days.

They had walked directly to the Floatarium from the nursery school. Little had been said, but Bertie had been left in no doubt that he was in disgrace. By the time they reached their destination, though, Bertie had been half-forgiven. Indeed, Irene had begun to smile – discreetly – over what had happened. It must have been an act of great self-liberation for him to climb onto one of the little chairs and write that message across the wall. And of course what he had written was accurate; indeed, it showed a real understanding of what was what to write an observation like that.

He had to learn, though, that some things are best kept to oneself. This was a difficult thing for children to master, she thought, as they were naturally frank. Duplicity and hypocrisy came later, instilled by adults; thus we learn to hide, to say one thing and mean another, to clad ourselves with false colours.

Irene reflected on these things as she lay in the darkness of the tank. Bertie had been left in the tank room with her, but not in a tank. He was seated on a chair with a colouring book which the proprietor of the Floatarium had thoughtfully provided for him. Of course, this would not be capable of diverting him, and he had rapidly abandoned it in favour of a magazine. Bertie had never seen the sense of colouring things in. Why bother?

Irene's mind wandered. It was completely quiet within the tank, and the absence of sensory distraction induced a profound sense of calm. One did not feel confined by the walls of the tank; rather, one felt weightless and without boundary, independent of any physical constraint, freed of the attachment that came with gravity. I could lie here forever, thought Irene, and forget about the world and its trials.

Her sense of detachment was suddenly interrupted by a knocking on the side of the tank.

"Bertie?"

A muffled voice came from outwith. "Irene?"

"Yes, I'm here, Bertie. In the tank, as you know. I'm relaxing. You can have a little go at the end."

"I don't want to float. I'll drown."

"Nonsense, darling. The specific gravity of the water is such that you can't sink. You'll like it."

"I hate floating."

Irene moved her hands gently in the water, making a slight splashing sound. This was rather irritating. Bertie was ruining the floating experience.

"Let Mummy float in peace a little longer, Bertie," she called out. "Then we'll go and have a latte. You can float some other time, if you want to. Nobody's *forced* to float."

There was silence for a moment and then a sudden shout that made Irene start.

"*Non mi piace parlare Italiano!*"

"Bertie?" called out Irene. "What was that you said?"

"*Non mi piace parlare Italiano! Non mi piace il sassofono! No! No!*"

Irene sat up, banging her head on the top of the chamber. Pushing open the lid, she looked out, to see Bertie standing defiantly in the middle of the room, a ripped-up magazine on the floor before him.

"Bertie!" she exclaimed. "What is this? You're behaving like a little boy! What on earth is wrong with you?"

"*Non mi piace parlare Italiano!*" shouted Bertie again. "I don't like speaking Italian!"

Irene climbed out of the chamber and reached for her towel.

"This is complete nonsense," she said. "You're upset – quite understandably – about what happened. That's all. You'll feel better once we've had a nice latte. Italian's got nothing to do with it. And I can't understand why you should say you don't like the saxophone. You love your saxophone."

"*No! No!*" shouted Bertie, stamping his feet on the ground. His face was red with rage now, and his fists were clenching and unclenching.

"Bertie, just calm down," said Irene. "If you want to talk, we can do so over latte. You mustn't make a noise here in the Floatarium. There are other people floating."

"I hope they sink!" shouted Bertie.

Irene took a deep breath. "That's a very, very nasty thing to say. What if somebody did sink? How would you feel then? You'd feel very bad, wouldn't you?"

Bertie did not reply. He was looking down at the ground now, and Irene noticed that his shoulders were heaving. Bertie was sobbing, but in silence.

She reached forward and embraced him, hugging the little boy to her.

"You'll feel better soon, Bertie," she said. "That smelly nursery must be very boring for you. We'll send you somewhere better. Perhaps St Mary's Music School. You like their Saturday mornings, don't you? There are some nice boys and girls there. And you might even get into the choir and dress up, like the rest of the Episcopalians. That would be nice, wouldn't it?"

"No," sobbed Bertie. "No."

38. Mother/Daughter Issues

Barely a mile from the Floatarium, where Bertie was protesting, Sasha Todd, wife of Raeburn Todd, was sitting down for morning coffee with her daughter, Lizzie. Sasha had chosen Jenners' tearoom for this meeting, because Jenners made her feel secure, and had always done so. Other shops might come and go, and one or two *parvenus* had indeed recently set up in the city, but she, quite rightly, remained loyal to Jenners. There was nothing unsettling about Jenners, as she had cause to reflect whenever she approached Edinburgh on a train from the west and saw the satisfying sign Jenners Depository. This signalled to the world that whatever one might find on the shelves of Jenners itself, *there was more in the depository, round the back.* This was reassuring in the most fundamental way.

There was nothing reassuring about Lizzie. She was twenty-three now, and had done very little with her life. At school she had been unexceptional; she had never attracted negative attention, but nor had she attracted any praise or distinction. Her reports had been solid – "might get a B at Higher level, provided she puts in more work"; "almost made it to the second team this year – a solid effort" and so on. And then there had been three years at a college which gave her a vague, unspecified qualification. This qualification had so far produced no proper job, and she had moved from temporary post to temporary post, none of which seemed to suit her.

Both Sasha and Todd thought that marriage was the only solution.

"We can't support her indefinitely," said Todd to his wife. "Somebody else is going to have to take on the burden."

"She's not a burden," said Sasha. "All she's doing is looking for herself."

"She should be looking for a husband," retorted Todd.

"Possibly," said Sasha. "But then, it's not easy these days. These young men one meets don't seem to be thinking of marriage."

Todd shook his head. "Yet marriages take place. Look at the back of *Scottish Field*. What do you see? Wedding photographs. Nice fellows in their kilts getting married in places like Stirling and Balfron."

Sasha sighed. What her husband said was true. Such a world existed – it had certainly existed in their time – but their own daughter seemed not to be part of it. Was there anything wrong with her, she wondered. There had been no signs of anything like that – no *unsuitable* friends with short-cropped hair and a tendency to wear rather inelegant jackets – so at least that was not the problem. Thank heavens they did not have to face the problem faced by friends in the Braids whose daughter, an otherwise reasonable girl, had brought home a female welder. What did one talk to a female welder about, Sasha wondered. Presumably there was something one could say, but she had no idea what it might be.

Now, in the tea-room at Jenners, scene, over so many years, of such rich exchanges of gossip, Sasha fixed Lizzie with the maternal gaze to which her daughter was so accustomed.

"You're looking thin," Sasha said. "You're not on one of those faddish diets, are you? Really, the damage those people do! Doctor what's-his-name, and people like that. I'm not suggesting that one should over-eat, but one wants to have something to cover one's poor skeleton."

She pushed the plate of iced cakes over the table towards her daughter.

Lizzie pushed them away. "No thanks. And I don't think I'm looking particularly thin. In fact, I'd say I'm about the right weight for my height."

Sasha raised an eyebrow. Lizzie was flat-chested in her view, and a judicious coating of plumpness might help in that respect. But of course she could never raise the issue with her daughter, just as she could say nothing about the dowdy clothes and the lack of make-up.

Taking a cake, Sasha cut it in half. Marzipan: her favourite. Battenberg cakes were hard to beat, particularly when dissected along the squares; she had little time for chocolate cake – sticky, amorphous, and over-sweet substance that it was.

"You know," she said, discreetly licking at her fingers, "you could do rather more with yourself than you do. I'm not being critical, of course. Not at all. I just think that if you paid a little bit more attention to your clothes . . ."

"And my face," interjected Lizzie. "Maybe I should do something about my face."

"There's nothing wrong with your face," said Sasha. "I said nothing about your face. You have a very nice face. I've got nothing against your face."

"In fact," said Lizzie, "people say that I look quite like you. In the face, that is."

Sasha picked up the second half of her cake and examined it closely. "Do they?" she said. "Well, isn't that nice? Not that I see it myself, but perhaps others do. Surprising, though."

"You don't sound very enthusiastic," said Lizzie.

Sasha laughed lightly. "Now," she said, "that's enough about faces. I've got something much more important to talk to you about."

39. The Facts of Life

"Something important?" asked Lizzie. There was doubt in her voice: what was important to her mother was usually rather unimportant to her.

"Very," said Sasha, glancing about her, as if those at neighbouring tables might eavesdrop on some great disclosure. "You will have heard that the ball is coming up. Soon."

"The ball?"

"You know," said Sasha. "The Conservative ball. The South Edinburgh Conservative Ball."

Lizzie looked bored. "Oh, that one. That's nice. You'll be going, I take it. I hope that you enjoy yourselves."

"We shall," said Sasha, firmly. "And we'd very much appreciate it if you would come in our party. Both Daddy and I. We'd both appreciate it. Very much." She fixed her daughter with a stare as she spoke. A message was being communicated.

Lizzie looked at her mother. She was so sad, she thought. Imagine living a life in which the highlight of one's existence was a political ball. How sad. "Depends," she said. "Depends when it is."

"Next week," said Sasha. "I know I haven't given you much notice, but it's next Friday, at the Braid Hills Hotel. It's such a nice place for it."

Lizzie pursed her lips. She was in a difficult situation. She did not want to go to the ball, but she was realistic enough to understand her position. Her parents paid her rent and gave her an allowance. She accepted this, in spite of her pride, and she understood that in return there were a few duties that she had to discharge. Attendance at the Conservative Ball had always been one of these. This was what her mother's look meant.

"All right," she said. "I'll come."

Sasha looked relieved. "That will be very nice." She picked up her table napkin – paper! – and removed a crumb of marzipan from the edge of her lower lip. She would have liked to lick her lips, and would have done so at home, but she couldn't in town. "We'll make up a small party. Daddy's arranged that."

Lizzie, who had been looking out of the window, turned to face her mother. "A party?"

Sasha smiled. "Yes, of course. A small party. Just the three of us and . . ."

"That's fine. The three of us. That's fine."

"And a fourth."

Lizzie said nothing. She tried to meet her mother's gaze, but Sasha looked away.

"A young man," said Sasha. "A very charming young man from the office. He's called Bruce. We thought it would be a good idea to ask him to join us."

Lizzie sighed. "Why? Why can't we just go by ourselves?"

Sasha leaned forward conspiratorially. "Because there's hardly anybody going," she whispered. "Nobody has bought a ticket – or virtually nobody."

Lizzie looked at her mother in frank astonishment. "Nobody?"

"Yes," said Sasha. "Even the people on the committee have found some excuse or other. It's appalling."

"Well, then, why don't you cancel it? Surely that would be simplest?"

Sasha shook her head. "No, it's not going to be cancelled. Imagine if people heard about that. We'd be the laughing stock. The ball is going ahead. Your father has made up his mind."

Lizzie thought for a moment. "And Bruce? What about him?"

Sasha answered quickly. "Very charming. A good-looking young man too. He lives down in the New Town somewhere." She paused, and then added: "Unattached."

For a moment there was a silence. Then Lizzie laughed. "So," she said. "So."

"Yes," said Sasha. "So. And it's about time, if I may say so, that you started to think of finding a suitable man. It's all very well enjoying yourself, but you can't leave it too late."

Lizzie closed her eyes. "I'm on the shelf, am I?"

Sasha picked up her coffee and took a sip. She would remain calm in this conversation; she was determined about that. "You know very well what I'm talking about. There are some people who just miss the bus. You may think that you've got plenty of time, but you haven't. The years go by. Then you suddenly realise that you're thirty-something and the men who are interested in getting married aren't interested in you any more – they're interested in girls in their mid-twenties. Oh yes, you may laugh, but that's the truth of the matter. If you want a husband, don't drag your feet – just don't drag your feet."

Lizzie waited until her mother had finished. Then: "But you're assuming that I want a husband."

Sasha stared at her daughter. "Of course you want a husband."

Lizzie shook her head. "Actually, I don't have much of a view on that. I'm quite happy as I am. There's nothing wrong with being single."

Sasha put down her coffee cup. She would have to choose her words carefully. "All right. You're single. Where does the money come from? You tell me that. Where does the money come from?"

Lizzie did not respond, and after a few moments Sasha provided the answer herself.

"Money comes from men," she said.

40. In Nets of Golden Wires

Carried down on the Jenners escalator, mother and daughter, one step apart, but separated by a continent of difference. *I must be patient with her*, thought Sasha; and Lizzie, for her part, thought exactly the same. *She'll come round to our way of thinking – it's just a question of time*, thought Sasha; and Lizzie said to herself: *God help me from ever, ever becoming like her. She actually said it. She said: money comes from men!* She felt herself blush at the thought, a warm feeling of shame, mixed with embarrassment, for Sasha. If her mother thought this, then what did her parents' marriage amount to? An agreement as to property? That would make her the by-product of an arrangement of convenience; no more than that.

They descended from the first floor in silence. Then, halfway down, Lizzie turned to the left and saw, standing on the ascending escalator, a young man, perhaps her age, perhaps a year or two older; a young man who was wearing a dark-olive shirt and a grey windcheater, and whose face reminded her, more than anything else, of one of those youths who stood as models for Renaissance painters. Had he been naked, and pierced by arrows, then he was Saint Sebastian in full martyrdom; but his expression was not one of agony, or even of anxiety; he had something to do in Jenners, and was going about his business calmly. *Look at me!* willed Lizzie. *Look!* But he did not seem to notice her, and his gaze remained fixed ahead.

They passed one another in seconds, and Lizzie, transfixed, turned round to watch him disappear behind her. She noticed the shape of the shoulders, and the neck, so vulnerable, so perfect, and the colour of his hair, and she was filled at that moment with a sudden sense of longing. The vision of male beauty which had been vouchsafed her struck her with sudden and great force, and she knew that she had to see this young man again; she had to speak to him.

She had been standing in front of her mother, and so she got off the escalator first when they reached the bottom and turned to face Sasha.

"We might try some perfumes," said Sasha. "My bottle of Estée

Lauder is almost empty and I thought I might try something else. You could help me choose."

Lizzie thought quickly. "You go," she said. "There's something I want to look for upstairs. Sorry, I forgot."

"What is it?" asked Sasha.

Lizzie thought for a moment. She was tempted to reply: *a man*, but did not, saying instead: "Oh, I just wanted to look around. But don't you worry about it, you go ahead."

She moved forward to give Sasha a quick peck on the cheek, and then, without waiting for her mother to protest, she stepped back onto the ascending escalator. Looking up, she saw that the young man had disappeared, but presumably he had taken the next escalator up; there was nothing for men on the mezzanine floor. So she strode up the steps, turning quickly to wave to Sasha, who was still standing, in puzzlement, staring up at her.

She knew that what she was doing was ridiculous. It was ridiculous to see somebody – on an escalator, too – and fall in love with him. People did not do that sort of thing. And yet she had. She had seen this man and she ached to see him again. Why? Because of the beauty of his expression? Because she knew, just to look at him, that he would be kind to her? How absurd, utterly absurd. And yet that is exactly how she felt. *I am caught by love in nets of golden wires.*

When she reached the first floor, she looked about her quickly. There was no sign of the young man, and she decided, again, that he must have gone further up. The food hall; that was it; that was where a young man would be going. He would be planning a dinner party for some friends and needed something special. He was used to Jenners, having been taken there with his mother – one of those matrons in the tea-room – and now he was coming back to do his own shopping.

Lizzie rushed to change escalators and arrived, slightly breathless, on the second floor. She made her way to the food hall and looked down the aisles. There were rows of shortbread tins and traditional oatcakes; lines of marmalade jars; nests of pickles and spices. A be-aproned woman came up to her with a tray and offered her a small piece of cheese on a stick. Lizzie took it, almost automatically, and thanked her.

"I'm looking for a man," she said.

"Aren't we all?" said the woman, offering her another piece of cheese.

Lizzie smiled. "He came up the escalator, and he seems to have disappeared. A young man in a grey windcheater. Tall. Good-looking."

The woman sighed. "Sounds ideal. He'd suit me fine."

"Did you see him?"

"No."

Lizzie wandered off. The store was too big. The world was empty. She had lost him.

41. Your Cupboard or Mine?

"I'm not sure," said Pat. "I'm not sure if that's a very good idea."

Matthew looked surprised. It seemed obvious to him, but then sometimes he discovered that others found it hard to grasp the self-evident. This had given rise to difficulties during his business career, such as it was. He had assumed that staff would understand the reasons for doing things in a particular way, only to discover that they had no idea. This meant that he had to spell things out to them, and this, in turn, seemed to irritate them. He had wondered whether he was going about it in the right way, and had discussed the issue with his father, but even his father had not seemed to grasp the point that he was trying to make.

"It really is the best thing to do," he assured her. "We talked about it over coffee. Everybody agreed that it would be better for the Peploe? to be looked after somewhere else. It was Pete's idea, actually, but Ronnie and Lou liked the idea too."

"But why? Why can't you take it back to your place and put it in a cupboard? Why put it in my cupboard?"

They were sitting at Matthew's desk in the gallery, and Matthew had his feet up on the surface of the desk while he leaned back in his leather captain's chair. Pat noticed his shoes, which were an elegant pair of brogues, leather-soled. Matthew noticed her looking at his shoes and smiled. "Church's," he said. "They make very good shoes for men. They last. But they're pricey."

Pat nodded. "They're very smart. I don't like big clumping shoes, like some of the shoes that you see men wearing. I like thin shoes, like those. I always look at men's shoes."

"But do you know how much these shoes cost?" Matthew asked. "Do you want to know?"

"Yes."

"Two hundred and fifty pounds," he said, adding: "That's for two."

He waited for Pat to laugh, but she did not. She was looking at his shoes again. "What sort of shoes do you think the First Minister wears?" she asked.

Matthew shrugged. It was a curious question to ask. He had no interest in politicians, and he would have had some difficulty in remembering the name of the First Minister. Come to think of it, who was he? Or was that the previous one? "We never see his feet, do we? Are they keeping them from us?"

"Maybe."

Matthew, slightly self-consciously, now lifted his feet off the desk. "I expect he buys his shoes in Glasgow," he said. "Not Edinburgh."

They sat in silence for a moment, while this remark was digested. Then Pat returned to the issue of the cupboard. "But why can't you keep the Peploe? in your cupboard . . . along with your Church's shoes?"

Matthew sighed. "Because it will be obvious to whoever is trying to steal it that it could be at my place. I'm in the phone book. They could look me up and then do my place over. Whereas you . . . well, you're not exactly in the phone book, I take it. They won't know who you are."

I'm anonymous, thought Pat. I'm not even in the phone book. I'm just the girl who works in the gallery. A girl with a room in a flat in Scotland Street. A girl on her *second* gap year . . .

"All right," she said. "I'll take it back to Scotland Street and put it in a cupboard down there. If that's what you want."

Matthew stood up and rubbed his hands together. "Good," he said. "I'll wrap it up and you can take it back with you this evening."

He walked across to the place where the Peploe? was hanging and lifted it off its hook. Then, bringing it back to the desk, he turned it over and they both examined the back of the painting. The stretcher, across which the canvas had been placed, had cracked in several places and was covered with dust. A label had been stuck on the top wooden strut, and Matthew now extracted a clean white handkerchief and rubbed the dust off this.

"You can tell a lot from labels," he said knowingly. "These things tell you a great deal about a painting."

Pat glanced at him. His pronouncement sounded confident, and for a moment she thought that he perhaps knew something about art after all. But it was all very well knowing that labels told you something, the real skill would lie in knowing what it was that they told you.

"There's something written on it," said Matthew, dabbing at the dust again. "Look."

Pat peered at the faded surface of the label. Something had been written on it in pencil. As Matthew removed more grime, the writing became more legible, and he read it out.

"It says: Three pounds two and sixpence."

They looked at one another.

"That was a long time ago, of course," said Matthew.

42. Gallery Matters

Matthew's problem, thought Pat, was that he very quickly became bored with what he was doing. That day was an example. After they had finished their discussion about what to do with the Peploe?, he had turned to a number of tasks, but had completed none. He had started a crossword, but failed to fill in more than a few clues and had abandoned it. He had then written a letter, but had stopped halfway through and announced that he would finish it the following day. Then he had begun to tidy his desk, but had suddenly decided that it was time for lunch and had disappeared to the Café St Honoré for a couple of hours. Pat wondered whether he had finished his meal, or only eaten half of it. Had he finished his coffee at Big Lou's, or had he left his cup half-drained? She would have to watch next time.

Of course, part of the reason for Matthew's behaviour, she thought, was that he was bored. The gallery did virtually no business and what else was there to do but sit and wait for customers?

"Perhaps we should hold an exhibition," she said to him when he returned from lunch.

Matthew looked at her quizzically. "Haven't we got one on at the moment?" he said, gesturing to the walls.

"This is just a random collection of paintings," Pat explained. "An exhibition involves a particular sort of painting. Or work by a particular artist. It gives people something to think about. It would draw them in."

Matthew looked thoughtful. "But where would we get all these paintings from?" he asked.

"You'd contact an artist and ask him to give you a whole lot of paintings," she said. "Artists like that. It's called a show."

"But I don't know any artists," said Matthew.

Pat looked at him. She wanted to ask him why he was running a gallery, but she did not. Bruce had been right, she told herself. He is useless. He hasn't got a clue.

"I know some artists," she said. "We had an artist in residence at school. He's very good. He's called Tim Cockburn, and he lives in Fife. There are a lot of artists in Pittenweem. There's Tim Cockburn, and then there's somebody called Reinhard Behrens, who puts a little submarine into all his paintings. He's good too. We could ask them to do a show."

Matthew was interested, but then he looked at his watch. "My God! Look at the time. And I'm meant to be playing golf with the old man. I'm going to have to shoot."

Left by herself for the rest of the afternoon, Pat dealt with the few customers who came in. She sold a D.Y. Cameron print and dealt with an enquiry from a woman who wanted to buy a Vettriano for her husband.

"I went into another gallery and asked them the same question," she said to Pat. "And they told me that they had no Vettrianos but that I could paint one myself if I wanted. What do you think they meant by that?"

Pat thought for a moment. There was an endemic snobbery in the art world, and here was an example.

"Some people are sniffy about him," she said. "Some people don't like his work at all."

"But my husband does," protested the woman. "And he knows all about art. He even went to a lecture by Timothy Clifford once."

"About Vettriano?" asked Pat.

"Perhaps," said the woman, vaguely. "It was about the Renaissance. That sort of thing."

Pat looked at the floor. "Vettriano is not a Renaissance painter. In fact, he's still alive, you know."

"Oh," said the woman. "Well, there you are."

"And I'm sorry, but we do not have any Vettriani in stock. But how about a D.Y. Cameron print? We have one over there of Ben Lawers."

Pat almost sold a second D.Y. Cameron print, but eventually did not. She was pleased, though, with the other sale, and when she left the gallery at five that evening, the Peploe? wrapped in brown paper and tucked under her arm, she was in a cheerful mood. She had agreed to meet Chris that evening, of course, and she had her misgivings about that, but at least she was going out and would not have to endure Bruce's company in the flat. And it would do him no harm, she thought, to know that she had been asked out by a man. He condescended to her, and probably thought that his own invitation to the pub was the only social invitation she was likely to receive. Well, he could reflect on the fact that she was going out that evening to a wine bar, and at the invitation of a man.

Back in the flat, Pat opened the hall cupboard and inspected its contents. There were a couple of battered suitcases, some empty cardboard boxes, and a bicycle saddle. Everything looked abandoned, which it probably was. This was a perfect place to hide a painting, and Pat tucked it away, leaning against a wall, hidden by one of the cardboard boxes. It would be safe there, as safe, perhaps, as one of those missing masterpieces secreted in the hidden collections of South American drug barons. Except that this was Edinburgh, not Asunción or Bogotá. That was the difference.

43. The Sort of People You See in Edinburgh Wine Bars

She was due to meet Chris at seven, in the Hot Cool Wine Bar halfway along Thistle Street. She arrived at ten past, which was just when she happened to arrive, but which was also exactly the right time to arrive in the circumstances. Quarter past the hour would have made her late, and any closer to seven would have made her seem too keen. And she was not keen – definitely not – although he was presentable enough and had been polite to her. The problem was the way he had said *hah*, *hah*; that had been a bad sign. So now she was there out of duty; having agreed to meet him she would do so, but would leave early.

She looked around the bar. It was a long, narrow room, decorated in the obligatory Danish minimalist style, which meant that there was no furniture. She had always thought that Danish minimalism should have been the cheapest style available, because it involved nothing, but in fact it was the most expensive. The empty spaces in Danish minimalism were what cost the money.

In true minimalist style, everybody was obliged to stand, and they were doing so around a long, stainless-steel covered bar. Above the bar, suspended on almost invisible wires, minimalist lights cast descending cones of brightness onto those standing below. This made everybody look somewhat stark, an impression that was furthered by the fact that so many of them were wearing black.

There were about twenty people in the bar and Pat quickly saw that Chris was not among them. She looked at her watch and checked the time. Had he said seven? She was sure that he had. And had it been the Hot Cool? She was sure of that too. It was not a name one would mix up with anything unless, of course – and this caused a momentary feeling of panic – he had meant the Cool Hot, which was in George Street, and was a very different sort of bar (non-minimalist). But the Cool Hot was ambivalent – was it not? – and this place was . . . She looked at the group of people closest to her. There were two men and two women: the men were standing next to one another and the women were . . . No, they were definitely not *ambivalent*.

She moved over to the bar, and signalled to the bartender.

"I was meeting somebody called Chris," she said.

The barman smiled at her. "Lots of Chrises here. Just about everybody's a Chris this year. What sort of Chris is yours? Architect Chris? Advocate Chris? Media Chris? The Chris whose novel is just about to be published by Canongate? Actually there are lots of those. So which Chris is it?"

She was about to say Police Chris, but stopped herself. This was, after all, the Hot Cool and it sounded inappropriate. So she said: "I'll wait for him. And I'll have a glass of white wine."

The barman went off to fetch a glass, and Pat, her hands resting nonchalantly on the counter, glanced at the other drinkers. They were mostly in their mid- to late-twenties, she thought; clearly affluent, and dressed with an expensive casualness. One or two older people, some even approaching forty, or beyond, were occupying the few available bar-stools, and were talking quietly among themselves; to the other drinkers in the bar these people were largely invisible, being of no sexual or social interest.

The barman returned with her drink, which was served in a smoked-green glass, inexplicably, but generously, filled with ice. Pat sipped at the chilled wine and then glanced over her shoulder. A young man, wearing a cord jacket and open-neck black shirt, who was standing at the other end of the bar, caught her eye and smiled at her. Uncertain as to whether or not she knew him, she returned the smile. Having been at school in Edinburgh, she found that there were numerous people who remembered her vaguely, and she them; people she had played hockey with or danced with in an eightsome at the school dance. This young man seemed slightly familiar, but she could not think of a name, or a context. Heriot's? Watson's? It was difficult to *tribe* him. Was he one of these Chrises referred to by the barman?

The barman walked past on the other side of the bar, drying a glass with a large, pristine white cloth.

"I hope he's not going to stand you up," he said. "The number of people who are stood up, you wouldn't believe. It happens all the time."

"I don't mind," said Pat. "I don't particularly want to see him. I'm only here because I agreed to a drink. I wasn't thinking."

The barman chuckled. "Don't you like him, then?"

"Not particularly," said Pat. "It's the way he says *hah*, *hah*. That's the big turn-off. *Hah*, *hah*."

"Hah, hah!" said a voice behind her. "So there you are! Hah, hah!"

44. Tales of Tulliallan

Had he heard her? Pat felt herself blushing with embarrassment. It was that most common of social fears – to be overheard by another when passing a remark about that very person – but Chris gave no appearance of having heard. This, she concluded, was either because he had not heard, or because he wished to save her feelings. The barman, who had realised what was happening, gave Pat a sympathetic look and shook his head discreetly. This meant that in his view at least, Chris had not realised that he was being discussed. Pat felt the warm flush of embarrassment subside.

"I'm very sorry I'm late," said Chris. "I was late getting off duty. Something cropped up in the afternoon and it went on and on. Sorry about that."

"I don't mind," Pat said. "I was a bit late myself."

"Well, here we are," said Chris breezily. "The Hot Cool."

He ordered a beer from the barman, who exchanged a knowing look with Pat.

"What's with him?" asked Chris, nodding his head in the direction of the barman as he went off to fetch the drink. "A private joke? Something I should be laughing at? Hah, hah!"

"It's nothing," said Pat quickly. "Nothing much." She lifted her glass to take a sip of her drink and looked at Chris. In the descending minimalist light he was certainly attractive – more attractive than he had been in the uniform of the Lothian and Borders Police – but she was sure that she would not revise the opinion that she had formed earlier. There was something unsubtle about him, something obvious, perhaps, which frankly bored her. *He's of no interest to me*, she found herself thinking. *There could never be anything between us.*

Chris's drink arrived, and he raised his glass to toast her. "*Cheerio*," he said, and Pat winced. This was another point against him. Now there was nothing he could say or do that would rescue the situation.

They spent the next fifteen minutes talking about that morning's break-in. There was a counselling service for people who had been broken into, Chris explained. The council provided it free, and one could go for as many sessions as one felt one needed. "Some people go for months," he said. "Some of them even look forward to being broken into again so that they can get counselling."

"And you?" said Pat. "Do the police get counselling after investigating break-ins?"

"We do if we need it," answered Chris. He had taken the question literally and frowned as he answered. "We were taught some counselling skills at Tulliallan."

"Tulliallan?"

"The Scottish Police College," explained Chris. "We all go there to be trained. Right at the beginning. But then we have courses from time to time. That's where we had our Art Squad course."

Pat was interested in this, and asked him to explain.

"It was quite a big course," said Chris. "There were twenty people from other forces, and ten of us from Edinburgh, although not all of us were assigned to art afterwards. Some got traffic and one, who was really useless at art, was moved to the dog squad. But I did quite well, I think, and I got in, along with two others.

"The course lasted a week. To begin with, they tested us for colour-blindness, and if you were too red–green blind they sent you back. We were all fine. Then they started on the lectures. We had five a day, and they were pretty tough, some of them.

"We learned about forgery techniques and how to spot a fake. We learned about what they can do in the labs – paint analysis and all the rest. And then we had art appreciation, which was really great. I liked that. We had two hours of that every day and we all wished that we had been given more. We used Kenneth Clark's *Civilisation* as our text book, but there were quite a few lectures on Scottish art. McTaggart. Crosbie. Blackadder. Howson. All those people. And a whole hour on Vettriano. That was the most popular session of the course."

"Vettriano?" asked Pat. "A whole hour?"

"Yes," said Chris. "And then, right at the end, we had a test. They dimmed the lights in the lecture room and flashed up slides on the screen. There were slides of Vettriano paintings and slides of Hopper paintings. You must know his stuff – Edward Hopper, the American artist who painted people sitting at the counters of soda bars or whatever they call them. You'd know them if you saw them.

"So they flashed up these slides in any order and we had to call out Vettriano! or Hopper! Depending on which it was. It was great training. Good bonding too. I'd recommend it to anyone. I really would." He was silent for a moment. Then he added: "I'll never forget the difference – never. I can still tell, just with one look.

Show me a picture by either of them – doesn't matter what – and I'll call out straightaway. Hopper! Vettriano! And I'll always get it right. Every time."

Pat looked at him mutely. They had not bonded.

45. More Tulliallan Tales

Chris was enjoying himself, talking about Tulliallan and his experiences there on the Art Squad training week. But there was more to come about that particular week.

"On the final day," he continued, "we had a visit from a really important person from the art world in Edinburgh. Really important. He came to speak to us on the Saturday afternoon, and we were told all about it the day before. The inspector who was in charge of the course said that we were very lucky to get him, as he was often away in places like Venice and New York. That's where these people go, he explained. They feel comfortable in places like that. And that's fair enough, I suppose. Imagine if they had to go to places like Motherwell or Airdrie. Just imagine.

"He arrived in the afternoon, an hour or so before he was due to give his lecture, which was at three. It was a fine day – broad sunshine – and most of us were sitting out at the front after lunch, as we were off-duty until the lecture. The college had sent a car to fetch him from Edinburgh, and we saw it coming up the drive, with two police motorcycle outriders escorting it. They came to a halt outside the front of the main building and the driver got out to open the door. Then he stepped out and acknowledged the driver's salute with a nod of his head.

"When he came into the lecture room we all stood up. The inspector, who was introducing him, indicated for us to sit down and then he began to lecture. He started off by saying how agreeable the building was, but that it was a pity that it had not been decorated more sympathetically. He suggested ways in which this could be improved by restoring the original features of the house. He even suggested colours for the carpets and the wallpaper.

"Then he said something about how the Scottish psyche had suffered from the iconoclastic doings in the Reformation. He said that there was a wound in the Scottish soul which came about from the denial of beauty. He said that the Scottish soul would only come to terms with itself if beauty were acknowledged. Then he said something about how Scottish police uniforms were dull, and that we could take a leaf out of the Italians' book.

"He said: 'Look at the carabinieri, with their gorgeous, really gorgeous, cap badges. Those great burning flames. And all you people have is your black and white squares. How sad! How unutterably sad!'

"We didn't quite know how to take this, but we sat there entranced. He went on like this for an hour or so before he looked at his watch and nodded to the inspector. The inspector stood up and thanked him for his talk. He said that he had given us a great deal to think about and that Tulliallan would never be the same again. Then they went out and the police car which had been waiting for him took him back to Edinburgh. We talked in hushed voices for the rest of the afternoon. We felt that we had somehow been touched by greatness, and we were very grateful. It was almost as if Lord Clark himself had been there. Almost, but not quite."

Chris had now stopped, and Pat was silent. She looked at him, at the shadow on his face from the curious overhead lighting. She felt strangely moved by the story of this visit, and she wanted to say something to him, but she could not decide what it was that she had in mind. How strange the visit must have been; rather like the visit she had read about in an Italian short story that her father had drawn to her attention. An immensely aristocratic count visits an archaeological site with his aides and speaks in a voice so distinguished that nobody can understand a word of what he is saying. *Beh andiatah reh ec brar* . . . and so on. But in spite of the fact that nobody could understand, they were all impressed with the visitor and felt honoured that he had condescended to be there. This is how they must have felt on that day at Tulliallan.

She stared at Chris, who looked back at her in silence. For a moment a smile played about his lips, and then he looked down at his glass of beer.

"I heard what you said about me," he said quietly. "This isn't going to work, is it?"

Pat said nothing. She was mortified that he had heard her unkind comments, and now she began to stutter an apology.

"I didn't mean it to sound like that," she said. "You know how sometimes people say things that get on your nerves, for no real reason at all. It happens to all of us."

"Except that in this case there is a reason," said Chris, his voice level and controlled. "I'm a bit of a joke to you, aren't I, because I don't fit in with your world. I just can't. Every single person I've met in this art job – every single one – has condescended to me. Oh they're nice enough, particularly if they need me to do something, but that's about it. This is a city of snobs, that's what it is. A city of utter snobs. And this place here is full of them. Wall to wall."

46. Humiliation and Embarrassment

Pat did not stay long at the Hot Cool after Chris had made his self-pitying declaration. It had not surprised her that he had been offended by her dismissal of him – any dismissal was offensive to the one on the receiving end – but there was something uncomfortable about the way in which he had included her in his blanket condemnation of the Edinburgh art world. She realised that he must have imagined her to be part of that world – and she was part of that world, in a very attenuated sense – but he had no right to make such sweeping statements about the attitudes of other people. How did he know anything about her views, other than that she did not think that there was much chance of developing a relationship with him, and this on the grounds of her objection to the use of the expression *hah, hah*? Anybody might object to that, just as they might object to any overused phrase, and it seemed quite unreasonable for him to accuse her – and so many others – of being snobbish. It was not snobbish, she thought, to object to those who said *hah, hah*. That was an entirely personal reaction, and we were entitled, surely, to personal reactions to a mannerism. We did not have to like the way other people walked, or talked, or the way they drank their coffee or combed their hair. Or did we have to like everything? Was it *inclusive* to like everything?

They had parted in a civil fashion. After a small amount of rather stiff conversation, Chris had looked at his watch and remembered another commitment, just seconds before Pat had been planning to recover from a similar lapse of memory.

"Maybe we'll meet again," he had said, looking dubiously around at the décor of the wine bar and at the other customers. "You never know."

"Maybe," said Pat. "And I'm really sorry if I offended you. I really am . . ."

He raised a hand. "Water under the bridge. Don't worry. It's just that this place gets me down from time to time. It's not your fault. Maybe I should go back to Falkirk."

"You can't go back to Falkirk," said Pat. She said this and then stopped: it sounded as if she was expressing a major truth about life, and about Falkirk, which was not the case.

Chris looked at her quizzically. "Why not?"

"Well, maybe you can. Maybe Falkirk's all right to go back to, if you come from there to begin with, if you see what I mean. What I wanted to say was that in general, in life, you can't go back."

He looked at his watch. "I actually do have to see somebody," he said. "I really must go."

After Chris had gone, Pat stood by herself at the bar for a short while. The barman, who had observed the scene, came over towards her, casually wiping the bar with a cloth.

"Chris gone?" he asked.

Pat looked down into her glass. "He did hear," she said quietly. "He heard what I said about his laugh. I feel terrible."

The barman reached over and touched her lightly on the wrist.

"You shouldn't. That was nothing. You should hear some of the things that are said in this place. Horrible things. Cruel things. What you said was nothing."

Pat looked at him. "But he was upset. He said that's how people are in this city."

"He's a bit marginal if you ask me," said the barman. "I see all types in this job, and I know. He's a cop, by the way. Did you know that?"

"Yes, I did. But how did you know? Had you met him before?"

The barman winked at her. "I can tell a mile off. And it's not a good idea to get too involved with cops. They can be difficult." He paused. "Anyway, you see that guy at the end there, the one in the cord jacket? He's been wanting to talk to you all evening. But take my advice, don't."

Pat glanced at the young man, who had remained at his place further down the bar throughout her ill-fated encounter with Chris. He was picking at a small dish of olives before him, looking ahead, although now he glanced at her quickly, and then looked away again.

"Why?" asked Pat.

"Just don't," said the barman. "I know. Just don't."

The barman turned away. He had customers to deal with and Pat, left by herself, finished the last of her drink, and walked out of the wine bar. She noticed that the young man in the cord jacket watched her as she left, but she kept her eyes on the door and did not glance in his direction. It was fine outside, and night was just beginning to fall. She looked up at the sky, which was clear. It was still blue, but only just, and in minutes would shade into darkness.

47. Irene and Stuart: a Breakfast Conversazione

It was a Saturday, and there was no need for Stuart to rush to catch the bus to work, yet he was an early riser and by the time that Irene got up he had already chopped the nuts and sliced the bananas for the Bircher muesli. He had also gone out to the newsagent for the papers, and was reading a review when Irene came into the kitchen.

"Anything?" asked Irene, making for the pot of coffee on the edge of the Aga.

"Practically nothing. A new biography of James the Sixth," said Stuart. "It's getting a good review here from somebody or other."

Irene opened the kitchen blind and looked out onto Scotland Street.

"I have no idea," she said, "no idea at all why people continue to write royal biographies. They go on and on. Even about the Duke of Windsor, about whom there was nothing to be said at all, other than to make a diagnosis."

Stuart lowered the paper. "Some of these kings were influential," he said. "They ran things then."

"That's not what history is about," snapped Irene. "History is about ordinary people. How they lived. What they ate. That sort of thing."

Stuart looked down at the review. "And ideas," he said, mildly. "History is about ideas. And monarchs tended to have some influence in that direction. Take Jamie Sext, for example. He had ideas on language. He was quite enlightened. He would have enjoyed the newspapers, if they had been around."

Irene stared at him. "Which newspaper?" she asked. But he did not answer, and she continued: "What a peculiar thing to say!"

"No," said Stuart. "Not really. In fact, it's quite interesting to speculate what people would have read if these papers had existed. Queen Victoria, for example, read *The Times*, but what would Prince Albert have read?"

"The *Frankfurter Allgemeine*?" ventured Irene.

They both laughed. This was undoubtedly very funny.

"And was she amused by *The Times*?" asked Stuart.

"No," said Irene. "She was not."

Irene joined him at the table.

"Enough levity," she said. "We must talk about Bertie. We have to do something. I can't face going back to that awful Macfadzean woman. So Bertie's going to have to go elsewhere."

"Couldn't he wait?" asked Stuart. "He knows a great deal as it is. Couldn't we give him a gap year?"

"A gap year?"

Stuart seemed pleased with his suggestion. "Yes, a gap year between nursery and primary school. So what if he's only five? Why not? Gap years are all the rage."

Irene looked pensive. "You know, you might have something there. It could be a year in which he did his Grade seven theory and one or two other things. It would take him out of the system for a while and allow him to flourish. We could make a programme."

"Send him abroad? Perhaps he could work in a village in South America, or Africa even."

Irene thought for a moment, as if weighing up the suggestion. "Hardly. But it would be a rather good way of letting him develop without having to look over his shoulder at other children. I'm sure he'd benefit. And perhaps I could take him to Italy – to perfect his spoken Italian."

Stuart laid aside his newspaper. "I was thinking of taking the pressure off a bit, rather than adding to it. I thought of a year out, so to speak. Perhaps we should leave Italian for the time being."

This suggestion did not go down well with Irene. "It would be a criminal waste of everything we've done so far if we let his Italian get rusty," she said coldly. "And the same goes for the saxophone and theory of music. For everything in fact."

"But perhaps at this age we should concentrate on his *langue maternelle*," said Stuart. "Italian is a very beautiful language, admittedly, but it isn't his *langue maternelle*."

"Neither here nor there," said Irene dismissively. "There is evidence – ample evidence – that the development of linguistic skills in the early years leads to much greater facility with language when one's older. Every minute is precious at this age. The mind is very plastic."

Stuart opened his mouth to say something, but thought better of it and was silent. He knew that he could not win an argument with Irene, and nine years of marriage to her had convinced him that he should no longer try.

"I'll think about it further," said Irene. "The only decision we have to make now is not to take him back to that woman and her so-called nursery school. And I don't think we should."

"*D'accordo*," said Stuart.

Irene looked satisfied. "In that case, I shall have a look around and see what's possible. I'll do this after we've started his therapy."

Stuart gave a start. This was new information. Had therapy been discussed before? He could not recall anything being said about it, but then sometimes he stopped paying attention when Irene was talking. He might have missed the discussion.

Irene, noticing his puzzlement, explained. "The Scottish Institute of Human Relations," she said. "We have an appointment there on Monday. A Dr Fairbairn. He's been highly recommended and he'll be able to advise us on why Bertie has suddenly started playing up."

"Do we really need all this?" asked Stuart.

Irene stared at him. No response was necessary, or at least no verbal response.

48. *Plans for the Conservative Ball*

On the other side of the city, in their house in the higher reaches of the Braids, Raeburn Todd and his wife, Sasha, had finished their breakfast and were now drinking a cup of coffee in the conservatory. This was where they liked to sit after breakfast at weekends, particularly on a fine day, such as this was. The Braids could be cold, with their extra three hundred feet or so, but that morning the weather was warmer than normal and they had even opened a window of the conservatory. It was the day of the South Edinburgh Conservative Ball, and Todd, who was the chairman of the ball committee, was reviewing the prospects for that evening's entertainment. He had made a list of things to do and was going through this with Sasha.

"First thing," he said in a businesslike fashion. "First thing is hotel bits and pieces. Meal and ballroom."

"All fine," said Sasha, who composed the rest of the committee, the other members having sent their apologies. "The menu's approved and the hotel said they would look after the flower."

Todd smiled. "Flower? Only one?"

Sasha nudged him playfully. "You know what I meant. Flowers. The fact that we have very few people coming doesn't mean we're only going to have one flower."

Todd looked down at the list in front of him and shook his head. "On which subject," he said, "this is really very disappointing. Nothing's come in this morning, I take it? Nobody else signing up?"

Sasha shook her head. "When the phone went before breakfast I hoped that it would be somebody. But it was the dress shop about my dress. So it looks like that's it." She paused. "Are you still sure that we should go ahead? Couldn't we come up with some other explanation for a late cancellation?"

Todd's reply was firm. "No. Absolutely not. We've been through this before. And, anyway, other parties have their problems with parties, so to speak. Have you ever been to a Labour Party do? Awful. Dreadfully dull events. Like a primary school parents'

124

evening, but not quite so much fun. And the Liberal Democrats have these terrible dinners where everybody wears woolly pullovers and rather shabby dresses. And as for the SNP, well, everybody's usually tight at their events, rolling all over the floor. Ghastly. No, we don't do too badly, I'm telling you!"

"Even with . . . how many is it?"

Todd consulted his list. "I make it six," he said. "You, me, Lizzie, that young man from the office, and Ramsey and Betty Dunbarton. They've confirmed, so that's six."

Sasha picked up her coffee and took a sip. "We could have just one table, then," she said. "We could all sit together."

This idea did not appeal to Todd. "No," he said. "I think we should have two tables. Table One and Table Two. This is because it would look rather odd just to have one table, and then I'm not sure if we want to spend the whole evening with the Dunbartons, charming company though they undoubtedly are. It's just that he's such a bore. And I'm sorry, but I can't stand her. So, no. Let's have two tables. We'll be at Table One, and they can be at Table Two."

Sasha accepted the reasoning behind this, and moved on to raise the issue of the band and the dances. "I've spoken to the man who runs it," she said. "They come from Penicuik, I think, or somewhere out that way. I've told him that we want middle-of-the-road dance music to begin with and then something suitable for reels. He said that's fine. He said they could do anything."

Todd nodded his agreement and was about to go on to another matter, but stopped. "Reels?" he asked. "Eightsomes and the like?"

"Yes," said Sasha. "People love that."

"But there are only going to be six of us," Todd pointed out. "How will we be able to do an eightsome if there are only six people there? And Ramsey Dunbarton is pretty frail these days. I can't imagine him doing an eightsome. The old boy would probably drop down stone dead. Then there'd only be five of us."

"There are other dances," said Sasha quickly. "A Gay Tories, for example, I mean a Gay Gordons! You only need two for that. And there's the Dashing White Sergeant. That needs three for each set, so there could be two sets."

Todd thought for a moment. "But don't you go in opposite directions with the Dashing White Sergeant, and then meet up? If three of us went off in one direction and three in another – always assuming that Ramsey Dunbarton is up to it – then we would only meet once we've danced round the whole room. The band would have to adapt. They'd have to play on and on until we got all the way round the room and met up on the other side. Wouldn't that be a bit odd?"

"Some of these bands are rather good," said Sasha.

49. Tombola Gifts

Todd left Sasha in the house while he went off to play golf. His golf partner had declined to buy a ticket for the ball, and Todd intended to reproach him for this, although he knew that there was no possibility of his relenting. He was reconciled now to the idea of a ball of six, which was, in his view, quorate. Even two would have been enough; had he and Sasha been the only people there, they would have persisted and danced in the face of adversity. That was the only way in politics. A ball with six people one year could be a ball with sixty the next year, and then six hundred the year after that. Political fortunes shifted, and it was no good throwing in the towel because of temporary set-backs. The Scottish Conservative Party would rise again and be the great force that it once had been in the affairs of the nation; it was only a question of time. And then people would be clamouring for tickets to the South Edinburgh Conservative Ball and he, Todd, would take great pleasure in turning them away.

After her husband had left for the Luffness Golf Club (Gullane, but not Muirfield), Sasha made her way into the dining room, where the prizes for the tombola were laid out on and around the large, four-leaf table. The members of the local party association had been generous, even if they had declined to attend the ball, and there were at least forty prizes waiting to be listed. Sasha sat down at the head of the table and began to compile a catalogue and assign a number to each prize. These numbers would then be put into a hat, and those at the ball – and those alone – would then be permitted to buy the tickets.

She dealt first with the items on the table. There was a Thomas Pink shirt, in candy stripes, with a collar size of nineteen and a half. Now this was a fine shirt, well-made and with double cuffs, but the collar size was rather large. Todd took size seventeen, and even that was sometimes a bit large for him; he was a big man and presumably this shirt would fit an extremely well-built man. Was there anybody in the Conservative Party quite that large? There was Mr Soames, of course, but he was probably the sort of man who had enough shirts already. So this might not be the most useful of prizes.

She assigned the shirt a number and turned to the next prize. This was a set of six fish knives and forks, made by Hamilton and Inches, and a very handsome prize for somebody. This would be popular at a Conservative function, but would be useless at a Labour Party event. They had no idea, she believed, of the use of fish knives and forks and used the same cutlery for everything. That was part of the problem. The Liberal Democrats, of course, knew what fish knives and forks were all about, *but pretended they didn't care!* Liberal Hypocrites, thought Sasha.

There were many other fine prizes. A digital radio, still in its box; a round of golf at the Merchants Golf Course; a large caddy of Old Edinburgh Tea from Jenners; and, now, what was this? – yes, the finest prize of all: lunch with Malcolm Rifkind and Lord James at the Balmoral Hotel! That was a splendid prize and it occurred to Sasha that she would dearly love to win that herself.

This thought made her abandon her task of cataloguing for a few minutes and ponder the implications of this tombola. If there were forty prizes and there were only going to be six people at the ball, then that meant that each person would get at least six prizes. That assumed, of course, that each person bought an equal number of tickets (which would be limited to forty in all). If that happened, then everybody present at the ball would do rather well, and would certainly win prizes which very much exceeded in value the cost of the ticket.

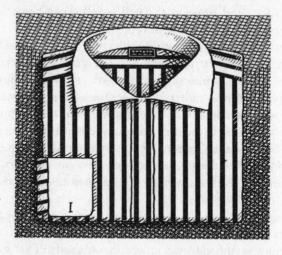

In these circumstances, Sasha reasoned, it would be permissible, perhaps, for the organiser – herself – to ensure that *sensitive* prizes were won by the right people. Now that would mean that the round of golf should not go to Ramsey Dunbarton, who was pretty unsteady on his legs and who could hardly be expected to play. So that, perhaps, could be *directed* towards Bruce, as a reward for agreeing to accompany Lizzie. Or perhaps, even more appropriately, he could win the dinner for two at Prestonfield House and take Lizzie with him, to give them a chance to get to know one another a bit better. That would be very satisfactory, and indeed the fairest outcome. The Ramsey Dunbartons could win the tea, which would suit them far better.

That left the lunch with Malcolm Rifkind and Lord James. In Sasha's view, the best possible person to win that would be herself. This was not because she was selfish, and wanted the glamorous prize, but because she wanted to protect the two generous donors from having to put up with Ramsey Dunbarton. It would be too much for them; they simply shouldn't have to face it. And for this reason – the best of all possible reasons – Sasha decided that she would have to ensure that she won this prize herself.

50. Bruce Prepares for the Ball

When Bruce received Sasha's call that morning – to invite him to pre-ball drinks at the house – he was about to leave 44 Scotland Street to buy himself a new dress shirt. His previous one, which had been a bargain, had washed badly, and looked grey, even under artificial light.

"There isn't going to be a big crowd there," said Sasha, "but the Braid Hills Hotel does a very good dinner, and I hear that the band is excellent."

"How many are coming?" asked Bruce.

There was a short silence at the other end of the line. "Not many. Probably fewer than fifty."

Bruce was polite. "I'm sure it'll be fine. And I don't like those really big affairs. You can't hear what you're saying to anybody."

"We'll have a lot of fun," said Sasha.

He doubted that – at least for himself – but did not say anything. With any luck, he thought, he might be able to get away shortly after twelve – Conservatives probably went to bed early – or at least Bruce's parents, both members of the Crieff Conservative Association, tended to retire by ten. So if it all came to an end in reasonable time, he would be able to get to a club and see what was going on there.

"One thing," said Sasha, before she rang off. "We're having a tombola. We've been given a lot of good prizes, but if you can bring a little something along to add to it, please do."

"I'll try," said Bruce.

He left the flat, feeling slightly restless. He found his life rather unsatisfactory at the moment. He had finished all the institute examinations, and so he was free of that particular burden, but it seemed as if nothing much else was happening. Part of the trouble was the absence of a girlfriend. I need somebody to hang about with, he thought. I need company. There was that girl in the flat, of course – Pat – but he found her a bit irritating. She seemed cool, indifferent even, although he suspected that this was a bit of an act. She's probably pretty interested in me, he thought. She probably wants me to take notice of her, but the poor girl's got a long wait ahead of her. Far too young, too unsophisticated. Pretty green. As he walked up to George Street, he glanced at his reflection in the occasional shop window. What a waste, he muttered. There I am looking like that, and no girlfriend. What a waste.

The shirt purchased, he returned to Scotland Street and spent the afternoon on his bed, watching videos of classic rugby matches. There was Scotland against Ireland at Murrayfield of a few years previously – a great Scottish victory, with a fine try from a player whom Bruce had known at Morrison's Academy. Then there was the Springboks playing Fiji, a terrific game in which four players were taken off to hospital in the first half! And Scotland meeting France in Paris, when France scored seventy points and Scotland scored three. That was not such a good game, Bruce thought, and he turned it off at half-time.

At five o'clock he went into the bathroom, ran a hot bath, and after a few moments in front of the full-length mirror, immersed himself in the deep, soapy water. He felt more cheerful now. That Todd girl would cramp his style, no doubt, but there might be other girls to dance with there; he wouldn't be stuck with her all night. And one of these other girls might be just right for him. There were stranger places to meet women than at a Conservative Ball. Such as . . . He wondered about that. Where was the most unlikely place to meet somebody? A dentist's surgery? Warriston Crematorium?

Bruce dressed himself with care. Gel was applied to the hair and cologne to exposed flesh. Then there was a quick inspection. Perfect. Great.

He left his room and went out into the hall. It was at that point that he remembered Sasha's request for a contribution to the tombola. This was irritating, but perhaps there would be some bric-à-brac in the cupboard. So he opened the door and looked inside. There were things which had been left there over the years by a succession of tenants. There might be something.

He found the parcel, and opened it. He held the painting up to examine it under the light. He did not like it. The colours were too bright and there was not enough detail. This was the problem with amateurs – they couldn't draw properly. You had to scratch your head to find out what they were trying to portray. Bruce liked Vettriano. He knew how to draw. Still, this would do for the tombola. It was obviously the work of somebody's aunt, long forgotten and abandoned in this cupboard. But at least he would not arrive empty-handed. So he slipped it back into its wrapping, picked up his coat, and left for the Todd house in the Braids, the painting under his arm.

51. Velvety Shoes

Groaning inwardly, Lizzie Todd walked up the short path that led to the front door of her parents' house in the Braids. She had grown up in this house, but she felt little of the affection that one was supposed to feel for the place in which one spent one's early years. Indeed, when she had left home to go to Glasgow Caledonian University to take her degree in Indeterminate Studies, she had done so with such a measure of relief that it was visible.

"Do you think she'll miss us?" Todd had said to his wife shortly after her departure. "She looked so happy. It was almost as if she was pleased to go."

Sasha sighed. "She's a strange girl. I'm not sure if I understand her, but I'm sure she'll miss us."

Todd had been silent. He had wanted a son, who would play

rugby for Watson's and who would in due course join the firm. But life rarely worked out as one planned it and when no further children had arrived he had accepted his lot, to be the father of a daughter who seemed each year to become more distant from him, and increasingly uninterested in his world. He looked to his wife for an explanation, and a solution, but it seemed that she was as incapable as he was of communicating with their daughter. It crossed his mind that it was dislike – as simple as that – a failure of the intricate, inexplicable chemistry that makes one person like or love another. But that was a bleak conclusion, and was only once, very briefly, articulated when Todd had said to the then sixteen-year-old Lizzie: "I suppose you'd like me more, wouldn't you, if I were Sean Connery?" And she had looked at him blankly, perplexed, and had said: "But you aren't," before she added: "And I suppose you'd like me more if I were Gavin Hastings." It had not been a profitable exchange.

Years on now, Lizzie slipped her key into the lock and opened the parental door. She sniffed at the air. This was the familiar smell of home, but not a smell that she particularly liked. Her mother's cleaner used a lavender-scented furniture polish and the smell of this pervaded the house. It had always been there, from the earliest days of Lizzie's childhood, and it had ruined lavender for her, forever.

From within the house there came the sound of a bath being run. Todd was late back from the golf course and needed a bath before changing into his kilt. Sasha, by contrast, was always ready well in advance, and was making her way down the corridor, fully dressed, when she heard Lizzie come in. When the two of them met in the hall, Sasha glanced quickly at Lizzie's dress. Had she made an effort? That was the issue. It would be typical of her to agree to come to the ball and then do nothing about looking her best for the occasion.

The verdict was positive. "That's a very pretty dress, dear," said Sasha. "And those shoes . . ."

They were standing at the entrance to the drawing room and Lizzie now turned away and walked towards the window that looked out over the distant rooftops of Morningside.

"They hurt my feet," she said. "I'm going to have to take something else with me."

"I can lend you a pair," Sasha said brightly. "I bought them just a few weeks ago. They'd go very nicely with that dress."

.She went off to fetch the shoes, while Lizzie stared moodily out of the window.

"Here," said Sasha, holding out the shoes. "Slip into these. They'll be much more comfortable."

Lizzie looked at the pair of velvety, bejewelled shoes which Sasha was holding out to her. There was a slight movement of her nose, almost undetectable, but insofar as it could be detected, upward.

"Where did you buy those?" she asked. And then, before Sasha could reply, Lizzie continued, "I saw a pair just like that in Marks and Spencers the other day. Did you get them at Marks?"

Sasha froze. "Marks? Marks?" Her voice wavered, but then became steely. "Certainly not. I got these from a shoe boutique in William Street. If you care to look at the label, you'll see exactly where they're from."

Lizzie reached out and took the shoes from her mother. She

looked inside and shrugged when she saw the boutique's label.

"Not really the sort of shoe I like to wear," she said. "Of course, they might suit you. In fact, I'm sure they do. Don't get me wrong."

"I'd never force you to wear my shoes," Sasha retorted.

Lizzie smiled. "Just as well," she said. "I'm a six and you're, what are you – size eight?"

Sasha did not reply. In one sense she was an eight, but she could fit perfectly well into a six-and-a-half, provided she did not have to walk. But she was not going to be drawn into a discussion with Lizzie about shoe sizes. It was typical of her daughter, she thought, just typical, that she should walk into the house on a day like this, a special day when they should all be getting ready to enjoy themselves, and start an argument about shoe sizes. It was all so *under-mining* of her, and so unfair. She had never criticised her daughter's dress sense, in spite of obvious temptations, and yet all she could do was reject every attempt that she made to help and advise her. Lizzie was beyond pleasing, she concluded, and this meant, she thought grimly, that she would never find a man, as no man was perfect; far from it, in fact – just look at Raeburn.

52. Silk Organza

Todd glanced at his watch. Bruce might arrive at any moment, but there was time for a whisky before that. He had picked up some of Sasha's anxiety over the evening, which was inevitable, he supposed, in view of the fact that they were the organisers; a whisky would reassure him. He poured himself a small glass of Macallan and wandered into the drawing room where Lizzie was standing by the window.

"I'm very grateful to you," he said quietly. "I know that you don't always enjoy these things. But it means a lot to your mother that you're coming tonight. So thank you."

Lizzie continued to look out of the window. "I don't mind," she muttered. "I didn't have anything else on."

"Even so," said Todd. "It's good of you."

He heard a door close behind him and he turned round to see Sasha coming into the room, holding a plate of sliced brown bread and smoked salmon. She put the plate down on a table and came to his side.

"You look so good in your kilt," she said, turning to Lizzie. "Your father does look good in it, doesn't he?"

"Yes," said Lizzie, without any great enthusiasm.

Todd shot her a glance. He did not mind if she was lukewarm about what he was wearing, but it would be nice, would it not, if for once she complimented her mother.

"And your mother looks good too, doesn't she?" he said. "With that magnificent dress. And the shoes."

Lizzie looked Sasha up and down. "Silk organza. Fish-tail hem, I see," she said.

"Fish what?" asked Todd.

"Fish-tail hem," repeated Lizzie, pointing at Sasha's dress. "You'll see that it's higher in the front – shows her knees – and then goes down at the back like a fish tail. Very popular among the twenty-somethings."

Todd looked at Sasha, who was staring at her daughter. "Well, I like it very much," he said. "Twenty-something, forty-something – what's the difference?"

"Twenty years," said Lizzie.

Sasha bent down and picked up a piece of buttered brown bread with its small covering of smoked salmon. For a moment Todd wondered whether she was going to use it as a weapon, but she popped it into her mouth and quickly licked the tips of her fingers.

"Actually," Sasha said, "I had this dress made up for me from a photograph I saw in *Harpers*. And, if I remember correctly, the person wearing it in the magazine was *not* in her twenties."

"Teens?" asked Lizzie.

Sasha looked at Todd. He saw that she had coloured, and that her lower lip was quivering. He turned to his daughter.

"Do you have to be like this?" he asked. "Do you have to say cruel things? Do you have to upset your mother?"

Lizzie's expression was one of injured innocence. "But I didn't say anything," she protested. "I merely said that that sort of dress was very popular among younger people. What's wrong with that? It's just an observation."

"Except that you think that I'm too old to be wearing it," Sasha blurted out. "That's it, isn't it? You're never happy unless you make me feel small. You'll be forty-four one day, you know."

"Forty-five," said Lizzie.

At this remark, Sasha turned sharply away and walked out of the room, leaving her husband and daughter staring mutely at one another. Todd lifted his glass of whisky and drained it.

"I think you should say you're sorry," he said. "It's a big night for your mother, and I really don't think that you should ruin it for her. Couldn't you just go through there and say that you're sorry? Would it cost you that much effort?"

Lizzie shrugged. "She could say sorry to me," she said. "She could say sorry for making me feel so bad all those years. For nagging me. For making me do things that I never wanted to do. For ruining my life."

He spoke quietly. "For ruining your life?"

"Yes," she said.

He looked down at his sporran and at his patent-leather Highland dancing pumps. This is what it has come to, he thought. This is what all their effort had brought forth: the accusation that they had ruined her life.

"I'm sorry," he said. "I really am very sorry if you think that. And I take it that you think the same of me – that I've done the same."

Lizzie shook her head. "Not really. I don't blame you for it. You can't help the way you are."

"And what, may I ask, is that? What way am I?"

Lizzie looked up at the ceiling, as if bored by the task of explaining the obvious.

"All of this," she said. "All this respectability. This whole Edinburgh bit. All of that."

Todd tried to look her in the eye as she spoke, but she avoided

136

his gaze. "All right," he said. "You've made your speech. Now please just try for the rest of the evening. That young man is walking up the path out there and I would prefer it if he didn't witness a family row. I'm going to fetch your mother. Please try. Please just try. I'm not asking you to approve of us, but please just try to be civil. Is that too much to ask? Is it?"

53. Bruce Fantasises

"You'll remember my wife," said Todd. "And my daughter Lizzie, of course."

Sasha, smiling and holding out her hand, advanced upon Bruce, who shook hands with her formally. Lizzie, who had been standing at the window, half turned to their guest and nodded. She made no move to shake hands.

"Well," said Todd, rubbing his hands together. "I must confess that I've jumped the gun. I've had a dram already. What about you, Bruce? Whisky? Gin? A glass of wine?"

Bruce asked for a glass of wine and while Todd went off to fetch it, Sasha took Bruce by the arm and led him to a sofa at the far end of the room. She sat down, and patted the sofa beside her. And it was at this point that Bruce suddenly realised that in his haste to leave the flat he had dressed inadequately. He had donned his full, formal Highland outfit, his Prince Charlie jacket with its silver buttons, his Anderson kilt, the dress sporran that his uncle had given him for his twenty-first birthday, his white hose from Aitken and Niven in George Street, and, of course, his new dress shirt. But he had forgotten to put on any underpants.

Bruce knew that there were those who refused to wear anything under the kilt as a matter of principle. He knew, as everybody did, that there were traditions to this effect, but they were old ones, and he had never met anybody who followed them. It was not just a question of comfort, and warmth, perhaps, in the winter; it was a question of *security*. And now he felt that security issue very acutely as he prepared to sit down on the sofa beside Sasha.

He lowered himself carefully, keeping his knees close together and making sure that the folds of the kilt fell snugly along the side of each leg. Then he looked at Sasha, who was watching him with what he thought was a slightly bemused expression. Had she guessed, by the way that he had sat down? He remembered, blushing, the last time this had happened when, as a thirteen-year-old boy, he had similarly rushed off to a school function and had been laughed at by schoolgirls, who had pointed to him and giggled. One might have thought that such painful episodes were well and truly in the past, but now here he was reliving the burning awkwardness of adolescence.

Sasha raised her glass, although her husband had not yet come back with a drink for Bruce. "We haven't seen one another for a long time, have we?" she asked. "Was it last year, at the office dinner at Prestonfield House?"

"I think so," said Bruce vaguely. He had worn his kilt on that occasion too, but had wisely donned underpants then. How on earth had he managed to forget to put them on tonight? What could he possibly have been thinking about?

Sasha looked across at Lizzie – a glance which was intercepted by Bruce. There was a feeling between these two, he thought; mothers and daughters were often at one another's throats, he had found; something to do with jealousy, he thought. Bruce's theories of female psychology were simple: women competed with one another for men and there was great distrust between them. Women did not like one another, he had decided – unlike men, who had easy friendships, with none of the ups and downs and moodiness of women's relationships.

Bruce was used to being fought over, and relished the experience. If he was in a room with two women, then he would imagine that both of them would be vying for his attention, and he liked to look for the signs of this subtle, under-the-surface competition. It was easy to miss, but if you kept your eyes open you could see it. In these particular circumstances, Lizzie would be glowering at her mother because the older woman had invited Bruce to sit beside her and now she was talking to him in this familiar way. This would be annoying Lizzie, because she, quite naturally, would be wanting Bruce to notice her, not her mother. Bruce smiled. How delicious! Mother and daughter are both interested in me, and she, the older one, is the boss's wife.

He looked at Sasha. She's crammed herself into that dress, he thought, but she's not all that bad-looking in the right light. And there was a certain brassiness to her which he rather liked, a suggestion that she understood what it was to have fun. Interesting. Now for the daughter. Well, what a frump, with that frown and that way of slumping her shoulders. He knew the sort well enough; she would have given up, that's what she would have done – she would just have given up on the prospect of finding a man. So she would have decided to behave as if she did not care, which of course she did. How sad. If she made an effort then she could probably be reasonable-looking, and might appeal to some man or other.

Bruce wondered. He was free at the moment, and he would be doing a service for this rather unhappy-looking girl if he paid her a bit of attention. She might do for a few weeks, to bridge the gap, so to speak, before somebody a bit more suitable turned up. He could even look on it as a form of community service of the sort that was handed out at the sheriff court. You are sentenced to one hundred and forty hours with Todd's daughter. You are warned that if you don't comply with the terms of this order then you will be brought back to the court to explain yourself to the sheriff.

And he would say to the sheriff: "My lord, have you *seen* her?" And the sheriff would look down from the bench and shake his head and say: "Young man, that's what community service is all about. But I see what you mean. You are free to go."

That's what Bruce thought. He found the fantasy rather amusing, and smiled again; a smile which was misinterpreted by Sasha, who thought: this dishy young man is smiling at me! It's not too late, obviously. It's not too late to have some fun in this life.

54. Supporting Walls

"This is a nice place you've got, Todd," said Bruce to Todd as he was handed his glass of wine.

Todd smiled warmly. "It's a very good corner of town," he said. "We've been here for – what – sixteen years now and I don't think we're planning to move, are we Sasha?"

Sasha shook her head. "I couldn't move," she said. "I've put so much effort into the garden and if you go further into town these days it's so noisy. Students and the like. All sorts of people."

Bruce nodded in sympathy. He knew all about students and the noise they made, although it was only a few years since he had been a student, and had made a lot of noise himself, if one were to be strictly honest. Mind you, he reflected, the noise he made was not from music being played at full throttle, it was rather from parties, particularly after rugby internationals. Those parties had produced a sort of *roar* which was far more acceptable than the sort of noise that came from student flats these days.

"Marchmont's impossible," he said. "I was pleased when I moved down to Scotland Street. It's much better."

Todd, who had taken a few paces back from the sofa and was standing with his back to the fireplace, gestured to the room around them. "Of course, we had to do a lot to this place when we moved in," he explained. "It was typical of those houses they built in the Twenties – the rooms were just far smaller than they needed to be. This room, for example, was two rooms. We took a wall out over there – right down the middle, and made it into a decent-sized drawing room."

Bruce looked about him. He could see where the earlier wall had been, as there was still a detectable line across the ceiling and one of the light fittings had clearly been moved. For a few moments he stared up at the ceiling, his surveyor's instinct asserting itself. Was that a bulge running where the wall must have been? And did the ceiling not seem to sag slightly in the middle? He looked over at the far wall, where the now-disappeared wall would have met the room's perimeter. It seemed to him that there was clear evidence of buckling.

He looked at Todd, who was running a finger around the rim of his whisky glass. "It's a very comfortable room," he began. "But that wall . . . would it not have been a supporting wall? I suppose that you had an engineer look at it?"

Todd snorted. "Engineer? Just for a partition wall in a bungalow? Good heavens, no. I looked at it myself. It was absolutely fine. I'm pretty sure that it wasn't load-bearing."

Bruce looked back at the ceiling and at the bulge. "Are you sure?" he said. "Hasn't there been a bit of movement?"

Todd frowned. "What exactly are you saying? Are you suggesting that the house is going to fall down about our ears?"

Sasha picked up the tension which had arisen between the two men, and made an attempt to defuse it. It was bad enough, in her view, to have Lizzie behaving like a sulky child without having an atmosphere develop between her husband and Bruce.

"I'm sure he doesn't mean that," she interjected. "Heavens no!"

Lizzie now spoke. "If your ceiling did come down," she said, "you would have lost a room, but you would have gained a court-yard. Think of that."

Sasha turned her head to stare at her daughter and Bruce, who now regretted raising the issue of the possible collapse of the Todd house, started to cross his legs, but stopped in embarrassment, and brought his knees together sharply. Lizzie, however, had been looking at him – or so he feared – and he saw her surprised expression. This made him blush, and Sasha, thinking him embarrassed by Lizzie's general attitude, reached over and touched him lightly on the sleeve.

"Everything will be fine," she whispered.

The conversation resumed, avoiding surveying issues, and focusing instead on Scotland's prospects in the forthcoming rugby season. Todd revealed that he had debenture seats at Murrayfield and spent some time extolling the virtue of their position in the West Stand. There then followed some disparaging remarks about dirty play by the French and the Italians. Bruce agreed with Todd's analysis of this, which seemed to relieve the tension considerably, and earlier remarks about structural unsoundness seemed now to be forgotten, or at least shelved.

When Todd looked at his watch and declared that it was time for them to start off for the Braid Hills Hotel, Bruce rose to his feet, carefully. Could he visit the bathroom quickly before they left? Of course, of course; down the corridor. Last door on the left.

He made his way down the corridor. The bathroom, which he noted had hunting prints on the wall, was more or less what he had expected, and he took the opportunity of looking at himself quickly in the mirror. This restored his confidence. One might have no underpants on, but what did it matter if one had the looks? Not at all. You don't really need underpants if you have the looks, Bruce thought to himself, and almost laughed out loud at the very idea.

He walked back down the corridor. The door next to the bathroom was open, with the light switched on. It was a drying room, with washing machine and tumble dryer, and a clothes-horse. On which there were several pairs of underpants.

55. Discovered

As he peered into the Todds' drying room, Bruce felt more than the normal curiosity (mild in the case of most) which we feel when we look into the drying rooms of others. After all, a drying room is hardly Chapman's *Homer* . . . nor is it a peak in Darien. This drying room, in fact, was of little interest, apart from the fact that there were at least four pairs of underpants on the clothes-horse and Bruce was conscious of the fact that social embarrassment might await him at the ball in his current state of incomplete dress. A simple solution would be to borrow – and it would just be borrowing – a pair of these underpants, obviously Todd's, slip into them when some suitable opportunity presented itself at the ball, and then return them, laundered, a few days later. This would not be theft; it would be borrowing of an entirely understandable and justifiable sort.

Of course the means of return would have to be considered. Borrowed items could normally be returned openly, but those that were borrowed *informally*, or borrowed with implicit consent, might have to be returned in a more discreet way. The clothing could be put into the post, perhaps, with an anonymous thank-you note – or with one signed in an illegible hand – or it might just be slipped into Todd's in-tray in the office when nobody was looking.

Bruce looked over his shoulder. The corridor was quite empty and he could hear the murmur of conversation coming from the drawing room. It was highly unlikely, he thought, that anybody would come this way: they were waiting for him to return before setting off for the Braid Hills Hotel. He could take as long as he liked, and be quite safe.

He stepped forward into the drying room and reached for a pair of underpants from the clothes-horse. As he did so, he saw that the pair which he had chosen had a large hole in the seat; how mean of Todd! It was typical of him – he was mean with stationery supplies in the office and he was always going on about keeping costs down. So he applied that philosophy to his clothing as well!

Bruce replaced the rejected pair of underpants on the clothes-horse and reached for another pair. This was better. Although the garment was certainly too large, the elastic would hold it in place. So he quickly folded the pants, stuffed them into his sporran and turned to go back out into the corridor.

He stopped. There, standing in the doorway, was Todd, an empty whisky glass in his hand.

Bruce swallowed. "Todd," he said, in strangled tones. "Todd."

Todd was staring at him, and Bruce noticed, for the first time, how the whites of his eyes were unnaturally large.

"Yes," he said.

Bruce swallowed again. "Well, I'm more or less ready to go," he said. "We don't want to keep people."

Todd blinked. "The bathroom is further along," he said. "This is the drying room."

Bruce laughed. "Oh, I found the bathroom all right," he said airily. "I took a wrong turning on the way back and ended up . . ." He paused, and then gestured around the drying room, "here. I ended up in here."

Todd moved back from the doorway in order to allow Bruce to come out into the corridor. "A rather odd mistake to make," he said. "After all, this is not a particularly confusing house. The corridor runs fairly straight, wouldn't you say? It goes up there, and then comes back. Frankly, I don't see how one can get lost in this house."

Bruce smiled. "I have a very bad sense of direction," he said quickly. "Terrible, in fact."

Todd said nothing, and so Bruce, forcing the best smile he could manage, began to walk back down the corridor towards the drawing room. His insouciance was misleading; the encounter had been deeply embarrassing. It was bad enough to be found in the drying room, but he wondered whether Todd had seen him pocket, or sporran, the underpants. Would he have said anything, had he seen him? The answer to that was far from obvious. If he had seen him, then one could only speculate as to what he would have thought. Presumably he would have thought of him as being one of those unfortunate people who steal the clothing of others for reasons too dark, too impenetrable, to discuss. That would be so unjust: the thought that he might harbour a trait of that sort was inconceivable. After all, he was a rugby enthusiast, a recently-admitted member of the Royal Institution of Chartered Surveyors, and . . . It was difficult to put one's finger on other badges of respectability, but they were certainly there.

Well, there was nothing that he could do about it. What did it matter if Todd thought that of him? He reached the drawing room before he managed to provide himself with an answer to that question.

"Bruce got lost," said Todd in a loud voice, behind him. "He ended up in the drying room."

Sasha, who had been talking to Lizzie, looked up in surprise.

"Lost in our house?" she exclaimed. "How did you manage that?"

144

"I took a wrong turning," said Bruce. He turned to look reproachfully at Todd. A host had no excuse to embarrass a guest like this, even if the host was the guest's boss.

"Very strange," said Lizzie, looking coolly at Bruce. "So you ended up among all the family underwear?"

Sasha's head swung round sharply, and Lizzie found herself fixed with a hostile stare from her mother. Bruce, who was now blushing noticeably, turned to look out of the window.

"I hope it doesn't rain," he said.

56. *At the Braid Hills Hotel*

"The nice thing about this job," observed the functions manager of the Braid Hills Hotel, "is that it has its surprises."

His assistant, surveying the room in which the South Edinburgh Conservative Association Ball was to be held, nodded his agreement. The room, although well-decorated with several sprays of flowers, had only two tables, one with four chairs around it and one with two. And even if the hotel had fielded its best napery –

starched and folded to perfection – and chosen bright red glassware – there was a distinctly desolate feel to the almost-empty room.

"You'd think that they would have sold just a few more tickets," said the assistant, adding, "in an area like this."

The manager shrugged. "I'm sure that they did their best. Still, I cannot understand why they've insisted on keeping the tables apart. Surely it would have been much better for all six of them to sit together – somehow less embarrassing."

When Sasha had called round earlier that day to review arrangements, he had suggested to her that the tables be put together, but she had firmly refused.

"I wouldn't mind in the least," she said. "But my husband has views on the matter."

So the tables had remained apart, and they were still apart when the first guests, Ramsey and Betty Dunbarton, arrived in the hotel bar, several minutes before the arrival of the Todd party.

Ramsey Dunbarton was a tall, rather distinguished-looking man who was only now beginning to stoop slightly. He thought of himself as being slightly on the Bohemian side, and had been a stalwart of amateur dramatic circles and the Savoy Opera Group. On more than one occasion he had appeared on the stage of the Churchill Theatre, most notably – and this was the height of his stage career – as the Duke of Plaza-Toro in *The Gondoliers*.

Betty Dunbarton was the daughter of a Dundee marmalade manufacturer. She had met Ramsey at a bridge class at the Royal Overseas League, and they had ended up marrying a year or so later. Their marriage had been childless, but their life was a full one, and the Conservative Ball was just another event in a busy social round. The following day they were due to go to lunch at the Peebles Hydro; the day after that there was a meeting of the Friends of the Zoo (with lunch in the Members' Pavilion); and so it went on.

Ramsey and Betty were standing near the bar when the Todd family, accompanied by Bruce, came in. Ramsey noticed that Todd did not smile at him, which was hurtful, he thought. That man doesn't like me, he said to himself. I've done nothing to deserve it, but he doesn't like me. And as for that daughter, that Lizzie, she was such a fright, wasn't she? What could one say about her? – one could really only sigh.

Introductions were made and drinks were bought before they went through to the function room.

"It's a pity there are not more of us," said Ramsey Dunbarton, looking at Todd. "Perhaps we should have made more of an effort with the tickets."

Todd glared at him. "Actually, we did our best," he said. "Not that we had much help from the rest of the committee, or from any members, for that matter."

"There are some things you just can't sell," muttered Lizzie.

They all looked at her, apart from Bruce, who was staring at the line of whiskies behind the bar. One way through the evening would be to get drunk, he thought, but then again . . .

"It doesn't matter that there are so few of us," said Sasha breezily. "The important thing is that we have a good time. And there'll be lots of room to do some dancing."

"A sixsome reel?" asked Lizzie.

This time, Bruce looked away from the bar and caught her eye. She doesn't want to be here either, he thought. And who can blame her? He smiled at her, encouragingly, but she did not respond.

They moved through to the room itself.

"Oh look!" exclaimed Betty Dunbarton. "Look at that pretty glassware. Just like the cranberry-ware which my cousin used to collect. Remember those glasses, Ramsey? Remember the jug she had in the display cabinet in Carnoustie – the one which was shaped like a swan? Remember that?"

"I always thought it was a duck," said Ramsey Dunbarton. "In fact I could have sworn it was a duck."

"No," said Betty, turning to Sasha, as if for support. "Its neck was too long for it to be a duck. It was a swan. And when you poured, the liquid would go all the way down the swan's neck and out of its beak."

"Wonderful," said Todd. "But look, we'd better get to our tables. I think that's yours over there."

147

Betty Dunbarton shook her head. "No," she said. "They've arranged it in a very silly way. Let's put the tables together so that we can talk. Ramsey, you go and ask that waiter over there to put the tables together."

Ramsey complied. He was sure that it had been a duck; he was sure of it. But now was not the time.

57. The Duke of Plaza-Toro

Once seated, Ramsey Dunbarton leaned across the table to address Bruce. They were separated by one place, occupied by Lizzie, and by a plate of cock-a-leekie soup which the Braid Hills Hotel had decreed should be the first course.

"I always think that soup's a good start to an evening," he said.

Bruce looked at his bowl of cock-a-leekie. They had started every evening meal with soup at home, and when they went out, to the Hydro or to the Royal Hotel in Comrie, they had soup too. Soup reminded him of Crieff.

"There are some people," Ramsey Dunbarton continued, "who don't like starting a meal with soup. They say that you shouldn't build on a swamp." He paused. "They think, you see, that having soup first makes the swamp – only a figure of speech, of course. Not a real swamp."

Bruce glanced at Lizzie, who was staring fixedly across the table at the arrangement of flowers. Had she noticed that he had no underpants? It was difficult to tell. And what did it matter, anyway? A certain level of recklessness sets in when one is not wearing underpants, and Bruce was now experiencing this. It was an unusual feeling to experience – in Edinburgh, at least.

"I had an aunt who was a wonderful cook," said Ramsey Dunbarton. "I used to go and stay with her down in North Berwick, when I was a boy. We used to go down there in the summer. I was sent with my brother. Do you know North Berwick?"

Bruce shook his head. "I know where it is. But I don't really know it as a place. You remember it, I suppose?"

"Oh yes," said Ramsey Dunbarton. "I remember North Berwick very well. I don't think one would forget North Berwick very readily. I wouldn't, anyway. North Berwick and Gullane too. We used to go to Gullane a great deal – from North Berwick, that is. We used to go and have lunch at the Golf Hotel and then we would go for a walk along the beach. There are sand dunes there, you know. And a wonderful view over the Forth to Fife. You can see places like Pittenweem and Elie. That's if the weather is clear enough. But it's often a bit misty. You get a bit of a haar sometimes. Do you know Elie?"

"I know where Elie is," Bruce replied. "But I don't really know Elie as a place." He turned to Lizzie in an attempt to involve her in the conversation. "Have you been to Elie?"

Lizzie looked down at her soup, which she had yet to touch. "Where?" she snapped. Her tone was that of one whose train of thought had been wantonly interrupted.

"Elie," said Bruce.

"Where?" Lizzie asked again.

"Elie."

"Elie?"

"Yes, Elie."

"What about it?"

Bruce persisted. She was being deliberately unpleasant, he thought. She's a real . . . What was she? A man-hater? Was that the problem? "Do you know it?" he asked. "Have you ever been to Elie?"

"No."

Ramsey Dunbarton had been following the exchange with polite interest and now resumed with further observations on Elie. "When I was a bit younger than you," he said, nodding in Bruce's direction, "I used to have a friend whose parents had a place over there. They went there for the summer. His mother was quite a well-known figure in Edinburgh society. And I remember I used to go over there with my friend and we'd stay there for a few days and then come back to Edinburgh. Well, I always remember that they had a very large fridge in the basement of their Elie house and my friend opened it one day and showed me what it contained. And what do you think it was?"

Bruce looked at Lizzie to see if she was willing to provide an answer, but she was looking up at the ceiling. This was unnecessarily rude, he thought. All right, so this old boy was boring them stiff but it was meant to be a ball and it was probably the highlight of his year and it would cost her nothing to be civil, at least.

"I really can't imagine." He paused. "Explosives?"

Ramsey Dunbarton laughed. "Explosives? No, goodness me. Furs. Fur coats. If you keep them in the fridge the fur is less likely to drop out. The fridge was full of fur coats. People used to buy them from the Dominion Fur Company in Churchill. This lady had about ten of them. Beautiful fur coats. Mink and the like."

"Well, well," said Bruce.

"Yes," said Ramsey Dunbarton. "The Dominion Fur Company was just over the road from the Churchill Theatre. We used to do Gilbert and Sullivan there. First in the University Savoy Opera Group and then in the Morningside Light Opera. I played the Duke of Plaza-Toro, you know. A wonderful role. I was jolly lucky to get it because there was a very good baritone that year who was after the part and I thought he would get it. I really did. And then the casting director came up to me in George Street one day, just outside the Edinburgh Bookshop, and said that I was to get the part. It was a wonderful bit of news."

Sasha, who was seated beside Bruce, and who had been talking to Betty Dunbarton, had now disengaged and switched her attention to the conversation between Bruce and Ramsey. But in the course of this change, she had heard only the mention of the Duke of Plaza-Toro.

"The Duke of Plaza-Toro – do you know him?" she asked.

Ramsey Dunbarton laughed politely. "Heavens no! He's in *The Gondoliers*. Not a real duke."

Sasha blushed. "I thought . . ." she began.

"There aren't all that many dukes in Scotland," Ramsey Dunbarton observed, laying down his soup spoon. "There's the Duke of Roxburghe, our southernmost duke, so to speak. No, hold on, hold on, is the Duke of Buccleuch more to the south? I think he may be, you know, come to think of it. Is Bowhill to the south of Kelso? I think it may be. If it is, then it would be, starting from the south, Buccleuch, Roxburghe . . . let me think . . . Hamilton, then Montrose (because he sits on the edge of Loch Lomond, doesn't he, nowhere near Montrose itself), Atholl, Argyll, and then Sutherland. Hold your horses! Doesn't the Duke of Sutherland live in the Borders? I think he does. So, he would have to go in that list between . . ."

Bruce looked around the table. All eyes had been fixed on Ramsey Dunbarton, but now they had shifted. Todd, who was still smarting over the moving together of the tables – against his explicit instructions – was glowering at Sasha, who was looking at Bruce, but in a way that he had not noticed; for he was looking at Betty Dunbarton, whose eyes, he saw, went in slightly different directions, and so could have been looking at anything; while Lizzie looked at the waiter who was watching the bowls of soup, ready to whisk them away and allow the service of the next course, and the course after that, so that the dancing could begin.

58. Catch 22

"Tories," muttered Jim Smellie, leader of Jim Smellie's Ceilidh Band. "And gey few of them too! Look, one, two . . . six altogether. See that, Mungo? Six!"

Mungo Brown, accordionist and occasional percussionist, drew on a cigarette as he looked across the dance floor to the table where the guests were sitting, waiting for the arrival of their coffee. "Don't complain," he said, smiling. "This bunch won't stay up late. We'll be out of here by eleven-thirty."

"Aye," said Jim, gazing across the empty dance floor. They were still deep in conversation, it seemed, and he wondered what they were talking about. In his experience there were two topics of conversation that dominated bourgeois Edinburgh: schools and house prices.

At the table, Betty Dunbarton turned to Todd, who was looking about anxiously, waiting for the coffee to be served. The service had been very good – one could not fault the Braid Hills Hotel, which was an excellent hotel, and it was certainly nothing to do with them that the two tables had been placed together – but it was now time for coffee, distinctly so, and then they could get out on the dance floor and he could get away from this woman at last.

"I do hope that we get a piece of shortbread with our coffee," Betty remarked. "Although, you know, I had a very bad experience with a bit of shortbread only last week. Ramsey was down at Muirfield . . ."

Todd turned round sharply. "Muirfield?"

"Yes," said Betty brightly. "He plays down there at least once a week these days. He's a little bit slow now, with his leg playing up, but he always gets in nine holes. He has the same foursome, you know. David Forth, you know, Lord Playfair . . ."

"Yes, yes," said Todd irritably. The mention of Muirfield had annoyed him. How long had Ramsey Dunbarton been on the waiting list, he wondered. Probably no time at all. And what was the use of his being a member? He would surely get as much enjoyment from playing somewhere closer to town.

"You know him?" asked Betty. "You know David?"

"No, I don't," said Todd. "I know who he is. I don't know him."

"I thought that you might have met him out at Muirfield," she said. "Do you get out there a great deal?"

Todd looked over his shoulder in an attempt to catch the waiter's eye. "No," he said. "I don't. My brother plays there, but I don't. I play elsewhere."

"Wouldn't it be nice to be in the same club as your brother?" asked Betty.

Todd shrugged. "I'm perfectly happy," he said. "And I really don't get the chance to play much golf these days. You know how it is. Not everyone wants to be a member of Muirfield, you know."

Betty laughed – a high-pitched sound which irritated Todd even more. It would be impossible to be married to a woman like this, he thought, and for a moment he felt sympathy for Ramsey, but no, that was going too far.

"I was going to tell you about this shortbread," said Betty. "I was sitting down for a cup of tea while Ramsey was out at Muirfield, with David and the others, and I decided to have a piece of short-bread. Now the shortbread itself was interesting because it had been baked by no less a person than Judith McClure, who's head-mistress of St George's. You know her?"

Todd stared at her glassily. "No," he said. "But I know who she is."

"Well," continued Betty, "I had gone to a coffee morning at St George's, in the art centre, with a friend, who's got a daughter there – a very talented girl – and I'm friendly with her mother, who lives over in Gordon Terrace, and she very kindly invited me to come to the coffee morning. Anyway, we went off and there was a stand with all sorts of things which had been baked by the girls and by the staff too. They were selling scones and the like to raise money for a school art trip to Florence. So I decided to buy something to add my little contribution to the cause. I love Florence, although Ramsey and I haven't been there for at least twenty years.

"Mind you," she went on, "there are lots of people who say that Florence is ruined. They say that there are now so many visitors that you have to queue more or less all morning to get into the Uffizi in the afternoon. Can you believe that? Standing there with all those Germans and what-not with their backpacks? All morning. No thank you! Ramsey and I just wouldn't do that.

"But I suppose if you're an Edinburgh schoolgirl and you're young and fit, then it's fine to stand about and wait for the Uffizi to open. So anyway I dutifully went over to the stall and bought a packet of shortbread which said: *Made by Dr McClure*. I was quite tickled by this because I had heard that he's the cook, you know. Roger. He's a fearfully good cook and he's writing a long book on

153

the lives of the popes at the moment. So maybe that means there's less time for cooking. Or perhaps one can do both – one can write a history of the papacy during the day and then cook at night. Something like that.

"The shortbread was delicious. I had several pieces over the next few days and then, without any warning, while I was eating the very last piece, a bit of tooth broke off. It had nothing to do with the shortbread, of course. I wouldn't want her to think that her shortbread broke my tooth – it didn't. It was just that this tooth was ready to break, apparently. There must have been a tiny crack in it and this was the time that it chose to break. One can't plan these things in life. They just happen, don't they?"

She did not wait for an answer. "I felt it immediately. If I touched the bit that had broken off, I felt a very sharp pain, like an electric shock. And so I telephoned the dental surgery, but it was a Sunday, and I got a recorded message telling me to phone some number or other. But the problem was that the person who left the message on that tape spoke indistinctly – so many people do these days – and I just couldn't make out the number! So what could I do? Well, I'll tell you. I had heard that there was an emergency dental service down at the Western General hospital, and so I phoned them up and asked whether I could come down and have the tooth looked at. And do you know what they said? They said that if I was registered with a dentist then I wouldn't be allowed in the door! That's what they said. So I said to them that I couldn't make out the emergency number and therefore couldn't get in touch with my own dentist, and they just repeated what they'd said about my not being able to go to their emergency clinic if I was registered elsewhere. Can you believe it! I'd fallen into some sort of void, it seemed. It's, what do they call it? A catch 23."

"Catch 22," said Todd quietly.

"No, I'm sure it's 23," said Betty. "Same as the bus that goes down Morningside Road. The 23 bus."

Todd looked at his watch. It was only 10.22. No, 10.23.

59. The Dashing White Sergeant

"Let's have some fun," whispered Jim Smellie to Mungo Brown. Taking the microphone in his hand, he held it up and called the ball to order. "Ladies and Gentlemen! Ladies and Gentlemen! I'm Jim Smellie and this is Jim Smellie's Ceilidh Band! Would you kindly arise and take your partners for an eightsome reel!"

Mungo drew out the bellows of his piano accordion and played an inviting major chord. At the table, Todd rose quickly to his feet and gestured, almost in desperation, to Sasha. She stood up too, cutting Ramsey Dunbarton off in the middle of a sentence. Bruce then rose, turning to Lizzie as he did so.

"Shall we?" he said.

She turned down her mouth. "I don't see how we can do an eightsome. Has anybody told the band that there aren't enough people for an eightsome?"

Bruce looked over at the band, the three members of which now seemed poised to play. This was ridiculous, he thought, but if nobody was going to do it, then he would have to go across and have a word with them.

He strode across the floor and approached Jim Smellie, who was smiling at him, his fiddle tucked under his chin.

"Look, we can't do an eightsome," said Bruce. "There are only six of us."

"Six?" asked Smellie, affecting surprise. "Are you sure?"

"Yes, of course I am," said Bruce, the irritation showing in his voice. "So we'll have to start with something else. What about a Gay Gordons?"

Smellie looked at Mungo. "Anything gay?" he asked. "This young man wants something gay."

Mungo raised an eyebrow. "Yes, I suppose so. Gay Gordons then?"

Bruce cast an angry glance at Smellie. "That'll do," he said.

The band struck up and the dancers went out onto the floor. There were only three couples, of course, and the floor seemed wide and empty. Bruce stood beside Lizzie, his arm over her shoulder, as the dance required. Had she shuddered when he had touched her? He had the distinct impression that she had, which was very rude of her, he thought. If it weren't for the fact that she was Todd's daughter, and Todd was, after all, his boss, then he would have given her a piece of his mind well before this. Who did she think she was?

"What do you put on your hair?" she asked suddenly. "It smells very funny. Like cloves, or pepper, or something like that."

Bruce winked at her. "Men's business," he said. "But I'm glad that you like it."

His response went home. "I didn't say . . ." She was unable to finish. The band had started and the small line of couples began to move round the perimeter of the floor. There was no more time for conversation, although Todd seemed to be trying to whisper something to Sasha, who looked over her shoulder and then whispered something back.

The Gay Gordons went on for longer than usual, or so it seemed to the dancers. Then, when the music finally came to an end,

Smellie seized the microphone and announced a Dashing White Sergeant. Sasha looked anxiously at Ramsey Dunbarton – the Gay Gordons had been energetic, and he seemed to have coloured. Was he up to another dance, she wondered.

She leaned over to Todd and whispered in his ear. "Do you think it wise . . . ?" she began. "He looks exhausted."

Todd shrugged. "He should know his limits. He seems to be all right."

In spite of their doubts, Ramsey Dunbarton was busy organising everybody for the next dance. Todd and Bruce were to join Betty in one set, and he would be flanked by Lizzie and Sasha.

Smellie watched, bemused, while the two sets prepared themselves, and then, with a nod to Mungo, he started the music. Off they went, dancing in opposite directions, all the way round the hall, to seemingly interminable bars before they encountered one another, bowed, and went through the motions of the dance. Mungo Brown smiled and looked away; he had never seen anything quite as amusing in thirty years of playing at ceilidhs.

"This is cruel," he mouthed to Smellie, and Smellie nodded and smirked as the two groups of dancers went off again in their wide, lonely circling of the dance floor.

At the end of the Dashing White Sergeant the dancers returned to their table while the band embarked on *The Northern Lights of Old Aberdeen*. Nobody wanted to dance to this, in spite of an exhortation from Jim Smellie that a waltz should be attempted.

Todd looked at his watch. They might do a few more dances – two at the most – and then they could bring the whole thing to an end. Honour would have been satisfied; they would have had their ball and nobody would be able to say that they could not muster support for one. Did the South Edinburgh Labour Party have a ball? They did not. Of course, they didn't know how to dance, thought Todd, with satisfaction. That's what came of having two left feet. He paused. That was really amusing, and he would have to tell Sasha about it. He might even tell it to Bruce, who liked a joke, even if his sense of humour was rather strange. Anything, of course, was better than those awful Dunbartons, with her wittering away about dentists and breaking her tooth and about Dr McClure's shortbread. What nonsense.

He looked at Bruce, noticing how the exertion of the dance had made his hair subside; it was still *en brosse*, but at a reduced angle of inclination. Todd stared at Bruce's head. Was it something to do with the melting of whatever it was that he put on his hair? Perhaps that stuff – whatever it was – stopped supporting hair when it became warmer. Brylcreem – good old-fashioned Brylcreem, of the sort that Todd had used when he was in his last year at Watson's, and which you could use to grease your bicycle chain if needs be – was a much simpler, and more masculine product. And it had used that very effective advertising jingle, which he could still remember, come to think of it. Brylcreem – a little drop will do you!/ Brylcreem – you'll look so debonair!/ Brylcreem – the girls will all pursue you/ They'll love to run their fingers through your hair!

That young man is a bit of a mystery, thought Todd. He was up to something when I saw him in the drying room. And whatever it was, he had no business to be there. It was all very suspicious.

60. *The Tombola*

It was now time for the tombola at the Annual Ball of the South Edinburgh Conservative Association. Jim Smellie's Ceilidh Band had made valiant efforts to provoke more dancing, but the guests, exhausted by the Gay Gordons and the Dashing White Sergeant, had decided that they would dance no more. Jim Smellie and the band played a few more tunes and then, after a maudlin rendition of "Good-night Irene", sung by Mungo Brown in a curious nasal drone, the band had packed up and gone home.

At their combined table on the other side of the room, the six guests sat, still feeling rather lost in the vastness of the empty function room, but enjoying nonetheless the drinks which Todd had generously purchased everyone after the last dance.

"We've had a wonderful evening," announced Sasha, looking around the table lest anybody venture to disagree.

Lizzie gave a snort, but not so loud that it could be heard by anyone other than Bruce, who was seated immediately beside her. "Speak for yourself," she muttered.

Bruce turned to her. "She is, actually," he said. "She is speaking for herself."

Lizzie said nothing for a moment, digesting the barely-disguised rebuke. She had tolerated Bruce thus far – and it had been an effort – but she was not sure if she could continue to do so. There was something insufferable about him, an irritating self-confidence that begged for a put-down. The problem, though, was that it was far from easy to put down somebody who was quite so pleased with himself. And what could one say? Could anything penetrate the mantle of self-satisfaction that surrounded him, like a cloak of . . . like a cloak of . . . There was no simile, she decided, and then she thought *cream*.

She turned to him. "You're like the cat who's got the cream," she said.

Bruce met her gaze. "Thank you," he said. And then he gave quite a passable imitation of a purr and rubbed his left leg against her, as might an affectionate cat. "Like that?" he asked.

Any response that Lizzie might have given was prevented by Sasha's standing up and announcing that the time had come for the tombola.

"We have marvellous prizes," she said. "And since it's only a modest crowd here tonight, there'll be plenty for everybody."

"Hear, hear," said Ramsey Dunbarton, raising his glass of whisky. "Plenty for everybody – the Party philosophy."

"Quite," agreed Sasha. "Now, to save the bother of a draw, I simply divided the tickets – on a totally random basis, of course – into six groups. I then put each group in a separate envelope and wrote a name on the outside. On payment of six pounds – one pound per ticket – you will each get your envelope. And then you can open it up and when you tell me the numbers, I will tell you what you've won."

"Sounds fair," said Bruce, but he noticed that Ramsey Dunbarton looked doubtful. Did he suspect Sasha of cheating? Bruce wondered. Surely that would be inconceivable. And yet she would have had every opportunity to dictate which tickets went into which envelope, and thus effectively determine who won what.

The Ramsey Dunbartons, slightly reluctantly, handed over twelve pounds and were given two white envelopes with *Ramsey* and *Betty* written on the outside. Then Lizzie completed the same transaction, in her case with an ostentatious show of boredom. Bruce, by contrast, handed over six pounds with good grace and smiled as he took the envelope from Sasha.

"Right," said Sasha. "Betty, if you would like to start by calling out the numbers on your tickets, I'll tell you what you've won."

While she was organising the tickets, Todd had gone out of the room and now he wheeled in a large trolley. This was covered with a sheet, which he took off with a theatrical gesture. There, stacked high in munificence, were the prizes – the silver fish knives and forks from Hamilton and Inches; the decanter from Jenners; the envelopes containing the vouchers for golf and dinner and other treats. All was laid out before them, and the guests immediately realised that this tombola represented remarkable value for the six pounds that each of them had been asked to pay.

The fish knives and forks went to Betty Dunbarton, who received them with exclamations of delight.

"Hamilton and Inches," said Sasha knowingly.

"Wonderful," said Betty. "Ramsey loves Hamilton and Inches."

The other prizes she won were less exciting, but still represented a good haul. And when it came to Ramsey's turn, although he was unmoved by the prize of the round of golf at Craiglockhart, he was extremely pleased with the two free tickets to the Lyceum Theatre to be followed by dinner (up to the value of twenty-five pounds) in the Lyceum Restaurant. His final prize was the picture which Bruce had brought as his contribution.

"A view of somewhere over in the west," announced Sasha as she handed the Peploe? over to him. "A very nice prize indeed, thanks to Bruce."

Ramsey and Betty nodded in Bruce's direction in acknowledgment of his generosity. Then they placed the Peploe? with the fish knives and forks and waited for the next stage of the draw. This saw Lizzie win the dinner at Prestonfield ("too fattening," she said), a jar of pickled red peppers from Valvona and Crolla ("can't stand red peppers," she remarked) and a copy of the latest novel by a well known crime-writer ("Ian who?" she asked). When it came to Sasha's turn, she won, of course, the lunch with Malcolm Rifkind and Lord James at the Balmoral Hotel. This brought some envious muttering from Ramsey Dunbarton, who clearly would have liked to have won that, but this merely confirmed Sasha's conviction that she had done the right thing. "I couldn't have imposed him on them," she said to Todd later. "Imagine them having to sit there and listen to stories about North Berwick and broken teeth."

Laden with prizes, the party began to break up. The Ramsey Dunbartons' taxi arrived to take them the short distance back to Morningside Drive and Bruce telephoned for a cab back to Scotland Street. Then he remembered the underpants. He had intended to slip into them earlier on, but had almost forgotten his state of undress. Now, as he remembered that the pants were in his sporran, it occurred to him that the simplest way of returning them to their owner would be to put them in the pocket of Todd's coat, which he knew had been hung in the cloakroom on the ground floor.

Making his excuses, Bruce left the small knot of guests around the table and made his way to the cloakroom. There, as he had expected, was Todd's black Crombie coat with its velvet collar. Bruce crossed the room quickly, extracting the underpants from his sporran as he did so. Then, fumbling in the folds of the coat, he slipped the pants into the right-hand pocket.

"Did you enjoy yourself?"

It was Todd, standing at the door.

"That's my coat," said Todd. "Yours is over there, isn't it?"

Bruce laughed nervously. "I must have had too much to drink," he said. "So it is!"

He moved over towards his coat and took it off the hook. Then he turned and looked at Todd, who was watching him suspiciously.

As he put on his coat, he felt Todd's eyes remain on him. It was very disconcerting. Bruce was used to being looked at – in an admiring way – but this was different.

61. Bertie Begins Therapy

For Irene Pollock, the mother of that most talented five-year-old, Bertie, the decision to seek advice from the Scottish Institute of Human Relations was an entirely appropriate response to a trying set of circumstances. Bertie's sudden outburst at the Floatarium – when he had so unexpectedly declared his opposition to speaking Italian and learning the saxophone – had been only the first sign of a worryingly rebellious attitude. Although it was difficult to put a finger on any particular incident or comment (other than his extraordinary behaviour at the Floatarium, which followed hard on the heels of the graffiti incident) there was no doubt that he was less co-operative than he used to be. An indication of this attitude was his subtle abandonment of the first names which he had been encouraged to use when addressing his parents; *Irene* and *Stuart* had come so naturally to him, and seemed so right; now it was *Mummy* and *Daddy* – terms which were acceptable when used by Irene or Stuart themselves, but which seemed disturbingly hierarchical – even reactionary – when uttered by Bertie.

And then there had been a shift in attitude towards his room. One afternoon she had gone into his room – which she called his *space* – to discover Bertie standing in the middle of his rug, staring disconsolately at the walls. He had not said anything at first, but she had formed the distinct impression that he was thinking about the colour – a reassuring pink – and might even have been imagining the walls in another colour.

"You're very lucky to have a space like this," said Irene, pre-emptively. "You really are."

Bertie looked at her briefly, almost in reproach, and had then turned away. "Other boys have different spaces," he said. "They have trains and things."

"Other boys are not as lucky as you are," Irene countered. "Other boys are forced into moulds, you know. Forced to play football, for example. Horrid things like that. Do you understand what I mean? We're giving you something very different, Bertie. We're giving you the gift of freedom from gender roles."

"Trains are free," muttered Bertie.

Irene struggled to contain her frustration. It was not easy, but she succeeded. "Are they?" she asked gently. "Why are trains free, Bertie? Why do you say that?"

Bertie sighed. "Trains go out into the night. Remember Mr Auden's poem, Mummy, the one you read to me once. *This is the night mail crossing the border/ Bringing the cheque and the postal order.*"

Irene nodded. She had given him W.H. Auden rather than A.A. Milne in the belief that the insights of Auden would be infinitely better for him than middle-class juvenile nonsense about being halfway up the stairs or changing the guard at Buckingham Palace and all the rest.

"I could read you more Auden, if you like," she said. "There's that lovely poem about . . ."

"*Streams*," interrupted Bertie. "I'd like the poem about streams because he talks about two baby locomotives, remember it? He says the god of mortal doting is pulled over the lawn by two baby loco-motives."

Irene stared at Bertie. Where on earth did this obsession with trains come from? Neither she nor Stuart talked about trains very much, if ever, and yet he seemed to think of nothing else. She closed her eyes for a moment and imagined herself arriving at Waverley Station at some time in the future, say ten years from now. And there, standing on the platform, notebook in hand, wearing a blue anorak, would be Bertie, trainspotting, in the company of several other Aspergeresque youths.

She left the room, the space, quietly. If there was nothing that could be done about it, then this retreat of Bertie into a rejection of everything she and Stuart stood for would be a bitter pill to swallow. But there was something they could do – there was a great deal *she* could do. Therapy – solid, Kleinian therapy – would move Bertie through this dangerous period; therapy would deal with the envy and the other ego issues which were causing this flowering of hate and negativity. And then all would be well. Even if the therapy were to take a year – and she well understood how slow analysis could be – there would still be plenty of time to have Bertie's ego development sorted out by the time he was due to begin at the Rudolf Steiner School. All that was required was love and patience; the love of a parent who knew that it was only too easy to become a harsh figure, and the patience of one who understood that bad behaviour was merely the product of frustrated longing for that which one wanted to love. Bertie wanted to love the Italian language and the saxophone; in his heart of hearts he associated those with that fundamental object of affection, the good breast, and he would return to a more fulfilling relationship with these things, the things of the mind and the soul, once he had resolved his Oedipal issues.

And so it was that Irene dressed Bertie in his best OshKosh dungarees and set off for an appointment with Dr Hugo Fairbairn at the Institute. They had time on their hands, and they took a circuitous route, walking along Abercromby Place so that they might look down into the gardens.

"Look, Bertie," said Irene, pointing to a shrub that was displaying a riot of blossom. "Look at the little flowers on that bush."

Bertie looked down, and then turned away sharply. "Mahonia," he said. "I hate mahonia. I hate flowers."

Irene caught her breath. There was no doubt but that this visit to the therapist was coming not a moment too soon.

62. The Rucksack of Guilt

Dr Hugo Fairbairn was unrelated to the distinguished psychoanalyst Ronald Fairbairn, whose colourful son, the late Nicholas Fairbairn, had so enlivened the Scottish firmament with his surprising remarks and invigorating attitudes. Not many people now knew about Fairbairn père, but his name still counted for something in the history of the psychoanalytical movement, along with names such as Winnicott, Ferenczi, and, of course, Klein. For Hugo Fairbairn, the name was something of a professional asset, as others would make the false assumption of relationship and assume that he was too modest to mention it. This gave him authority in the psycho-analytical movement – with its dynastic tendencies – and had undoubtedly helped him in establishing his practice. Aided by his name, his rise to eminence had been rapid; he had appeared on conference platforms at the Tavistock, and had been referred to in several articles in *The Analytical Review*. In due course, his elegantly-written case-history, *Shattered to Pieces: Ego Dissolution in a Three-year-old Tyrant*, had become something of a classic. Indeed, one reviewer had gone so far as to suggest that Fairbairn's three-year-old tyrant, Wee Fraser, might be heading for the same sort of immortality as that famous patient whose analysis was written up by Freud – Little Hans, who had feared that the Viennese dray horses might bite him. This, of course, was a grossly inflated claim – no case, ever, anywhere, could be as important as those upon which Freud himself had pronounced – but it was still true that there were some very interesting aspects of Wee Fraser's troubled psyche. This boy had none of Hans's neurotic dreads – and that was what made him so interesting. Rather than fear that he might be bitten, Wee Fraser had himself bitten a number of others, including a Liberal Democrat councillor who had called at the door and Dr Fairbairn himself, thus eliciting that famous line in the case history: "The young patient then attempted the oral incorporation of the analyst."

Irene, of course, had heard of Dr Fairbairn, and had attended a lecture which he had given on Wee Fraser at the Royal Scottish Museum. She had every confidence in him and in his ability to get to the heart of Bertie's malaise, and she secretly entertained thoughts of Bertie in due course appearing in the psychoanalytical literature. *A Remarkably Talented Boy and his Problems in Adjusting to a Mediocre Society*. That would be a possible title; and the text itself would be extremely interesting. There would have to be, of course, a complete exposure of Christabel Macfadzean and her lack of understanding of Bertie (and children in general). She, poor woman, would stand for the essential poverty of the bourgeois imagination, a cipher for everything that was wrong with Edinburgh itself.

She allowed herself the luxury of these thoughts as they completed their journey, Bertie trailing slightly behind her, hands in his pockets, still, she noticed, trying to avoid standing on the cracks.

"Where are we going anyway?" muttered Bertie.

"We're going for therapy," said Irene. She had never concealed anything from Bertie and this, of all occasions, was one on which a frank explanation was required.

"What happens at therapy?" asked Bertie, a note of anxiety now entering his voice. "Do other boys have therapy? Will there be other boys there?"

"Of course other boys have therapy," said Irene, reassuringly. "You may not see other boys, but they do go there. Lots of boys have therapy."

Bertie thought for a moment. "Am I having therapy because I'm suspended?" he asked.

Irene frowned. "Your suspension from nursery was a nonsense," she said. "You mustn't feel that you have been suspended at all. Just ignore it."

"But am I suspended?" asked Bertie. "Like a cancelled train? Am I cancelled?"

"No," said Irene, gritting her teeth at the persistent, worrying train references. "That woman tried to suspend you, but I withdrew you before she could do so. You can't be suspended if you're withdrawn." She paused. They were now standing outside the entrance to the Institute, and it was time to go in.

"We can talk about all that later on," she said. "Now we must go in and meet Dr Fairbairn. I'm sure that you'll like him." And there was certainly nothing forbidding in Dr Fairbairn's manner when the two of them were shown into his consulting room. He was dressed in a loose-fitting cord jacket and a pair of slightly rumpled charcoal slacks. He greeted them warmly, bending down to shake hands with Bertie and addressing Irene formally as Mrs Pollock.

Irene knew that she would like him. She usually made snap judgments of people – it had taken her no more than a few minutes to get the measure of Christabel Macfadzean, for example – and she seldom revised her opinions after she had formed them. People were, in her experience, either possible or impossible. Hugo Fairbairn was clearly possible, and she would have judged him so even had she been unaware of his background and his writings.

Dr Fairbairn gestured to a small circle of easy chairs at one side of the room. "Let's sit down," he said, smiling at Bertie as he spoke. "Then we can have a little chat."

They took their places and Irene glanced at Dr Fairbairn. In spite of her interest in these matters, she had never actually consulted a psychotherapist before (analysis was ruinously expensive, Stuart had pointed out; the cost of a mortgage, more or less). If she had been able to afford it, Irene would have shown no hesitation in undergoing analysis, not that she had any *issues* to resolve – there was nothing wrong with her, in her view – but the whole process of discovery of that which drives one would be fascinating, would it not? A whole range of new resentments might surface; new understandings of what one's parents were doing to one; renewed access to those little secrets of childhood; light upon the dark furniture of the mind.

But that was not what Bertie needed. His conflicts were fresh and current, not buried deep in the experience of the past. But how would Dr Fairbairn elucidate these things? Through Kleinian play therapy?

"What's the trouble then?" asked Dr Fairbairn, rubbing his hands together as he spoke. "Been a naughty boy?"

Irene could not prevent herself from gasping. This was a very direct approach, almost naïve in its directness, and yet he must know what he was doing. This was, after all, the author of *Shattered to Pieces*.

Bertie stared at Dr Fairbairn. For a moment he did nothing, and then he winced, as if bracing himself for a slap.

Dr Fairbairn's eyes narrowed. He threw a glance at Irene, who was looking at Bertie and frowning.

"You aren't here to be punished," said Dr Fairbairn. "Did you think I was going to smack you?"

"Yes," said Bertie. "I thought that you were going to smack me for thinking bad thoughts."

Dr Fairbairn smiled. "No, Bertie, I'd never do that. Analysts don't smack people."

"Not even if they deserve it?" asked Bertie.

"Not even then," replied Dr Fairbairn. He was about to continue, when he stopped, and appeared to think of something.

When he had been bitten by Wee Fraser, he had in fact smacked him sharply on the hand. Nobody had seen it and of course it was not mentioned in the case report. But he had done it, and now he felt guilt, like a great burden upon his back. *The Rucksack of Guilt*, he thought.

63. Irene Converses with Dr Hugo Fairbairn

"There's something troubling you," said Irene when she saw the pained expression cross Dr Fairbairn's face. "You looked almost tormented just then."

Dr Fairbairn turned away from Bertie to face Irene.

"You're very observant," he said. "And indeed you're right. I felt a great pang of regret. It's passed now, but yes, it was very strong."

"The emotions always register so clearly," said Irene. "Our bodies are not very good at concealing things. The body is far too truthful."

Dr Fairbairn smiled. "Absolutely. That's the great insight which Wilhelm Reich shared with us, isn't it? Reich was a bit odd in some of his views, I'm afraid, but he was right about character armour. Are you familiar with what he says about that?"

Irene nodded. "The idea we create a carapace of posture and gesture to protect the real us. Like Japanese Noh actors and their masks."

"Precisely," said Dr Fairbairn.

For a short while nothing was said. During the exchange between his mother and Dr Fairbairn, Bertie had been watching the adults, but now he turned away and looked out of the window, up at the sky, which was deep and empty. A tiny vapour trail cut across the blue, drawn by an almost invisible plane. How cold it must be up there in that jet, thought Bertie, but they would have jerseys and gloves and would be kept warm that way. Planes were good, but not as good as trains. He had travelled on a plane the previous year, to Portugal for their holidays, and he still cherished the memory of looking out of the window and seeing the ground fall away below him. He had seen roads, and cars, as small as toys, and a train on a railway line . . .

"You looked anguished," said Irene. "It must have been a very painful memory."

"Not for me," said Dr Fairbairn quickly. "Well, the smack was painful for him, I suppose."

"For whom?"

Dr Fairbairn shook his head. "I don't want to talk about it," he said.

Irene laughed. "But surely that's exactly what you get other people to do – you get them to talk about things."

Dr Fairbairn spread his hands in a gesture of helplessness. "I have talked about it in the past," he said. "I certainly told my own analyst."

"And did that not draw the pain?" asked Irene gently.

"For a short time," said Dr Fairbairn. "But then the pain returned. Pain comes back, doesn't it? We think that we have it under control, and then it comes back to us."

"I understand what you mean," said Irene. "Something happened to me a long time ago which is still painful. I feel an actual physical pain when I think of it, even today. It's like a constriction of the chest."

"We can lay these ghosts to rest if we go about it in the right way," said Dr Fairbairn. "The important thing is to understand the thing itself. To see it for what it really is."

"Which is just what Auden says in that wonderful poem of his," said Irene. "You know the one? The one he wrote in memory of Freud shortly after Freud's death in London. *Able to approach the future as a friend, without a wardrobe of excuses* – what a marvellous insight."

"I know the poem," said Dr Fairbairn.

"And so do I," interjected Bertie.

Dr Fairbairn, whose back had been turned to Bertie, now swung round and looked at him with interest.

"Do you read Auden, Bertie?"

Irene answered for him. "Yes, he does. I started him off when he was four. He responded very well to Auden. It's the respect for metre that makes him so accessible to young people."

Dr Fairbairn looked doubtful, but if he had been going to contest Irene's assertion he appeared to think better of it.

"Of course, Auden had some very strange ideas," he mused. "Apropos of our conversation of a few moments ago – about psychosomatic illness – Auden went quite far in his views on that. He believed that some illnesses were punishments, and that very particular parts of the body would go wrong if one did the wrong thing. So when he heard that Freud had cancer of the jaw, he said: *He must have been a liar*. Isn't that bizarre?"

"Utterly," said Irene. "But then people believe all sorts of things, don't they? The Emperor Justinian, for example, believed that homosexuality caused earthquakes. Can you credit that?"

Dr Fairbairn then made an extremely witty remark (an Emperor Justinian joke of the sort which was very popular in Byzantium not all that long ago) and Irene laughed. "Frightfully funny," she said.

Dr Fairbairn inclined his head modestly. "I believe that a modicum of wit helps the spirits. Humour is cathartic, don't you find?"

"I know a good joke," interjected Bertie.

"Later," said Dr Fairbairn.

Irene now resumed her conversation with the analyst. "I've often thought of undergoing a training in analysis," she said. "I'm very interested in Melanie Klein."

Dr Fairbairn nodded encouragingly. "You shouldn't rule it out," he said. "There's a crying need for psychoanalysts in this city. And virtually nobody knows anything about Klein." He paused for a moment. "It's a totally arbitrary matter – the supply of analysts. There's Buenos Aires, for example, where there is an abundance – a positive abundance – and here in Scotland we are so few."

Irene looked thoughtful. "It must be very hard for analysts in Argentina, with their economic crisis and everything. I gather that some analysts have seen their savings wiped out entirely."

"Yes," said Dr Fairbairn. "It's been tough for analysts there. Firstly the generals, Videla and that bunch. They banned the teaching of psychoanalysis, you know. For years people had to be discreet. Freud unsettles people like generals. Military types don't like him."

"Not surprising," said Irene. "People in uniform don't like to be reminded of the fact that we're all vulnerable underneath. Uniforms are a protection for fragile egos.

"I would never, ever, send Bertie to a school that required a uniform," said Irene firmly. "There are no uniforms at the Steiner School."

They both looked at Bertie, who looked back at them.

"But I want a uniform," he said. "Other boys have uniforms. Why can't I have a uniform too?"

The question was addressed to Irene, who said nothing in reply.

She would normally have refused a request for a uniform out of hand, but now she looked to Dr Fairbairn for a lead.

The analyst smiled at Bertie. "Why would you want a uniform, Bertie? Would it make you feel different?"

"No," said Bertie. "It would make me feel the same, which is what I want."

64. Post-analysis Analysis

Bertie's hour with Dr Fairbairn passed extremely quickly – or so it seemed to Irene. She was very impressed with the psychotherapist, who quite lived up to her expectations of what the author of *Shattered to Pieces* would be like. They had discovered that they had a great deal in common: an appreciation of Stockhausen (not a taste shared by everyone; indeed, Irene had admitted that one had to work at Stockhausen), an enthusiasm for Auden, and a thorough knowledge of the works of Melanie Klein. All of this had taken some time to establish, of course, and this had left little time for Dr Fairbairn to say anything to Bertie, after their brief – and somewhat disturbing – exchange over Bertie's fears that Dr Fairbairn would smack him.

That had been a potentially embarrassing moment and Irene had been concerned that the psychoanalyst might conclude that Bertie was used to being smacked by his parents. That, of course, would have been a terrible misunderstanding. Irene and Stuart had never once raised their hands to Bertie, not even when, shortly after the incident in the Floatarium, he had deliberately set fire to Stuart's copy of *The Guardian* while he was reading it in his chair. That had been a dreadful moment, but they had kept very cool about it, which was undoubtedly the right thing to do. Rather than let Bertie think that they were upset by this, they had pretended to be completely unconcerned.

"Daddy doesn't care," Irene had said insouciantly. "It makes no difference to him."

Bertie had looked at his father, as if for confirmation.

"No," said Stuart. "I don't need to read the newspaper. I know what it would have said anyway."

Irene had been momentarily concerned about this, but had let the remark pass. She hoped, though, that Bertie would not interpret it as suggesting that *The Guardian* was predictable. That would never do. And he should certainly not develop ideas like that before he went to the Steiner School, where *The Guardian* was read out each day at school assembly.

Now, before going back to Scotland Street with Bertie, she decided that they would make the short detour to Valvona and Crolla, to stock up on porcini mushrooms. Bertie liked this shop, with its rich smells and its intriguing shelves, and she would be able to talk to him over a latte in the café. And it was always possible that one might meet somebody interesting in the café, and have a conversation about something important. She had recently met a well-known food-writer there and she had learned a great deal about olive oil – things she had never known before. Edinburgh was full of interesting people, Irene thought, provided one knew where to go to meet them. Valvona and Crolla was a good start, because interesting people liked to eat interesting food. Then there was Ottakars Bookshop in George Street, and Glass and Thompson in Dundas Street, where interesting people went for a latte.

She found herself thinking about Dr Fairbairn, who was unquestionably interesting. She had never seen him in Valvona and Crolla, which was surprising, but perhaps he bought his olive oil in a delicatessen in Bruntsfield – that was always possible – or even in a supermarket, although that was unlikely. One would not expect to turn a corner in one of those ghastly supermarkets and see the author of *Shattered to Pieces* peering into the refrigerated fish section.

Where did Dr Fairbairn live, she wondered? This was a crucial, and very difficult question. The best place for a person like him to live was the New Town, although the better part of Sciennes was certainly a suitable place for psychoanalysts. He could not live in Morningside (too bourgeois) nor the Grange (too haut-bourgeois). This left very few locales in which Dr Fairbairn could be imagined, unless, of course, he lived in Portobello. That, Irene had to concede, was just possible. The most surprising people lived in Portobello, including at least some creative people.

And was Dr Fairbairn married, with children perhaps? This was even more difficult to determine than the question of where he might live. She had glanced at his left hand and had seen no ring, but that meant nothing these days. There were even some people who put rings on the relevant finger in order to flout convention or to throw others off the scent, whatever the scent was. And Dr Fairbairn might not be married at all but might have a partner, and children by that partner. Or he might not be interested at all.

That, of course, was the most difficult issue to determine. Irene knew that there were people who were just not interested at all, just as there were people who were not in the slightest bit interested in tennis. This did not mean that they were resentful of people who played tennis, or of people who liked to watch tennis; it's just that tennis *meant nothing to them*.

They made their way slowly towards Valvona and Crolla. Bertie was still cautiously avoiding stepping on the lines in the pavement, frowning with concentration on the task, but this was unnoticed by Irene, who was still lost in speculation over the private life of

Dr Fairbairn. There was something about him which suggested that he did not have a wife or partner. It was difficult to put one's finger on this, but it was a rather lost look, a look of being uncared for. One sometimes saw this in men who had no women to look after them. Gay men were different, Irene thought. They looked after themselves very well, but straight men tended to look dishevelled and slightly neglected if they had nobody.

Mind you, she thought, that young man at the top of the stair, Bruce, looked far from neglected. He put that substance on his hair – what was it, lubricant? – and he was always rather smartly dressed. She had talked to him on several occasions and he had been perfectly civil. He had once even let Bertie touch his *en brosse* hair after Bertie had made a remark about how good it looked. Bruce had bent down and said to Bertie as the little boy had gingerly reached out to touch his head: "You could look like this one day too – if you're lucky!"

It had been an odd remark, but they had all laughed. Afterwards Bertie had asked several questions about Bruce, but Irene had answered them vaguely. Little boys liked to have heroes, as Melanie Klein pointed out, and she was not sure whether that young man was a suitable choice. Nor did she encourage Bertie's open admiration for that Macdonald woman's Mercedes-Benz. Bertie had enquired whether they might ask if he could have a ride in it one day, and she had given an unequivocal no to that request.

"We have our own car," said Irene. "A much more sensible car than that, I might add."

"But we never go in our car," complained Bertie. "Where is it?"

"It's parked," said Irene curtly.

"Where?" asked Bertie. "Where is our car parked?"

Irene did not know. Stuart had parked it somewhere or other a few weeks ago and she had no idea where this was. So she gave a simple reply. "Outside," she said, as they arrived at their destination.

65. A Meeting in Valvona and Crolla

They walked past the shelves in Valvona and Crolla, each looking at the items at his and her particular eye-level. Irene gazed at packets of pasta; not ordinary, hard pasta of the sort that one might see in a supermarket, vulgar spaghetti and the like, but obscure, complicated egg-rich pastas – tagliatelle and other rare varieties. These cost twice as much as vulgar pasta, but tasted infinitely better. Vulgar pasta tasted like cardboard, Irene thought, and she could never understand how people could actually eat it. Probably because they knew no better, she decided. Ordinary people – as Irene called them – were remarkably in the dark, and often simply did not realise how in the dark they were. Fortunately, ordinary people were beginning to develop more sophisticated habits, brought about, in part, by overseas travel, not that Spain helped very much, thought Irene.

Down at his eye-level, Bertie saw tinned fish and sea-food, Portuguese sardines and Sicilian octopus. The pictures on these tins were intriguing. The Portuguese sardines were portrayed as swimming contentedly in a small shoal near the surface of the sea, while in the background there was a wild coast with high cliffs and mountains behind. Bertie had been to Portugal, and some of it, he recalled, had looked just like that. They had eaten sardines there, too, every night, though the sardines had looked less happy than those portrayed on the tin.

After they had completed their shopping, they had gone through to the café and latte had been ordered.

"Well, Bertie," said Irene cheerfully. "What did you think of Dr Fairbairn?"

Bertie appeared to think for a moment. "He was very kind," he said. "He didn't smack me when he called me a naughty boy."

Irene's eyes widened. "He did *not* call you a naughty boy," she protested. "He asked you whether you had been a naughty boy, that's all. And I didn't think that he meant it."

"Why did he say it then?" asked Bertie. "Why did he call me a naughty boy?"

Irene drew in her breath. This would require very careful

handling. It had been unwise of Dr Fairbairn to use the term "naughty boy" in the first place, but then he probably had not realised just how bright Bertie was. Other boys would have seen this remark as a bit of harmless banter – a joke really – but Bertie was far too sensitive for that. Bertie had cried when he had seen a picture of the unfinished parliament building in the newspapers. That showed real sensitivity. "It's so sad," he had said. "All that building and building and it's never finished. Can we not help them, Mummy?"

She would have to mention to Dr Fairbairn – very tactfully, of course – that he was sensitive to suggestion, unlike Wee Fraser perhaps. Wee Fraser had not been a sensitive boy, by all accounts, and even when his ego had been re-assembled at the end of the analysis, he had not seemed to have developed any particularly sensitive traits. He had stopped biting people, of course, which amounted to a slightly more sensitive approach to life, but in other respects one could probably not hope for much change.

"Bertie," she began, "when Dr Fairbairn asked you – asked you, mind – whether you had been a naughty boy, he was referring to how other people might have reacted to your behaviour. This is different from saying that you had been a naughty boy. His tone was ironic. If he really thought that you had been naughty, then he wouldn't have used those words. You do understand that, don't you?"

Bertie said nothing. He had been naughty, he thought: he had written on the nursery walls. Surely that was quintessentially naughty. And he wanted to be naughty. That was the whole point. If they kept making him learn Italian and play the saxophone and all the other things, he would show them. He would punish them, and they would stop. That was how grown-ups, people like Mrs Klein, whose book he had read, thought. And this Doctor Fairbairn person, who had hardly talked to him at all and who hadn't even been interested in his joke – the only way to make him take any notice would be to do something really naughty. Perhaps I should bite him, thought Bertie. Then he will really take notice and tell them to drop the Italian and the saxophone. They might even be persuaded not to send me to the Steiner School and send me to

Watson's instead, where there are uniforms and rugby and things like that. And secret societies too, Bertie thought, although those might only be for after you've left.

Irene looked at her son. There was so much promise there – such an extraordinary level of ability – and she would not let her project for him be derailed. She stopped herself; train metaphors were *not* what she wanted here.

"Bertie," she said gently, "I want you to know that Stuart loves you very much. It's quite natural for boys to feel confused about their fathers and, well, I suppose one might say that it's natural for boys to feel threatened by their fathers. Dr Fairbairn will help you to get over this. That's what Dr Fairbairn is for."

Bertie looked at her. What was all this? He liked his father very much, and when he had set fire to his copy of *The Guardian* it had nothing to do with his feelings for his father. Why would they just not leave him alone? Why did they force him to do all these things? Those were the questions which worried Bertie.

Irene reached for her latte and took a sip. She glanced around her. The café was uncrowded, and she let her gaze run slowly over the few people who were there. There was a woman in her mid-thirties, a blonde, with hair held back with an Alice band. Irene noticed that she had that look about her which goes with bored affluence. Her husband, no doubt, was a fund manager or something similar. There would be a couple of children, and she was whiling away the hours before it was time to collect them from school. The children would be exactly like her, thought Irene, right down to the Alice band (if they were girls). She smiled. People were so predictable.

Her gaze moved to the next table. There was a young couple poring over *The Scotsman* property section. Irene looked at their faces. Yes, they were anxious, she thought. How difficult for them, struggling to find a place to live in that competitive, overpriced market. And what would they find at the end of the day? A two-bedroomed flat for the price of a small farm in Australia. Mind you, she had no idea what small farms cost in Australia, but she imagined that it was not very much. She had read somewhere that people sometimes gave such farms away, just to get off them. I would never, ever farm in Australia, she said to herself, and shuddered at the thought. Heat. Dust. Drought.

Then she stopped. A man was sitting by himself at the table beyond that. He was reading a newspaper, and nursing a small cup of espresso. There was a file with some papers sticking out of it on the table in front of him, but his attention was fixed on the newspaper.

"Bertie," she whispered. "That man over there. The one reading the paper. Do you recognise him? He looks very familiar."

Bertie followed his mother's gaze.

"Yes," he said. "I've seen his picture in the paper. I know who that is."

"Who is it then?" asked Irene. She had thought that Bertie would know. He was a very attentive boy.

"That's Mr Dalyell," said Bertie.

66. Mr Dalyell's Question

Although Bertie was Irene's creation, in both the biological and the metaphorical sense, she was constantly astonished by the things that he knew and that he occasionally revealed so casually. His recognition of Tam Dalyell, purely from newspaper photographs, was a case in point. How many five-year-olds were there in Edinburgh, or anywhere else for that matter, who would recognise the redoubtable politician? None, she imagined. It was even possible that there were many adults who would not know the name, given the contemporary obsession with an entirely superficial celebrity. People had no difficulty in recognising rock musicians and actresses, people for whom Irene had the most profound distaste, but they had great difficulty in recognising those who actually did things of value. So while they would know who all the current actors and footballers were (or at least the good looking ones like Mr Grant

179

and Mr Beckham), they could not be expected to know about people who did something to change the world for the better. Except Bertie, it would seem: Bertie knew.

Irene gazed at her son with pride. There had been moments in the last few days when she had even begun to doubt the whole Bertie project. Her thoughts had been dangerously seditious; perhaps it would have been better not to teach him Italian, nor the saxophone. She actively thought that, but quickly corrected herself: what a waste that would have been, what a criminal waste! And so she had overcome those temptations – temptations of mediocrity, or ordinariness – and persisted. And now, quite unexpectedly, had come the reward: the recognition of Mr Dalyell in Valvona and Crolla.

"Did you read about him, Bertie?" she asked, her voice lowered lest Tam Dalyell hear them talking about him.

Bertie, who had been served a latte with a generous portion of chocolate sprinkled across the surface, took a sip of the creamy liquid, sucking in the chocolate froth with puckered lips.

"Don't make that noise," began Irene automatically, but stopped. Private noises were inevitable with children and she had read they should not be unduly inhibited. Those who were stopped from making these ordinary human noises took it out on the world later on – Irene had read that somewhere and had been impressed by the insight. It was so true, she thought. Oppression was the preserve of the oppressed. The child who is scolded into silence makes others silent later on. It was so true, and yet it was so difficult to rid oneself of the censorious urge when it came to children. They made such a noise. They smelled. And little boys were so brutal in their approach to the world, kicking and shoving and breaking things, just as men did; it was so tempting to subdue these little boys with rules and reproach.

"I know all about Mr Dalyell," said Bertie, wiping the chocolate residue from his lips. "He asked a famous question."

Irene listened to this without any great interest. Scottish politics were of no consequence to her – even Scottish politics in the Westminster context. Although she had been born in Scotland and had been educated there, her outlook transcended that background. She belonged to that sector of society which somehow did not regard itself as located anywhere in particular. To be located, thought Irene, was to be provincial and narrow. She was *above* location.

Bertie looked again in the direction of the man at the table. Then he took another sip of his latte and turned to Irene.

"Or it's Mr Harper," he said.

Irene looked puzzled. "Or?"

"Yes," said Bertie, as if explaining something very simple to one who could not be expected to grasp the self-evident. "Mr Harper is the leader of the Greens. Mr Dalyell is one of the Reds. That man over there is either Mr Dalyell or Mr Harper. It's difficult to say, Mummy."

Irene cast a glance over in the direction of the mysterious politician. Bertie was right: there might well be a strong resemblance between Tam Dalyell and Robin Harper, and certainly if one asked the average five-year-old to say which was which one would not expect a clear answer. But there was nothing average about Bertie, of course.

Now she was uncertain herself. It was very unsettling, really, not being sure whether one was confronted with Mr Dalyell or Mr

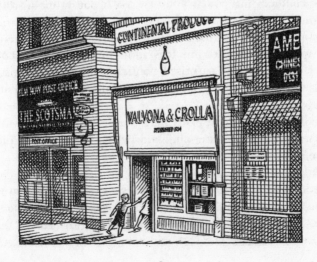

Harper, and, really, should one find oneself in this position? Robin Harper was younger than Mr Dalyell, who was a very senior politician, and one might be expected to distinguish on those grounds. But Mr Dalyell did not really show the years at all, and both had a rather, how should one put it, *enigmatic* look to them, as if they knew the answer to some important question, and we did not. And both, of course, were good men, of whom there was a very short supply.

She smiled. How was the matter to be resolved, short of asking him directly? But what would one say? "Are you, or are you not, Tam Dalyell?" sounded a bit accusing, as if there was something *wrong* in being Tam Dalyell. And if one were to be given a negative answer, would one proceed to say: "In that case, are you Robin Harper?" That sounded as if it was somehow second best thing to be Robin Harper, which of course it would certainly not be, at least if one were Robin Harper in the first place. Presumably Robin Harper was quite happy about being Robin Harper. He certainly looked contented with his lot.

It was Bertie who proposed a solution. "May I ask him, Mummy? May I ask him the answer to his question? If it's Mr Dalyell, then he could give us the answer."

Irene smiled. "Of course you may ask him, Bertie. Go and ask him what's the answer to his famous question."

Bertie immediately rose to his feet and approached the other table, where he stood on his toes and whispered something into the ear of the slightly surprised politician. There then ensued a brief conversation, during which Bertie nodded his head in understanding.

"Well?" pressed Irene when Bertie returned. "Who was it?"

"It was Mr Dalyell after all," said Bertie. "And he told me the answer."

"And?" said Irene.

Bertie looked at his mother. She was always forcing him to do things. She made him learn Italian. She made him play the saxophone. Now she was forcing him to give her the answer to the West Lothian Question. He would have to punish her again.

"I'm not going to tell you," he said simply. "Mind your own business."

67. *Playing with Electricity*

Pat returned to the flat that evening slightly later than usual. The gallery had been unusually busy and she and Matthew had been obliged to deal with a series of demanding customers. When they had eventually closed the gallery, Matthew had suggested that they go for a drink in the Cumberland Bar. Pat had hesitated; she was beginning to like Matthew, but she thought that on balance she would keep her relationship with him on a strictly business level; there was nothing else there, and she would not want to give him any encouragement. If she went for a drink with him, he might misread the situation and it would then become embarrassing to extricate herself. But had Matthew given any sign of interest in her? She thought perhaps he had, although it was difficult to put one's finger on precisely why she should think this.

But what was more significant was her desire to get back to the flat. She had found that as the afternoon drew on, she had thought increasingly frequently of the prospect of returning that evening and seeing Bruce. A few days ago, this would have brought on a sense of irritation; now it was something different. She wanted to see him. She was looking forward to going back to Scotland Street and finding him there. Even the smell of cloves, the scent of his hair gel which signalled his presence, was attractive to her.

She did not reflect on this to any extent; indeed she hardly dared admit it to herself. I do not like him, she told herself; I cannot like him. I have disliked him right from the beginning. He's self-satisfied; he thinks that every woman fancies him; in reality he's just . . . What was he, now that she came to search for an adjective that would sum Bruce up? And why, in the midst of this deprecation should the word gorgeous come to mind?

Matthew did not seem to be too disappointed when she declined his invitation. "I'm going to the Cumberland anyway," he said. "Walk that far with me. It's on your way."

They made their way down Dundas Street in companionable silence. A few of the shops were still open; others were closed and shuttered. The fact that Matthew said nothing did not make Pat feel awkward. He was easy company, and it did not seem necessary to say anything. It would have been different with Bruce, she thought; she could not imagine being silent with him. And that surely was a bad sign. There is no point in cultivating the friendship of those with whom we feel we have to talk. And yet, and yet . . . friendship was one thing; was she thinking of something altogether different? I am playing with electricity, she thought. And what happens to those who play with electricity? Zap!

When they reached the end of Cumberland Street, Matthew said goodnight and disappeared into the bar. Pat continued her way through Drummond Place and turned down into Scotland Street. She glanced up at their windows, hoping to see a light, but the flat was in darkness. Bruce was not back yet. This knowledge brought with it a pang of disappointment.

She walked up the stairs, past Irene and Stuart's door, with its anti-nuclear sticker. From within the flat there drifted the sound of a saxophone, and she stood for a moment and listened. She had not heard Bertie for the last few days, but now he had resumed, even if the playing seemed quieter and more subdued. She strained to hear the tune: it was not "As Time Goes By", but it was still familiar. "Play Misty for Me", she thought. The playing suddenly stopped and she heard the sound of voices, a scream, she thought; a small voice crying *No! No!* and then silence. Then there came an adult's voice – Irene's, she imagined – and then *No! No!* again.

Pat smiled. She remembered how she herself had resisted piano lessons as a child and had been forced to practise for half an hour a day. That had paid off, as her parents knew it would, and she had become a competent pianist. But she had often wished to cry *No! No!* in protest against the playing of scales and arpeggios. In Bertie's case it must be so much worse. She had heard from Domenica just how pushy his mother was, and she felt a pang of sympathy for the small boy, burdened with that heavy tenor saxophone that must be almost the same size as himself.

She continued up the stairs and let herself into the flat; as she had expected, there was no sign of Bruce. She turned on a light in the hall. A few letters lay on the floor. She picked these up and glanced at them. One was for her – a letter from a friend who had gone to live in London and who was always having boyfriend trouble. The others were for Bruce, and she put these down on the hall table.

Bruce's door was open. This was not unusual; he usually left the flat before her, in a rush, as he tended to get out of bed late and lingered in the bathroom – in front of the mirror, she had always assumed. So he often did leave his door open in his rush to get out of the flat, and Pat, who had never gone into his room, had been given glimpses of what it contained. Now she decided she would have a closer look.

It was a strange feeling going into Bruce's room uninvited. She paused at the door and almost turned back, but she now felt a delicious feeling of daring, of sweet risk, and she reached for the light switch near the door and flicked it on.

The room before her was relatively Spartan, and tidier than she had imagined it would be. In her experience, young men let their rooms deteriorate into near-squalor. Clothes would be tossed down as they were removed, and left to fester. Books would be strewn around tables. There would be unwashed coffee cups, and tapes, and ancient running shoes with their characteristic acrid smell. In Bruce's room there was none of this. In one corner there was a bed, neatly made, with an oatmeal-coloured bedspread. Opposite, against the wall, was a desk with a laptop computer, a neat row of books, and a container of paper clips. Then there was a chair across which a coat had been draped and a wardrobe. A jar of hair gel, half used; the slightest smell of cloves.

Pat stood still for a moment, looking around her. The broad picture of the room now taken in, she began to notice the finer details. She saw the picture of the Scottish rugby team; she saw the green kit-bag that contained his gym things; she saw the disc of the Red Hot Chilli Peppers tour. All this was very ordinary, but to her surprise she found herself excited by the sight. Everything here belonged to him, and had that strange extra significance in which we vest the possessions of those to whom we are attracted. Items which belong to them become potent simply because they are theirs. They are talismans. They are reminders.

She felt an emptiness in the pit of her stomach. It was familiar to her. She had felt it when she had become infatuated as a sixteen-year-old with a boy at school. It had been a painful, heart-breaking experience. And now she felt it again, like a powerful drug; taking hold of her, dulling her defences. She wanted to be with him. She wanted Bruce. Electricity. Electricity.

She lay down on his bed and looked up at the ceiling. The bed was comfortable; just right, whereas hers was slightly on the soft side. She closed her eyes. There was that faint smell of cloves again, no doubt from the hair gel which had rubbed off on his pillow. She took a deep breath. Cloves. Zanzibar. And electricity.

68. Boucle d'Or

Goldilocks, or Boucle d'Or, as Bruce might have called her, lay asleep on the bed in the cottage when suddenly she opened her eyes and saw the bears. "Who's been sleeping in my bed?" said a gruff voice.

"And who's this sleeping in my bed?" asked Bruce, standing above her, looking down, bemused.

Pat opened her eyes and saw not the ceiling, to the sight of which she had closed them, but Bruce's face, and she shut them again. But it was, of course, true; she was on his bed, uninvited, and now he had found her there. He looked mildly quizzical, she noticed, if not completely surprised; he was the sort of person, she thought, who imagined that people would gladly lie down on his bed, as a privilege, perhaps – a treat.

She sat up and swung her legs over the edge of the bed. "I'm sorry," she said. "I came in here and lay down on your bed. I dropped off to sleep."

He laughed. He did not mind. "But what were you doing?"

Pat stared at the floor. She could hardly tell him that she came in because she wanted to see his things, to get a sense of him. And so she mumbled something else altogether. "I wanted to see what your room was like – whether it was different from my own."

Bruce raised an eyebrow. "Well . . . ?"

"I know it sounds odd," said Pat. "And I'm sorry. I'm not really nosy, I'm really not."

"Of course not," said Bruce, taking off his jacket and flinging it down on a chair. "Make yourself at home. Don't mind me. Make yourself at home."

For a moment Pat thought that he was going to take his clothes off, as he had moved away and was now undoing buttons; but he only stripped to the waist, moving towards the cupboard, from which he extracted a clean, folded shirt. And his undressing happened so quickly, before she had time to get to her feet and leave the room. It was all very casually done, but was it intended as some sort of show?

She glanced at him, quickly, so that he should not see her look, and she noticed the smooth, tanned skin, almost olive, and the ripple of muscles. He was utterly confident, utterly physically at home in the space he occupied, as is any creature of beauty. For a moment she thought of Michelangelo's David, and she remembered the shock that she had felt when, on a school trip to Florence, they had wandered into the gallery in which David stood and had hardly dared look, but had looked nonetheless. "Remember, girls," a teacher had said. "Remember that this is art."

What, she had wondered, was that intended to mean? That young men in real life would not be like this, so noble, so marbly, so composed? Or that art might license the feminine gaze upon the male but that in real life one should not be so bold? She recalled this as

Bruce crossed shirtless to the window and stood there, looking out on to the street. For a few moments he did nothing, then he unfolded the clean shirt and slipped into it. She felt a pang of disappointment at this act; she wanted this display, crude as it was, to continue.

"I'm going out," he said, almost as an aside. "Otherwise I would have offered to cook a meal tonight. But I'm going out."

He turned to face her, and smiled at her in a way which struck her, surprisingly, as pitying. Was this pity because she had done such a silly, school-girlish thing as look at his room and lie on his bed? Or pity for the fact that he was going to disappoint her and go out?

"I've met a rather interesting girl," he said. "She's American. I'm taking her out to dinner."

Pat said nothing.

"She's called Sally," Bruce went on, looking in the mirror beside his wardrobe and stroking his chin. "Should I shave for Sally? What do you think?"

"It's up to you," said Pat.

"Some girls like a bit of designer stubble," Bruce said casually, peering again into the mirror. "What do you think?"

Pat got up and walked towards the door. "I can take it or leave it," she said, struggling to keep her voice even.

Bruce tore himself away from the mirror and watched her leave the room. "Sorry," he muttered, just loud enough for her to hear. "If I didn't have to go out . . ."

She left the room, shaken by what had happened and by her reaction to it. She did not know what to do, and went aimlessly into the kitchen and switched on a light. She would eat something, perhaps, or put on the kettle – anything to occupy herself for a few moments and take her mind off the encounter she had just had. Everything, it seemed to her, had changed. She had left the flat that morning as a different person; as a person who was in command of herself, and come back a person in thrall. It was profoundly unsettling, just as it was completely unexpected. And it was unwanted too.

She was aware of Bruce in the background, of the opening of

the bathroom door and its closing, of the sound of footsteps on the stripped pine floorboards, of the sound of a radio which he had switched on. She felt restless and confused. It was a good thing that he was going out, as this would stop her thinking of him; no, it was a bad thing, as she wanted him to be there. But I do not want him, she told herself; I do not want this. I do not.

On impulse, she left the kitchen and walked into the hall and opened the cupboard to retrieve the ironing board. She had some clothes to iron. It was a task that she never enjoyed, but it was domestic and mindless and it would take her mind off him.

She flicked the switch inside the cupboard. There was the ironing board and there, of course, would be the painting, the Peploe? that she was looking after. But it was not, of course, and she gasped at the discovery.

"Something wrong?"

He was standing immediately behind her, and she was aware of the freshly-applied hair gel.

"There was something I was looking after." Her voice faltered. "A painting . . ."

Bruce laughed. "Oh that. Well, I'm very sorry, I got rid of that. I didn't know it was yours. I thought . . ."

She turned to him aghast. Now he became defensive. "Don't look at me like that," he said. "If you leave things lying about in that cupboard they're fair game. Rules of the flat. Always have been."

69. The Turning to Dust of Human Beauty

Domenica opened the door of her flat to a neighbour clearly in distress. Wordlessly, she ushered Pat in.

"I feel that I don't even have to ask you," she said as she led Pat into her study. "It's him, isn't it? Bruce."

Pat nodded. She had fought back her tears while Bruce explained to her what had happened to the painting, but now they came, a cathartic flood. He had been unapologetic. "How was I to know?" he asked. "There are all sorts of things in there."

"Can you get it back? You must know who has it."

Bruce shrugged. "Some old couple won it. Ramsey something or other, and his gas-bag wife. I don't know anything about them. Sorry."

Pat felt outraged. "You could ask," she shouted. "That's the least you could do."

Bruce drew back, shaking a finger at her. "Temper! Temper!" He had done this to her before, after the incident with the hair gel, and the effect had been the same: the provoking of a seething anger. But she had said nothing more; she felt too weak, too raw to do anything, but the exchange had ended with a weak promise from Bruce to ask Todd for the Dunbarton telephone number. A few minutes later she had heard the front door close as he left the flat, and she sat in her room, her head in her hands. How was she to tell Matthew, as she would have to do? It occurred to her that she might lose the job at the gallery, and while she would be able to find something else, there was the ignominy of dismissal.

Telling Domenica helped.

"It's not the end of the world," she said, when Pat had finished. "You should be able to get it back. After all, these people who won it have no right to keep it. It was not Bruce's to give in the first place, and that means that they can't acquire any right to it. It's that simple."

This had encouraged Pat, although doubts remained. "Are you absolutely sure about that?"

"Of course," said Domenica. "Bruce effectively stole it from you. It's stolen property. And stolen property is stolen property."

Pat wiped at her eyes. "I feel so stupid," she said. "Coming in here and burdening you with all this."

Domenica reached out and laid a hand on her forearm. "You shouldn't feel that. I'm very happy to help. And anyway, we all feel weak and sniffly from time to time." She paused. "Of course, there is something else, isn't there?"

Pat looked at her. Domenica could tell, she knew, but she was not at all sure if she wanted to speak about that.

Domenica smiled. "He's got under your skin, hasn't he?"

Pat did not answer. She stared down at the floor. She was thinking of her anger, her irritation with Bruce, but then the image came back to her of him standing there before the window, his shirt off. She looked up. Domenica was watching her.

"I thought that it might happen," said Domenica. "I thought that it might happen in spite of everything. If one puts two people together and one of them is a young man like that, well . . ."

"I don't like him," said Pat. "You should hear what he says."

"Oh, I know what Bruce is like," said Domenica. "Remember that I've been his neighbour for some time. I know perfectly well what he's like."

"Well, why has this . . . why has this happened?"

Domenica sighed. "It's happened for a very simple reason," she said. "It's a matter of human reaction to the beautiful. It's a matter of aesthetics."

"I feel this way about Bruce because he's . . ." It was difficult for her to say it, but the word was there in the air between them.

"Precisely," said Domenica. "And that's nothing new, is it? That's how people react to beauty, in a person or an object. We become intoxicated with it. We want to be with it. We want to possess it. And when that happens, we shouldn't be the least bit surprised, although we often are.

"It's an age-old issue," she went on. "Our reaction to the beautiful occurs in the face of every single one of our intellectual pretensions. We may be very well aware that the call of beauty is a siren-call, but that doesn't stop it from arresting us, seizing us, rendering us helpless. A soul-beguiling face will make anybody stop in their tracks, in spite of themselves."

Pat listened in silence. Domenica was right, of course. Had Bruce not looked the way he looked, then she would have been either indifferent to him or actively hostile. He had done enough to earn her distaste, if not her enmity, with his condescension and his assumptions, and if it had not been for this aesthetic reaction, as Domenica called it, he would have been unable to affect her in this way. But the reality was that he had, and even now she cherished that moment of bizarre shared intimacy in his room, when he had removed his shirt and she had looked upon him.

"So," said Domenica briskly. "Do you want my advice? Or my sympathy? Which is it to be?"

Pat thought for a moment. She had not expected these alternatives. She had expected, at the most, that Domenica would listen sympathetically and make a few general remarks, instead of which she had provided what seemed to be a complete diagnosis and was now offering something more.

"Your advice, I suppose." She realised it sounded grudging, which was not her intention, but her tone seemed not to disconcert Domenica.

"Well," said Domenica. "It would seem to me that you have a clear choice. You can move out of the flat straightaway and endeavour never to see him again. That would be clean and quick, and, I suspect, rather painful. Or you can continue to live there and allow yourself to feel what you feel, but do it on your own terms."

"And what would that mean – on my own terms?"

Domenica laughed. "Enjoy it," she said. "Let yourself feel whatever it is that you feel, but just remember that at the end of the day he's not for you and that you will have to get rid of him. And there's another way in which this would be highly satisfactory."

"Which is?"

"You might have the additional satisfaction of teaching him a lesson. He's played with the affections of numerous young women – that's the type of boy he is. Teach him a lesson. Help him to moral maturity."

"But what if I still feel something for him?"

"You won't," said Domenica. "Believe me, there's nothing more brittle than human beauty. Encounter it. Savour it, by all means. Then watch how it turns to dust."

Pat sat quite still, watched by Domenica. "Anyway," said Domenica, rising to her feet. "I'm about to go off to listen to a lecture at the Portrait Gallery. I suggest that you come with me.

It'll take you out of yourself for a couple of hours, and there are drinks afterwards to which I'm sure you can come. How about it?"

Pat thought for a moment. She did not want to go back to the flat, which was cold and empty. So she said yes, and they went out together, out into Scotland Street and the night.

70. An Evening with Bruce

Bruce did not feel apologetic about the scene which had developed over the missing painting; he felt annoyed. There was no reason for him to reproach himself, he thought, because he had had every reason to assume that the painting had been abandoned. It was valueless, anyway. Pat had screamed something about it being by Peploe, whoever he was, but Bruce doubted that unless, of course, this Peploe person was somebody's uncle. He could tell when a painting was worth something, and that painting was definitely not worth the cost of the frame, which must have been pretty little anyway. What a fuss over nothing! You could get a painting like that any day of the week from one of those charity shops – useless pictures of the Trossachs or St Andrews or places like that. Completely useless. If she was so upset about it, then he might, just might, pick up something from one of those shops and give it to her to make up for it. But why should he? He had done no wrong, and her reaction was typical of a woman. They make the most ghastly fuss over little things; he had seen it all before and he had no time for it.

And what made it worse, he thought, was that that silly, half-hysterical girl was falling for him; her lying on his bed just confirmed the suspicions he had been entertaining for some time. Having had a great deal of experience of these things, Bruce could tell when somebody was falling for him. It was the way they looked at you; that slightly unfocused look. It was something to do with body chemistry, he imagined. The effect of pheromones made women's eyes go all watery. It was curious, but he had seen it so many times when women looked at him.

Bruce had decided that she would get no encouragement from him. Being mixed up with her would make his life too complicated. She would be possessive, he expected, and would cramp his style. It would be difficult, for example, to bring other girls back to the flat as she would always be there, thinking that she had a prior claim on him. No, he would have to play this very carefully.

He might give Pat the occasional thrill, of course, as he had done when he had removed his shirt. She had been watching him – he had felt her gaze – and there was no doubt about her interest. But that would be about as far as it would go. She could look, but she would not be allowed to touch.

Now, this newly-acquired girl, Sally, was a different proposition altogether. Bruce had met her in the Cumberland Bar when she had been brought there by friends of his, and he had become immediately interested in her. He had known at once that she was his type: a tall, willowy girl, with a good eye for casual elegance in clothes. She had attracted his attention right away and he had sidled up to her and asked for an introduction. She had looked him up and down appraisingly and had smiled at him, which was no more than he expected, of course.

"Yo!" Bruce said.

"Ya!" came the reply, and with these short, potent words the compact had been sealed. They had talked enthusiastically. Sally was American, and in Edinburgh for a year – long enough, thought Bruce – and was studying for a master's degree in economics.

"Cool!" Bruce said, and she had nodded.

"Yeah," she said. "Cool."

At the end of the evening they had agreed to meet the following evening, and now Bruce stood in the Cumberland Bar awaiting her arrival. There were one or two people he recognised in the bar, but he did not feel like talking to them. He had put the row with Pat out of his mind, and he was now thinking about something rather more important – his job. He was becoming bored with surveying, and was particularly disenchanted with Raeburn Todd, his boss, and the firm of Macaulay Holmes Richardson Black. This feeling had been building up and had been brought to a head by his experiences at the Conservative Ball. That had been a particularly depressing occasion from Bruce's point of view, as it had given him a vision of what might become of him if he did not make a change. Todd was the warning incarnate, thought Bruce: that is how I shall talk and behave if I remain where I am. I shall become exactly like Todd, with a wife exactly like Sasha, and a house in the Braids. No, that would not do: there must be an alternative.

But the identification of the rut was one thing; the finding of a way out was quite another. Bruce had thought of other possibilities, only to reject them. Many of his friends were accountants or lawyers – the Cumberland Bar was full of them. But it would take too long now for him to qualify for either of these professions, and the accountancy examinations were notoriously stressful. So those two options at least were firmly ruled out. What else was there? Finance was a possibility, but that was ruthlessly competitive and dominated by people with a background in mathematics. Bruce acknowledged that he was not very good with numbers, and so he would need to go for something where he could use his social skills. He looked about the bar, and at that moment the idea occurred. The wine trade. He knew a few people in wine, and they struck him as being very much his type. If they could do it, then there was no reason why he should not make a go of it. Bruce Anderson, MW, he muttered under his breath. Specialist in Bordeaux and California. He caught a glimpse of himself in a mirror behind the bar and he smiled. MW – Master of Wines. It would be considerably more impressive than being a surveyor.

He was still smiling when Sally came into the bar.

"You're looking great," he said.

"You too."

"*Gracias.*" He would normally have said *merci* to a compliment of this sort, but he remembered that she was American and that Americans tended to speak Spanish rather than French.

He bought her a drink – a glass of Margaret River Chardonnay – and they chatted easily, perched on stools at the bar. Half an hour later, Bruce looked at his watch.

"Do you feel like eating?"

Sally looked him up and down. "I could eat you up," she said.

Bruce laughed. "Cool."

71. At the Scottish National Portrait Gallery

While Bruce and Sally were engaged in culinary self-appraisal in the Cumberland Bar, Domenica and Pat were making their way up the stairs at the National Portrait Gallery in Queen Street.

"Such an edifying building," observed Domenica. "A wonderful mixture of Gothic and Italianate. There are two galleries I really love – this one and the Metropolitan Museum in New York. Do you know New York?"

Pat did not. "In which case," Domenica continued, "you should go there as soon as you get the chance. Such an exhilarating place. And the Metropolitan Museum is such a wonderful box of delights.

It has all those marvellous collections donated by wealthy New Yorkers who spend all their lives acquiring things and then give them away."

"Perhaps they feel guilty," suggested Pat.

Domenica did not agree. "The very rich don't do guilt," she said, adding, "as one might say today. President Bush said that he didn't do nuances. Isn't that wonderful! The verb 'do' does so much these days. Even I'm beginning to do 'do'."

They reached the top of the stairs and made their way into the hall where rows of chairs had been set up for the lecture. There was already a fair crowd, and they had to find seats at the back. Domenica waved to one or two people whom she recognised and then turned to address Pat, her voice lowered.

"Now this is interesting," she said. "This is a *very* interesting audience. There are some people here who are just *itching* to have their portraits painted. They come to everything that the gallery organises. They sit through every lecture, without fail. They give large donations. All for the sake of immortality in oils. And the sad thing is – it *never* works. Poor dears. They just aren't of sufficient public interest. Fascinating to themselves and their friends, but not of sufficient public interest."

Domenica smiled wickedly. "There was a *very* embarrassing incident some years ago. Somebody – and I really can't name him – had a portrait of himself painted and offered it to the gallery. This put them in a terrible spot. The painting could just have been lost, so to speak, which would have been a solution of sorts, I suppose, but galleries can't just lose paintings – that's not what they're meant to do. So they were obliged to say that he just wasn't of sufficient public interest. So sad, because he really thought he was of great public interest.

"Then there are people who are of some interest, but not quite enough, or at least not quite enough while they're still alive. It will be fine when they're dead, but the gallery can hardly tell them that the best thing to do is to die. That would be rude. It's rather like the way we treat our poets. We're tremendously nice to them after they're dead. Mind you, some poets are rather awkward when they're still alive. MacDiarmid could be a little troublesome after a bottle of Glenfiddich. He became much safer *post-mortem*.

"I can tell you the most remarkable story about MacDiarmid," Domenica continued. "And I saw this all happen myself – I saw the whole thing. You know the Signet Library, near St Giles? Yes? Well, I was working there one day, years ago. They had let me use it to have a look at some rather interesting early anthropological works they had. I was tucked away in a corner, completely absorbed in my books, and I didn't notice that they had set out tables for a dinner. And then suddenly people started coming in, all men, all dressed in evening dress. And I thought that I might just stay where I was – nobody could see me – and find out what they were up to. You know how men are – they have these all-male societies as part of their bonding rituals. Tragic, really, but there we are. Poor dears. Anyway, it transpired that a terribly important guest was coming to this one, none other than the Duke of Edinburgh himself. Frightfully smart in his evening dress. And there, too, was MacDiarmid, all crabbit and cantankerous in his kilt and enjoying his whisky. I was watching all this from my corner, feeling a bit like an anthropologist observing a ritual, which I suppose I was. A little later on, the Duke stood up to make a speech and I'm sorry to say that MacDiarmid started to barrack him. He was republican, you see. And what happened? Well, a very well-built judge, Lord somebody, lifted the poet up and carried him out of the room. So amusing. The poet's legs were kicking about nineteen to the dozen, but to no avail. And I watched the whole thing and concluded that it was some sort of metaphor. But I've never worked out what it was a metaphor for!"

"Is that true?" asked Pat.

Domenica looked severe. "My dear," she said, "I *never* make things up. But, shh, here comes our lecturer, the excellent James Holloway. We must listen to him. He's very good."

Pat had been distracted by Domenica's monologue and James Holloway was several minutes into his lecture before she began to concentrate on what he was saying. But as Domenica had predicted, it was interesting, and the time passed quickly. There was enthusiastic applause and then the audience withdrew to another room where glasses of wine and snacks were being offered.

Domenica seemed in her element. Acknowledging greetings from several people, she drew Pat over to a place near a window where a sallow, rather ascetic-looking man was standing on his own.

"Angus," she said. "This young lady is my neighbour, which makes her a neighbour, or almost, of yours." She turned to Pat. "And this, my dear, is Angus Lordie, who lives in Drummond Place, just round the corner from us. You may have seen him walking his dog in the Drummond Place Gardens. Frightful dog you've got, Angus. Frightfully smelly."

Angus looked at Pat and smiled warmly. "Domenica here is jealous, you see. She'd like me to take *her* for a walk in the Drummond Place Gardens, but I take Cyril, my dog, instead. Much better company."

Pat stared at Angus, fascinated. He had three gold teeth, she noticed, one of which was an incisor. She had never seen this before.

Domenica noticed the direction of her gaze. "Yes," she said loudly. "Extraordinary, isn't it? And do you know, that dog of his has a gold tooth too!"

"Why not?" laughed Angus.

72. *Angus Lordie's Difficult Task*

After a few minutes of coruscating conversation with Angus Lordie, Domenica was distracted by another guest. This left Pat standing with Angus Lordie, who looked at her with frank interest.

"You must forgive me for being so direct," he said, "but I really feel that I have to ask you exactly who you are and what you do. It's so much quicker if one asks these things right at the beginning, rather than finding them out with a whole series of indirect questions. Don't you agree?"

Pat did agree. She had observed how people asked each other

questions which might elicit desired information but which were ostensibly about something else. What was the point of asking somebody whether they had been busy recently when what one wanted to know was exactly what they did? And yet, now that she had been asked this herself, how should she answer? It seemed so lame, so self-indulgent, to say that one was on one's *second* gap year. And to say that one worked in a gallery was almost the same thing as saying outright that one was still on the parental pay-roll. But then there was a case for truthfulness – one might always tell the truth if in an absolute corner, Bruce had once remarked.

"I work in a gallery," she said with as much firmness as she could manage, "and I'm on my second gap year."

She noticed that Angus Lordie did not seem surprised by either of these answers.

"How very interesting," he said. "I'm a portrait painter myself. And I've done my time in galleries too."

Pat found herself listening to him very carefully. His voice was rich and plummy, deeper than that which one might have expected from an ascetic-looking man. It had, too, a quality which she found fascinating – a tone of sincerity, as if every word uttered was felt at some deep level.

She asked him about his work. Did he paint just portraits, or did he do other things too?

"Just portraits," he said, the gold teeth flashing as he spoke. "I suspect that I've forgotten how to paint mere things. So it's just portraits. I'll do anybody."

"How do you choose?" she asked.

Angus Lordie smiled. "I don't choose," he replied. "That's not the way it works. They choose me. People who want their children painted, or their wives or husbands, or chairmen for that matter. And I sit there and do my best to make my subjects look impressive or even vaguely presentable. I try to discern the sitter's character, and then see if I can get that down on canvas."

"Who do you like doing best?" Pat enquired.

Angus Lordie took a sip of his wine before he answered. "I can tell you who I don't particularly like doing," he said. "Politicians. They're so tremendously pushy and self-important for the most part. With some exceptions, of course. I'd like to do John Swinney, because he strikes me as a nice enough man. And David Steel too. I like him. But nobody has asked me to do either of these yet. Mind you, why don't you ask me who I like doing absolutely least of all?"

"Well?" said Pat. "Who is that?"

"Moderators of the obscure Wee Free churches," said Angus Lordie, shuddering slightly as he spoke. "They are not my favourite subjects. Oh no!"

"Why?" asked Pat. "What's wrong with them?"

Angus Lordie cast his eyes up to the ceiling. "Those particular churches take a very, how shall we put it? – a very restricted view of the world. Religion can be full of joy and affirmation, but these characters . . ." He shuddered. "There used to be a wonderful Afrikaans word to describe the position of rigid ideologues in the Dutch Reformed Church – *verkrampte*. It's such an expressive term. Rather like *crabbit* in Scots. All of these words are tailor-made for some of these Wee Free types. Dark suits. Frowns. Disapproval."

"But why do you paint them, then?" asked Pat.

"Well, I don't make a habit of painting them," answered Angus Lordie. "I've just finished painting my first one now. I'd love to paint a resolved Buddhist face or a flashy Catholic monsignor with a taste for the pleasures of the table, but no. These people – the Portrait Gallery people – are having an exhibition later in the year of portraits of religious figures. It's called Figures of Faith, or something like that. And I've drawn the short straw. I've got the Wee Free Reformed Presbyterian Church (Discontinued)."

Pat laughed. "What a name!"

"Yes," said Angus Lordie. "These Free Presbyterians are always having rows and schisms. Well, this Discontinued bunch is quite different from the mainstream Free Presbyterians, who are very nice people – nothing to do with them, or with any of the other well-known ones. But they've got a couple of hundred members, which isn't too bad even if it's the Church Universal."

Pat smiled. She was enjoying this conversation; there was

something appealing about Angus Lordie, something vaguely anarchic. He was fun.

"So I was asked," continued Angus Lordie, "to paint a portrait of a Reverend Hector MacNichol, who happens to be the Moderator of this particular bunch of Free Presbyterian types. I agreed, of course, and he came down to my studio for the first sitting. And that's when I found out that he more or less expressed, in the flesh, the theology of his particular church, which takes a pretty dim view of anything which might be regarded as vaguely fun or enjoyable. There he was, a tiny, crabbit-looking man – minuscule, in fact – who gazed on the world with a very disapproving stare. He noticed an open bottle of whisky in my studio and he muttered something which I didn't quite catch, but which was probably about sin and alcohol, or maybe about Sunday ferries, for all I know."

"It can't have been easy to paint him," said Pat.

Angus Lordie agreed. "It certainly was not. I sat him there in the studio and he said to me in a very severe, very West Highland voice: 'Mr Lordie, I must make clear that I shall under no circumstances tolerate any work being done on this portrait on a Sunday. Do you understand that?'

"I was astonished, but I made a great effort to keep my professional detachment. I'm sorry to say that the whole thing was destined – or pre-destined, as a Free Presbyterian might say – to go badly wrong."

"And did it?" asked Pat.

"Spectacularly," said Angus Lordie.

73. *A Dissident Free Presbyterian Fatwa*

Looking at his new twenty-year-old friend, Angus Lordie, member of the Royal Scottish Academy and past president of the Scottish Arts Club, reflected on how agreeable it was to have a young woman to talk to in a room of his coevals. He liked young women, and counted himself lucky to live in a city populated with so many highly delectable examples of that species, even if none of them ever bothered to talk to him.

"My dear," he said to Pat, touching her gently on the wrist, "you are so kind, so considerate, to listen to the conversation of an academician of my years – barely fifty, I might add."

"I'm interested in this story," said Pat. "This Moderator person sounds awful. And you had to paint him!"

"Indeed I did," said Angus Lordie. "But, do you know, as I began the task it seemed to me as if I had become possessed. It was almost as if I had been taken over by an entirely foreign energy. I had absolutely no difficulty in beginning. I saw the portrait in my mind's eye, even before I began.

"I had set up a large canvas, you'll understand – I normally paint portraits on a generous scale. But now, as I looked at this tiny, crabbit man, sitting there in his clerical black suit and staring at me with a sort of threatening disapproval, I found that I sketched in a tiny portrait, three inches square, right in the middle of the big canvas. This just seemed to be the right thing to do. He was a small-minded man, in my view, and it seemed utterly appropriate to do a small portrait of him.

"We had several sittings. I didn't let him see what I was doing, you'll understand, and so he had no idea of the picture which was emerging in the middle of the canvas – a picture which set out to express all the sheer malice and narrowness of the man. I thought it was very accurate. I had boiled down his spirit and it came to a tiny half-teaspoon of brimstone."

Pat listened in fascination. She could imagine what might have happened next; the Reverend MacNichol would see the picture – which is exactly what happened, as Angus Lordie explained.

"It was during the third sitting," said Angus Lordie. "I went out of the studio to answer the telephone, and while I was out MacNichol took it upon himself to get up and have a peek at progress so far. When I came back into the studio he was standing there, purple with rage, wagging a finger at me. 'How dare you insult a man of the cloth,' he yelled at me. 'You wicked, wicked man!'

"I tried to pacify him, but he would have none of it. He fetched his hat – a black Homburg which was far too big for a tiny man like that – shoved it down over his ears, and marched out of the studio. But as he left, he turned to face me and said: 'You will be sorry, Mr Lordie! You will find out what it is to incur the wrath of the Discontinued Brethren!' Then he left, and I sat down, somewhat shocked, and considered my position.

"What had happened, I was later told, was that he had pronounced some sort of Free Presbyterian *fatwa* on me. I was shocked. What exactly will they try to do to me? Put me to the sword? Burn me out of my studio? I have absolutely no idea what the implications are, as this happened only a few days ago."

Pat was silent. Many people find it hard to know what to say to one who has just had a *fatwa* pronounced on him, and Pat was one of these. Words somehow seem inadequate in such circumstances, and any further enquiry tactless. It might help to ask: "Is it a temporary *fatwa*, or a permanent one?" But Pat just shook her head in disbelief – not at the story, of course – but at the mentality of those who would pronounce a *fatwa* on another.

Angus Lordie sighed. "Still," he said. "One must not complain. Portraiture has its risks, and I suppose a dissident Free Presbyterian *fatwa* is one of them. Not that one would expect to encounter such a thing every day . . . But, to more cheerful subjects. Would you like to visit my studio some time? I'm just round the corner from Scotland Street, on the same side of the square as Sydney used to be – Sydney Goodsir Smith, of course. And Nigel McIsaac too. Nigel was a very fine artist – lovely, light-filled pictures – and I still see Mary McIsaac in the square from time to time."

He looked over towards the other side of the room where a young man was circulating with a bottle of wine, refreshing glasses. "I'm so bad at catching the eyes of young men at parties," he said airily. "Such a limitation! Perhaps you could do it for me?"

Pat looked across the room and immediately attracted the attention of the waiter, who came over to them and refilled Angus

Lordie's glass. Pat, who was generally abstemious, asked for only half a glass.

Angus Lordie looked again at Pat. His gaze was intense, Pat felt, and it was almost as if he were appraising her. But she did not feel threatened in any way – why? Because he was an artist looking at a potential subject, rather than a middle-aged roué looking at a girl?

"Yes," he said, resuming the interrupted conversation. "Sydney was one of the lights of this city, one of our great makars. Would it be rude of me to say that I assume that you've not read any of his work? No? Well, there's a treat for you. He was a great man – a great man. He loved his drink, you know, as all our poets have done. If the Scottish Arts Council had any imagination, it would have a system of whisky grants for poets, rather like the Civil List pension that Grieve got. Each poet would receive a couple of bottles a month – once they had produced a decent work between covers. What a gesture that would be!

"Sydney sometimes had these sessions that would last all night and into the morning. Conversation. Friendship. Wonderful ideas bouncing about. Beautiful invented words. And, do you know, he had this terribly funny toast that he would give from time to time. He'd raise his glass and say: '*Death to the French!*' Wonderfully funny."

Pat frowned. "But why would he say that?"

Angus Lordie looked at her in astonishment. "But, my dear, he didn't mean it! Good heavens! Do you think any of us here –" and with a gesture he embraced the entire room and the northern part of the city from Queen Street onwards – "do you think any of us here actually mean anything we say? My dear!"

"I do," said Pat.

"You mean everything you say?" Angus Lordie exclaimed. "My dear, how innocent you are!" He paused. Then: "Would you mind posing for me – in my studio? Would you mind?"

74. *A Man's Dressing Gown*

Domenica and Pat left the reception at the Scottish National Portrait Gallery shortly before nine. Pat was hungry but she nevertheless turned down Domenica's invitation to join her in her flat for a mushroom omelette. She liked her neighbour, and enjoyed her company, but she knew that if she accepted then she would not get to bed before eleven at least, as Domenica liked to talk. Her conversation ranged widely and it was entertaining enough, but Pat felt emotionally exhausted and she wanted nothing more than to take to her bed with a sandwich, a glass of milk, and a telephone. She had not spoken to her father for some time and she felt that a chat with him would help, as it always did.

She said goodbye to Domenica on the landing.

"I hope you're feeling better," said the older woman. "And remember what I said. Whatever you do, don't let him upset you. Just don't."

Pat smiled at her. "I won't," she assured her. "I promise you."

"Good," said Domenica, and leaned forward and planted a kiss on Pat's cheek. Her lips felt dry against her skin and there was a faint odour of expensive perfume. For a moment Pat stood still; she had not expected this intimacy – if it was an intimacy. Everybody kissed one another these days; kisses meant nothing.

Then the moment of uncertainty passed, and she thanked Domenica for the evening. "You've been so kind to me," she said.

"I haven't," said Domenica, turning her key in the door. "I've been a neighbour, that's all. And you're a sweet girl."

Domenica's door closed behind her and Pat went into her own flat. The hall was in darkness as she entered and she reached to switch on a light. Then she stopped; light was emanating from under Bruce's door. So he's back, she thought. He can't have had much of an evening.

The thought pleased her. She wanted him to be there – as in a sense that meant that he was with her. And that was what she wanted; she wanted it against all the promptings of the rational part of her being.

She stood still for a moment, in the darkness of the hall, debating with herself what to do. She and Bruce had parted on awkward terms that evening. She had been angered by his failure to apologise for giving away her painting, and she had stormed out of the kitchen. Now she felt that she wanted to make it up with him; she should tell him that she was not holding it against him and that all she wanted was for him to give her the telephone number of the people who had won the picture. Getting it back from them might not be easy, and Bruce's support might be needed in that, but in the meantime she could do all that was necessary.

She decided to knock on his door and speak to him. Perhaps he would suggest that they have coffee together or that . . . What do I really want? she asked herself.

She now stood before his door and knocked gently. There was silence inside, and then, hesitantly, Bruce's voice called out. "Pat?"

There was something in the tone, in the way he answered, that made her realise immediately that he was not alone in the room. And the realisation filled her with embarrassment, that she had disturbed them, and with intense, searing jealousy.

Horrified, she moved away from Bruce's door and ran over the hall to her own room, slamming the door behind her. She thought she heard Bruce's door open, but she was not sure, and she wanted to shut out all sound from that quarter. She threw herself down on the bed, her hands over her eyes.

She lay there for over half an hour, doing nothing, her eyes closed. She felt as if she was paralysed by misery, and that even the effort of lifting the telephone and keying in her parents' number would be too much. But somehow she managed that, and heard her father answer at the other end.

"Are you all right?"

She took a moment to answer; then, "Yes. I'm all right. I suppose."

"You don't sound very convinced."

She made an effort to sound more cheerful. "I've lost something at work – something that was entrusted to me."

"Tell him," said her father simply. He had the ability to

diagnose problems even before they were explained. "Tell your boss about it. Own up."

"I was going to do that," she said. "But that doesn't make it any easier."

Her father paused before answering. "There is nothing – and I mean nothing – that doesn't look less serious if confessed, or shared. Try it. Tell your boss tomorrow what has happened. Tell the truth, and you'll see how the world carries on. Just try it."

She spoke to her father for a few minutes longer before ringing off. She felt slightly better just for having spoken to him, and now she got off the bed and walked towards the door. She did not want to go out of her room but she would have to cross the hall to get to the bathroom. She could not bear the thought of seeing Bruce – not just now – but she thought that he would be unlikely to come out.

She crossed the hall to the bathroom. The light still showed under Bruce's door – *At least they aren't in there together in the dark*, she thought – but no sound came from the room. *And what does that mean?* she asked herself.

Inside the bathroom, she stood in front of the mirror and brushed her teeth. Then she washed her face, splashing it with cold water afterwards.

"Hallo."

She spun round. A tall young woman, with streaky blonde hair, was standing in the door. She was wearing Bruce's dressing gown and her hair was dishevelled.

Pat stared at the young woman.

"What do you want?" she asked. She did not intend to sound as brutally rude, but that was how the question emerged.

The other girl was taken aback, but recovered quickly. "Nothing," she said. "At least, nothing from you."

She turned on her heel and disappeared and Pat stared into the mirror. At least she had seen her face, and this would enable her to answer the question which every jealous person wishes to have answered. *Is she/he more attractive than I am?*

And the answer in this case, she thought, was yes. And there was

208

something else – another respect in which she was outclassed; another respect in which she could not compete. She could never wear a man's dressing gown like that, with such complete shamelessness.

75. News of a Loss

There was every temptation to put off the moment when she would confess to Matthew that the Peploe? was no longer in her possession, but Pat resisted this firmly and successfully. When Matthew came into the gallery the following morning – twenty minutes after Pat had arrived – he barely had time to hang up his coat before she made her confession.

Matthew listened carefully. He did not interrupt her, nor did his expression reveal any emotion. When Pat had finished, she looked down at the ground, almost afraid to look back up at him, but then she did and she saw that the anger she had expected simply was not there.

"It's not your fault," Matthew said evenly. "You couldn't have imagined that he would do such an inconsiderate thing." He paused, and shook his head in puzzlement. "Why on earth did he assume that the painting belonged to nobody? Somebody had to have put it there."

"He assumes a lot," said Pat. "He's a little on the arrogant side." As she spoke, she wondered where Bruce would be now, and what he would be doing. She had never wondered that before, but now she did.

"I think I've met him," said Matthew. "He goes to the Cumberland, doesn't he? Tall, with hair like this . . ."

Pat nodded. Bruce was tall, and his hair did go like that; and why should it make her catch her breath just to think of him?

Matthew sat down at his desk and looked at Pat. "We'll get it back," he said. "As you've just said, it still belongs to us, doesn't it?"

"That's what my neighbour pointed out," said Pat. "I hope she's right."

"I'm sure she's right," said Matthew. "So all we need to do is to find out who these people are – the people who won it – and ask them to give it back."

Pat waited for Matthew to say something more, to censure her, perhaps, but he did not. Instead he spoke about some paintings which somebody had brought in for sale the previous day and which they were planning to take a look at that morning. Neither of them thought that there would be anything worth very much, but they were looking forward to spending a few hours searching for the names of artists in the books and relating them, if possible, to the paintings before them. Some names, of course, would simply not occur; would have faded into complete obscurity.

"Why do people insist on painting?" asked Matthew as they stared at a late nineteenth-century study of an Arab dhow.

"It's their response to the world," muttered Pat, peering at the signature below the dhow. "People try to capture something of what they see. It's like taking a photograph. Why do people take photographs?"

Matthew had an immediate answer. "Because they can't look at what's before them and think about it for more than two seconds. It's a sign of distraction. They see, photograph, and move on. They don't really look."

Pat looked at him, and noticed the way that the hairs lay flat against the skin of his wrist, and the way that one of his eyebrows was slightly shorter than the other, as if it had been shaved off. And she noticed, too, his eyes, which she had never really looked at before, and the way the irises were flecked with grey. And Matthew, for his part, suddenly noticed that Pat had small ears, and that one of them had two piercings. For a few moments neither spoke, as each felt sympathy for the other, as the same conclusion – quite remarkably – occurred to each: here is a person, another, who is so important to himself, to herself, and so weak, and ordinary, and human as we all are.

They worked quietly together, looking carefully at the paintings, before Matthew stood up, stretched, and announced: "Nothing here. Nothing."

And Pat had to agree. "I can't imagine that we could sell any of these for more than . . . forty, fifty pounds."

"Exactly," said Matthew. "Let's say thank you, but no." He glanced at his watch. It was early for coffee, but he felt that he wanted to get out of the gallery, which suddenly seemed oppressive to him. That feeling would pass if he could get out and see his friends in Big Lou's coffee bar.

With Matthew across the road at Big Lou's, Pat picked up the telephone and dialled the office number that Bruce had given her when he had reluctantly agreed to find out how to contact the Ramsey Dunbartons. She listened anxiously as the telephone rang at the other end and when Bruce answered, with a gruff "Anderson", she almost put down the receiver. But she mastered her feelings, and asked him whether he had obtained the necessary information from Todd.

"I have," said Bruce. "And here's the number." He paused. "I don't know whether they'll be terribly pleased."

"Why not?" asked Pat. "Surely they'll understand that there's been a mistake."

"Yes," said Bruce quickly. "Your mistake."

Pat ignored this. "We'll see," she said.

Bruce laughed. "Right, we'll see. Now, is there anything else you wanted to say?"

Pat was on the verge of saying that there was not, but then, for reasons which she could not understand, and before she could stop herself, she said: "That girl – that girl, Sally – do you like her?"

There was a silence at the other end of the line, and Pat felt herself tense with embarrassment. It was a ridiculous question, which she had no right to ask, and Bruce would have been quite entitled to tell her to mind her own business. But he did not, and replied quite brightly: "What do you think?"

"Do you mean what do I think of her?" It was a question that she could have answered with a remark about how she wore his dressing gown and the flaunting that this entailed, but she said instead: "Or what do I think you feel?"

"Yes," said Bruce. "What do you think I feel?"

"You hate her," said Pat. "You can't stand her."

Bruce whistled down the line. "Very wrong, Patsy girl. Very wrong. I want to marry her."

76. Remembrance of Things Past

Neither Ronnie nor Pete had arrived at Big Lou's when Matthew came in that morning. As Matthew approached the counter, Big Lou, who had been tidying the fridge, looked up and greeted him warmly. There was nobody else in the coffee bar – indeed Matthew was the first customer that morning – and she was pleased to have somebody to talk to.

She prepared Matthew's coffee and brought it over, sitting down next to him in the booth.

"Those other two are late," she said. "Not that I mind. They never have anything interesting to say – unlike you."

"And I just have bad news today," said Matthew, rather gloomily. "My Peploe?"

"Not a Peploe?" asked Big Lou. "Somebody's looked at it?'

"It may be a Peploe," said Matthew. "But whatever it is, it's gone."

Big Lou drew in her breath. It did not take her long to work out that Pete must have heard the discussion about it going to the flat in Scotland Street, and must have stolen it from there. She was sure that he was in league with that man, the man whom he described as John, but whom he then denied knowing. Well, she for one was not fooled by that.

"I'll wring his neck when he comes in," said Big Lou. "He's your man. Pete's taken it – or he's mixed up in it."

"It's not him," said Matthew. "It's somebody from the South Edinburgh Conservative Association."

Big Lou was trying to work out the meaning of this puzzling

remark when Matthew explained about the tombola.

"That's not too bad," she said. "At least you know where it is – and you're still the owner."

Matthew nodded. Everybody seemed confident about the recovery of the painting, and perhaps they were right. It was a stroke of good fortune that it had fallen into the hands of the Conservative Party, as they would always behave with honour and integrity. He wondered what would have happened if the painting had ended up at a Scottish Socialist Party function. They would have cut it up into little squares and shared it round all those present. The thought made him smile.

"Do you think that great art only comes into existence when there is surplus wealth?" he asked Big Lou.

Big Lou frowned. "You have to have time to create art," she said. "If you're busy surviving, then art probably doesn't get much of a look in. Look at Proust."

"Proust?"

"Yes," explained Big Lou. "Marcel Proust wrote an awfully long novel. Twelve volumes, wasn't it? Or there are twelve volumes in the set I have down in Canònmills. If Proust actually had to work – to earn his living – then he would not have had the time to write *A la recherche du temps perdu*. Nor, come to think of it, would he have had any of those people to write about if they had been obliged to do any real work."

Matthew raised an eyebrow. He had never read Proust, although he knew one quote which he had been able to use from time to time. Proust, he had read, had said that steamships insult the dignity of distance, and Matthew had occasionally mentioned this to others, and had enjoyed their discomfort. He had said it to his father once, when he had been taking a close interest in one of his son's failed business ventures – the travel agency, that was – and that had stopped him in his tracks. Proust was useful that way.

"Should I read Proust, Lou?" he asked.

"Aye," she replied. "If you've got the time. I'm on volume five now, and I like it. Combray reminds me of Arbroath."

Matthew nodded. What was Proust about? He decided to ask Lou, as it was not the sort of question one could raise in the presence of Ronnie and Pete.

"A lot of things," said Big Lou. "Not much actually happens in Proust, or rather it takes a long time to happen. Marcel writes a lot about things that remind him of something else. That's what happened when he ate those little Madeleine cakes and the taste brought back to him the memory of Combray."

Matthew sipped at his coffee. Did that remind him of anything? He closed his eyes, and took another sip. Yes! Yes! He was transported back to a period of greater happiness, when he was twelve and was visiting his grandfather in Morningside. They had a house behind the Royal Edinburgh, a large house with a garden, the house now long since demolished and the garden built over with flats with ridiculous, inappropriate names like Squire's Manor (built by an English builder who had no idea that squires and manors did not exist in Scotland). But it was not the flats that he thought of, but that house, that great, rambling Victorian house with its turrets and shutters and high ceilings.

His grandfather had sat with him in the morning room, which looked out over the lawn, and which smelled of nasturtiums and coffee and damp India paper of the books that lay out there on his reading trolley. And Matthew had listened, while the old man tried to talk. He had been badly affected by a stroke, and many of his words had gone from him, but he had managed to whisper to the boy, in a painfully slow fashion, each word punctuated by long silences, *"Never trust anybody from Glasgow."*

And Matthew had looked at the old man, and smiled in disbelief, and asked why should one not trust anybody from Glasgow. His question had brought a puzzled look to his grandfather's brow, and this was followed by a further search for words.

"I can't remember," the old man had said eventually, disappointed at the loss of precious knowledge. "I can't."

And then Matthew had sipped at the coffee which his grandfather had given him – coffee which was stone cold, but strong – and which tasted just like the coffee which Big Lou now served him.

214

"I've had a Proustian moment," Matthew said, bringing himself back to reality.

"That happens all the time," said Big Lou. "We all have Proustian moments, but don't really know about it until we read Proust."

77. *Into Deep Morningside*

Pat sat at her desk in the gallery, numbed by the effect of Bruce's words. He hardly knew that girl, she thought. He had met her the day before the dressing-gown incident, which said something about the speed with which she had allowed the relationship to progress. What a tart!

And what exactly did he see in her, she wondered. She was undoubtedly attractive, but there were numerous girls just as attractive, if not more so. Bruce would only have to go into the Cumberland Bar and stand there for twenty minutes or so and he would be *mobbed*, yes mobbed, by girls who would be only too anxious to develop a closer acquaintance with him. So surely the mere factor of physical attractiveness would not be enough to make Bruce talk about marriage.

Was it something to do with her being American? Some people were impressed with that, because they felt that the Americans were somehow special, a race apart. That used to be how the British regarded themselves when they bestrode the world; perhaps it was not surprising that Americans should have a similar conceit of themselves now that they were the great imperial power – a special race, touched with greatness. And there would be people like Bruce who might share this self-evaluation and think that it would be something privileged, something special, to be associated with an American.

She thought of all this, her despair growing with each moment. I hate him, she said to herself. He's nothing to me. But then she thought of him again and she felt a physical lurch in the pit of her stomach. I want to be with him. I want him.

I'm ill, she thought. Something has happened to my mind. This is what it must be like to be affected by one of those illnesses which her psychiatrist father had told her about.

"People who are brewing a psychotic illness often have some degree of insight," he had said to her. "They know that something strange is happening to them, even if the delusions are powerful and entirely credible once they are experienced."

Perhaps this was what was happening to her; she had been overcome with a powerful delusional belief that Bruce was desirable, and even if she knew that this was a destructive belief, she still felt it – it still exercised its power over her. So may an addict feel when confronted with the substance of his addiction: well aware that the drug will harm him but unable to do anything about it. And so may an addict deprived feel when he realises that what he craves is not available to him; the emptiness, the panic that she now felt.

Matthew, when he returned, was a welcome distraction from this discomfort.

"I've telephoned Mr Dunbarton," said Pat.

Matthew looked at her with anticipation. "And?"

"He was very good about it," she said.

Ramsey Dunbarton appeared to have been pleased to receive her call, having initially assumed that she was from Party

216

Headquarters, and that she was enquiring about the success of the event.

"It was a very satisfactory evening," he had said. "Nice of you to ask. The turnout was modest, perhaps, but that didn't appear to dampen spirits. And we had some of the younger members there too. A charming fellow with . . . with hair, and that Todd girl, the one who was studying over in Glasgow but who's now back in Edinburgh.

"My wife bumped into her, actually, a few times at the Colinton tennis courts. You know the ones just off the Colinton Road, just after that Mercedes garage. No, hold on, is it a bit before? – I find that bit of Colinton Road a bit confusing. I suppose it depends on whether you're coming from the direction of town or from the other direction, you know, the road which goes up to Redford and to Merchiston Castle School.

"Funny that you should mention Merchiston. I was there, you know, a good time ago. We had a great time, although, my goodness, it was fairly Spartan in those days, I can tell you. A bit like a prison camp, but that didn't bother us boys. I see nothing wrong with communal showers, and some boys actually liked them. Why not? Things are very different now – much more comfortable, and a very good school altogether. But I hope that the boys don't go too soft.

"My godson, Charlie Maclean, went there, along with his two brothers. Charlie had a splendid time and right at the end he went to a cadet camp in Iceland. There was a bit of a row there, and the master who was in charge of the cadets, who was some sort of captain or major, got into a terrible stramash with the boys. Anyway, the long and the short of it was that there was a mutiny, led by Charlie. This master said: 'Maclean, you're expelled!' Whereupon Charlie said: 'But I've just left school anyway. You can't expel me!' Whereupon this character shouted: 'Then you're forbidden to join the Old Merchistonian Association!' What a hoot!"

It was at this point that Pat interrupted him, and explained what she was calling about. Ramsey Dunbarton listened, and then laughed.

"I would have been delighted to return it to you," he said. "Unfortunately, we've already given it away. I'm so sorry. It went down to a charity shop this morning. Betty knows the people who run it and they're always looking for things like that. But you could go and see them, no doubt, and get it back. They're the ones in Morningside Road. They're not all that far down from the Churchill Theatre. Do you know where that is? I used to take part in Gilbert and Sullivan there. *The Gondoliers*. Do you know *The Gondoliers*? I was the Duke of Plaza-Toro once. I was frightfully lucky to get the role as there was a very good baritone that year who was after it. Then I met the director outside the Edinburgh Bookshop and . . ."

78. Steps with Soul

At roughly the same time that Matthew returned to the gallery from his morning coffee, Domenica Macdonald was edging her custard-coloured Mercedes-Benz into a parking place at the foot of Scotland Street. She was observed by three pairs of eyes – those of the taxi drivers who sat in their cabs at the bottom of the street and ate their early lunch before setting off for their next call. One of the taxi drivers knew her, as he had occasionally exchanged a few words with her in the street, and he smiled as he remembered a witty remark that Domenica had so casually and cleverly made, something about pigeons and local councillors; terribly funny, as he recalled it, although he could not remember the punchline, nor indeed how the story began. What would it be like to be married to a clever woman like that, he wondered. Could he take her to the taxi-drivers' ball at the Royal Scot Hotel on the Glasgow Road? Hardly. The men talked about golf at the taxi-drivers' ball, and the women inevitably talked about the pros and cons of self-catering accommodation in Tenerife. This woman would not want to talk about things like that – he could tell.

There were those who had something to say about Tenerife, and those who did not.

Domenica brought the car to a halt and switched off the ignition. She had been for a drive around Holyrood Park – exercise for the car, as she called it – and had been thinking as she drove. What, she had been wondering, would Edinburgh be like if it were not so beautiful? If Edinburgh looked, for instance – well, one had to say it, like *Glasgow*? Would it be inhabited by the people who currently lived there – that is, by people of taste (there was no other expression for it – it just had to be said) – or would it be inhabited by the sort of people who lived in Glasgow – that is by people who . . . ? She stopped herself. No, this was not the sort of thought that one should allow oneself. Those sorts of attitudes – of condescension towards Glasgow – were decidedly dated. When she was younger it had been perfectly acceptable for people to think that way about Glasgow – to turn up their metaphorical noses at it – but now it seemed that nobody thought like that any more. Edinburgh was different from Glasgow, it was true, but it was no longer considered *helpful* to remark on the differences to any great extent, even if here and there were to be heard faint echoes, very faint, of the old attitudes. Her aunt, for example, who was Edinburgh through-and-through, had even possessed a map which she had drawn as a schoolgirl in which Glasgow simply did not feature. It was not there. Dundee was marked, as was Aberdeen, but where Glasgow was there was simply a void. And the map had been marked by the geography teacher, who had placed a large red tick on the side, and had written underneath: *A very fine map indeed. Well done.*

Why, she asked herself, was Edinburgh so beautiful? The question had come to her as she rounded the corner on the high road, round the crumbling volcanic side of Arthur's Seat, and saw the Old Town spread out beneath her – the dome of the Old College with its torch-carrying Golden Boy; the domestic jumble of Old Town roofs, the spires of the various spiky kirks – such beauty, illuminated at that very moment by shafts of light from breaks in the cloud. This was beauty of the order encountered in Siena or

Florence, beauty that caused a soaring of the spirit, a gasp of the soul.

It was a privilege to be a citizen of such a place, thought Domenica. The beauty of the New Town had been created by those who believed in the physical embodiment, in stone and glass and slate, of order, of reason, and this had found expression in architectural regularity. And yet surely it was more than a matter of mere proportion; for the regular features of the male film star, the broad forehead, the neatly-nicked chin, the equal eyebrows, are actually rather repulsive – or so at least Domenica thought. Those regularly-featured Hollywood males made her feel slightly nauseous; and the same could be said for their female equivalents, hardly intellectuals they. These people had regular features but were actually *ugly* because they tended to be so completely vacuous. Regularity without some metaphysical value behind it, some beauty of soul or character, was more disappointing – and indeed repulsive – than the honestly haphazard, the humanly messy. It was more disappointing because it promised something that was not there: it should engage the soul, but did not. It was shallow and meretricious. So Mother Teresa of Calcutta, with her weepy eyes and her lined face, was infinitely more beautiful than . . . ? Than the current icons of feminine beauty? Than that woman who called herself Madonna (whoever she was)? Of course Mother Teresa was more beautiful – infinitely so. Only a culture with a thoroughly upside-down sense of values could think otherwise. And that, mused Domenica ruefully, is precisely the sort of culture we have become.

Now that girl, Pat, her new neighbour whom she was getting to know rather better; she had harmonious features, a reasonably pretty face one might say, but was far more beautiful than girls who might appear to be more attractive. That was because Pat had character, had a depth of moral personality that ostensibly more glamorous girls almost always lacked. And Bruce? Domenica herself had described him as beautiful in her recent conversation with Pat, but was that strictly true? Did Bruce have anything of substance behind his Greek-god features? That was difficult to say. He was not vacuous; he was irritating. So at least there was something there.

Domenica stepped out of her car and began to make her way along the pavement to the door of No. 44. The subject of beauty would be shelved for the time being, she decided, as she now had to think about lunch. There was some mozzarella in the fridge, and that would go rather nicely with tomatoes. But did she have any basil? Probably not, but then basil was not essential. There were some who lived entirely without basil, she reflected; some who had never heard of it; and smiled at the thought, absurd though it was, like a line from the pen of Barbara Pym.

She opened the front door and began to climb up the stone steps. They were well-trodden steps, and the stone had been worn away in the middle so that the treads were uneven. This did not matter, of course, because these steps, although irregular, were still beautiful. And why were they beautiful? Because they had character. Steps with soul. Barbara Pym again. She would have to be careful.

79. A Meeting on the Stair

On her way up the stairs, Domenica found herself directly outside Stuart and Irene's flat when the door was opened by Irene, who was on the point of leaving the flat with Bertie. Both women were taken aback, although there was no real reason for surprise. Doors opened onto the stair, which people used regularly, and it was inevitable that these doors should sometimes be opened at precisely the time that others were passing by. But for some reason it seemed to happen rather rarely, and Domenica was now offered a glimpse into a flat which she had never before seen. Irene had never invited her in because she disliked her, and she had similarly omitted to include Irene and her husband in any of her sherry parties. What contact there had been between them had been in the street outside, or sometimes at the bottom of the stair – brief, civil exchanges, but concealing only-guessed-at depths of mutual antipathy.

For a moment both women stood there in silence, mouths slightly open, Irene just inside the flat, with Bertie at her side, and Domenica directly outside, one foot on the coir doormat which resided just outside the door.

Domenica broke the silence. "Well," she said, "it's certainly a good morning to be going out. I've just been round Holyrood Park and the city looked gorgeous." As she spoke she took the opportunity to glance beyond Irene and Bertie into the flat. She noticed a bowl of papyrus grass on a hall table – curious, she thought – and a large framed poster of a Léger painting on the wall behind. Even more curious. Why Léger?

Her composure recovered, Irene noticed Domenica's glance and shifted slightly to obscure her view. What a cheek, she thought. It was typical of this woman's arrogance, that she should imagine that she had the right to stare into her hallway. And what would she be doing? Making a socio-economic judgment, probably, which is what these Edinburgh-types simply couldn't resist doing. And how dare she go on about her car, her gross, flashy, fuel-guzzling piece of German machinery!

"I take it you walked," said Irene quickly. "One wouldn't *drive* in Holyrood Park these days, would one?"

This was an opening salvo, but from such opening shots might spring a full-scale war. "Oh no," Domenica said airily. "I drove. In my Mercedes. It was lovely. You've seen my nice big car, Bertie? The custard-coloured one? Would you like a ride in it one day?"

Bertie's eyes lit up. "Oh yes please, Mrs Macdonald," he said.

This brought a sharp intake of breath from Irene. "I'm sorry Bertie," she said. "We can't go for a ride in any and every car." She lowered her voice to a whisper, but one still quite audible to Domenica. "And, anyway, she's not Mrs Macdonald. She's *Miss* Macdonald."

Domenica smiled, even if somewhat icily. "Actually, it's perfectly all right for Bertie to call me Mrs Macdonald. I don't mind in the slightest. I was married, you know, some time ago. Strictly speaking, though, I should be called Mrs Varghese. I went back to my maiden name, although I am not, if I may make this clear, a maiden."

Irene affected polite interest. "Mrs Varghese? What an exotic name!"

"Yes," said Domenica. "Perhaps I should use it again. You won't know India, of course, but it comes from the South, from Kerala." She turned to Bertie. "And why aren't we in nursery school today, Bertie? Is it a holiday?"

"I'm suspended," said Bertie. "I'm not allowed to go back."

Domenica raised an eyebrow. She looked at Irene, who was frowning down on Bertie and about to say something. "Suspended?" said Domenica quickly, before Irene had the time to speak. This was delicious. Dear little Mozartino suspended! "For doing something naughty?"

"Yes," said Bertie. "I wrote on the walls."

"Oh dear," said Domenica. "I'm sorry to hear that. But I'm sure that you're sorry for what you did."

Irene, who now looked agitated, was again about to say something, but Bertie spoke before she had the chance to start. "And now I'm going to psychotherapy. That's where we're going right now. We're going to see Dr Fairbairn again. He makes me talk about my dreams. He asks me all sorts of questions."

"Therapy!" exclaimed Domenica.

"That's enough, Bertie," snapped Irene. Then, turning to Domenica, she said: "It's nothing really. There was a bit of difficulty with a rather limited teacher at the nursery school. Unimaginative really. And now we're giving Bertie a bit of self-enhancement time."

"Psychotherapy," said Bertie, gazing down at the floor. "I set fire to Daddy's *Guardian*." He paused, and looked up at Domenica. "While he was reading it."

"*The Guardian*!" exclaimed Domenica. "How many times have I wanted to do that myself! Do you think I need psychotherapy too?"

"We really must get on," said Irene, pushing Bertie through the door. "You must excuse us, Domenica. We have to walk to Bertie's appointment." She paused, before adding pointedly: "We don't use our car in town, you see."

"I think our car's been lost," said Bertie. "Daddy parked it somewhere when he was drunk and forgot where he put it."

"Bertie!" said Irene, reaching out to seize his arm. "You must not say things like that! You naughty, naughty boy!" She turned to face Domenica. "I'm sorry. He's confabulating. I don't know what's got into him. Stuart would never drive under the influence. Bertie's imagining things."

"Well, where is it then?" asked Bertie. "Where's our car, Mummy? You tell me where it is."

Domenica looked at Irene politely, as if waiting for an answer.

"Our car is parked," said Irene. "It is parked in a safe place somewhere. We do not need to use it very much as we happen to have a sense of responsibility towards the environment. Some people . . . some people may choose to act otherwise, but we do not. That's all there is to it."

"Of course if you have lost it," said Domenica, "it'll probably be down in the car pound. That's where they take irresponsible cars."

"Our car is not irresponsible," said Irene. "It is a small car."

"Easy to lose, I suppose," said Domenica.

"It is not lost!" said Irene, chiselling out each word. "Now come, Bertie, we mustn't keep Dr Fairbairn waiting."

"I don't care," said Bertie, as he was hustled past Domenica, but still within her hearing. "You're the one who wants to see him, Mummy. You're the one who likes to sit and talk to him. I can tell. You really like him, don't you? You like him more than Daddy. Is that right, Mummy? Is that what you think?"

80. Male Uncertainty, Existential Doubts, New Men etc.

Matthew called the taxi while Pat wrote out a notice saying that the gallery would be closed for an hour.

"It won't take us much longer than that," said Matthew. "We'll nip up to Morningside Road, buy the painting back, and be back down here in no time."

"Buy it?" asked Pat. "Isn't it still ours?"

Matthew gazed up at the ceiling. "It may be ours technically. But it may be simpler just to pay whatever they're asking. It can't be very much."

Pat was doubtful. It might not be as simple as Matthew imagined. She had heard that charity shops were more astute than one might think, and the days when one might find a bargain, an misidentified antique or a rare first edition, were over. "Sometimes these places send anything interesting off for valuation," she pointed out. "They do that with books, for example. Anything that looks as if it might be worth something is looked at – just in case. First editions, you see. Some of these first editions can be pretty valuable, and these charity shop people know it."

Matthew smiled. "Not these Morningside ladies," he said. "That place will be staffed by Morningside ladies. You'll see. They won't know the first thing about art."

Like you, thought Pat, but did not say it. And she was not so sure about Morningside ladies, who tended, in her experience, to be rather sharper than people might give them credit for. Peploe was exactly the sort of painter of whom such ladies might be expected to have heard – Peploe and Cadell. These ladies might not like Hockney – "He paints some *very* unsuitable subjects," they might say – but they would like Peploe: "Such nice hills. And those lovely rich tones of the flowers. So very red." – and Cadell: "Such lovely hats they wore then! Just look at those feathers!"

Faced with a Peploe? it was perfectly possible that they might have set the painting aside for valuation, and if they had done that it would be impossible to get it back from them. They would have to contact a lawyer, perhaps, and take the matter to court. That would take a long time and she wondered whether Matthew would have the stomach for it. Even if he did, then at the end of the day if the painting turned out not to be a Peploe, they would have wasted a lot of time and money on something quite valueless. Not that Matthew had much to do with his time, of course. His day, as far as she could make out, consisted of drinking coffee, reading the newspaper, and doing one or two tiny little tasks that could easily be fitted into ten minutes if he really exerted himself.

What was it like to be Matthew? This rather interested Pat, who often wondered what it would be like to be somebody else, even if she was not entirely sure what it was like to be herself. That, of course, is something that one is not sure about at twenty, largely because one is not yet sure who one is. Being Matthew must be, well, it must be rather dull. He did not appear to believe in anything with any degree of passion; he did not appear to have any real ambitions; there was no sense of disappointment or loss – it was all rather *even*.

Matthew did not seem to have a particular girlfriend either. His evenings, as far as she could ascertain, were spent with a group of friends that she once glimpsed in the Cumberland Bar. There were two young women – slightly older than Pat – and three young men. Matthew called them "the crowd" and they seemed to do everything together. The crowd went to dinner; it went to see the occasional film; it sometimes went to a party in Glasgow over the weekend ("One of the crowd comes from Glasgow," Matthew had explained). And that, as far as Pat could work out, was Matthew's life.

The taxi arrived and they set off for Morningside Road.

"Holy Corner," said Matthew, as they traversed the famous crossroads with its four churches.

"Yes," said Pat. "Holy Corner." She did not add anything, as it was difficult to see what else one could say.

Then they passed the Churchhill Theatre, scene of Ramsey Dunbarton's triumph all those years ago as the Duke of Plaza-Toro in *The Gondoliers*.

"The Churchhill Theatre," observed Matthew.

Pat did not say anything. There was no point in contradicting the obvious, and equally little point in confirming it. Of course if one did not *know* that this was the Churchhill Theatre, one might express surprise, or interest. But Pat knew.

The taxi crested the hill, and there, dropping down below them, was Morningside Road. At the end of the road, beyond the well-set houses, the Pentland Hills could be seen, half wreathed in low cloud. It was a reminder that the city had a hinterland – a land-scape of soft hills and fertile fields, of old mining villages, of lochs and burns. She looked away, and saw Matthew staring down at his hands. It occurred to her then that he was nervous.

"You mustn't worry," she said. "We'll get your painting back."

He looked at her, and smiled weakly. "I'm such a failure," he said. "I really am. Everything I touch goes wrong. And now there's this. The one painting of any interest in the gallery, and it ends up in a charity shop in Morningside! I'm just thinking what my old man would say. He'd split his sides laughing."

Pat reached out and took his hand. "You're not a failure," she said. "You're kind, you're considerate, you're . . . ."

The taxi driver was watching. He had heard what Matthew had said and now he witnessed Pat's attempt to comfort him. This was not unusual, in his experience. Men were in a mess these days – virtually all of them. Women had destabilised them; made them uncertain about themselves; undermined their confidence. And then, when the men fell to pieces, the women tried to put them together again. But it was too late. The damage was done.

The taxi driver sighed. None of this applied to him. He went to his golf club two or three times a week. He was safe there. No women there; a refuge. I am certainly not a new man, he thought – unlike that wimp in the back there. Good God! Look at him! What a wimp!

81. Morningside Ladies

"See," whispered Matthew as they stood outside the charity shop. "There they are. Morningside ladies."

Pat peered in through the large plate-glass window. There were three ladies in the shop – one standing behind the counter, one adjusting a rack of clothing and one stacking a pile of books on a shelf.

She glanced at the contents of the window. A wally dug, deprived of its mirror-image partner, and lonely; an Indian brass candlestick in the shape of a rearing cobra; several pieces of mock-Wemyss chinaware; an *Oor Wullie* annual for 1972; and then a painting, but not the Peploe?. Yet the subject of this painting was uncannily similar to that of the painting they sought – a view of a shore and hills behind it. Pat nudged Matthew, who was peering through the window into the depths of the shop.

"Look at that." She pointed to the painting.

"Not ours," said Matthew gloomily.

"I know, but it looks so like it," said Pat.

"Everybody paints Mull from Iona," said Matthew. "There are hundreds of those paintings. Virtually every house in Edinburgh has one."

"And in Mull?" asked Pat.

"They have pictures of Edinburgh," replied Matthew. "It's rather touching."

They stood for a few moments more outside the shop before Matthew indicated that they should go in. As he pushed open the door, a bell rang in the back of the shop and the three women turned round and looked at them. The woman who had been stacking the books abandoned her task and came over to them.

"Are you looking for anything in particular?" she asked pleasantly. "We've just received a new consignment of clothing and there are some rather nice things in it. We could let you have first look if you like."

Pat glanced at the clothes on the rack. *Who could possibly wear that?* she thought as her eye was caught by a brown suede fringed jacket. And Matthew, looking in the same direction, noticed a loud red tie and shuddered involuntarily.

The woman intercepted their glances. "Of course they're not to everybody's taste," she said quickly. "But students and people like that often find something they like."

Pat was quick to reassure her. "Of course they will," she said. "I have a friend who gets all her clothes from shops like these. She swears by them."

The woman nodded. "And it all goes to a good cause. Every penny we make in this shop is put to good use."

Matthew cleared his throat. "We're looking for a painting," he began. "We wondered . . ."

"Oh we have several paintings at the moment," said the woman keenly. "We can certainly find you a painting."

"Actually, it's a very specific painting," said Matthew. "You see, it's a rather complicated story. A painting that belongs to me was inadvertently given to the South Edinburgh Conservative Association. Then unfortunately . . ."

The woman frowned. "But how can one give a painting to the Conservatives inadvertently?" she interrupted. "Surely one either knows that one is giving a painting to the Conservatives, or one doesn't."

Matthew laughed. "Of course. But you see in this case the painting was given by somebody who had no right to give it. He effectively stole the painting – stole it inadvertently, that is."

The woman pursed her lips. She cast a glance at Pat, as if to seek confirmation from her that there was something strange about the young man with whom she had entered the shop.

Pat responded to the cue. "What my friend means to say is that somebody took the painting, thinking it belonged to nobody, and gave it as a prize at the Conservative Ball at the Braid Hills Hotel."

The mention of the Braid Hills Hotel seemed to reassure the woman. This was a familiar landmark in the world map of Morningside ladies; like a shibboleth uttered at the beginning of some obscure social test, the name of the Braid Hills Hotel signalled respectability, shared ground.

"The Braid Hills Hotel?" the woman repeated. "I see. Well, that's quite all right. But how do we come into it?"

Pat explained about the prize and the conversation that she had had with Ramsey Dunbarton. At the mention of this name, the woman smiled. Now all was clear.

"Of course," she exclaimed. "Ramsey himself came in this morning. Such a nice man! He was once the Duke of Plaza-Toro, you know, in *The Gondoliers*. And . . ."

"And?" prompted Matthew.

"And he was in several other musicals. For quite some time . . ."

Pat stopped her. "Did he bring in a painting?"

The woman smiled. "Yes he did and . . ." she paused, looking hesitantly at Matthew. "And we sold it almost immediately. I put it in the window and a few minutes later somebody came in and bought it. I served him myself. He came right in and said: "That painting in the window – how much is it?" So I told him and he paid straightaway and took the painting off. I'm terribly sorry about that – I really am. I had no reason to know, you see, that it was your painting. I assumed that Ramsey Dunbarton had every right to have it sold. But of course *nemo dat quod non habet*. Perhaps if you speak to him about it, perhaps . . ."

Pat glanced at Matthew, who had groaned quietly. "You wouldn't know who bought it, would you?" It was unlikely, of course, but she could ask. The purchaser might have written a cheque, and they could get the name from that. Or he might have said something which would enable them to identify him. It was just possible.

The woman frowned. "I don't actually know him," she said. "But I had a feeling that I knew him, if you know what I mean. I'd seen him somewhere before."

"In the shop?" asked Pat. "Would anybody else here know who he was?"

The woman turned to her colleague, who was standing at the cash desk, adding a column of figures.

"Priscilla? That painting we sold this morning to that rather good-looking man. The one who hadn't quite shaved yet. You know the one."

Priscilla looked up from her task. She was a woman in late middle-age, wearing a tweedy jacket and a double string of pearls. There was an air of vagueness about her, an air of being slightly lost. When she spoke, the vowels were pure Morningside, flattened so that *I* became *ayh*, *my* became *may*.

"Oh my!" said Priscilla. "The name's on the tip of my tongue! That nice man who writes about Mr Rebus. That one. But what is his name? My memory is like a sieve these days!"

Matthew gave a start. "Ian Rankin?" he said.

"That's his name," said Priscilla. "I don't read his books personally – they're a bit *noir* for me – but I suppose those stronger than I read them. Still, *de gustibus non disputandum est*, as one must remind oneself, and believe me, I do! How could one possibly survive these days without repeating that particular adage all the time? You tell me – you just tell me!"

82. On the Way to Mr Rankin's

Ian Rankin! This revelation took Matthew and Pat by surprise, but at least they now knew where the painting had gone and whom they would have to approach in order to get it back. Once the name had been established, the third woman in the shop was able to tell them where Ian Rankin lived – not far away – and they prepared to leave. But Pat hesitated.

"That painting," she enquired, pointing at the window display. "Would you mind if I looked at it?"

Priscilla went forward to extract the painting from its position in the window and passed it to Pat. "It's been there for rather a long time," she said, fingering her pearl necklace as she spoke. "It was brought in with a whole lot of things from a house in Craiglea Drive. Somebody cleared out their attic and brought the stuff in to us. I rather like it, don't you? That must be Mull, mustn't it? Or is it Iona? It's so hard to tell."

Pat held the painting out in front of her and gazed at it. It was in a rather ornate gilded frame, although this was chipped in several places and had a large chunk of wood missing from the bottom right-hand corner. The colours were strong, and there was something decisive and rather skilful about the composition. She looked for a signature – there was nothing – and there was nothing, too, on the back of the frame.

"How much are you asking for this?"

Priscilla smiled at her. "Not very much. Ten pounds? Would that be about right? Could you manage that? We could maybe make it a tiny bit cheaper, but not much."

Pat reached into the pocket of her jeans and extracted a twenty pound note, which she handed over to Priscilla.

"Oh!" said the older woman. "Twenty pounds. Will we be able to change twenty pounds? I don't know. What's in the float, Dotty?"

"It doesn't matter about the change," said Pat quickly. "Treat it as a donation."

"Bless you, you kind girl," said Priscilla, beaming with approbation. "Here, let me wrap it up for you. And think what pleasure you'll have in looking at that. Will you hang it in your bedroom?" She paused, and glanced at Matthew. Were they . . . ? One never knew these days.

They took the wrapped-up painting and left the shop.

"What on earth possessed you to buy that?" Matthew asked, as they left. "That's the sort of thing we throw out all the time. One wants to get rid of things like that, not buy them."

Pat said nothing. She was satisfied with her purchase, and could imagine where she would hang it in her room in the flat. There was something peaceful about the painting – something resolved – which strongly appealed to her. It may be another amateur daubing, but it was comfortable, and quiet, and she liked it.

They crossed the road at Churchill and made their way by a back route towards the address they had been given.

"What are we going to say to him?" asked Matthew. "And what do you think he'll say to us?"

"We'll tell him exactly what happened," said Pat. "Just as we told those people. And then we'll ask him if he'll give it back to us."

"And he'll say no," said Matthew despondently. "The reason why he bought it in the first place is that he must have realised that it's a Peploe?. Somebody like him wouldn't just pop into a charity shop and buy any old painting. He's way too cool for that."

"But why do you think he knows anything about art?" asked Pat. "Isn't music more his thing? Doesn't he go on about hi-fi and rock music?"

Matthew shrugged. "I don't know. It's just that I've got that bad feeling again. This whole thing keeps giving me bad feelings. Maybe we should just forget about it."

"You can't," said Pat. "That's forty thousand pounds worth of painting. Or it could be. Can you afford to turn up your nose at forty thousand pounds?"

"Yes," said Matthew. "I don't actually have to make a profit in the gallery, you know. I've never had to make a profit in my life. My old man's loaded."

Pat was silent as she thought about this. She had been aware that Matthew did not have to operate according to the laws of real economics, but he had never been this frank about it.

Matthew stopped walking and fixed Pat with a stare. Again she noticed the flecks in his eyes.

"Are you surprised by that?" he said. "Do you think the less of me because I've got money?"

Pat shook her head. "No, why should I? Plenty of people have money in this town. It's neither here nor there. Money just is."

Matthew laughed. "No, it isn't. Money changes everything. I know what people think about me. I know they think I'm useless and I would never have got anywhere, anywhere at all, if it weren't for the fact that my father can buy me a job. That's what he's done, you know. He's bought me every job I've had. I've never got a job, not one single job, on merit. How's that for failure?"

Pat reached out to touch him on the shoulder, but he recoiled, and looked down. She felt acutely uncomfortable. Self-pity, as her father had explained to her, is the most unattractive of states, and it was true.

"All right," she said. "You're a failure. If that's the way you feel about yourself." She paused. Her candour had made him look up in surprise. Had her words hurt him? She thought that perhaps they had, but that might do some good.

They began to walk again, turning down a narrow street that would bring them out onto Colinton Road. A cat ran ahead of them, having appeared from beneath a parked car, and then shot off into a garden.

"Tell me something," said Matthew. "Are you in love with that boy you share with? That Bruce? Are you in love with him?"

Pat made an effort to conceal her surprise. "Why do you ask?" she said, her voice neutral. It had nothing to do with him, and she did not need to answer the question.

"Because if you aren't in love with him, then I wondered if . . ."

Matthew stopped. They had reached the edge of Colinton Road and his voice was drowned by the sound of a passing car.

Pat thought quickly. "Yes," she said. "I'm in love with him."

It was a truthful answer, and, in the circumstances, an expedient one too.

83. But of Course

He was sitting in a whirlpool tub in the walled garden, wisps of steam rising from the water around him. A paperback book was perched on the edge of the tub, a red bookmark protruding from its middle.

"I find this a good place to think," he said. "And you feel great afterwards."

Matthew smiled nervously. "I hope you don't mind us disturbing you like this," he said. "We could come back later if you like."

Ian Rankin shook his head. "Doesn't matter. This is fine. As long as you don't mind me staying in here."

There was a silence for a few moments. Then Pat spoke. "You bought a painting this morning."

A look of surprise came over Ian Rankin's face. "So I did." He paused. "Now, let me guess. Let me guess. You've heard all about it and you want to buy it off me? You're dealers, right?"

"Well we are," said Matthew. "In a way. But . . ."

Ian Rankin splashed idly at the water with an outstretched hand. "It's not for sale, I'm afraid. I rather like it. Sorry."

Matthew exchanged a despondent glance with Pat. It was just

as he had imagined. Ian Rankin had recognised the painting for what it was and was holding on to his bargain. And who could blame him for that?

Pat took a step forward and leaned over the edge of the tub. "Mr Rankin, there's a story behind the painting. It's my fault that it ended up in that shop. I was looking after it and my flatmate took it by mistake and gave it as a raffle prize and then . . ."

Ian Rankin stopped her. "So it's still yours?"

"Mine," said Matthew. "I have a gallery. She was looking after it for me."

"What's so special about it?" Ian Rankin asked. "Is it by somebody well-known?"

Matthew looked at Pat. For a moment she thought he was going to say something, but he did not. So the decision is mine, she thought. Do I have to tell him what I think, or can I remain silent? She closed her eyes; the sound of the whirlpool was quite loud now, and there was a seagull mewing somewhere. A child shouted out somewhere in a neighbouring garden. And for a moment, inconsequentially, surprisingly, she thought of Bruce. He was smiling at her, enjoying her discomfort. *Lie*, he said. *Don't be a fool. Lie*.

"I think that it may be by Samuel Peploe," she said. "It looks very like his work. We haven't taken a proper opinion yet, but that's what we think."

The corner of Matthew's mouth turned down. She's just destroyed our chances of getting it back, he thought. That's it.

Ian Rankin raised an eyebrow. "Peploe?"

"Yes," said Pat.

"In which case," said Ian Rankin, "it's worth a bob or two. What would you say? It's quite small, and so . . . forty thousand? If it were bigger, then . . . eighty?"

"Exactly," said Pat.

Ian Rankin looked at Matthew. "Would you agree with that?"

"I would," said Matthew, adding glumly, "Not that I know much about it."

"But you're the dealer?"

"Yes," said Matthew. "But there are dealers and dealers. I'm one of the latter."

"I'm just going to have to think about this for a moment," said Ian Rankin. "Give me a moment."

And with that he took a deep breath and disappeared under the surface of the water. There were bubbles all about his head and the water seemed to take on a new turbulence.

Pat looked at Matthew. "I had to tell him," she said. "I couldn't lie. I just couldn't."

"I know," said Matthew. "I wouldn't have wanted you to lie."

He wanted to say something else, but did not. He wanted to tell her that this was exactly what he liked about her, even admired – her self-evident honesty. And he wanted to add that he felt strongly for her, that he had come to appreciate her company, her presence, but he could not, because she was in love with somebody else – just as he had feared – and he did not expect, anyway, that she would want to hear this from him.

Ian Rankin seemed to be under the water for some time, but at last his head emerged, dark hair plastered over his forehead, the keen, intelligent eyes seeming brighter than before.

"It's in the kitchen," he said. "But of course you can have it back.

Go inside and I'll join you in a moment. I'll get it for you."

Matthew began to thank him, but he brushed the thanks aside, as if embarrassed, and they made their way into the house.

"I didn't think he'd do that," Matthew whispered. "Not after you said what it could be worth."

"He's a good man," said Pat. "You can tell."

Matthew knew that she was right. But it interested him nonetheless that a good man could write about the sort of things that he wrote about – murders, distress, human suffering: all the dark pathology of the human mind. What lay behind that? And if one thought of his readers – who were they? The previous year, on a trip to Rome, he had been waiting for a plane back to Edinburgh and had been queuing behind a group of young men. He had observed their clothing, their hair cuts, their demeanour, and had concluded – quite rightly as their conversation later revealed – that they were priests in training. They had about them that air that priests have – the otherworldliness, the fastidiousness of the celibate. Matthew judged from their accents that they were English, the vowels of somewhere north – Manchester perhaps.

"Will you go straight home?" asked one.

"Yes," his friend replied. "Straight home. Back to ordinary parish liturgy."

The other looked at the book he was holding. "Is that any good?"

"Ian Rankin? Very. I read everything he writes. I like a murder."

And then they had passed on to something else – a snippet of gossip about the English College and a monsignor. And Matthew had thought: Why would a priest like to read about murder? Because good is dull, and evil more exciting? But was it? Perhaps the reason the good like to contemplate the deeds of the bad is that the good realise how easy it is to behave as the bad behave; so easy, so much a matter of chance, of fate, of what the philosophers call moral luck. But of course.

84. An Invitation

Immensely relieved at the recovery of the Peploe?, Matthew and Pat returned to the gallery in a taxi, the painting safely tucked away in a large plastic bag provided by Ian Rankin. Matthew's earlier mood of self-pity had lifted: there were no further references to failure and Pat noticed that there was a jauntiness in the way he went up the gallery steps to unlock the door. Perhaps the recovery of a possible forty thousand pounds meant more to Matthew than he was prepared to admit, even if the identity of the painting was still far from being established. In fact all they knew – as Pat reminded herself – was that she thought that it might be a Peploe, and who was she to express a view on such a matter? Her pass in Higher Art – admittedly with an A – hardly qualified her to make such pronouncements, and she was concerned at having raised everybody's hopes prematurely.

"It's probably worthless," she had said to Matthew in the taxi. "I don't think Ian Rankin really believed that it was worth anything. That's probably why he let us have it back."

Matthew was not convinced. "He gave it back because he thought it was the right thing to do. I could tell that he thought it was a Peploe too. I'm pretty sure you're right."

"And what are we going to do with it now?" asked Pat. "I'm not sure if I should take it back to the flat again."

Matthew laughed. "That's all right. I'll take it back to my place. Or even to the old man's place. He's got a safe." He paused. "Shall we have a celebration? What are you doing this evening?"

Pat considered this for a moment. She had no plans for that evening, and there was every reason to celebrate, but she was not sure how Matthew would interpret an acceptance of his invitation. There had been a purpose behind his asking about her feelings for Bruce – she was convinced of that – and she did not want to encourage him. If he was falling for her, then that would be messy. He was her employer; he was some years her senior – almost thirty, was he not? – and there was another major reason why it would not work. She felt nothing for him, or, rather, not very much. He was decent, he was kind; but there was no attraction beyond that.

He would be perfect for somebody who wanted a reliable, unde-manding boyfriend, for somebody in *the crowd*. Surely there must be a girl there who would love Matthew to take an interest in her? They could go to the Dominion Cinema together and sit in the more expensive seats and then, on the way out, look at the kitchen-ware in the kitchenware shop on the corner of Morningside Road. Pat had seen young couples doing that – standing in front of that window and gazing at the stainless steel cafetières and the Le Creuset saucepans. What would it be like to stand there with some-body else – a man – and look at the pots and pans that seemed to be such potent symbols of future domestic bliss? What would it be like to stand there with Bruce . . . ?

With Bruce? She stopped herself. The thought had come into her mind unbidden, as delicious, tempting thoughts do. Bruce would be wearing his Aitken and Niven rugby sweater and his olive green mock-moleskin trousers, and he would have his hand against the small of her back, and they would be thinking of their kitchen . . . No! No!

"Well?" said Matthew. "Are you doing anything tonight? I thought we could go to the Cumberland for a drink to celebrate. It'll be on me."

Pat brought herself back from fantasy to reality. It would be churlish to refuse Matthew, and an outing to the Cumberland Bar would hardly be compromising. Plenty of people dropped in at the Cumberland with their workmates and nothing was read into the situation. It was not as if he was proposing an intimate *diner à deux* in the Café St Honoré.

"And then we could go and have dinner in the Café St Honoré," Matthew said. "That is, if you've got nothing else on."

He looked at her, and she saw the anxiety in his eyes. But she could not accept; she could not.

"Let's just go for a drink," she said. "I have to . . ." What lie could she come up with to put him off? Or could she tell the truth?

"I want to see Bruce later on," she said. And as she spoke she realised that she had told the truth. She did want to see Bruce; she wanted to be with him again; it was physical, like a nagging pain in the pit of her stomach. And it alarmed her, for what he wanted was not what she wanted.

Matthew lowered his eyes. He's disappointed, she thought; and it would have been so easy for me to have dinner with him and make him happy, and now I have disappointed him.

"What about your crowd?" she asked brightly. "Will they be there?"

Matthew shrugged. "They may be. Maybe not. One's going off to London for a few days this week – he may already have gone. And another has a heavy cold. So if the crowd turns up there won't be many of them."

He looked at her again, and she wondered what he was thinking. She had not lied to him, and so she could look back at him, meeting his gaze with all the satisfaction of one who has told the truth. She did want to see Bruce.

"Why are you so keen on him?" Matthew asked. "I thought – from something you said some time ago – that he got on your nerves. Isn't he vain? Didn't you say something about that?"

"Yes," said Pat. "Yes, he's vain."

Matthew looked impatient, as if there was something that was not being explained to him clearly enough. "How can you like him if he's vain?" he asked. "Doesn't that turn you off?"

Pat smiled. "It should," she said. "Yes, it should. But it doesn't, you know."

"Very peculiar," said Matthew. "Very peculiar."

Pat said nothing. She did not disagree.

Sexual attraction, thought Matthew. The dark, anarchic force. More powerful than anything else. Always there. Working away, but not for me.

85. In the Cumberland Bar

Carrying the discreetly-wrapped Peploe? under his arm, Matthew escorted Pat to the Cumberland Bar for their celebratory drink. Any disappointment he had felt at the turning down of his invitation to dinner was, if still felt, well concealed. Matthew was used to being turned down by women, and had come to expect it. He was not sure why he should be so unlucky, but had a suspicion that it was something to do with his eyes. He knew that they had strange grey flecks in them and he feared that there was something about that which disturbed women – some primeval signal that warned them off men with grey-flecked eyes. He had noticed women looking into his eyes and then frowning; indeed, he had seen Pat do that when they had had that conversation on the way to their encounter with Ian Rankin.

It was very unfair. There was Pat, who was attractive in every sense, throwing herself away on that vain flatmate of hers, who presumably had an insufferable conceit of himself. And there he was, Matthew, who only wanted to give Pat some fun and take her to dinner at the Café St Honoré and spoil her. Bruce would treat her badly – that was obvious – and she would be horribly upset. He would treat her well and maybe, just maybe, there would be some future in it for both of them. There would be no future with Bruce.

He almost wanted to tell her, to warn her, but it would seem odd to speak like that, like an older brother, or even a parent. And so he was silent, at least on that subject, and she spoke no more of it either.

The Cumberland Bar, when they reached it, was already filling with early-evening drinkers.

"Busy," said Matthew, scanning the heads for signs of the crowd. None of them was there, which rather pleased him. He wanted to be with Pat, and the presence of members of the crowd could distract her attention.

They found a couple of seats together and Matthew went to the bar to buy Pat the glass of Chardonnay she had requested. Then, glasses in hand, he made his way back to their table and sat down beside her.

"Do you know many of these people?" asked Pat, looking at the crush of figures that was forming around the bar.

"A few," said Matthew, raising his glass of Guinness in a toast. "Here's to you. Thanks for getting the picture back."

"To Ian Rankin," Pat replied. "What a nice man."

"A real softie," said Matthew.

Pat was not sure what to make of this. Did Matthew consider him a softie because he had given the painting back? That was nothing to do with being a softie. That was to do with principles. For a few moments she felt irritated. Who was Matthew to call anybody a softie, when he so obviously was the softie? No, Ian Rankin was no softie, what with his designer stubble and the black tee-shirts.

She decided not to say anything about this. "And now what?" she said. "What do we do about that painting? Shouldn't we get an opinion on it now?"

Matthew agreed with her. He was not sure, though, who they would get to do this. That would require some thought because he did not like the idea of being humiliated by some condescending art expert. He had already secretly imagined the scene in which the expert, looking down his nose, would sneer at him. "Peploe? You must be joking! What on earth makes you think this is a Peploe?"

She was waiting for Matthew's reply when she looked up to see a familiar figure coming towards her. For a moment she had difficulty placing him, but then she remembered: Angus Lordie, the man she had talked to at the Scottish National Portrait Gallery after the lecture. He had come into the bar, looked around him, and seen her at the table. She noticed, too, that it was not just him, but his dog as well – a black collie with a lop-sided ear and sharp eyes.

Angus Lordie had entered the Cumberland Bar in low spirits, but seeing Pat he broke into a wide smile.

"My dear!" he exclaimed, as he approached their table. "Such a perfect setting for you! Even a bar in the St-Germain could do no more justice than this simple establishment! And at your side, your young gallant . . ."

"This is Matthew," said Pat quickly. "I work with him at his gallery."

Angus Lordie nodded in Matthew's direction and extended a hand. "I would normally not shake hands with a dealer, sir," he said with a smile. "But in your case, I am happy to do so. Angus Lordie."

Matthew rose from his seat and shook the outstretched hand. Pat noticed that he did not seem to be very enthusiastic, and for a moment she felt pity for him. Their private celebration, it would seem, was over.

"And now," said Angus Lordie, handing his dog's lead to Pat, "if you wouldn't mind holding Cyril for a moment, I'll go and get myself a drink."

Pat took the end of the lead and tugged gently to bring Cyril towards the table. The dog looked at her for a moment and then, to her astonishment, gave her a wink. Then he took a few steps forward and sat down next to her chair, turning to look up at her as he did so. Again he winked, and then bared his teeth in what looked like a smile. Pat noticed the glint of the gold tooth which Domenica had mentioned at the reception.

Pat leant over towards Matthew. "This is a very strange dog," she said. "Do you see his gold tooth?'

Matthew looked down into his Guinness. "I had hoped that we would be able to have a celebration. Just you and me. Now it looks as if . . ."

Pat reached out and touched him gently on the forearm. "I'm sorry," she said. "I didn't ask him to join us."

"Well, now we're stuck," said Matthew sulkily. "And that dog smells."

Pat sniffed. There was a slight smell, she had to admit, but it was not entirely unpleasant – rather like strong mushrooms.

Angus Lordie returned now, a glass of whisky in one hand and a half-pint glass of darkish beer in the other. He put the whisky down on the table and then set the glass of beer on the floor next to the dog.

"Cyril drinks," he explained. "It's his only bad habit. That, and chasing after lady dogs, which is more of a call of nature than a bad habit. Here we are, Cyril – make it last."

Pat and Matthew watched in astonishment as Cyril took a few sips of beer and then looked up and gave Pat a further wink.

"Your dog keeps winking at me," said Pat.

"Yes," said Angus Lordie, pulling a chair across from a neighbouring table. "Mind if I join you? Thanks so much. Yes, Cyril has an eye for the ladies, don't you, Cyril?"

86. On the Subject of Dogs

"On the subject of dogs," said Angus Lordie, taking a sip of his whisky, "I've just discovered the most marvellous book. I came across it quite by chance – *The Difficulty of Being a Dog*. It's by a French writer, Roger Grenier, who was a publisher apparently. He knew everybody – Camus, Sartre, Yourcenar – all of them, and he had a wonderful dog called Ulysse. The French title was *Les Larmes d'Ulysse*, The Tears of Ulysses, which was rather better, in my view, than the one they used in English. But there we are. You don't know it, by any chance?"

Pat shook her head. Was it all that difficult to be a dog? Dogs had a rather pleasant existence, as far as she could make out. There were miserable dogs, of course: dogs owned by cruel and irresponsible people or dogs who were never taken for walks, but most dogs seemed contented enough, and often seemed rather happier than the humans attached to them.

"It's a remarkable book," Angus Lordie continued, glancing down at Cyril, who was inserting his long pink tongue into the glass to get to the dregs of his beer. "It's full of extraordinary snippets of information. For example, did you know that Descartes thought of dogs as machines? Outrageous. Wouldn't you agree, Cyril?"

Cyril looked up from his beer glass and stared at Angus Lordie for a few moments. Then he returned to his drink.

"You think that he looked at me because he heard his name,"

mused Angus Lordie. "But then it's always possible that he looked at me because he heard the name Descartes."

"Descartes?" said Pat, raising her voice.

Cyril looked up and winked at her.

"There you are," said Angus Lordie. "Cyril has good taste. He has a low opinion of Descartes because of his views of animal-machines, and he has a correspondingly high view of Voltaire, who sided with the dogs against Descartes, and also, I might add, of Kant, who disposed of Descartes' argument like that – pouf! – in a footnote. Kant said that dogs think in categories, and therefore aren't machines." He paused, and looked down at Cyril who looked back up at him, his gold tooth exposed. "Of course it's typical of the Germans that they should argue in terms of categories of thought, whereas Bentham said that dogs weren't machines because they were capable of suffering in the same way in which we do. The English are much more down to earth, you know."

Pat cast a glance at Matthew, who had a glazed expression. She was not sure what to do. It would not be easy to get rid of Angus Lordie, and yet she could understand how Matthew must feel. He could not compete with the older man, with his easy garrulousness and his tirade of facts about dogs.

She tried to include Matthew in the conversation. "Do you have a dog, Matthew?"

Matthew shook his head. "No dog,' he muttered.

"No dog?" asked Angus Lordie brightly. "No dog? Poor chap. I couldn't live without a dog. I've had Cyril here ever since I rescued him from some crofters in Lochboisdale. I happened to be in the pub there and I heard two crofters talking about a dog who was no good with sheep. They were going to put him down the following day, as there was no point in keeping him. I overheard this, and I offered to take him off their hands. They agreed, and the next day was the beginning of Cyril's life with me. He's never looked back."

Pat wondered about his gold tooth, and asked Angus Lordie how this came about.

"He bit another dog in the tail," came the explanation. "And his

245

tooth broke off. So I took him to my own dentist, who's a drinking pal of mine. He was a bit unsure about treating a dog, but eventually agreed and put it in. Not on the National Health, of course; I paid seventy quid to cover the cost of the gold and what-not. We had to do it at night, when there were no other patients around, as people might have objected to seeing a dog in the dental chair that they had to use. People are funny that way. There's Cyril paying his full seventy quid and some would say that he would have no right to treatment. Amazing. But people aren't entirely rational about these things."

Matthew suddenly rose to his feet. "I'm sorry," he said, looking at Pat but not at Angus Lordie. "I'm sorry, but I have to go."

Angus Lordie looked at his watch. "How late is it? My goodness, the evening's young. Can't you stay?'

Matthew ignored his question. Still addressing himself to Pat, he told her that she could have the following morning off, if she wished. "We haven't really been able to celebrate,' he went on. "So take the morning off."

"Please don't go yet," she said, glancing sideways at Angus Lordie as she spoke.

Matthew shook his head. "No. Sorry. I have to be on my way."

He turned on his heels, and although he nodded cursorily at Angus Lordie, it was clearly not a warm farewell.

"Sorry about that," said Angus Lordie, lifting his glass of whisky. "I hope that I haven't broken up your party."

Pat said nothing – she was watching Matthew leave the bar, sidling past the group of raucous drinkers who were effectively blocking the door. Her sympathy for Matthew had grown during the short time they had been in the bar. He was not like Angus Lordie, who had confidence, who had style. There was something vulnerable about Matthew, something soft and indecisive. He was the sort of person who would go through life never really knowing what he wanted to do. In that respect he was typical of many of the young men she had met in Edinburgh. That type grew up in comfortable homes with all the opportunities, but they lacked strength of character. Was that because they had never had to battle for anything? That must be it. And yet, thought Pat, have I had to fight for anything? Am I not just the same as them? The thought discomforted her and she left it there, at the back of her mind – one of those doubts which could be profoundly disturbing if it were allowed to come to the fore.

Reaching the door, Matthew turned back and looked in her direction. She caught his eye, and smiled at him, and he did return the smile as he disappeared through the doorway into the night. Pat stared at the doorway and was still staring when Bruce came in, together with Sally, laughing at some private joke. She had her arms about his shoulders and was whispering into his ear.

87. The Onion Memory

"Know them?" asked Angus Lordie, noticing the direction of Pat's stare.

For a moment Pat said nothing, and she watched Bruce and Sally squeeze past the knot of people at the doorway and go over to the bar. This manoeuvre brought them closer to the table at which she was sitting with Angus Lordie, and so she averted her gaze. She did not want Bruce to see her, and any meeting with that American girl would be awkward – after the incident with the dressing gown.

"Do I know them?" she muttered, and then, turning back to face Angus Lordie, she replied: "Yes, I do. He's my flatmate. He's called Bruce Anderson."

"Terrific name," said Angus Lordie. "You might play rugby for Scotland with a name like that. Cyril's name – Cyril Lordie – would be useless for rugby, wouldn't it? The selectors would choke on it and pass you by! You just can't play rugby if you're called Cyril, and that's all there is to it. It's got nothing to do with being a dog."

Pat said nothing to this. Of course Bruce's name was wonderful:

Bruce – a strong, virile, confident name. Bruce and Pat. Pat and Bruce. Yes. But then cruel reality intruded: Bruce and Sally.

Pat looked at Angus, who smiled at her. His conversation was extraordinary. Many of the things he said seemed to come from nowhere, and seemed so eccentric; it appeared that he looked at things from an entirely different angle, which was fun, and exhilarating. He was the opposite of boring, the opposite of poor Matthew. And that, she thought, was why Matthew had felt obliged to leave. This man made him feel dull, which Matthew was, of course.

Angus Lordie was looking towards the bar, where Bruce and Sally were standing, Bruce in the process of ordering drinks. "That girl," he said. "His girlfriend, I take it? You know her?"

Pat cast a glance at Bruce and Sally, and then looked quickly away. "Not very well," she said. "In fact, I've only met her once. She's American."

"American? Interesting." Angus Lordie paused. "What do you think she sees in him?"

He waited for Pat to answer, and when she did not, he answered his own question. "He's very good-looking, isn't he? With that hair of his. He's got something on it, hasn't he? Yes. Well, I suppose that if I looked like that I'd have American girls hanging on my arm too."

Pat looked at Angus Lordie. Did he really still think like that – at the age of fifty, or whatever he was? It was sad to think that he still wanted to be in the company of girls like Sally because that would doom him to a life of yearning after people who inevitably would be interested in younger men and not in him. Mind you, he was good-looking himself, and if one did not know his real age he could pass for rather younger – forty perhaps.

She suddenly stopped herself. It had occurred to her that Angus Lordie might actually be interested in her. He had smiled when he had seen her, and had made his way straight to their table. Did this mean that he . . . that he had *designs* on her, as her mother would put it? In her mother's view of the world, men had

248

designs, and it was the responsibility of women to detect these designs and, in most cases, to thwart them. It was different, of course, if designs were honourable; in that case, they ceased to be designs *sensu stricto*.

Angus Lordie had stopped looking at Bruce and Sally. He sighed. "I knew an American girl once," he said. "A lovely girl. It was rather a long time ago, when I lived up in Perthshire. I had left the Art College and had moved into an old mill house in our glen – yes, we had half a glen in those days – my father, I may as well tell you, was one of those Perthshire pocket lairds – and there I was, twenty whatever, thinking that the London galleries would come knocking at my door at any moment. I lived *la vie bohème*, Perthshire version, but in great comfort actually. I used to get up at eleven and paint until three or so. Then I'd go for a walk and have people round for dinner in the evening. Life was pretty good.

"Then this American girl turned up. She was staying with some people in Comrie, wandering around Europe in general and had ended up there. She used to come over and see me and we would sit and talk for hours at the kitchen table. I made her mugs of tea in some wonderful old Sutherlandware mugs I had, beautiful things. And the air outside smelled of coconut from the broom in blossom and there were those long evenings when the light went on forever. And, I tell you, I could have conquered the world, conquered the world . . ."

He broke off, looking up to the ceiling. His glass of whisky, half empty now, was in his hand. Pat was silent, and indeed it was as if the whole bar was silent, although it was not.

After a moment, Angus Lordie looked at Pat. She noticed that his eyes were watery, as if he were on the verge of tears.

"It is the onion memory that makes me cry," he said quietly. "Do you know that line?"

Pat replied gently. "No. But it's a lovely image. The onion memory."

"Yes," said Angus Lordie. "It is, isn't it? I think it comes from a poem by Craig Raine. A fine poet. He talks about a love that was not to last, and thinking about it makes him cry. Such a good thing to do, you know – to cry. But forgive me, I shouldn't talk like this. You have everything before you. There's no reason for you to feel sad."

Pat hesitated. There was something about Angus Lordie that invited confidence; there was an intimacy in his manner that made one want to speak about things which mattered.

"I do feel a bit sad," she said, toying with her glass as she spoke. "I feel sad because that boy over there, Bruce . . . he's with another girl, and . . ."

Angus Lordie reached out and patted her on the arm. "My dear, you need say no more. I understand." He glanced over at Bruce and Sally. "This must be very painful for you."

"It is."

"Of course it is." He picked up his glass and downed the last of his whisky. "Let us leave this place. Let us leave this place and visit our dear friend, Domenica Macdonald. She is most hospitable and she is always, always, very good at driving away regrets of every sort. Cyril can wait outside, tied to a railing. He loves Scotland Street. It's the smells, I think. So much smellier than Drummond Place."

88. Big Lou Receives a Phone Call

As Angus Lordie was proposing to Pat that they leave the comfortable purlieus provided by the Cumberland Bar, Big Lou, coffee bar proprietrix and autodidact, was standing in her flat in Canonmills, looking out of the window. She normally ate early, but that evening she had not felt hungry and was only now beginning to think of dinner. She had been reading, as she usually did when she returned from work, and was still immersed in Proust.

The bulk of Big Lou's library consisted of the volumes which she had acquired when she had purchased the second-hand bookstore out of which she had made her coffee bar. There were books, however, which she bought herself from the dealers in whose shops she had taken to browsing on Saturday afternoons, when the coffee bar was closed. There were several shops in the West Port which she now frequented, although the increasing number of rowdy and vulgar bars in the vicinity was beginning to distress her. Lothian Road, not far away, was now an open sewer as far as Big Lou was concerned – innocent enough during the day, but at night the haunt of bands of drunken young men and girls in impossibly short skirts and absurd high heels. And at the entrance to each of these bars stood threatening men with thick necks, shaved heads, and radio mikes clipped onto their ears. There had been nothing like that in Arbroath, and very little of it in Aberdeen. Mind you, she thought, Aberdeen is too cold to hang about on street corners. And those girls with their very short skirts would freeze quickly enough if they tried to wear them on Union Street in the winter. Was climate the reason why Scotland had always been so respectable?

Big Lou was beginning to have doubts about Proust. She was proud of her edition, which was the Scott-Moncrieff translation, published in a pleasing format in the early Fifties (Big Lou liked books which *felt* good). She was now on volume six, and was reading about the Duchesse de Guermantes and her decision to travel to the Norwegian fjords at the height of the social season. Proust said that this had an effect on people which was similar to the discovery, after reading Kant, that above the world of necessity there was a world of freedom. Was this not a slight exaggeration? Big Lou asked herself. But with whatever levity Proust invoked images of determinism, Big Lou herself took the subject seriously enough. She had several books on the subject in her collection, and after reading them – not with a great deal of enjoyment – she had come out in favour of free will. She was particularly persuaded by the argument that even if we cannot be shown to be free, we have to behave as if freedom of the will existed, because otherwise social life would be impossible. And that meant, in her view, that determinism was false, because it did not fit the facts of human life.

There was no good in having a theory that bore no relation to reality as it was understood and acted upon by people. That is what she thought about determinism. But then she asked herself about God, and became confused. If it were the case that people thought that they needed a concept of God in order to get by in life, then would that mean that only those theories of reality which had a place for God would be defensible? This, she thought, was doubtful. Unless, of course, one made a sharp distinction between social theories – which need not be provable, but which must at least work for the purposes we require of them – and other theories, which can be true and correct but which we do not need to be able to apply to day-to-day life. That was it, she thought.

The problem was that some people preached social philosophies that paid no attention to reality. Some French philosophers had a tendency to do this, Big Lou had noted: they did not care in the slightest if their theories could have disastrous consequences – because they considered themselves to be above such consequences. It was perfectly possible to portray scientific knowledge as socially determined – and therefore not true in any real sense – when one was safe on the ground in Paris; but would you ask the same question in a jet aircraft at thirty-five thousand feet, when that same knowledge underpinned the very engineering that was keeping one up in the air? By the same token, French philosophers had been able to admire Mao and his works because they did not have to live in China at the time. And they knew, too, that what they preached would never be put into effect.

Big Lou stood before her window and remembered the young man who had come into her coffee shop wearing a tee-shirt with a picture of Castro on it. She had served him his coffee and then pointed at the picture.

"Do you really admire people who put others in prison for speaking their mind?" she had asked. "Would you wear that shirt if you lived under him?"

The young man had looked at her and smiled. "You're so naïve," he had said, and taken his coffee to his table. And then, to follow this remark, he had turned to her and said: "Have you ever heard of false consciousness?"

"Aye," said Big Lou. "I have."

But the young man had laughed and turned to the reading of a magazine he had brought with him. Of course she had thought later of the things that she might have said to him, but she had remained silent and had merely gone to the door and locked it, discreetly. Ten minutes or so later, the young man had got up to leave – he was the only customer at the time – and had tried the handle of the door. When he realised it was locked, he had turned to her and demanded that she let him out, which she had done.

He had looked indignant, as she had taken her time to walk to the door and unlock it. So might the jailer in a prison swagger to his task. And as she opened the door for him she said: "You're a university student, aren't you? I've never been that, you know. But don't you think that I've just been able to teach you a lesson about freedom?"

She smiled at the memory – it had been a moment of gentle victory – and was smiling still when her telephone rang. She walked across the room to answer it and heard the voice of the man from Aberdeen, her chef, the man whose letter she kept in that special drawer, and whose voice she had not thought she would hear again.

"I'm in Edinburgh, Lou," he said. "Can I take you out for dinner? Are you free?"

She thought of determinism. Of course she was free.

89. Big Lou Goes to Dinner

Eddie was the name of Big Lou's friend from Aberdeen. He was waiting for her, as he promised he would be, in Sandy Bell's Bar in Forrest Road. He was a tall man in his early forties, with dark, lank hair and an aquiline nose. She saw him immediately she entered the bar, and he smiled at her and nodded. For Big Lou this was a moment of great significance, as it always is when we see one whom we loved a long time ago, and might love still; it had been years, and she had thought of him often – if not each waking day, then almost every day; and now here he was, unchanged, it seemed, and standing there smiling at her as if they were friends who had not seen one another for a mere week or so.

She made her way over towards him, squeezing past a group of young men who were listening earnestly to something being said by one of their number. And in the far corner, sitting at a table, a fiddler worked his bow through a tune that could just be heard above the hubbub of conversation. The notes were jagged and quick, and she remembered that they had sat in a similar pub one evening in Aberdeen when a Shetland fiddler had been playing, and her heart gave a lurch and she wondered whether he would remember that too. Men did not remember these things; or they had their own memories.

When she reached him he put his glass down on the bar and leaned forward to kiss her lightly on the brow.

"Well," he said. "It's been a long time, hasn't it, Lou?"

She nodded. She would not cry, she had determined, but there were tears to be fought back. Discreetly, unseen by Eddie, Big Lou bit her lip.

"Aye, it's been a good long time. And now . . ."

"And now here we are," said Eddie.

She said nothing and glanced at the bartender, who was hovering. Eddie ordered her a drink – "I remember that you like Pernod, Lou. Pernod! Yes, I remember that well."

"I don't drink it very much any more," she said. "But thanks, Eddie."

They looked at one another. She noticed that he had put on a bit of weight, but not much, and that there were a few grey hairs above his ears. His hair looked a bit neater, too, but that was because he had been in America, and people worried more about their grooming there.

"How are you doing, Eddie?" she asked. "Are you still in Galveston? In Texas, or wherever it is?"

He smiled, somewhat awkwardly, and looked down at his feet. "I meant to write to you again, Lou, and tell you. I'm not the best letter-writer, you know. You did get my letter, didn't you?"

Big Lou reached for the glass which the bartender was offering. "Yes, I got your letter, Eddie." If he knew, she thought; if he knew how many times I have read that letter, and how I have preserved it, a token, for there were no other tokens.

"I stayed in Galveston for a few years," said Eddie. "Then I moved to Mobile, Alabama. Great place. That's where I am now. You'd like it, you know."

Big Lou listened carefully. He had said that she would not like Galveston, that she should not join him out there. Now he was saying that she would like Mobile. Did this mean that he wanted her to go back there with him; that he wanted her again? And why would he assume that she would be available? But of course he would know that; of course he would.

He asked her what she was doing, and she explained. He said that she would be good at running a coffee bar – he had always thought that she should be in the catering industry, he said – and she thanked him for that. And was he still cooking? He was, but not for oil men.

"I'm a real chef now," he said. "Cooking in the oil industry is just industrial. Big helpings for these big guys. Lots of carbo-hydrates. No finesse."

She imagined him again in his kitchen whites, with the cap that he liked to wear, which hid his greasy hair. She had given him a special shampoo once, which claimed that it would end greasy hair, but either it had not worked or he had stopped using it.

They finished their drinks and then went over the road to the

Café Sardi. He had booked a table there, and asked her whether she knew it. She did not, but she liked it when she went in. She liked restaurants with pictures on the walls and there was something about Italian restaurants which was always welcoming.

They sat at a table near the wall. He looked at the menu and told her about some of the dishes that he cooked now. Americans had a sweet tooth, he said, and so he was obliged to sprinkle icing sugar on things which would be savoury in Scotland.

"Is it very different over there?" asked Big Lou. "Would I like it, do you think?"

He fiddled with the edge of the tablecloth. 'It's very different in some ways," he said. "You have to look after yourself. If you're down, you're down. Nobody's going to come and pick you up. But if you want to work, then it's a great place to be."

"Maybe I should come and see you," said Big Lou. She spoke tentatively, because he had not invited her yet, in spite of his saying that she would like Mobile. What a strange name, she thought: Mobile, and he pronounced it *Mobeel*, which must be the right way to say it. Eddie was good on these details; he had always been like that.

"There's something I should tell you, Lou," said Eddie. "I'm married now. I married a girl I met there. We run a restaurant together."

Big Lou said nothing. She started to speak, but said nothing. She looked down at the cutlery, at her side plate, at the single flower in the tiny vase, at the way the candle flame flickered in the draught.

90. Poetry of the Tang Dynasty

There are, said Auden (and Tolstoy), different types of unhappiness. For Big Lou, the revelation that Eddie had married a woman in Mobile, Alabama, made her unhappy. She had never had very much, and losing what little she had was at least a suffering to which she was fairly accustomed (Auden's phrase about the poor). For Pat, who had been loved a great deal, and knew it, the sight of Bruce in the Cumberland Bar, his attention entirely given over to his American girlfriend, provided a new sort of unhappiness. This was the unhappiness of knowing that you simply cannot have what you want to have – an unhappiness which is a bitter discovery for the young. The young rarely believe that they will not be able to get what they want, because there is always an open future. I may not be beautiful today, but I shall be beautiful tomorrow. I may not have much money today, but that will all change. Not so.

As he escorted Pat out of the Cumberland Bar, Angus Lordie was aware that she was feeling miserable. One with less psychological insight than he might have attempted to cheer her up with distracting remarks, or with observations on the fact that there were plenty of other young men. But he knew what it was to love without hope, and knew that the only way to deal with that bleak state was to look one's unhappiness in the face. And it was important, he thought, to understand that the last thing that the unhappy wish to be reminded of is the greater unhappiness of others. Telling a person with toothache that there are others with greater toothache than their own was no help at all.

So he said to Pat, as they left the Cumberland: "Yes, it's very uncomfortable, isn't it? You want him and he doesn't want you – because he's got another girl. Oh yes. Very unfortunate. And, of course, even if he didn't have her, he might not want you anyway."

Pat did not consider this helpful and was about to tell him that she did not want to talk about it. But he continued. "I can understand what you see in him, you know. I can understand the attraction of male beauty. I'm an artist, and I know what beauty is all about. That beautiful young man has worked a spell on you. That's what beauty does. We see it and it puts a spell on us. It's most extraordinary. We want to merge ourselves with it. We want to possess it. We want to *be* it. You want to *be* that young man, you know. That's what you want."

Pat listened in astonishment as they made their way round

Drummond Place towards the top of Scotland Street. As they walked past the house of the late Sydney Goodsir Smith, makar, Angus Lordie looked up at the empty windows and gave a salute.

"I like to acknowledge Sydney's shade," he said. "*Guidnicht, then, for the nou, Li Po/ In the Blythefu Hills of Tien-Mu.*" He turned to Pat. "Those lovely lines are by Sydney, God rest his great rambunctious soul. He wrote a lovely poem, addressed to the Chinese poet Li Po, about an evening's goings-on in an Edinburgh bar, *a cheerie howf,* peopled by a *crousi companie o' philosophers and tinks.* What a marvellous picture! And all this going on *while the world in its daithdance/ skudder and spun/ in the haar and wind o space and time.*"

He stopped and looked down at his dog. "Do you think this is awful nonsense, Cyril? Will you tell Pat that I don't always go on like this, but that sometimes . . . well sometimes it just seems the right thing to do. Will you tell her that, Cyril?"

Cyril stared at his master and then turned to look up at Pat. He winked.

"There," said Angus Lordie. "Cyril would have got on very well with Sydney. And he does like to hear about the Chinese poets too, although he knows that the Chinese eat dogs – a practice of which Cyril scarcely approves, tolerant though he is of most other human foibles. A dog has to draw a line.

"Do you enjoy Chinese poetry, Pat? No. I suppose that you've never had the pleasure. You should try it, you know. The Arthur Waley translations. These Chinese poets wrote wonderful pieces about the pleasure of sitting on the shore of their rivers and waiting for boats to arrive. Nothing much else happens in Chinese poetry, but then does one want much to happen in poetry? I rather think not."

They turned down Scotland Street, walking slowly in order to allow Cyril to sniff at every kerbstone and lamp-post.

"It's really rather easy to write eighth-century Chinese poetry," said Angus Lordie. "In English, of course. It requires little effort, I find."

"Make one up now," said Pat. "Go on. If you say it's so easy."

Angus Lordie stopped again. "Certainly. Well now, let us think."

He paused. Then turning to face Pat, he addressed her gravely:

I look across this street of stone,
This street which takes a country's name,
To the house with lights, where a gentle companion
Prepares her jug of wine, brings to mind
The hours that we have spent together
In that quiet room; each stair that lies
Between ourselves and her, will raise the heart a little,
Will tidy the unhappiness from your courtyard,
Will make you smile again. My unhappy friend;
I tell you so; I tell you this is true.

He finished speaking, and bowed slightly to Pat. "My Chinese poem," he said. "Not as good, perhaps, as that which might have been written by Li Po, if he were with us, which he is not, but capable perhaps of preparing you for an evening with Domenica and myself and conversation about things that really matter. And if, incidentally, this is balm for your undoubted unhappiness, then I shall consider myself to have done no more than any neighbour should do. *N'est-ce-pas*, Cyril?"

91. God Looks Down on Belgium

"And where," asked Domenica Macdonald, as she opened her door to them, "is your malodorous dog?"

Angus Lordie seemed not to be taken aback by what struck Pat as a less than warm welcome. But Pat's concern proved to be misplaced. The relationship between her neighbour, Domenica, and her newly-acquired friend, Angus Lordie, was an easy one, and the banter they exchanged was good-natured. In the course of the evening, Angus Lordie was to describe Domenica – to her face – as a "frightful blue-stocking", and in return she informed him that he was a "well-known failure", a "roué" and "a painter of dubious talent".

"If you are referring to Cyril," said Angus Lordie, "he is outside, tied to a railing, enjoying the smells of this odiferous street. He misses such smells in Drummond Place, with its rather better air. He is quite happy."

Domenica ushered them into her study. "I really am rather pleased that you came to see me," she said, as she took a half-full bottle of Macallan out of a cupboard. "I've been worrying about this *fatwa* of yours, Angus. Have those dissident Free Presbyterians shown their hand yet?"

Pat remembered the talk about the dissenting Free Presbyterian *fatwa* imposed upon Angus Lordie as a result of his uncomplimentary portrait of their Moderator. Angus Lordie had not mentioned anything more about it, and certainly his demeanour was not that of one labouring under a *fatwa*.

"Oh that," said Angus Lordie, accepting the generous glass of whisky which Domenica had poured for him. "Yes, they've done one or two things to signal their displeasure, but I think that the whole thing will probably blow over."

"And what precisely have they done?" asked Domenica.

"A group of them came and sang Gaelic psalms outside my door," he replied. "You know those awful dirges that they go in for? Well, we had a bit of that. I went out and thanked them afterwards and they looked a bit disconcerted. They mumbled something about how I would hear from them again, but they didn't seem to have much heart for it."

"It's so difficult to sustain a *fatwa*," said Domenica. "One has to be so *enthusiastic*. I'm not sure if I could find the moral energy myself."

"Cyril howled when he heard the Gaelic psalms," said Angus Lordie. "And they thought that he was joining in. He sounded so like them! Quite uncanny! Of course he does come from Lochboisdale and he's probably heard Gaelic psalms before. Perhaps it made him feel homesick."

"Oh well," said Domenica. "These things all add to the gaiety of nations. That's the nice thing about life in Scotland. It's hardly dull. I'm immensely relieved that I don't live in a dull country."

"Such as?" asked Pat. Her gap year had taken her to Australia and then, briefly, on to New Zealand. New Zealand was perhaps somewhat quiet while Australia had proved to be far from dull; at least for her.

"Oh, Belgium," said Domenica. "Belgium is extremely dull."

Angus Lordie nodded his head in agreement. "I've never quite seen the reason for Belgium," he said. "But I certainly agree with you about its dullness. Remember that party game in which people are invited to name one famous Belgian (other than anybody called Leopold) – that's pretty revealing, isn't it?"

"I have a list of famous Belgians somewhere," said Domenica rather absently. "But I think I've mislaid it."

"It'll turn up," said Angus Lordie, taking a sip of his whisky. "These things do. Did I tell you, by the way, that I composed a hymn about Belgium? The Church of Scotland has been revising its hymnary and was asking for more modern contributions. I composed one of which I was really rather proud. I called it *God looks down on Belgium*."

"And the words?" asked Domenica.

Angus Lordie cleared his throat. "The first verse goes as follows," he began:

God's never heard of Belgium,
But loves it just the same,
For God is kind
And doesn't mind –
He's not impressed with fame.

After he had finished, he folded his hands and looked at Domenica. Pat felt uncertain. Was this serious? She had enjoyed the Chinese poem which he had declaimed to her in Scotland Street, but this hymn seemed . . . well, he couldn't possibly mean it.

Domenica looked at Angus Lordie and raised an eyebrow. "Did the Church of Scotland use it?" she asked.

"Inexplicably, no," said Angus Lordie. "I had a very polite letter back, but I fear that they feel that it's not suitable. I suppose it's something to do with comity within Europe. We have to pretend to take Belgium seriously."

"We live in such a humourless age," Domenica remarked. "It used to be possible to laugh. It used to be possible to enjoy oneself with fantasies – such as your ridiculous hymn – sorry, Angus – but now? Well, now there are all sorts of censors and killjoys. Earnest, ignorant people who lecture us on what we can think and say. And do you know, we've lain down and submitted to the whole process. It's been the most remarkable display of passivity. With the result that when we encounter anybody who thinks independently, or who doesn't echo the received wisdoms of the day, we're astonished."

"In such a way is freedom of thought lost," said Angus Lordie, who had been listening very attentively to Domenica. "By small cuts. By small acts of disapproval. By a thousand discouragements of spirit."

They were all silent for a moment as they reflected on what had been said. Domenica and Angus Lordie appeared to be in agreement, but Pat was not so sure. What was the point about being rude about Belgium? Surely we had made moral progress in recognising the sensitivities of others and in discouraging disparaging comments? What if a Belgian were to hear the words of that hymn? Would a Belgian not be gratuitously offended? And surely one should never criticise people for things that they cannot help – such as being Belgian?

Pat was thinking this when she became aware that the eyes of the other two were on her.

"You must understand something, my dear," Domenica said to her. "Angus is not to be taken seriously."

Angus Lordie nodded. "Absolutely right," he said. "But listen, Domenica, I'm feeling bored and I want some excitement. I was wondering whether you would care to show Pat here and me the tunnel. I get a distinct feeling this is a night for exploration – of every sort."

Domenica glanced at Pat. It was a glance that was rich in moral warning.

92. In Scotland Street Tunnel

Pat had heard that Scotland Street – the street itself – was built over a Victorian railway tunnel. Bruce had pointed out to her that the basements on either side of the street went appreciably lower than was normal for the New Town – that was because the street was supported by the roof of the tunnel.

"I know quite a lot about these things," he said. "Just ask me if there's anything you want to know."

Now, accompanied by Domenica and Angus Lordie, she stood outside a low door in the space outside the lowest basement floor of their block. Above them, arched like broad flying buttresses, were the stone steps that led to their front door and to the door of the upper basement. Cyril, who had been retrieved by Angus Lordie from his station at the railings, was eagerly sniffing at the door.

"I thought this was a coal cellar," said Pat.

"Indeed it is," said Domenica, pushing the door open with her foot. "But it is something over and above that – something which only I and one or two other long-term residents know about."

She shone the beam of her flashlight into the dark space behind the door.

"It still smells of coal," she said. "As you will notice. But that door at the back there gives access to the tunnel. And if you follow me, we can go inside and take a walk."

Domenica stepped forward decisively. Angus Lordie indicated to Pat that she should follow her and that he and Cyril would bring up the rear. "Cyril is utterly without fear," he said, "which unfortunately suggests that he has little imagination. The brave are usually somewhat unimaginative, don't you find?"

There was no time to discuss this intriguing proposition, as Domenica was now inside the tunnel and the light from her torch was playing against the opposite wall. Crouching, as the cellar door was not high enough to walk through unbent, Pat made her way into the tunnel, feeling immediately the cooler air on her skin, smelling the slightly musty odour, not unlike the smell of a garden shed that has been left unopened for some time.

She looked up. Domenica was directing the torchlight towards the roof of the tunnel. There, growing from the blackened masonry, were clusters of small stalactites, white against the dark background, like colonies of fungi. The tunnel was high – over twenty feet, Pat thought – and it was broad too, to allow for a footpath on either side of the track.

Domenica shone the torch up the tunnel, in the direction of Drummond Place. "We should start walking," she said. "And watch your feet as you go. This is fairly steep. The gradient is actually one in twenty-seven. And the distance in this tunnel, by the way, is measured in chains."

"You are immensely well-informed, as ever," said Angus Lordie. "Where did you pick up this arcane knowledge?"

"From the organist at St Giles," replied Domenica. "My friend Peter Backhouse. He knows everything there is to be known about railways, and he knows all about the old lines of Edinburgh. He can tell you all about Bach and Pachelbel and so on, but he also knows all about track gradients and signalling systems and the Edinburgh, Leith and Granton Railway Company. Remarkable, isn't it? I'm always impressed by people who know a lot about trains."

"I've always thought that the Church of Scotland was a bit unsound on railways," said Angus Lordie. "Did you ever hear Professor Torrance talk about trains when he was moderator? You did not. And now that we have a female moderator, well, I'm afraid there's likely to be little improvement. Women tend not to be interested in trains in quite the same way that men are. Or at least some men. I have no interest in trains myself, of course."

"That's because there is a large part of the female in your psyche," said Domenica. "You're in touch with your feminine side. You're a new man, Angus."

For a few moments they walked on in silence. It did not seem to Pat that Angus Lordie was a new man at all; in fact, it seemed to her that he was quite the opposite. And Cyril was certainly not a new dog – not with his liking for beer, his reputed chasing after lady dogs, and his tendency to wink. None of these was the attribute of a new dog.

"Where does this tunnel lead?" asked Pat suddenly. She did not usually feel claustrophobic, but now she began to feel a slight unease as she realised that they were getting some distance from the cellar door which had admitted them. They only had one torch with them – what would happen if that torch failed? Would they have to feel their way along the side of the tunnel until they found the opening? And what if there were places where the floor had collapsed, which they would not see in the darkness?

Domenica answered her question. "It goes all the way up to Waverley Station," she said. "It ends opposite platforms 1 and 19. It's bricked up there, I'm afraid, and so we shall have to come back by the same route."

Pat reflected on this and then asked where the trains went.

"Down to Granton," said Domenica. "Peter Backhouse showed me a map once which made it very clear. The trains set off from Canal Street Station in the centre of the city and went down the tunnel purely by the force of gravity. Coming up the other way, they were pulled by a rope system, which was powered by a stationary engine. When they came out at Scotland Street Station they made their way down to Granton. You could get a ferry there to take you over to Fife. There was no Forth Bridge in those days, you see."

Cyril barked suddenly, and Domenica swung the beam of the torch round to illuminate him.

"He's seen something," said Angus Lordie. "Look at the way his nose is quivering. What have you picked up, boy – what have you sniffed?"

Cyril growled. "He's never wrong, you know," said Angus Lordie. "He's found something. Shine the beam in the direction he's looking in, Domenica."

Domenica moved the beam of the torch to the side. They were all silent as the light moved and then there came a gasp from Domenica. She was the first to see it – the first to understand what they were looking at. And then the others realised too, and they looked at Domenica, on whose face a small part of the light of the torch was falling. And they waited for guidance – for an explanation.

93. A Further Tunnel – and a Brief Conversation About Aesthetics

Domenica broke the silence that followed Cyril's extraordinary discovery. And it was Cyril's discovery, as everybody later agreed – one for which he should be given all due credit. Had he not barked to alert them to the change in the smell of the air, then they would have walked right past the largely-concealed mouth of the side-tunnel. But Cyril, detecting a new whiff, gave them warning, and when Domenica turned her torch in the right direction, they had seen the much smaller tunnel sloping off to the west.

"Peter Backhouse said nothing about this," muttered Domenica, as she took a step towards the mouth of the smaller tunnel.

"It has no doubt been forgotten about," said Angus Lordie, reaching out to twist off a piece of the board that had been used to block the entrance. The wood came away in his hand, and immediately another piece fell off the now-crumbling barrier.

"I suspect that this is a service tunnel of some sort," said Domenica, directing the beam up the very much narrower passage.

"Shall we?" said Angus Lordie. "Would it be safe to walk up a little? Heaven knows what we might find."

The idea of fresh exploration seemed attractive to Domenica and Angus Lordie – and immensely so to Cyril, who was straining on his lead to enter this territory of uncharted smells. Pat was not so enthusiastic. It was one thing to walk down a well-known tunnel, and quite another to explore a tunnel which nobody appeared to know about. Again she worried about the possible failure of the torch. It would have been bad enough having to navigate down the central tunnel in complete darkness, but if they entered what might well be a warren of service tunnels, then they might be lost indefinitely, wandering around beneath the streets of Edinburgh until hunger and fatigue claimed them and they failed. There would be no prospect of rescue, then, as nobody knew that they had ventured into the Scotland Street tunnel in the first place. Their disappearance would thus be a complete mystery, rather like the disappearance of that party of Australian schoolgirls who were swallowed up by the earth at Hanging Rock. That had not been a successful picnic, on the whole.

"Do you think this is safe?" she asked. Her voice in the darkness sounded very weak, and she wondered whether anybody had heard her. But Domenica had, and she reached out and grasped her arm.

"Don't worry. This won't go very far. And if it were going to cave in, it would have done so a long time ago."

"Quite right," added Angus Lordie. "Safe as houses."

They made their way down the side-tunnel, walking more slowly, as there was less room, and they could barely fit two abreast. The tunnel was not quite straight, and from time to time it veered slightly to the left or right, but its general direction was westwards.

Pat shivered. The air was cooler now, and she began to regret not having fetched a jersey or a coat from the flat before they began their expedition. But she had been unwilling to go into her flat in case she should disturb Bruce and Sally, and so she had come lightly dressed. Of course there was no reason to believe that Bruce and Sally would be there: they were probably still in the Cumberland Bar, for all she knew, or having dinner together, over a candle-lit table. Would they be talking about her? she wondered. Of course they would not – there was no reason for them to be interested in her. Bruce tolerated her – that was all – and Sally disliked her. So she was nothing to them, and they would have no reason even to think about her, let alone discuss her.

She was aware of Angus Lordie walking beside her, while Domenica was a few steps ahead, the light from her torch bobbing up and down as she walked.

"What an adventure!" Angus Lordie whispered. "Did you imagine that we would find ourselves taking a subterranean promenade together?"

"No," she said. "I did not."

He sighed. "I am conscious, of course, that there are many others with whom you would prefer to take such a walk. That young man in the bar, for example." He paused for a moment. "Don't throw your heart away, my dear. I recognise the signs so well. An impossible passion. Don't waste your time on him."

She was going to remain silent, but her answer slipped out, almost without her willing it.

"It's not so easy," she said. "I'd like to stop, but I find that I can't. You can't stop yourself feeling something for somebody else. You just can't."

"Oh yes, you can," said Angus Lordie, his voice raised slightly. "You can stop yourself from loving somebody perfectly well. You simply change the way you look at them. People do it all the time."

Domenica now joined in. "I'm sorry," she said. "But you can't really expect to have a confidential conversation in a tunnel. I have heard every word you've whispered, and I feel that I must agree with Angus. Of course you can change the way you feel about something or somebody. But it requires an effort of the will – a conscious decision to recognise what you have missed."

"Precisely," said Angus. "And this is exactly what the Professor of Aesthetics at Harvard did. She decided that she found palm trees beautiful – before that she thought them an unattractive sort of tree. Then she discovered that she liked the way that their fronds made striped light. And after that, palm trees were beautiful."

This conversation on aesthetic theory might have continued, and indeed Angus Lordie was mentally marshalling arguments in favour of his position – and that of the Professor of Aesthetics at Harvard – when Domenica suddenly drew to a halt.

"Are we reaching the end?' asked Pat. It was difficult to see what lay ahead, as the beam of the torch was, as she had feared, becoming rather weaker. But it seemed as if there was a blockage of some sort there.

"I think we are," said Domenica. "Look, it seems to go fairly sharply upwards."

They moved forward cautiously, Domenica playing the beam of the torch up towards the ceiling of the tunnel. Suddenly, and without warning, she flicked the switch of the torch and the beam of light disappeared. They were not in total darkness, though – weak rays of yellow light came from above them, emanating from what appeared to be cracks in the roof above them. There was not a great deal of light, but it was sufficient for them to see one another's faces, and to see the few chunks of fallen masonry that littered the tunnel floor around them.

Pat saw Domenica beckon them to her, and she and Angus Lordie drew near.

"We're under a room," said Domenica, pointing upwards. They had been stooping as they walked, and now, by standing straight, their heads almost touched the roof.

"There's something happening up there," whispered Domenica. "Let's take a look. But do keep your voices down and, Angus, whatever you do, don't let that dog of yours bark."

"But where are we?" whispered Pat. They had walked some distance – perhaps the equivalent of two blocks on Princes Street – but it was difficult to calculate distance in the darkness. They might have done many more chains than that.

"By my calculation," said Domenica, *sotto voce*, "we are more or less directly underneath the New Club!"

94. An Interesting Discovery

Moving carefully, so as not to make any sound, Domenica, Angus Lordie and Pat took up positions directly under the cracks in the ceiling. It was not easy to see what was going on above, but by the careful placing of an eye to a crack – a manoeuvre which involved pushing the side of one's face against the rough masonry, and suppressing the urge to sneeze that inevitably followed – they were able to see up into the room above.

It was not a perfect view. It is, in general, easier to look down rather than to look up (a proposition which may be applied to a range of human activities, including literature and journalism). The view from Parnassus gives one a greater sense of power, one might assume, than the view of Parnassus from the plains below. But even from their disadvantaged and uncomfortable position, the sight which greeted their eyes was one which amply repaid the effort.

The cracks in the ceiling were cracks in the floor of a large room. They were directly below an impressive table, which was probably why they had been undiscovered. And around this table were seated some twenty people – forty sets of legs, male and female – forty shoes with accompanying ankles. And that was about all they could see, such were the limitations of their vantage point.

Pat stared at the shoes. Most of them were men's shoes, but there were women's shoes here and there, including a pair that was very close to her eye. She stared at the shoes: they were made of expensive leather, and had fashionable, finely honed square-tip toes. As she stared, one of the feet lifted slightly and the shoe came down on the edge of the crack through which Pat was looking. Had she wished to do so, she could have poked the tip of her little finger through the crack and touched the shoe. But she did not.

She looked at some of the other legs and saw that one set of ankles, placed up at the top of the table, was clad in a pair of extremely bright red socks. The shoes involved were fine ones – black brogues with a high shine on the toe-caps, influential shoes – which made the colour of the socks seem all the more surprising. Pat lowered her head for a moment and tapped Domenica on the shoulder.

"Did you see those red socks?" she whispered. "Up at the end of the table."

Domenica pressed her face to the crack and looked again. Then she turned back to Pat. Her expression was excited; as if she had made a great discovery.

"I know who that is!" she whispered. "There's only one person who wears socks like that."

Pat thought that she had heard the name, or seen it in the papers, but was not sure.

"He was chairman of a whisky company, I think," said Domenica. "Highland Distillers. Then he's on the board of the Bank of Scotland, and he's chairman of the National Galleries of Scotland. He's a very nice man. I've met him several times. Those feet over there must be his – I'm sure of it. And it looks as if he's in the chair!"

"And can you recognise anybody else?" asked Pat.

"I can," whispered Angus Lordie. "Take a look at those feet halfway along on the far side. Look at the shoes."

They all peered through the cracks to examine the shoes that had been pointed out to them. They looked ordinary enough though, and Pat and Domenica were wondering what special features had enabled Angus Lordie to identify them when there came a sound from above, a coughing, and then the sound of a gavel being struck on the surface of the table.

"Chairman, are you ready?" a voice asked.

"I was right," whispered Domenica. "I was right! I know that voice. I know it!

"The secretary of the New Club," she said. "That's him!"

"Chairman," repeated the voice, "would you like me to read the minutes of the last meeting?"

"No," said another voice, from the end of the table. "I think we've all read them. Any matters arising?"

There was a silence. "How are things progressing with the . . . with you know what."

"What?" asked another voice.

"You know," someone replied. "That delicate business."

"Oh that!" somebody said. "I had a word with the person in question and it's all sorted out."

"But what if it gets out?" asked a woman's voice. "What if *The Scotsman* gets to hear of this?"

"They won't get to hear of it," said the first voice. "And anyway, it's just a social matter. Nobody else's business."

"Good," said a woman. "You've handled it all very well."

"Just as you handle everything," said somebody.

"Thank you. But I think it's a committee thing. I think we can all take a bit of credit for that."

There was silence for a moment. Pat looked at Domenica, who smiled at her. Her expression was triumphant.

"I knew it!" said Domenica quietly. "I knew it all along!"

"Now," said a more authoritative voice. "Now, I think we should get on with things and look at the draft mission statement. I'm not sure whether we should have a mission statement – or at least not a public one. But I suppose it would be useful to have one just for ourselves, so that we can remind ourselves of what we're about. What does everybody else think?"

Some of the feet moved. Ankles were crossed, and then uncrossed.

"I think we should have one," said somebody halfway down the table. As long as it can sum up our essential ethos. That would be useful."

"And how would we sum that up?" asked a low, rather indistinct voice.

"Essentially we exist in order to . . ." said a voice which was too quiet to be heard properly, ". . . namely by ourselves."

There were murmurs of assent, and then, to the horror of those below, Cyril, who had been standing patiently beside Angus Lordie, uttered a loud bark.

For a moment all was confusion. Angus Lordie bent down to stifle Cyril, who responded by giving a loud yelp of protest. Pat drew away from the crack through which she had been staring, to bang her head rather sharply against Domenica's forehead which was similarly moving away from the crack. But order soon re-established itself and the three of them moved quickly away from their secret vantage point.

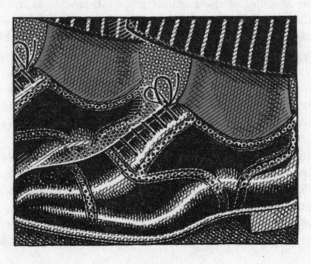

"Time to go!" said Domenica. "Most disappointing, but I think it would be diplomatic to leave."

They walked back down the new tunnel and soon emerged in the main railway tunnel. Then, the light of the torch getting feebler by the minute, although Domenica assured them there was enough power to see them back to Scotland Street, they began the journey home.

"Do you know what that was?' Domenica asked. "Do you two realise what we witnessed?"

"A meeting," said Pat.

"Yes," agreed Domenica. "But that was a very special meeting. That, you see, was the Annual General Meeting of the Edinburgh Establishment!"

95. Mr Guy Peploe Makes an Appearance

The next day Pat decided not to tell Matthew about her extraordinary experiences. She had thought that he would be particularly interested in their unexpected witnessing of the Annual General Meeting of the Edinburgh Establishment, as this was a story that any Edinburgh person might be expected to hear with particular relish. The Establishment could be seen in public, of course, at certain events, or on the golf course at Muirfield, but very few people would have imagined that it went so far as to convene an annual general meeting. Nor would most people know who the chairman of the Edinburgh Establishment was, and Pat had been looking forward to breaking that news to Matthew. But when she saw him, with his deflated look and his sense of defeat, she could not bring herself to reveal to him just how much excitement there had been the previous evening. If he asked her, she would say that she had done nothing very much, for that, she suspected, was what Matthew himself would have done.

The gallery was curiously busy that morning – or at least for the first part of the morning. Several sales were made, including that of a large and particularly fine McCosh study of ornamental fowls. This was, at least, a painting upon which Matthew could expound with knowledge and enthusiasm. He knew Ted McCosh, and was able to explain the trouble he took to mix his own paints and prepare his painting surfaces in exactly the way in which the seventeenth-century Dutch masters would have done, and the client, a large-bellied man from Angus, a ruddy-faced countryman who would have comfortably fitted in a Rowlandson etching, was delighted with his purchase. Could more such paintings be obtained? They could: Ted painted fowl industriously in his studio in Carrington. How contented the ornamental poultry looked in their sylvan setting. Indeed they did.

The sale of the McCosh lifted Matthew's spirits, with the result that he suggested that both he and Pat should go for coffee that morning. They could leave a note to the effect that anybody who needed them could find them in Big Lou's coffee shop.

Pat was relieved by the invitation. She was concerned that Matthew might be feeling resentful of her, and she was not sure whether she could manage to work with a disappointed suitor. But there was none of this as they crossed the street to the coffee bar and picked their way down Big Lou's hazardous steps, scene of a minor fall all those years ago by Hugh MacDiarmid on his way to what was then a bookshop.

Big Lou welcomed them from behind her counter. There were one or two customers there already, but no sign of Ronnie or Pete.

"The boys seem to be going somewhere else," said Big Lou, shrugging her shoulders. "Pete owes me fifty pounds, so I think that's the last I'll see of them."

"You shouldn't lend money," said Matthew. "You can see that they're a bad risk."

"You might not say that if you wanted to borrow off me," said Lou simply.

They sat down in one of the booths. Matthew stretched out, and smiled.

"Maybe we're turning the corner," he said. "Maybe the art market's picking up."

Pat smiled. She wanted Matthew to be a success, but she doubted whether it would be as the owner of a gallery. Perhaps there was some other business for which he would show a real aptitude. Perhaps he could . . . perhaps he could be a consultant. There were plenty of people who advertised themselves as consultants, but were rather vague about what exactly it was that one might consult them about. These people offered advice, and people appeared to pay for this advice, although the basis on which the advice was offered sometimes seemed a little bit questionable. There was a boy from Pat's year at school who was already a consultant at the age of twenty. She had seen him featured in the style section of a newspaper as a "successful consultant". But how could he advise anybody on anything, when he had not had the time to do anything himself?

Poor Matthew – sitting there with his cappuccino and his label-less shirt, looking pleased with himself because they had sold a few paintings – it would be good, Pat thought, to be able to help him find somebody, a girlfriend who would appreciate him; but how dull it would be for her, how dreary to wait for something to happen, when nothing ever would.

It was while Pat was thinking this, and Matthew was staring dreamily at the froth on the top of his cappuccino, that they heard Big Lou greet another customer.

"Mr Peploe," she said loudly.

At the mention of the name, Matthew sat up and looked round at the newcomer. He saw a dark-haired man somewhere in his mid-thirties, with a strong face and with eyes that seemed to be amused by something.

Big Lou caught Matthew's eye. "This is Guy Peploe," she said, reaching for a cup from her counter. "Yes! This is Mr Peploe himself!"

Matthew looked confused. "Peploe?" he said weakly.

Big Lou laughed. "I met Mr Peploe a few days ago. He's from the Scottish Gallery over the road. He said that they usually have their own coffee in the gallery, but that he would pop in and try mine. So here he is!"

"I see," said Matthew. He looked at Pat for reassurance. This was dangerous.

"And I told him about your painting," went on Big Lou. "And he said that of course he would look at it for you. He said you shouldn't be shy. He's always looking at paintings for people. And if it's a Peploe, he'll know. He's Samuel Peploe's grandson, you see."

"Oh," said Matthew weakly. "I haven't got it with me. Sorry."

"But you brought it in this morning," said Pat. "I saw it. I'll go and fetch it."

Guy Peploe smiled politely. "I'd be very happy to take a look," he said. "I'm very interested."

It was difficult for Matthew to do anything but agree. So Pat went back across the road to fetch the Peploe?, leaving Matthew sitting awkwardly under the gaze of Guy Peploe, who seemed to be quietly summing him up.

"I think I was at school with you," mused Guy Peploe. "You were much younger than I was, but I think I remember you."

"No," said Matthew. "Somebody else."

96. Mr Peploe Sees Something Interesting

Pat came back with the Peploe? under her arm. On entering Big Lou's coffee bar, she saw that Guy Peploe was now sitting opposite Matthew, engaged in conversation. She slipped into the booth opposite Guy Peploe and placed the wrapped painting on the table.

Matthew glanced at her, almost reproachfully. "I don't think that it's a real Peploe," he said. "I've never thought that, actually. It's Pat who said it was."

Pat felt irritated that he should seek to cover his embarrassment by blaming her, but she said nothing.

Guy Peploe was staring at the wrapping. "We'll see," he said. "I take the view that the best way of authenticating a painting is to look at it. Wouldn't you agree? It's rather difficult to say anything unless you've got the painting in front of you."

Matthew laughed nervously. "Yes, I find it very difficult when people phone me up and describe a painting that they have. They expect me to be able to value it over the phone."

"People are funny," said Guy Peploe. "But you can never turn down an opportunity to look at something. You never know. You remember that Cadell that turned up in a charity shop a few years ago. Remember that?"

"Yes," said Matthew, who did not remember.

"So perhaps we should take a look at this one," said Guy Peploe patiently. "Shall I unwrap it?"

Matthew reached for the painting. "I'll do it," he said.

He pulled off the sealing tape and slowly unfolded the wrapping paper. Pat watched him, noticing the slight trembling of his hands. It was, for her, a moment of intense human pity. We are all vulnerable and afraid, she thought – in our different ways.

Matthew removed the last of the wrapping paper and silently handed the picture over to Guy Peploe. Then he glanced at Pat, and lowered his eyes. At the counter, Big Lou stood quite still, her cloth in her hand, her gaze fixed on the Peploe? and Peploe.

Guy Peploe looked at the painting. He held it away from himself for a few moments, narrowing his eyes. Then he turned it round and looked at the back of the canvas. Then he laid it down on the table.

"I'm sorry," he said. "I'm a Peploe – this isn't."

Matthew and Pat had both been holding their breath; now they exhaled together, and it seemed to Pat as if Matthew would continue to lose air until he deflated completely, leaving just his skin, like an empty balloon. Instinctively she reached out for his hand, which, when she found it, was clammy to the touch.

"It doesn't matter," she whispered. "You never really thought it was. It's all my fault for raising your hopes."

Guy Peploe looked at Matthew. "Yes," he said. "I can well see how you could have thought it was by Peploe. You must have a good eye."

This kind remark may have been meant, or it may not; Pat could not tell. She thought it likely that he was just being kind, and certainly it was a generous thing to say. It would have been easy for him to have dismissed their hopes out of hand, and thus belittled Matthew; but he had not done that. Instead, he had been courteous.

Guy Peploe now picked up the painting and touched it gently with his forefinger. "The paint's all wrong, I'm afraid," he said. "My grandfather painted on absorbent surfaces. This meant that the linseed oil was drained out of the paint and as a result the surface has a lovely, scratchy texture to it. He worked on board, you know. He bought pieces of wood which he would then put in the top of his paint box and work on right there. Sometimes there are grains of sand in the paint because he would be painting on the beach.

"And then there's the subject. This is Mull, of course, but it's not quite the right angle for Peploe's work. My grandfather used to go up to the northern part of Iona and paint Mull from there. There were one or two beaches that he liked in particular. All the paintings he did of Mull from Iona are from that perspective." He paused, squinting at the painting before him. "Now that over there is definitely Ben More, but it's Ben More from a rather strange angle. I'm not sure if this view is real at all. It's almost as if somebody has taken bits of Mull and stuck them together. I'm sorry, but that's what it seems like to me."

"But what about the signature?" asked Pat. "That SP in the corner there."

Guy Peploe smiled. "Signatures can be misleading. Some artists never signed their work and yet signatures appear on them later on. That doesn't mean that the picture in question is a forgery – it's just that somebody has added a signature."

"Why would they do that?" asked Matthew.

"Because they think that the painting's genuine," explained Guy Peploe. "And it may well be genuine. But then they think that the best way of shoring up their claim that it's by the artist in question is to add a signature – just to add an extra bit of certainty!"

"And did Peploe sign?" asked Pat.

"Yes," said Guy Peploe. "He signed works that he was particularly pleased with. He did not use SP, as far as I know."

As he spoke, Guy Peploe suddenly leaned forward and examined the painting closely. "You know, there's something rather interesting here," he muttered. "Yes, look. I'm pretty sure that this is an overpainting. I think that there's another painting underneath." He held the painting up so that the light fell upon it from a different angle. "Yes, look at that. Look just above Ben More there. Can you see the shape of . . . yes, the shape of an umbrella?"

They looked, and yes, at a certain angle, there appeared to be the shape of an umbrella. But what would an umbrella be doing above Ben More? The West did indeed get a lot of rain – but not *that* much.

97. *More about Bertie*

Irene and Bertie always arrived punctually for Bertie's session of psychotherapy with Dr Fairbairn, and the famous analyst, author of that seminal study on Wee Fraser, was always ready for them. They saw him jointly, which Dr Fairbairn explained was the best way of dealing with an issue in which two parties were involved.

"I could ask you about Bertie, and Bertie about you," he said. "And in each case I would get a very different story, quite sincerely put. But if I speak to both of you at the same time, then we shall get closer to the truth." For a moment he looked doubtful, and added: "That is, if there is such a thing as the truth."

This last comment puzzled Bertie. Of course there was such a thing as the truth, and it seemed inexplicable that an adult, particularly an adult like Dr Fairbairn, should doubt its existence. There were fibs and then there was the truth. Could Dr Fairbairn not tell the difference between the two? Was Dr Fairbairn perhaps a fibber?

"I fully understand," said Irene. She was pleased that Dr Fairbairn had invited her to sit in on the therapy sessions, as she enjoyed listening to the sound of his voice, and she delighted in his subtle, perceptive questioning. His manner was suggestive, she had decided; not suggestive in any pejorative sense, but suggestive in the sense that he could elicit responses that revealed something important.

That morning, as Dr Fairbairn ushered them into his consulting room, she noticed that there was a new copy of the *International Bulletin of Dynamic Psychoanalysis* lying on the top of his desk. The sight thrilled her, and she tried, by craning her neck, to make out the titles listed on the cover. *Mother as Stalin*, she read, *A New Analysis*. That looked interesting, even if the title was slightly opaque. It must be all about the need that boys are said to feel to get away from the influence of their mothers. Yes, she supposed that this was true: there were boys who needed to get away from their mothers, but that was certainly not Bertie's problem. She had a perfectly good relationship with Bertie, as Dr Fairbairn was no doubt in the process of discovering. Bertie's problem was . . . well, she was not sure what Bertie's problem was. Again, this was something that Dr Fairbairn would illuminate over the weeks and months to come. It was, no doubt, his anxieties over the good breast and what she had always referred to as Bertie's *additional part*. Boys tended to be anxious about their additional parts, which was strange, as she would have imagined an additional part was something to which one might reasonably be quite indifferent, in the same way one was indifferent to other appendices, such as one's appendix.

And then there was another, quite fascinating article: *Marian Apparitions in Immediate Post War Italy: Popular Hysteria and the Virgin as Christian Democrat*. That looked very interesting indeed; perhaps she could ask Dr Fairbairn whether she could borrow that once he had read it. The Virgin tended to appear in all sorts of places and at all sorts of times, but there was sometimes a question mark over those who saw her. Rome urged caution in such cases, as did Vienna . . .

Bertie sat down next to Dr Fairbairn's desk while Irene sat on a chair against the wall, where Bertie could not see her while he was talking to the psychotherapist.

"How do you feel today, Bertie?" asked Dr Fairbairn. "Are you feeling happy? Are you feeling angry?"

Bertie stared at Dr Fairbairn. He noticed that the tie he was wearing had a small teddy-bear motif woven into it. Why, he wondered, would Dr Fairbairn wear a teddy-bear tie? Did he still play with teddy-bears? Bertie had noticed that some adults were strange that way; they hung on to their teddy bears. He had a teddy bear, but he was no longer playing with him. It was not that he was punishing him, nor that his teddy bear, curiously, had no additional part; it was just that he no longer liked his bear, who smelled slightly of sick after an unfortunate incident some months previously. That was all there was to it – nothing more.

"Do you like teddy bears, Dr Fairbairn?" asked Bertie. "You have teddy bears on your tie."

Dr Fairbairn smiled. "You're very observant, Bertie. Yes, this is a rather amusing tie, isn't it? And do I like teddy bears? Well, I suppose I do. Most people think of teddy bears as being rather attractive, cuddly creatures." He paused. "Do you know that song about teddy bears, Bertie?"

"*The Teddy Bears' Picnic?*"

"Exactly. Do you know the words for it, Bertie?"

Bertie thought for a moment. "*If you go down to the woods today . . .*"

"*You're sure of a big surprise!*" continued Dr Fairbairn. "*If you go down to the woods today/ You'd better go in disguise.* And so on. It's a nice song, isn't it Bertie?"

"Yes," said Bertie. "But it's a bit sad, too, isn't it?"

Dr Fairbairn leaned forward. This was interesting. "Sad, Bertie? Why is *The Teddy Bears' Picnic* sad?"

"Because some of the teddy bears will not get a treat," said Bertie. "Only those who have been good. That's what the song says. *Every bear who's ever been good/ Is sure of a treat today*. What about the other bears?"

Dr Fairbairn's eyes widened and he scribbled a note on a pad of paper before him. "They get nothing, I'm afraid. Do you think that you would get something if you went on a picnic, Bertie?"

"No," said Bertie. "I would not. The teddy bears who set fire to their Daddies' copies of *The Guardian* will get nothing at that picnic. Nothing at all."

There was a silence. Then Dr Fairbairn asked another question.

"Why did you set fire to Daddy's copy of *The Guardian*, Bertie? Did you do that because guardian is another word for parent? Was *The Guardian* your Daddy because Daddy is your guardian?"

Bertie thought for a moment. Dr Fairbairn was clearly mad, but he would have to keep talking to him; otherwise the psychotherapist might suddenly kill both him and his mother. "No," he said. "I like Daddy. I don't want to set fire to Daddy."

"And do you like *The Guardian*?" pressed Dr Fairbairn.

"No," said Bertie. "I don't like *The Guardian*."

"Why?" asked Dr Fairbairn.

"Because it's always telling you what you should think," said Bertie. "Just like Mummy."

98. Irene and Dr Fairbairn Converse

With Bertie sent off to the waiting room where he might occupy himself with an old copy of *Scottish Field*, Irene and Dr Fairbairn shared a cup of strong coffee in the consulting room, mulling over the outcome of Bertie's forty minutes of intense conversation with his therapist.

"That bit about teddy bears was most interesting," said Dr Fairbairn, thoughtfully. "He had constructed all sorts of anxieties around that perfectly simple account of a bears' picnic. Quite remarkable."

"Very strange," said Irene.

"And as for that exchange over *The Guardian*," went on Dr Fairbairn. "I was astonished that he should see you as overly directional. Quite astonished."

"Absolutely," said Irene. "I've never pushed him to do anything. All his little enthusiasms, his Italian, his saxophone, are of his own choosing. I've merely facilitated."

"Of course," said Dr Fairbairn hurriedly. "I knew as much. But then children misread things so badly. But it's certainly nothing for you to worry yourself about."

He paused, placing his coffee cup down on its saucer. "But then that dream he spoke about was rather fascinating, wasn't it? The one in which he saw a train going into a tunnel. That was interesting, wasn't it?"

"Indeed," said Irene. "But then, Bertie has always had this thing about trains. He goes on and on about them. I don't think there's any particular symbolism in his case – he really is dreaming about trains *qua* trains. Other boys may be dreaming about . . . well about other things when they dream about trains. But not Bertie."

"But what about tunnels?" asked Dr Fairbairn.

"We have one in Scotland Street," said Irene. "There's a tunnel under the road. But nobody's allowed to go into it."

"Ah," said Dr Fairbairn. "A forbidden tunnel! That's very significant!"

"It's closed," said Irene.

"A forbidden tunnel would be," mused Dr Fairbairn.

They both thought about this for a moment, and then Dr Fairbairn, reaching out for his cup of coffee, returned to the subject of dreams. "I have never underestimated the revelatory power of the dream," he said. "It is the most perfect documentary of the unconscious. The film script of both the id and the ego – dancing their terrible dance, orchestrated by the sleeping mind. Don't you think?"

"Oh, I do," said Irene. "And do you analyse your own dreams, Dr Fairbairn?"

"Most certainly," he replied. "May I reveal one to you?"

"But, of course." Irene loved this. It must be so lonely being Dr Fairbairn and having so few patients – perhaps none, apart from herself – with whom he could communicate on a basis of intellectual and psychoanalytical equality.

"My dream," said Dr Fairbairn, "occurred some years ago – many years in fact, and yet my memory of it is utterly vivid. In this dream I was somewhere in the West – Argyll possibly – and staying in a large house by the edge of a sea loch. The house was a couple of hundred yards from the edge of the loch, and it was set about with grass of the most extraordinary verdant colour. And this grass was touched with the golden light, as of the morning sun.

"The woman who lived in this house had a name, unlike so many people who come to us in our dreams. She was called Mrs Macgregor – I remember that very distinctly – and she was kind to the guests. There were other people there too, but I did not know them. Mrs Macgregor was gentle and welcoming – she made a tray of tea and then took me gently by the hand and led me across the lawn to a shed beside the loch. And I can remember the smell of the air, which had that tangle of seaweed that you get in the West and that softness too. And I did not want her to let go of my hand.

"We came to the shed and she opened it for me, and do you know, there inside was a lovingly preserved art-nouveau typesetting machine. And I marvelled at this and turned round, and Mrs Macgregor was walking away from me, back towards the house, and I felt a great sense of loss. And that is when I awoke, and the house and the grass and the sea loch faded, but left me with the most extraordinary sense of peace – as if I had been vouchsafed a vision.

"Many years later, I was in a restaurant in Edinburgh, with a largish group of people after a meeting. We were sitting there waiting for our dinner to be served and the subject of dreams arose. I decided to narrate my dream, and there was a sudden hush in the restaurant. Everybody had started to listen to it – the other diners, the waiters, the Italian proprietor of the restaurant, Pasquale, as he was called – everybody.

"And there was a complete silence when I finished. Then, one of the other members of the party – a most distinguished Edinburgh psychiatrist, broke the silence. He said: *Mrs Macgregor is your mother!*

"And of course Henry was right, and everybody in the restaurant started to talk again, loudly, with relief, perhaps, because they were reassured that their mothers were with them too – their mothers had not gone away."

Irene was touched by this story, and she was silent too, as had been the diners in that restaurant. She wondered whether she dared tell Dr Fairbairn about her own dream, that had come to her only a few nights previously, in which she had been in the Floatarium, in the flotation tank, and there had been a knocking on the door, and she had opened the lid and seen a blonde child standing outside, like that figure of Cupid in the painting *Love Locked Out*. And now she realised that BLONDE CHILD could be translated, in Scots, or half in Scots, to make FAIR BAIRN.

She could not tell him this, because this was dangerous, dangerous ground. So she closed her eyes instead, and thought of her life. She was married to Stuart, and she was the mother of Bertie. And yet she was lonely, hopelessly lonely, because there was nobody with whom she could talk about these things that mattered so much to her. Perhaps things would change when Bertie went to the Steiner School, as he was due to do shortly. Then there would be other Steiner mothers, and she could talk to them. There would be coffee mornings and bring-and-buy sales in aid of the new personal development equipment for the school. And she would not have to go to the Floatarium and float in isolation but would be part of something bigger, and more vibrant, and accepting, as communities used to be, before our fall from grace, the shattering of our Eden.

99. Bruce Takes a Bath, and Thinks

In the bathroom of his flat at 44 Scotland Street, Bruce Anderson stood before the mirror, wearing only the white boxer shorts which his mother had given him for his last birthday. The light in the bathroom was perfect for such posing – light from a north-facing skylight which, although clear, was not too harsh. This light allowed for the development of interesting shadows – shadows which brought out the contours of the pectorals, which provided for shades and nuances in the shoulders and the sweep of the forearms.

Bruce was not unaware of his good looks. As a small boy he had become accustomed to the admiring glances which he attracted from adults. Elderly women would reach out and pat him on the head, ruffling his hair, and muttering *little angel* or *wee stunner*, and Bruce would reward them with a smile, an act of beneficence on his part which usually brought forth more exclamations from his admirers. As he became older, the women who patted his head began to desist (although they still felt the urge), as one does not pat every teenage boy on the head, no matter how strong the temptation to do so. The looks of adults were now supplemented with the wistful glances of coevals, particularly the teenage girls of Crieff, for whom Bruce seemed some sort of messenger of beauty – a sign that even in Crieff might one find a boy so transcendentally exciting that all limitations of place, all frustrations at the fact that one lived in Crieff and not in Edinburgh, or Newport Beach, or somewhere like that, might be overcome.

Beauty, of course, has its moment, which may sometimes be very brief, but in Bruce's case the looks which had driven so many of those girls in Crieff and surrounds to an anguish of longing, survived; indeed they mellowed, and here he was, he told himself, more attractive than ever before; a picture, he thought, of the young man at the height of his powers.

He moved closer to the mirror, and standing sideways, he pressed his right arm and side against its cold surface. This brought him closer to himself, like a conjoined twin. He moved his arm up, and his handsome twin's arm moved up too. He smiled, and his brother smiled too, in immediate recognition. Then he turned round and faced himself in the mirror – so close now that his breath clouded the glass, a white mist that came and went quickly, and was strangely erotic. He moved his lips closer to the lips in the mirror, and for a moment they stayed there, almost, but not quite touching, united, for there was something that was beginning to worry Bruce. With whom, exactly, was he in love?

Sally, he said to himself as he turned away from the mirror – a wrench, of course, but he did turn away – with Sally, the girl he had even thought of asking to marry him. She would be keen on that, he imagined, and would naturally accept, but then he had thought that perhaps it was premature. Certainly he liked her – he liked her a great deal – but marriage was perhaps taking it a bit far.

He slipped out of the boxer shorts and then lowered himself into the water. Lying there, he could look up through the skylight and watch the clouds scudding across the evening sky. He liked to do this, and to think; and now he was thinking about his job and how the time had come to move on. He had decided that he had had enough of being a surveyor for Macaulay Holmes Richardson

Black. He had had enough of working for Todd, with his pedantic insistence on set office procedures and his tendency to lecture. What a narrow universe that man inhabited! The Royal Institution of Chartered Surveyors! The world of clients and their selfish demands and complaints! Was this what lay ahead of him? Bruce found himself thoroughly depressed by the thought. He would not allow it. He was cut out for a wider, more interesting world than that, and he now had a clear idea of how he would achieve it.

He would have lingered longer in the bath, but the thought of that evening's engagement stirred him. Hardly bothering with the mirror, he dressed quickly, gelled his hair, and went into the kitchen. He had eaten very little for lunch and made a sandwich for himself before going out: a piece of French bread sliced down the middle, into which he inserted a piece of the cheese which he had purchased the day before from one of Ian Mellis's cheese shops. Bruce liked that particular shop; he liked the way one of the girls behind the counter smiled at him and offered him samples of cheese. Bruce leaned forward over the counter and allowed her to slip the slivers of cheese into his mouth, which she obviously enjoyed; and it was a small thing, really, giving her that thrill – no trouble to him and it clearly meant a lot to her.

There was no sign of Pat as he left the flat. Poor girl, he thought. He had seen her in the Cumberland Bar the other evening with that man who had the strange dog, but he had pretended not to see her, as he did not want her to feel any worse than she must already feel. It could not be easy for her – seeing him with Sally while all the time she fancied him terribly, even going to the extent, as she had, of lying on his bed when he was not there. That was amazing, but that's how women behaved, in Bruce's experience. He would never forget that girlfriend of his when he was eighteen – the one who had gone to India for three months and who had taken a pair of his boxer shorts with her so that she could sleep with them each night under her pillow. That was disconcerting, and Bruce had been embarrassed that she had written and told him about this on a postcard which anybody, including that nosy postman in Crieff, could have read. The postman had looked at him sideways, and smiled, but when Bruce had accused him of reading his postcards he had become belligerent and had said: "Watch your lip, Jimmy." That was not the way the postal authorities were meant to behave when faced with a complaint, but the postman was considerably bulkier than Bruce and he had been obliged to say nothing more about it.

He left the flat and went downstairs. A friend at work had arranged the meeting for him, and now he was bound for the wine bar, where Will Lyons would be waiting. Will was the man to give him advice, he had been told, about the new career that Bruce had mapped out for himself. The wine trade. Smart. Sophisticated. Very much more to his taste – and waiting at his feet.

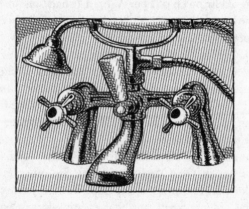

100. Bruce Expounds

Will Lyons had agreed to meet Bruce at the request of his friend, Ed Black. Ed knew a colleague of Bruce's through Roddy Martine, who knew everybody of course, even if he was not absolutely sure whether he knew Bruce. There was a Crieff connection to all this. Roddy Martine had attended a party at the Crieff Hydro, which was run by the cousin of Ross Leckie, a friend of Charlie Maclean, who had been at the party and who had introduced him to Bruce, who knew Jamie Maclean, who lived not far from Crieff. It was that close.

Will knew about wine, as he had spent some years in the wine trade. Bruce had been told this, and wanted to get some advice on how to get a job. He was confident that this could be arranged, but he knew that contacts were useful. Will could come up with introductions, although he did not want to ask him for these straightaway. So this meeting was more of a general conversation about wine. Will would see that Bruce knew what he was talking about and the rest would follow, but all in good time.

Will was waiting for him in the wine bar. Although they had not met before, Bruce had been told to look out for the most dapper person in the room. "That'll be Will," Ed had said.

They shook hands.

"You must let me do this," said Bruce, reaching for his wallet. "Glass of wine?"

"Thank you," said Will, reaching for the wine menu.

Bruce picked up a copy of the menu and looked down it. "Not too bad." He paused, and frowned. "But look at all these Chardonnays! Useless grape! Flabby, tired. Did you see that article in *The Decanter* a few weeks ago? Did you see it? It was all about those ABC clubs in New York – Anything But Chardonnay. I can see what they mean – revolting against Chardonnay."

"Well," said Will quietly, "there are some . . ."

"I never touch it myself," said Bruce. "It's fine for people who get their wine in supermarkets. Fine for women. Hen parties. That sort of thing. Fine for them. But I won't touch it. May as well drink Blue Nun."

"Do you like champagne?" Will asked politely.

"Do I like champagne?" replied Bruce. "Is the Pope a Catholic? Of course I do. I adore the stuff."

"And Chablis?"

"Boy, do I love Chablis! I had the most marvellous bottle the other day. Fantastic. Flinty, really flinty. Like biscuits, you know. Just great."

Will was about to point out that the Chardonnay grape is used to make both champagne and Chablis, but decided not to. It was fashionable, amongst those who knew very little, to decry Chardonnay, but it was still a great variety, even if its reputation had been damaged by the flooding of the market with vast quantities of inferior wine.

"Of course I'm much more New World than Old World," Bruce went on, scanning further down the list. "France is finished in my view. Finished."

Will looked surprised. "France? Finished?"

Bruce nodded. "Washed out. They just can't compete with the New World boys – they just can't. If you sit down with a bottle of good California – even a modestly-priced bottle – and then you sit down with a bottle of Bordeaux, let's say, the California wins every time – every time. And a lot of people think like me, you know."

Will looked doubtful. "But don't you think that these New World wines wane after two or three mouthfuls?"

"No," said Bruce. "Not at all."

Will smiled. "But, you know, these New World wines give you a sudden burst of delight, but don't you think that they rather drown the flavour? French wines usually are much more complex. They're meant to go with food, after all."

"You can eat while you're drinking New World wines, too," said Bruce. "I often do that. I have a bottle of California and I find it goes well with pasta."

"Red or white?" asked Will.

"White with pasta," said Bruce. "All the time."

They both looked at the menu.

"Here's one for me," said Bruce. "I'm going to get a half bottle of Muddy Wonga South Australian. That's a big wine – really big."

Will looked at the Muddy Wonga listing. "Interesting," he said. "I've never heard of that. Have you had it before?"

"Lots of times," said Bruce. "It's got a sort of purple colour to it and a great deal of nose."

"Could be the mud," suggested Will quietly, but Bruce did not hear.

"And you?" asked Bruce. "What are you going to have?"

"Well," said Will. "I rather like the look of this Bordeaux. Pomerol."

"A left bank man," said Bruce.

"Actually, it's on the right bank," said Will quietly.

"Same river," said Bruce.

Will agreed. "Of course."

"Of course at least you'll get it with a cork in it," said Bruce. "None of those ghastly screw caps. Do you know I was at a restaurant the other day – with this rather nice American girl I've met – and they served the wine in a screw cap bottle. Can you believe it?"

"Screw caps are very effective," Will began. "There are a lot of estates . . ."

Bruce ignored this. "But can you believe it? A screw cap in a decent restaurant? I almost sent it back."

"Corked?" ventured Will.

"No, it had a screw cap," said Bruce.

They ordered their wine, which was served to them in a few minutes. Bruce poured himself a glass and held it up to his nose.

"Superb," he said. "The winemaker at Muddy Wonga is called Lofty Shaw. He had some training at Napa and then went back to Australia. Here, smell this."

He passed his glass under Will's nose.

"Blackcurrants," said Bruce. "Heaps of fruit. Bang."

Will nodded. "It's a big wine," he said.

"Huge," said Bruce. "Muscular. A wine with pecs!"

Will said nothing for a moment. Then he asked Bruce about his plans.

"I'm fed up to here with surveying," said Bruce. "So I thought I might try something in the wine trade. Something that will allow me to use my knowledge."

Will looked thoughtful. "You have to work your way up," he said. "It's like any business."

"Yes, yes," said Bruce. "But I know the subject. I would have thought I could start somewhere in the middle and then get my MW in a year or so."

"It's not that simple," said Will.

"Oh, I know," said Bruce. "But I'm prepared to wait. A year, eighteen months, max."

Will stared at Bruce. He was uncertain what to say.

101. Pat and Bruce: an Exchange

Bruce was quite pleased with the way in which the meeting with Will Lyons had gone. He had been able to set him right on one or two matters – including the primacy of New World wines – and he had also been able to change his mind, he was sure, about Chardonnay. It was strange, thought Bruce, that somebody like that should be prepared to drink Chardonnay when everybody else was getting thoroughly sick of it.

And the end result of all this was that Will had offered to speak to somebody and find out if there were any openings coming up in the wine trade. Bruce was confident that there would be such an opportunity, and had decided that he might as well hand in his resignation at Macaulay Holmes Richardson Black. He would probably have to work out a month or two of notice, but that would mean that he could take a holiday for a month or so before starting in the wine trade.

Todd would probably try to persuade him to stay, but he would refuse. He could just imagine the scene: Todd would talk about the training the firm had given him – "Does that mean nothing to you, Bruce?" – and he would try to appeal to his better nature. But all that would be in vain.

"I'm very sorry," he would say. "I'm very sorry, Mr Todd, but my mind is made up. I've got nothing against Macaulay Holmes and so on but I really feel that I need something more stimulating. Less dull."

That would floor Todd – to hear his world described as dull. Bruce relished the thought. He might go on a bit, although he would not really want to rub it in. "Being a surveyor is all right for some," he would say. "I'm sure that you're happy enough doing it, but some of us need something which requires, how shall I put it, a little bit more flair."

Poor Todd! He would have no answer to that. It would almost be cruel, but it needed to be said and it would make up for all the humiliation that Bruce had endured in having to listen to those penny-lectures from his employer. All that going on about professional ethics and obligation and good business practice and all the rest; no more of that for Bruce. And in its place would come wine-tastings and buying trips to California, and the opportunity to mix with those glamorous, leggy, upper-crust girls who tended to frequent the edges of the wine trade. What an invigorating thought! – and it was all so close. All that he needed to do was find the job.

It occurred to Bruce that it would be nice if he were to be interviewed for the job by a woman. Bruce knew that he could get women to do anything he wanted them to do, and if he could somehow engineer things that the job decision was to be made by a woman, then he was confident that he would walk into it.

He had returned to the flat and was sitting in the kitchen, thinking of this delicious future, when he heard the door open. That would be Pat, poor girl, coming home from a dull evening somewhere. He would be nice to her, he decided; he could afford to be generous, now that things were going so well for him.

When Pat came into the kitchen, Bruce gave her a smile.

"Cup of coffee?" he said. "I was going to make myself one."

Pat blushed. She tried to stop herself, but she blushed, and he noticed, for he smiled again. Poor girl: she can't look at me without blushing.

Bruce rose to his feet and went to the coffee grinder.

"I'll make you something really nice," he said. "Irish coffee. I learned how to do it in Dublin. We went over for a rugby tour once and one of the Irish guys taught me how to make Irish coffee. I'll make you a cup."

"I'm not sure," said Pat, faltering. "I'm a bit tired."

"Nonsense," said Bruce. "Sit down. I won't make it too strong."

Pat sat down at the kitchen table and watched him going about the business of making the coffee. She could not help but stare at the shape of his back and the casual way he stood; at his arms, half-exposed by the rolled-up sleeves of his dark-blue rugby jersey; and she thought: *I can't help myself – I just can't. I have to look at him.*

He turned round suddenly and saw her staring at him. He lowered his eyes, as if in embarrassment, and then looked up again.

"It's hard for you, isn't it?" he said.

She bit her lip. She could not speak.

"Yes, it must be hard for you to deal with," he went on. "Me and Sally. And there's you. Hard."

"I don't know what you're talking about," Pat muttered, her face burning with shame.

Bruce took several steps forward and stood next to her. He touched her on the shoulder, and then moved his hand across to lay it gently against her cheek.

"You're burning up," he said. "Poor Pat. You're burning up. Poor wee girl. You're on fire."

She moved a hand to brush him away from her cheek, but Bruce simply closed his hand about hers.

"Look," he said. "Let's be adult about this. I'm involved with this American girl, but not as involved as you might think. I'm not going to marry her after all. I'll still go out with her, but it's nothing permanent. So I can make you happy too. Why not? Share me."

For a moment Pat said nothing. Then, as the meaning of his words became clear to her, she gasped, involuntarily, and pulled her hand away from his grasp. Then she pushed her chair back, knocking it over, and stumbled to her feet. She looked at him, and saw him quite clearly, more clearly than she would have believed possible. And she was filled with revulsion.

"I don't believe it," she whispered. "I don't believe it."

Bruce smiled, and then shrugged. "Offer's on the table, Patsy girl. Think about it. My door is always open, as they say."

102. *Paternal Diagnosis*

In her misery, she hardly remembered the journey across town by bus, or the walk from Churchill to the family house in the Grange. Her father was alone in the house – her mother was in Perth for several days, visiting her sister – and he was waiting for her solicitously in the hall. She fumbled with her key and he opened the door to let her in, immediately putting his arm about her.

"My dear," he said. "My dear."

She looked up at him. He had realised from her telephone call that there was something wrong, and he was there, waiting for her, as he had always been. It had never been her mother who had comforted her over the bruises of childhood – she had seemed so distant, not intentionally, but because that was her way, the result of an inhibited, unhappy youth. Her father, though, had always been at hand to explain, to comfort, to sympathise.

They went through to the family living room. He had been reading, and there were several books and journals scattered across the coffee table. And there, near the chair, were his slippers – the leather slippers that she had bought him from Jenners for a birthday some years ago.

"I don't think I even have to ask you," he said. "It's that young man, is it not? That young man in the flat."

It did not surprise her that he should have guessed. He had always had an intuitive ability to work out what was happening, the ability to see what it was that was troubling people. She imagined that this came from years of experience with his patients, listening to them, understanding their distress.

She nodded. "Yes."

"And?"

"I thought I liked him. Now I don't."

"Are you sure?"

"I'm sure. But I'm . . . I'm a bit upset."

Her father took his arm from her shoulder. "Of course you're upset. Falling out of love is every bit as painful as falling out of a tree – and the pain lasts far longer. Most of us have shed pints of tears about that.

"From what you told me about that young man, I would say that he has a narcissistic personality disorder. Such people are very interesting. They're not necessarily malevolent people – not at all – but they can be very destructive in the way they treat others."

Pat had discussed Bruce with her father, briefly, shortly after she had moved into the flat in Scotland Street. He had listened with apparent interest, but had said nothing.

"He's just so pleased with himself," she said. "He thinks that everyone, everyone, fancies him. He really does."

Her father laughed. "Of course he does. And the reason for that is that he sees himself as being just perfect. There's nothing wrong with him, in his mind. And he thinks that everybody else sees things the same way."

Pat thought about this. By falling for Bruce – that embarrassing aberration on her part – she had behaved exactly as he had thought she would behave. It had been no surprise to him that she had done this; this was exactly what women did, what he expected them to do.

She turned to her father. "Is it his fault?"

Her father raised an eyebrow. "Fault? That's interesting. What's fault got to do with it?"

"Can he help himself?" Pat said. "Could he be anything other than what he is? Could he behave any differently?"

"I'm not sure if your personality is under your control," said Pat's father. "It's the way you are, in a sense, rather like hair colour or stature. You can't be blamed in any way for being short rather than tall, or having red hair."

"So Bruce can't be blamed for being a narcissist?"

Pat's father thought for a moment. "Well, we have some control over defects in our characters. For example, if you know that you have a tendency to do something bad, then you might be able to do something about that. You could develop your faculty of self-control. You could avoid situations of temptation. You could try to make sure that you didn't do what your desires prompted you to do. And of course we expect that of people, don't we?"

"Do we?"

"Yes, we do. We expect people to control their greed, their avarice. We expect people who have a short temper at least to try to keep it under control."

"So Bruce could behave less narcissistically if he tried?"

Her father walked to the window and looked out into the darkness of the garden. "He could improve a bit perhaps. If he were given some insight into his personality, then he might be able to act in a way which others found less offensive. That's what we expect of psychopaths, isn't it?"

Pat joined him at the window. She knew each shadow in the garden; the bench where her mother liked to sit and drink tea; the rockery which in recent years had grown wild; the place where she had dug a hole as a child which had never been filled in.

"Is it?" she asked.

He turned to her. She liked these talks with him. Human nature, sometimes frightening; evil, always frightening, seemed tamed under his gaze; like a stinging insect under glass – the object of scientific interest, understood.

"Yes," he said. "Most people don't understand psychopathy very well. They think of the psychopath as the Hitchcockian villain – staring eyes and all the rest – whereas they're really rather mundane people, and there are rather more of them than we would imagine. Do you know anybody who's consistently selfish? Do you know anybody who doesn't seem to be troubled if he upsets somebody else – who'll use other people? Cold inside? Do you know anybody like that?"

Pat thought. Bruce? But she did not say it.

"If you do," her father went on. "Then it's possible that that person is a psychopath. One shouldn't simplify it, of course. Some people resort to a check list, Professor Hare's test. It stresses anti-social behaviour that occurs in the teenage years and then continues into the late twenties. There are other criteria too."

Pat's father paused. "Tell me something, my dear. This young man – could you imagine him being cruel to an animal?"

Pat was hesitant at first, but then decided. No, he would not. One could not describe Bruce as cruel. Nor cold, for that matter.

"No," she said. "I can't see him being unkind in that way."

"Not a psychopath," said her father simply.

103. And Then

Pat went back to Scotland Street that night. Her father had asked her whether she wanted to stay at home, but she had already decided that she would go back. She could not go home every time something went wrong, and then, if she did not return, Bruce would have effectively driven her out. She could imagine what he would think – and say – about her: *Far too immature – couldn't cope. Fell head over heels for me and then disappeared. Typical!* No, Bruce would not be allowed that victory; she would go back to the flat and face him. There would be no row; she would just be cool, and collected. And if he alluded in any way to what had happened she would simply say that she was no longer interested, which was the truth anyway. She would be strong. More than that; she would be indifferent.

She walked up the stair at 44 Scotland Street, up the cold, echoing stair. She walked past the Pollock door, with its anti-nuclear power sticker and she thought for a moment of Bertie, whom she had not seen for some time and whose saxophone seemed to have fallen silent. It was a week or more since she had heard him playing, and on that occasion the music had seemed remote and dispirited, almost sad. It was, she recalled, a version of Eric Satie's *Gymnopédie*, a piece written for piano but playable on the saxophone by a dexterous player. It was haunting music, but in Bertie's hands had seemed merely haunted. It was not surprising, of course, if that little boy was unhappy; anybody would be unhappy with Irene for a mother, or so she had been told by Domenica, who felt that Bertie was being prevented from being a little boy. How different had Pat's own childhood been. She had been allowed to be whoever she wanted to be, and had taken full advantage of this, pretending for three weeks at the age of thirteen to be Austrian (trying for her parents) and then Californian (extremely trying). Mothers like Irene were bad enough for daughters, Pat thought, but were frequently lethal for boys. Daughters could survive a powerful mother, but boys found it almost impossible. Such boys were often severely damaged and spent the rest of their lives running away from their mothers, or from anybody who remotely reminded them of their mothers; either that, or they *became their mothers*, in a desperate, misguided act of psychological self-defence.

In spite of her determination to face up to Bruce, she found that her hand was trembling as she inserted her key into the front door of the flat. As she turned the key and began to push the door open, she felt that she was being watched, and spun round and looked behind her, at Domenica's flat across the landing. That door was closed, but the tiny glass spy-hole positioned at eye-level above Domenica's brass name plate suddenly changed from dark to light, as if somebody within, looking out onto the landing, had moved away from the door. Had Domenica been watching her? Pat turned away and then quickly looked over her shoulder again. The spy-hole was darkened again.

Pat closed the door behind her and switched on the light in the hall. It was eleven o'clock, and Bruce's door was shut. There was no light coming from beneath the door and she was emboldened to move forward slowly and silently. She thought that she could hear music coming from his room, but it was very faint and she did not wish to go right up to the door; or did she? Treading softly, she returned to the light switch and turned off the hall light, and stood there in the darkness, her heart beating violently within her. She closed her eyes. He was there, in that room, and he had said to her that his door was always open. But what did she feel about him? She had been overcome with revulsion by what he had said to her earlier that evening and she had gone away despising him, hating him. But she could not really hate him, not really. She could not be cross with him, however arrogant and annoying he was. She simply could not.

She slipped out of her shoes and crossed the hall again and stood directly outside his door. There was no music – that had been imagined or had drifted in from somewhere else. Now there was just silence, and the beating of her heart, and her breath that came in short bursts. Never before had she felt like this; never, and this in spite of everything that had been said to her by her father, all that clarity of mind and vision overcome by nothing more than mere concupiscence.

Very slowly, she reached for the handle of his door and began to turn it. The handle was silent, fortunately, and the door moved slightly ajar as she pushed at it. Hardly daring to breathe, astonished at what she was doing, at her brazen act, she moved slowly through the open door and stood there, just over the threshold, in Bruce's room.

The room was not in complete darkness, as the curtains did not quite meet in the middle and some light came in from outside; light that fell, slanted, upon the bed near the window. Bruce lay there, half covered by a sheet, his dark hair a deep shadow on the pillow, one arm crooked under his head, and one foot and ankle protruding from the sheet at the foot of the bed.

Pat looked and saw the rise and fall of his chest and the flat of his midriff and she felt as if she would sway and stumble. She could reach out easily, so very easily, and touch him, touch this vision of beauty; she could lay her hand upon his shoulder, or upon his chest, but did not do so, and just stood there quietly, struggling with the temptation which was before her. And as she did so, she thought of something that Angus Lordie had said when he had quoted from Sydney Goodsir Smith, who talked of the earth spinning around in the emptiness. Yes, the earth spun in a great void in which our tiny issues and concerns were really nothing, and what small pleasure or meaning we could extract from this life we should surely clutch before our instant was over.

She took a step forward, and was closer to him now, but stopped, and quickly turned away and walked out of the room. Bruce had been awake, and she had seen his eyes open at the last moment as she approached and the smile that flickered, just visible, about his lips.

104. The Place We Are Going to

Sitting on the top deck of a number 23 bus, bound for an interview at the Rudolf Steiner School, Irene and Bertie looked down on the passing traffic and on the pedestrians going about their daily business.

"It would have been easier to go by car," Bertie observed. "We could have parked in Spylaw Road. The booklet said there was plenty of parking in Spylaw Road."

"Travelling by bus is more responsible," said Irene. "We must respect the planet."

"Which planet?" asked Bertie. He had a map of the planets in his room – or his space as it was called – and he had learned the names of many of them. Which planet did his mother mean?

"Planet Earth," said Irene. "The one we are currently occupying, as you may have noticed, Bertie."

Bertie considered this for a moment. He had great respect for the planet, but he also respected cars. And it was still a mystery to him as to what had happened to their own car. He had last seen it five weeks earlier; now it had disappeared.

"Where is our car, Mummy?" he asked quietly.

"Our car is parked," Irene replied.

"Where?"

Irene's tone was short when she replied. "I don't know. Daddy parked it. Ask him."

"I did," said Bertie. "He said that you parked it somewhere."

Irene frowned. Had she parked the car? She tried to remember when she had last driven it, but it seemed so long ago. Deciding to leave the conversation where it stood, she looked out of the bus window, over Princes Street Gardens and towards the distant, confident shape of the Caledonian Hotel. This trip to the Steiner School for an interview had been Dr Fairbairn's idea, although she had accepted it, eventually.

"Bertie must be able to move on," said the psychotherapist. "We all need to move on, even when we're five."

Irene looked pained. If Bertie moved on, then where, in the most general sense, would he go? And where would that leave her, his mother? Bertie was *hers*, her *creation*.

Dr Fairbairn picked up her concern, and sought to reassure her. "Moving on means that you may have to let go a bit," he said gently. "Letting go is very important."

This did not help Irene, and her expression made her disquiet clear. Melanie Klein would never have approved of the term moving on, which had a distinctly post-modern ring to it. Nor did she speak of closure, which was another word that in her opinion was overworked and clichéd. She had imagined Dr Fairbairn to be above such terms, but here he was using the words as easily as he might talk about the weightier concepts of transference and repression. She decided to sound him out about closure.

"And closure?" she said hesitantly, as one might propose something slightly risqué.

"Oh, he certainly needs closure," said Dr Fairbairn. "He needs closure over that *Guardian* incident. And then we need closure on trains. *Bertie's trains need to reach their terminus.*"

Irene looked at Dr Fairbairn. This was a most puzzling remark to make, and perhaps he would explain. But he did not.

"First we should think of how he can move on," said Dr Fairbairn. "Bertie needs a sense of where he's going. He needs to have a horizon."

"Well," said Irene, slightly resentfully. "I can hardly be accused of not offering him a sense of his future. When I take him to saxophone lessons I point out to him how pleased he will be in the future that he worked at the instrument. Later, much later, it will be a useful social accomplishment."

Dr Fairbairn nodded vaguely. "Saxophone?" he said. "Is an ability to play the saxophone a social accomplishment or is it an anti-social accomplishment? No reason to ask that, of course; just wondering."

Irene was quick to answer. "Saxophones provide a lot of pleasure for a lot of people," she said. "Bertie loves his saxophone." (She was ignoring, or had forgotten perhaps, that awful scene in the Floatarium where Bertie had shouted, quite unambiguously, *Non mi piace il sassofono*.)

"Oral behaviour," muttered Dr Fairbairn. "One puts the saxophone mouthpiece *in the mouth*. That's oral."

"But you have to do that with a wind instrument," began Irene. "And even if you have no oral fixation might you not still want to play the saxophone? Just for the music?"

"One might think that," said Dr Fairbairn, "if one were being naïve. But you and I know, don't we, that explanations at that level, attractive though they may be, simply obscure the symbolic nature of the conduct in question. Let us never forget that the apparent reason for doing something is almost always not the real reason for doing it.

"Take the building of the Scottish Parliament," went on Dr Fairbairn, warming to the theme. "People think that the fact that it is taking so long is because of all sorts of problems with designs and plans and so on. But have we stopped to ask ourselves whether the people of Scotland actually *want* to finish it? Could it not be that we are taking so much time to finish it because we know that once we finish it we'll have to take responsibility for Scotland's affairs? Westminster, in other words, is Mother – and indeed doesn't it call itself the Mother of Parliaments? It does – the language itself gives it all away. So Mother has asked us to build a parliament and that is exactly what we are doing. But when we finish, we fear that Mother will ask us to go away – or, worse still, Mother will go away herself. Many people don't really want that. They want Mother still to be there. So they're doing everything they can to drag out the process of construction.

"And here's another thing. Why does the parliament building look as if it's been made out of children's wooden building blocks? Isn't that obvious? It's because we want to please Mother by doing something juvenile, because we know that Mother herself doesn't want us to grow up. That's why it looks so juvenile. We'll win Mother's approval by doing something which confirms our child-like dependence."

Irene listened to all this with growing enthusiasm. What a brilliant analysis of modern Scotland! And he was right, too, about saxophones; of course they were oral things and she was no doubt running a risk of fixing Bertie in the oral stage by encouraging him to play one. But at least she knew now, and the fact that she knew would mean that she could overcome the sub-text of her actions. So she could continue to encourage Bertie to play the saxophone, while at the same time helping him to progress through the oral stage to a more mature identity.

She looked at Dr Fairbairn. "What you say is obviously true," she said. "But I wonder: what shall I do to move Bertie on?"

"Give him a clear sense of where he's going next," replied Dr Fairbairn. "Take him to the place he's going to. That is what we all need – to see the place we're going to."

105. Bertie's Friend

Bertie sat in a small waiting room while Irene talked to the director of admissions at the Steiner School. He was not alone; on the other side of the simply-furnished room was a boy of about his own age, or perhaps slightly older, a boy with tousled fair hair, freckles around the cheek bones, and a missing front tooth. Bertie, who was wearing corduroy dungarees and his red lace-up shoes, noticed that this boy was wearing jeans and a checked shirt. It was a splendid outfit, thought Bertie – the sort of outfit which he would have seen cowboys wearing in cowboy films, had he ever been allowed to watch any.

For a time they avoided eye contact, staring instead at the brightly-coloured pictures on the wall and the pattern of the tiles on the floor. Every so often, though, one of the boys would sneak a glance at the other, and then quickly look away before he was noticed.

Eventually, though, they glanced at the same time, and their eyes locked together. Bertie opened his mouth to speak, but the other boy spoke first.

"My name's Jock," said the boy. "What's your name?"

Bertie caught his breath. Jock was a wonderful name to have – it was so strong, so friendly. Life must be easy if one were lucky enough to be called Jock. But instead they had called him Bertie, and of course he could hardly tell this boy that.

"I don't usually give my name," Bertie said. "Sorry."

Jock frowned. "You can tell me. I won't tell anybody."

Bertie looked Jock squarely in the eye. "You can't break promises, you know."

"I know that," said Jock. "And I never would."

"Bertie," said Bertie.

"Hah!" said Jock.

A short silence followed. Then Bertie said: "Are you going to Steiner's?"

Jock shook his head. "I've come here for them to look at me," he said. "But I don't think my parents will send me here. I'm going to go to Watson's."

Bertie's eyes narrowed. Watson's! That was where he wanted to go – that was where they played rugby and had secret societies. That was where real boys went; sensitive boys came to the Steiner School. The thought caused him a pang of anguish. He would have liked Jock to be his friend, but now it seemed as if they would be going to different schools. All Bertie wanted was a friend – another boy who would like the same sort of things that he liked – trains and things of that sort. And he had no such person.

"I envy you going to Watson's," said Bertie. "You're lucky. Will you play rugby?"

"Yes," said Jock. "I've already started going to rugby for the under-sixes."

The words stabbed at Bertie. Rugby was the game he wanted to play – like that nice man, Bruce, who lived on the stair. But he had never had the chance, and it was clear, too, that his mother disapproved of Bruce, and of Mrs Macdonald, and of everyone, really, except for Dr Fairbairn, who was mad, as far as Bertie could work out. Would Irene disapprove of his new friend, Jock? He thought she probably would.

"Do you like trains?" Bertie asked suddenly.

Jock took the sudden change of subject in his stride. "I love them," he said.

Bertie looked wistful. "Have you . . . have you ever been on a train?" he asked.

Jock nodded. "Of course," he said. "I went to London on a train, and back again. And I've been to Dundee. I went over the Forth Bridge and the Tay Bridge. Then we came back and went over the bridges again. That's four times over a bridge altogether. Or does that make five?"

"Four," said Bertie. What did it matter if Jock was no good at mathematics? – he played rugby and was just the sort of friend for whom Bertie had longed all his life.

"And I've got a model train set in my room," Jock went on. "I've got a Flying Scotsman. It goes under my bed and round the chair. I've got bridges too, and a station."

Bertie was silent for a moment. Then he spoke. "You're lucky," he said. And then repeated: "You're lucky."

Jock looked at him. Then he stood up and crossed the room to sit next to Bertie.

"You're sad about something," he said quietly. "What's wrong?"

Bertie looked into the face of his new friend, gazing at the freckles and the space where the tooth had been. "I don't have much fun," he said. "And I've got no friends."

"You've got me," said Jock. "We could become blood brothers. One of my babysitters read me a story about some boys who became blood brothers. They cut their hands just there and they mixed their blood together. And that makes you a blood brother."

"Doesn't it hurt?" asked Bertie.

"No," said Jock. "We could become blood brothers right now. I've got my penknife."

Bertie was astonished: he had never been allowed a knife, but now Jock took a bulky Swiss Army penknife out of his pocket and showed it in the palm of his hand. "See," said Jock. "See that."

Bertie gazed at the knife. There were numerous blades and devices on the knife; one could do anything with an implement like that.

"Here," said Jock, prising out a blade. "I'll cut myself first, if you like. You have to do it here, in this bit of skin between the thumb and this finger. Then you squeeze the blood out into the palm of your hand and you shake hands with your friend. That's how it works."

Bertie watched in fascination as Jock held the gleaming blade above the taut skin, and drew in his breath sharply as his new friend made a small incision. Small droplets of blood welled up, and were quickly smeared by Jock across his palm.

"Now your turn," said Jock, wiping the blade on the leg of his jeans.

Bertie held out his right hand, the forefinger pulled back from the thumb, revealing the waiting stretch of skin. Jock steadied the blade and looked at Bertie.

"Are you ready?" he asked. "Do you want to close your eyes?"

"No," said Bertie. "I don't mind. It won't hurt, will it?"

"No," said Jock. "It won't hurt."

And at that moment the door opened and Irene came out. For a moment she stood quite still, slow to absorb the extraordinary sight before her. Then she screamed, and rushed forward to snatch the knife from Jock's hand.

"What on earth are you doing?" she shouted.

Bertie looked down at the floor. He struggled against the tears, but in vain; he did not want Jock – brave Jock – to see him cry. He had longed for a friend like Jock, and now he was being taken away from him, snatched away by his mother. It had been so close, that ceremony of blood brotherhood, and it would have made all the difference to have had a blood brother. But it was not to be.

Bertie felt a great sense of loss.

106. Lunch at the Café St Honoré

Sasha had been shopping in George Street. She had spent more than she intended – over two hundred pounds, when one totted it up – but she reminded herself that money was no longer an object. A few days earlier, she had received a letter from a firm of solicitors to the effect that the residue of her aunt's estate, which had been left to her, amounted to over four hundred and eighty thousand pounds. When she had been first told that she was the residuary beneficiary, Todd had explained that the residue was what was left after everybody else had taken their share.

"It's unlikely to be more than a couple of hundred pounds," he had said. "The legacies are bound to swallow most of it up, not that the old trout had very much, I suspect."

The old trout, however, had been as astute an investor as her legacies had been mean. Five hundred pounds had been left to the Church of Scotland. Twenty-five pounds had been left to the Scottish Society for the Prevention of Cruelty to Animals; a further twenty-five pounds to the Gurkha Trust, and ten pounds to St George's School for Girls. The residue was to go to Sasha, and now that the estate had been ingathered by Messrs Turcan Connell it amounted to almost half a million pounds *after* the payment of duty.

It had taken some time for Sasha to accustom herself to the fact that she now had a considerable amount of money at her disposal. They had been comfortable enough before on Todd's drawings on the partnership of Macaulay Holmes Richardson Black, but having these uncommitted hundreds of thousands of pounds was material wealth on a scale which Sasha had previously not experienced. She was not a spendthrift, though, and this minor shopping spree in George Street had made her feel vaguely uncomfortable. If she spent two hundred pounds a day, every day, she wondered, how long would it take her to get through her fortune? About eight years, she calculated, allowing for the accumulation of interest.

She thought for a moment of what eight years of profligacy might be like. She could buy a new pair of shoes every day, and have at the end of that eight-year period more than two thousand pairs of shoes. But what could one do with such a mountain of shoes? This was the problem; there was a limit to what one could do with money. And yet here I am, she thought, feeling guilty about spending two hundred pounds.

She was thinking of this when she wandered into Ottakars Bookshop. Sasha was not a particularly keen reader, but she belonged to a book group that met every other month and she needed to buy the choice for their next meeting: Ronald Frame. At their last meeting they had discussed a novel by Ian Rankin, and one or two of the members had been slightly frightened. Sasha had been able to reassure them, though: nothing to worry about, she had said. Very well written, but nothing like that ever happens in Edinburgh. Or at least not in the Braids.

She moved to the Frame section in Ottakars. There was *The Lantern Bearers*, and there was *Time in Carnbeg*, the book group's choice. She picked it up and looked for a picture of the author. Sasha liked to know what the author looked like when she read a book. She did not like the look of Somerset Maugham, and had not read him for that reason. And she did not like the look of some of the younger woman novelists, who did nothing, it would seem, with their hair. *If they do nothing with their hair, then will they do much more with their prose?* she asked herself. And answered the question by avoiding these writers altogether. Such frumps. And always going on about how awful things were. Well, they weren't awful – and certainly not if one had four hundred and eighty thousand pounds (minus two hundred).

It was while she was examining the *Carnbeg* book for a picture of Ronald Frame that she became aware of another customer standing on her right, examining a shelf of wine books. And a further glance revealed that it was Bruce, the young man from the firm who had come to the Edinburgh South Conservative Association Ball at the Braid Hills Hotel. She had liked him even before the ball and his courteous behaviour on that evening – he had been extremely polite to Ramsey Dunbarton when he was going on about having been the Duke of Plaza-Toro in some dreadful operetta back in the year dot – had endeared him further to her. And he was terribly good-looking too, bearing in mind that he came from somewhere like Dunfermline, or was it Crieff?

She moved towards him and he looked up from the wine atlas he had been studying.

"Mrs Todd!"

"Please, not Mrs Todd," she said. "Please – Sasha."

Bruce smiled. "Sasha."

"You're looking at wine books," she said, peering at the atlas. "I wish I knew more about wine. Raeburn is quite informed, but I'm not."

Bruce smirked. Raeburn Todd would know nothing about wine, in his view. He would drink – what would he drink? Chardonnay!

"I find the subject very interesting," said Bruce. "And this atlas looks really useful. Look at this map. All the estates are listed in this tiny section of river bank. Amazing. Pity about the price, though. It's really expensive."

Sasha took the wine atlas from him and glanced at the back cover. Eighty-five pounds did seem like a lot of money for a book, but then the thought crossed her mind. Eighty-five pounds was not a great deal of money if you had over four hundred thousand pounds.

"Let me get it for you as a present," she said suddenly. And then she added: "And then let me take you for lunch at the Café St Honoré. Do you know it? It's just round the corner."

"But I couldn't," protested Bruce. "I couldn't let you."

"Please," she said. "Let me do this. I've just had wonderful good fortune and I want to share it. Please let me do this – just this once."

Bruce hesitated for a moment, but only for a moment. Women were always doing this sort of thing for him. They couldn't help themselves.

"All right," he said. "But at least let me buy us a bottle of wine at the restaurant. What do you like?"

"Chardonnay," said Sasha.

107. Confidences

They sat at a table for two, near the window. Bruce, who had completed a survey earlier than he had expected, was pleased to spend the few hours that he had in hand having lunch, and if this was in the company of an attractive woman (even if slightly blowsy) and at her expense, then all the better. The survey in question had been a singularly unpleasant chore – looking around a poky flat off Easter Road. The flat had been modernised by a developer in shim-sham style, with chip-board cupboards and glossy wallpaper. Bruce had shuddered, and had written in a low valuation, which would limit the price which the developer got for the property. Now, in the considerably more pleasing surroundings of the Café St Honoré, one might almost be in Paris, and he sat back and perused the menu with interest.

"I'm rather glad I bumped into you," said Sasha, fingering the gold bracelet on her wrist. "I had been wanting to talk to you."

Bruce raised an eyebrow. "I enjoyed the ball," he said. "Even if there were very few people there. More like a private party. Good fun."

Sasha smiled. "You were very good to poor old Ramsey Dunbarton," she said. "It can't have been much fun for you, listening to him going on about being the Duke of Plaza-Toro."

Bruce smiled. One could afford to be generous about the boring when people found one so fascinating. "It meant a lot to him, I suppose," he said. "Who was the Duke of Plaza-Toro anyway? Was he in the Tory Party?"

Sasha laughed. "Very droll," she said. "Now listen, did you talk to my daughter at all?"

"I did," said Bruce. "We got on rather well."

Sasha frowned. "That surprises me," she said. "She's been so contrary recently."

"I didn't notice that," said Bruce.

"Well, quite frankly, she worries me," Sasha went on. "And I wondered if you had any suggestions. You're in her age group. You might see something I'm missing."

Bruce scrutinised the menu. He was not sure whether he liked this line of conversation.

"Let me give you an example," Sasha went on. "At the ball, Lizzie won dinner for two at the Prestonfield Hotel. Now any normal girl would ask a friend along to join her. Lizzie didn't do that. No, she telephoned the hotel and asked them whether instead of a dinner for two she could have two separate dinners for one. Can you believe that?"

Bruce thought for a moment. "Perhaps she wasn't in the mood for company," he said. "We all feel like that sometimes."

"But that's how she seems to feel all the time," said Sasha, showing some exasperation. "She seems to make no effort to get friends. Or a decent job, for that matter."

"People are different," said Bruce. "She's not into drugs, I take it? She's not running around with a Hell's Angel, is she? Well then, what have you got to complain about? What do you want her to do anyway?"

"I want her to find a circle of friends," said Sasha. "Nice young people. I want her to have a good time. Maybe get a boyfriend. An outgoing type, who'd take her places. Give her some fun."

Bruce looked down at the table and moved his fork slightly, to make it parallel with his knife, as an obsessive-compulsive might do. She means somebody like me, he thought. Well, if the point about all this is to see whether I'm available, the answer will have to be no. There are limits to what one should do in the line of duty.

"She'll meet somebody," he said airily. "Give her the space. Let her get on with it."

"But she does nothing," said Sasha. "How can she meet somebody suitable if she won't go out with people? She needs to get into a group. You wouldn't be able to introduce her . . ."

Bruce did not allow her to finish her sentence. "I'm sorry," he said. "I'm very much involved with an American girl at the moment. I'm not really socialising in a crowd. I used to. But not now."

For a few moments the disappointment registered on Sasha's face, but she quickly recovered her composure. "Of course," she said. "I hadn't intended to ask you. I just wondered if you knew of anybody she might get to know. Parties, perhaps. That sort of thing."

"Sorry," said Bruce.

"Well, let's not think about it any more. I'm sure you're right. She'll sort herself out. Now, what are you going to have? Remember this is on me!"

They ordered their lunch, and a bottle of Chardonnay. They talked, easily, and in a friendly way. Sasha told a most amusing story about a scandal at her tennis club, and Bruce passed on a piece of office gossip which Todd had not mentioned to her – something about one of the secretaries. Then they talked about plans for the summer.

"Raeburn was thinking of going to Portugal," said Sasha. "We have friends with a villa there. It has a tennis court too."

"I like tennis," said Bruce. "I used to play a lot."

"I bet you were a strong player," said Sasha. She pictured him for a moment in tennis whites. His arms would be strong; his service hard to return.

"Moderately," said Bruce. "I need to work on my backhand."

"Don't we all!" said Sasha. "But look at your wrists. They're ideal for tennis. Look."

She reached out and took hold of his wrist playfully. "Yes," she said. "A real tennis player's wrist. You should keep up your game."

It was at that point that Todd came in. He had arranged to meet a colleague from another firm for lunch, to discuss, very tentatively, a possible merger. He did not see this colleague, who was late, but he did see his wife, sitting at a table in the window, holding hands with that young man from the office.

For a moment he did not move. Bruce looked up, and saw him,

and pulled his wrist away from Sasha's grasp. She looked round in astonishment and saw Todd, who was beckoning to Bruce.

Bruce stood up, shocked. "I'll explain to him," he mumbled.

Todd stared at Bruce as he came towards him. Very slowly, he lifted a hand and pointed directly at Bruce.

"You're history," he said quietly. "You're history."

"It's not what you think," said Bruce. "We were talking about tennis."

Todd did not seem to hear this. "You have an hour to clear your desk," hissed Todd. "You hear me? An hour."

"You can't dismiss people like that," said Bruce, his voice faltering. "Not these days."

"You listen to me," said Todd. "Some time ago you did a survey of a flat and said that you had looked into the roof space. Well, I went and checked – and you hadn't. You lied. I've been keeping that up my sleeve. You're history."

Bruce stood quite still. It was a strange feeling, being history.

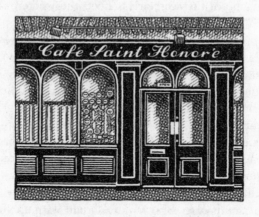

108. Action is Taken

One of Matthew's problems, thought Pat, was that he seemed unwilling to make decisions. The way he had behaved over the

Peploe? – now the non-Peploe – was an example of his chronic lack of decisiveness. Had it not been for the fact that Big Lou had met Guy Peploe, with the result that Matthew had been pushed into action, it was doubtful whether they would have identified the painting as being by somebody other than Peploe. Nor would they have discovered that it was probably an over-painting. That had been established by Guy Peploe himself, who had spotted the shape of an umbrella above a mountain.

Now that some progress had been made with the painting, the matter should be taken further. If it was indeed an over-painting, then what lay underneath could be of some interest – although still probably no more than the work of some gauche amateur. Pat had asked Matthew whether he was planning to do anything about it, but he had simply shrugged.

"Maybe," he said. "But I can't think of who would paint an umbrella."

"A French impressionist?" suggested Pat. "They were always painting people with umbrellas. There's that famous one in the Art Institute of Chicago. I saw it when we went there with the Academy Art Department. They were very good, you know, the art people at the Academy. Mrs Hope. Mr Ellis. Remember them? They took us to all sorts of places. They were inspirational. That's where I learned to love art."

She saw Matthew shift in his seat as she spoke. There was something funny about Matthew. He had got up to something at school – she was sure of it. But what? So many people had their secrets – secrets that we are destined never to find out. People had a past – she had Australia, but the least said about that the better. It was not her fault – she had never thought that – except for one or two people who had said that she should not have spoken to that person in the café and that she should have realised that the man with the eye-patch was not what he claimed to be. She reflected for a moment – now that she was home, it did not seem quite so bad. Indeed, it had been something of an adventure. Perhaps she should tell Domenica about it one of these days. She liked stories like that.

Matthew had changed the subject and nothing more was said about the non-Peploe until that afternoon, when the doorbell rang and Angus Lordie came into the gallery, followed by Cyril. When he saw Pat, Cyril wagged his tail with pleasure and winked.

"Passing by," said Angus Lordie. "I was taking Cyril for a stroll and I thought I might pop in and see what you have on the walls. Interesting stuff. That over there is a worth a quid or two, you know. You didn't? Well, I think it's a James Paterson."

Matthew stood up and joined Angus Lordie in front of a large painting of a girl in a field. "Are you sure?" he said.

Angus Lordie smiled. "Absolutely. If I had the wall space I'd buy it myself."

Matthew turned and glanced at Pat. "I thought it might be," he said.

"Well, it is," said Angus Lordie. "He lived in Moniaive, I think. Or somewhere down . . ." He paused. He had seen the non-Peploe, which was stacked casually against the side of Matthew's desk. "Well! Well! Look at that. Very intriguing!"

"Not a Peploe," said Matthew, smiling. He was warming to Angus Lordie now, having disliked him when he first met him in the Cumberland Bar with Pat. The identification of the Paterson had cheered Matthew. He had no idea who James Paterson was, but he would soon find out. And Matthew was not sure where Moniaive was either, but he could look that up too.

"Oh, I can tell it's not a Peploe," said Angus Lordie, walking across the room to pick up the painting. "What interests me is the shape I can make out – very vaguely – underneath."

"An umbrella," Matthew said quickly. "Rather like the umbrellas that the French impressionists painted. You'll know that one in Chicago, of course. The Art Institute. Wonderful place."

Pat said nothing. It was good to see Matthew's confidence growing. She looked at Cyril who was sitting near the door, his mouth half-open, the sun glinting off his gold tooth. Cyril was perfectly confident – quite at ease in the space he occupied, as every animal is, except us.

Angus Lordie held the painting at an angle to the light.

"Fascinating," he said. "The painting on the top is rubbish, of course, but a deft application of paint-stripper might show something rather interesting. Would you like me to do it for you? We could do it in my studio."

Matthew hesitated. "Well . . ."

"What a good idea!" exclaimed Pat. "Don't you agree, Matthew?"

Matthew turned and looked at Pat, reproach in his eyes. He did not like people making decisions for him, but this is what they inevitably did. One day I'm going to say no, he thought. I'm going to become myself. But then he said: "I suppose so. Yes, I suppose it would be good to see what's underneath."

"What about this evening?" said Angus Lordie. "You two come round to the studio. And bring Domenica. We'll make a party of it."

The time was agreed, and Angus Lordie, with Cyril at his side, set off up the road. As he walked, he thought of the painting. It was really very exciting. He had his ideas, of course, as to what lay underneath, and if he were proved right, then that would have major implications for Matthew. And it would be nice, too, to be credited with the discovery, just as Sir Timothy Clifford had got a lot of credit when he discovered a da Vinci drawing under a sofa in the New Club. (That had made the papers!) There would be mention of his own discovery in the newspapers and perhaps a photograph of himself and Cyril. He would be modest, of course, and would downplay the significance of what he had done. Anybody could have seen it, he might say. I just happened to be in the right place at the right time.

"But it required your expert hand to reveal the secret!" the reporter would say. And he would smile, and say, self-effacingly: "Yes, perhaps it did. Perhaps it did."

109. *A Most Remarkable and Important Discovery*

"Angus is an extremely good host," Domenica had said, and she was right. He welcomed his guests with a tray of devils on horseback and small oat-cakes on which thick-cut slices of smoked salmon had been balanced. Then there were crackers with boiled egg, ersatz caviar, and small circles of mayonnaise. All of this was provided in generous quantities.

His flat, which occupied the top two floors of a Drummond Place stair, was built with a generosity which escapes modern builders; the ceilings soared up to fifteen feet, the dark pine wainscoting reached waist-level, and the floor boards were a good twelve inches wide. And everywhere on the walls there were paintings and hangings – portraits, landscapes, figurative studies. A Cadell picture of a man in a top hat, raffish as the proprietor, smiled down above the fireplace in the drawing room. A large Philipson, crowded with cathedrals and ladies, occupied the expanse of wall to its side, and a magnificent Cowie, schoolgirls in a painter's loft, hung beside that.

And then there were the bookshelves, which filled the hall and the dining room; towering constructions with books stacked two and three deep. Domenica, drink in hand, stopped beside one of these and exclaimed with delight as she drew out a volume.

"Ruthven Todd!" she said. "Nobody reads him these days, and they should. Look at this. *Acreage of the Heart*, published by William McLellan. The Poetry Scotland series."

Angus Lordie came to her side, licking mayonnaise off his fingers.

"That contains a very fine poem, Domenica," he said. "*Personal History*. Do you know it?"

Domenica turned a page. "*I was born in this city,*" Domenica began to read aloud. "*Where dry minds . . .*"

"*Grow crusts of hate/ Like rocks grow lichen*", Angus Lordie took it up. "Such powerful, powerful lines."

Pat looked puzzled. "Why did he write that?"

"Because it's true," said Angus Lordie. "Or, at least it used to be true. Todd was born into haut-bourgeois Edinburgh, which used to be just like that. Brittle. Exclusive. Turned in on itself. And immensely snobbish."

"And still is a bit like that," said Domenica quietly. "In its worst moments."

"But much better than it used to be," Angus Lordie countered. "You very rarely see those real, cold Edinburgh attitudes these days. The arrogance of those people is broken. They just can't get away with it. That horrid disapproval of anything that moves – that's gone."

Domenica did not appear to be completely convinced. "I'm not sure," she said. "What makes Edinburgh different from other cities in these islands? It is different, you know. I think that there is still a certain hauteur, a certain intellectual crustiness. It's not nearly as marked as it was in Todd's day, but . . ."

Angus Lordie smiled. "But Domenica rather likes all that," he suggested mischievously. "She's a bit of a Jean Brodie, you see."

Pat looked at Domenica, wondering whether she would take offence. Hadn't Jean Brodie been a fascist? Wasn't that the whole point about Spain and the betrayal and all the rest? Matthew simply looked confused. What was this man talking about? And where was that peculiar dog of his?

They were all standing in the drawing room overlooking the Drummond Place Gardens. It was about nine o'clock, and the sky was still light. The branches of the trees moved gently against the sky and the stone of the buildings opposite, for there was a slight breeze. Pat sipped at the drink that Angus Lordie had given her – a gin and tonic flavoured with lime; she was happy to be here, with these people, with Matthew, whom she liked more and more for his gentleness; with Angus Lordie, who amused her and seemed so grateful for her company, and who was not a threat to anyone; and with Domenica, whom she admired. What a difference, she thought, between this company, interesting and sympathetic, and the company of Bruce and his friends in the Cumberland Bar. What a profound mistake to fall in love with that man – she realised that now. She had no feeling for him, not even revulsion; she felt nothing. At that crucial moment, when she had seen him awake and smiling at her, she had realised that she was free.

Angus Lordie interrupted her thoughts. "We should do something about the picture now," he said. "Let's go into my studio and get to work."

They followed him from the drawing room, down a book-lined corridor, and into a large room, two floors high, with large skylights set into the ceiling. Matthew, who had been clutching the painting, now handed it over to Angus Lordie and watched anxiously as their host laid it down on a table and reached for a large, opaque bottle. He placed the bottle beside him and then raised his glass of whisky to Matthew.

"Paint-stripper," he said. "In the bottle that is – not the glass! Hah!"

Matthew said nothing, but narrowed his eyes as Angus Lordie took the top off the bottle and sprinkled a viscous liquid across the painting. Then he rubbed this gently with a cloth.

"Draw near and see," said Angus Lordie. "We'll give this a moment to act, and then I'll give it a wipe. All should be revealed."

Slowly the surface of the painting began to blister and bubble. The shore of Iona disappeared, and then the coast of Mull. Next went the sea; those blue waves which had rather impressed Matthew became grey and then brown.

"Now a gentle wipe," said Angus Lordie. "That'll get rid of all this superfluous paint. Here we go."

They were all huddled over the painting now. Pat noticed that Matthew looked pale, and that his breathing was shallow. Domenica, catching Pat's eye, gave her a conspiratorial nod. And Angus Lordie, absorbed in his task, looked only at the surface of the painting, which was now changing colour markedly.

"Now then," Angus Lordie said, dabbing at a section of the painting. "Gently does it. Gently."

"An umbrella," whispered Domenica. "Look. An umbrella."

"Yes!" said Angus Lordie, triumphantly. "Yes! And look what we have here. A beach. Yes! And do we have people in evening suits dancing under that umbrella, which is being held up, is it not, by a butler? Yes we do! We do!"

Angus Lordie straightened up. "Yes!" he shouted. "Exactly as I had suspected! A Vettriano!"

110. Gain, Loss, Friendship, Love

Matthew was quietly pleased. He had lost a Peploe (which he had never really had, anyway) but he had gained a Vettriano (which he had never known he had). After the initial shock of the discovery, he turned to Angus Lordie and embraced him warmly. "I'm so glad that you offered to do this," he said. "I would never have imagined it. A Vettriano!"

Angus Lordie smiled, wiping his hands on a piece of cloth. "I was alerted by the shape of the umbrella," he said. "I just had a feeling that it was our friend Mr Vettriano underneath. I don't know why, but I had this feeling."

"Never underestimate the power of intuitions," said Domenica. "They are a very useful guide. They can show us the way to all sorts of things – including the way to being good."

Angus Lordie raised an eyebrow. "How so?" he asked. "What have intuitions to do with goodness?"

"Intuitions help us to know what is right and wrong," said Domenica. "If your intuitions tell you that something is wrong, then it probably is. And once you start to use your moral faculties to work out why it's wrong, you'll see that the intuition was right in the first place."

"Interesting," said Angus Lordie. "But I suspect that the intuition is merely a form of existing knowledge. You know something already, and the intuition merely tells you that the knowledge is buried away in your mind."

"But that's exactly what an intuition is," said Domenica. "That's exactly why they're so useful."

Angus Lordie replaced the cap on the bottle of paint-stripper. "Enough of all this," he said. "I propose that we go through to the drawing room and open a bottle of champagne. Leave the painting here, Matthew. It needs to dry a little. I'll come back in a moment and fetch it."

They followed their host back down the corridor and into the large, formally furnished drawing room. Angus Lordie busied himself with the opening of a bottle of champagne, which he took from a concealed fridge in a walnut cabinet. Then he poured a glass for each of them and they stood in the middle of the room, under the Murano chandelier, and raised their glasses to each other.

"To the successful sale of the Vettriano," said Angus Lordie, chinking his glass against Matthew's. "That is assuming that you will be selling it. Vettriano, of course, is not to everybody's taste. But the point is there's a strong market for them and it seems to be getting stronger."

Matthew looked into his glass. He did not like to talk about financial matters, but he was very curious to know what value Angus Lordie might put on his painting. "You wouldn't have any idea," he began.

"Of what it's worth?" said Angus Lordie.

"Yes."

"Well," said Angus Lordie. "Let's think. I think that this is a very early Vettriano, but it's an important one in terms of his development as a popular painter. It's his beach period, I would have thought – with touches of his umbrella period. So that makes it very interesting. And the value would be . . . Let's think. Perhaps, a hundred thousand. Something like that?"

Pat glanced at Matthew and noticed that his hands were shaking. She reached across and touched him gently on the shoulder. "Well done!" she whispered. "Well done!"

Matthew smiled back at her. He liked this girl, and he wondered if there was still a chance that she might like him too. Perhaps she had overcome her ridiculous attachment to that ghastly Bruce. Perhaps she would want somebody more settled, like me. That is what he thought, but he knew, even as he thought it, that he was hoping for too much. Nobody liked him in that way; they just didn't.

Angus Lordie put down his glass. "I'll go and fetch it," he said. "The light is slightly better through here at this time of the evening. We can take a close look at it."

He left them, and a short time later he returned, holding the painting out before him. He cleared his throat and started to say something, but no words came and they knew immediately that something was wrong.

Angus Lordie held the painting out to Matthew. "I'm terribly sorry," he said. "The paint-stripper appears to have continued to act. The Vettriano seems to have gone."

Matthew looked at the painting in dismay. The beach, the umbrella, the butler, the dancing couple – all had merged into a set of curiously-coloured streaks and puddles of paint. Matthew looked at Angus Lordie, and then he laughed. It was a laugh that surprised them all – except Pat. "I was never really too keen on Vettriano," he said. "Don't feel too bad about it." With that comment, that simple forgiving comment, Pat realised the depth of Matthew's goodness. She would not forget that.

Angus Lordie let out a sigh of relief. "That's very good of you," he said. "But I was thinking – you could still try to sell this as an abstract Vettriano. That's what it's become, you see. Vettriano put this paint on this canvas, and it certainly looks pretty abstract now."

Matthew smiled. "Perhaps."

Angus Lordie placed the abstract Vettriano down on a table and fetched another bottle of champagne from the fridge. Domenica, who had been silent since Angus Lordie had returned to the room with the news of the restoration mishap, now said: "Angus, you've been a rotten restorer, but you remain, in my view, a rather more competent poet. Cheer us all up with one of your impromptu pieces."

"Something Chinese?" asked Angus Lordie. "Late Scottish-Tang?"

"No," said Domenica. "Not that. Something else."

"Why not?" he said. "How about this?"

He moved to the window and then turned to face his guests. *Together again* he began.

Here in this place,
Of angled streets and northern light,
Under this particular moon, with Scotland
Quiet and sleeping behind and around us;
Of what may I speak but friendship,
And of our human wish for love – not just for me
But for friends too, and those who are not my friends;
So if you ask me, now, at this moment,
What is my wish: it is for love over Scotland,
Like tears of rain – that is enough.